The Queen of Sparta

The Queen of Sparta

T. S. Chaudhry

TOP HAT BOOKS

Winchester, UK
Washington, USA

First published by Top Hat Books, 2014
Top Hat Books is an imprint of John Hunt Publishing Ltd., Laurel House, Station Approach,
Alresford, Hants, SO24 9JH, UK
office1@jhpbooks.net
www.johnhuntpublishing.com

For distributor details and how to order please visit the 'Ordering' section on our website.

ISBN: 978 1 78279 750 0

A CIP catalogue record for this book is available from the British Library.

Design: Stuart Davies

The cover is based on the original design by Dan Prescott from Couper Street Type Co.
www.couperstreet.com

Printed in the USA by Edwards Brothers Malloy

'My task is to relate the stories that have been told; I do not necessarily have to believe in them.'
– Herodotus ('the Father of History')

Prologue – The Manuscript

Aornos, Swat Valley
Lands of the Indus
Summer, 327 BC

The forbidding stronghold, perched high on a peak, blazed against the cloudy night sky like a beacon. Down below, the old woman stood before her enemy, clasped in chains. Her gown was torn and tattered, her braided grey hair drenched in blood, her ferocious stare fixed on the man who had slaughtered her people and taken her land.

Alexander of Macedon had crossed over the high mountain range seeking the land the Persians called *Puraparaseanna,* 'beyond the mountains,' and what others described as the fabled lands of the Indus. He had thought that crossing into 'India' would be relatively easy, and indeed it had been, until he entered this valley. Here, everything had gone wrong. Alexander's men, who had won great victories for hundreds of miles across Asia, were now facing adversaries they could not easily conquer. This new enemy could appear out of nowhere to strike hard and fast, and then disappear without a trace.

There was something peculiar about this enemy. Unlike most of the Asiatic foes Alexander's force had faced before, these warriors fought with skill and discipline. A mere hundred of the enemy could hold off tens of thousands of Alexander's men in narrow defiles, on bridges over fast-flowing rivers, and in the thick pine forests. And their horsemen were the most proficient Alexander had seen, carrying out remarkable manoeuvres in mountainous terrain, so unsuited for cavalry. These were no highland brigands, no mere hill-tribesmen – but fierce warriors equal to, or perhaps better than, Alexander's conquering troops.

And then there was the valley. Its lush green hills awash with pine, oak, ash and cypress trees, dwarfed by magnificent snow-capped mountains; the varying shades of green flora contrasting with the grey-blue of the rivers flowing below. The effect was mesmerizing. Alexander's men called it *Paradeisos* – 'Paradise on earth'.

But the Macedonian conqueror had turned this paradise into hell. Where Alexander could not win by force, he resorted to guile, deceit and treachery. He made truces only to break them, attacking his enemies in their homesteads and settlements without mercy; destroying everything in his path. A quest for conquest had turned into a war of extermination. The resistance became only fiercer and the struggles more terrible. Still, one by one they fell, the fortified towns of Massaga, Ora and Barzius – and relentless slaughter followed. This last stronghold, rocky Aornos, had been the worst. It would have certainly been a defeat for the Macedonian King were it not for a mercenary commander, fighting for the enemy, who had opened the fortress gates for him.

Now, down below, hundreds of prisoners were gathered in front of the Macedonian camp. Wretched prisoners in tattered clothing huddled together by the banks of the fast-flowing Indus as rain began to fall.

Flanked by his commanders and advisors, Alexander was seated in front of these hundreds of prisoners on a field-chair. For all his fame, there was something was odd about the Macedonian conqueror. Short of height and slight of build, with golden curly hair, his face was smooth and soft; almost feminine. One of his eyes was blue and the other brown – which many regarded as a sign that he was touched by the gods, or was indeed a god himself.

Alexander gazed at the old woman who had led the resistance against him. In spite of her injuries, the woman stood erect, defiance blazing in her eyes. Though the hue of her skin was dark, her facial features were unmistakably European. The Macedonian King recalled the first time he had seen her, several weeks earlier, outside the walls of Massaga. When he sent out an emissary ordering her troops to lay down their arms, she had shouted back in Greek: *Molon Labe* – 'come and get them.'

'Name?' he asked, in a rather harsh, almost squeaky, voice.

'Cleophis,' she replied, unflinching.

'Your name is Greek. Where are you from?'

She replied in a language Alexander could not understand. He turned to his Asiatic interpreters, who shrugged their shoulders.

A Corinthian officer came forward and whispered in Alexander's ear. 'This is my home. Perhaps you are the one who is lost, Macedonian?'

Alexander frowned. 'What is she speaking?'

'A dialect of Doric Greek, Your Majesty,' explained the Corinthian. 'I have heard it spoken in Sparta, but only by royalty.'

'Damned Spartans,' muttered Alexander to himself. Of all the Greeks, they were the only ones who had refused to join his empire-building expedition. 'What is a Spartan woman doing here, by the banks of the Indus?' Alexander asked, motioning the Corinthian to translate.

'I was born here, not in Sparta,' Cleophis replied, 'though the royal blood of Sparta flows strong in my veins.'

'Ah…' Alexander smiled. 'A descendant of Leonidas, no doubt?'

Cleophis remained silent.

'Woman, do you know I have destroyed Persia against whom the Three Hundred Spartans made their stand at Thermopylae, a century and a half ago?'

The old woman scowled. 'It was the Greeks who fought the Persians then, not the Macedonians. Your ancestors served the Persians and later betrayed them. Your kind prefers treachery to courage.'

Alexander flew into a rage. 'I am Greek. My fore-fathers came from Argos. My ancestor, Alexander the First, son of Amyntas, helped the Greeks defeat the Persians. It was he and Leonidas of Sparta and Themistocles the Athenian who saved Greece from the Persian yoke. By destroying the Persians' Empire, I have only finished the work they began.'

Cleophis, in spite of her iron restraints, moved forward from the crowd of prisoners. 'What makes you think any of *them* saved Greece? You men think you are the centre of the universe, don't you? No, Macedonian, Greece was not saved by these men. She was saved by a woman.'

'This hag is mad!' said Alexander to himself. He got up in disgust.

As he rose to leave, Cleophis railed at him, 'Macedonian, you conquer for the sake of conquest. Your lust for power knows no bounds. You can take this land but you will not be able to hold it. Mark my words, your presence here is only ephemeral, but the children of the Sakas will be drinking from the waters of the Indus for thousands of years to come.'

Alexander surveyed the prisoners. The people of Aornos, in chains and in torn clothes; sobbing women and children among them. All standing in mud, their homes burning in the background. He looked at Cleophis one last time. Her angry expression had grown even fiercer. The Macedonian King turned and calmly gave the order to his troops as he walked to his tent.

By morning, all were dead.

* * *

The next day, Alexander rode with a cavalry escort to the nearby town of Min-angora. Though only mid-afternoon, it seemed like dusk. Dark clouds had descended over the valley, shrouding it in darkness. Violent thunder echoed as drizzle turned to heavy downpour. The shadowy figures of the Macedonian horsemen, faces obscured beneath hooded cloaks, crossed a wooden bridge, and followed a road that ran alongside a fast-flowing river. Ahead was the town. A large wooden palace stood on a gentle hill on the left bank of the river. As the horsemen approached the palace, they saw a small dark figure walking – or rather, hobbling – towards them. He smiled and bowed low.

Alexander snapped his finger. The only native rider in his Macedonian retinue dismounted his horse and hurried to the King's side. 'Ask him if he is the one I must thank for delivering Aornos to me,' ordered the King.

But before the native could frame his question, the small man replied in heavily accented Greek. 'Indeed, Majesty, it was I who arranged it. I am pleased to have been of service to you.'

The Macedonian King frowned. He could not understand why so many people, so far from Greece, could speak the language so fluently.

'My name is Vishnugupta Chanakiya,' the man continued. 'But you may call me *Kautilya*, 'the Crafty One'. The mercenary commander who betrayed Aornos to you is a compatriot of mine.'

Kautilya was a small bald man with deformed limbs. He had an unusually large hooked nose, bulging eyes, and his mouth revealed large misshapen, twisted teeth when he smiled. Still, his appearance was not without charisma.

Alexander nodded to one of his men, who rode out towards Kautilya and offered him a heavy purse. To the Macedonian King's surprise, Kautilya waved it away, shaking his head.

'Your Majesty's presence here is more important to me than gold,' explained Kautilya. 'You are the enemy of our enemies and thus our friend. King Ambhi of Taxila awaits your aid against his rival, King Porus of the Puravas, overlord of the Suraseni. And if you defeat Porus, all of India will fall at your feet.'

Finally, someone had said something that pleased Alexander. He smiled and dismounted his horse.

'Has King ... ah ... Omphis ... sent you, then? Is he the one you serve?'

'No, Majesty,' said Kautilya. 'I serve no master. I am an exile from a kingdom further to the east. King Ambhi has given me asylum. He allows me to use the university in Taxila for research, in return for my political advice. I have asked him to ally with you.' Kautilya escorted him inside the modest wooden palace. 'Rest now, Majesty. We shall talk later tonight.'

That evening, Alexander dined alone with Kautilya on the spacious terrace on the top floor of the palace. It was a pleasant place overlooking the river, furnished with beautifully carved wooden furniture, luxurious cushions and rich rugs. Jasmine vines hung over the wooden railing emitting the sweetest of fragrances, the rushing sound of the river's water was almost melodic, and the distant lights of the town danced in the wind.

Alexander reclined on a comfortable bed-like couch, while Kautilya squatted, cross-legged, on the carpeted floor in front of him. A low table full of tiny bowls was placed between them. He asked the Indian who were these people who had resisted him so fiercely. 'And why are there so many people in this land who speak Greek?'

Kautilya explained, 'Cleophis' ancestors settled here centuries ago. They once ruled over the lands spanned by the river Indus. But their dominion eventually broke up as they fought both their neighbours and each other. One by one, their petty kingdoms and republics fell to others. You have just destroyed their last remaining state – and thus helped rid us of a major enemy.'

'And the Greek connections,' the Indian continued, 'have been here for a while as well. Ambhi, the ruler of Taxila, also claims to be of Greek descent and even looks it. Taxila, like Min-angora, is virtually a Greek city, populated by Greek-speakers. People of Greek descent have been living here for well over a century. Some are said to be descended from Greek merchants who operated between here and the Asiatic Greek colonies of Aeolia and Ionia. Some say their ancestors were transplanted from the West and resettled here by Persian kings as punishment for rebellion. Others claim descent from Greek mercenaries who fought in civil wars between Persian princes. But then there are those who claim even stronger links with Greece, like Cleophis. Her tribe was called the *Ashkayavana* – the 'Horse Greeks' – who were ruled by people of royal Spartan blood.'

'Is that so? What was that hag saying about a woman defeating the Persians?'

Kautilya smiled. 'Majesty, I have in my possession a manuscript, written ... well, partly written ... by a prince from Sakala who travelled to Greece a hundred and fifty or so years ago. He is one of the two authors of the manuscript. I have no doubt that the other is the woman Cleophis spoke of.'

Alexander asked what language the manuscript was written in.

'Greek,' replied Kautilya, 'for reasons you will understand when you read the text.' He disappeared through the door of the balcony. Moments later he hobbled back, bearing a sheaf of parchments neatly strung together. Kautilya bowed low and handed the thick collection of parchments over to Alexander, across the low table. 'I shall look forward to hearing your views on this manuscript, Majesty. But for now, I wish you good night.' Kautilya bowed once more and left the company of the Macedonian King.

That night, Alexander began to read. Written in Attic Greek, the very dialect Alexander spoke, the manuscript began thus:

Even after all these years, I can still recall the calm after that cursed battle, as I walked among its dead. I can still taste that iron-tinged stench of blood that hung in the air. I began from the place where the heroes fell, my brother among them, by the entrance of the Great King's tent. And as I strode towards Leonidas' Wall, I passed a mound of bodies and shields. These were the last of the three hundred, their corpses riddled with arrows. And thereafter I came to the entrance of the pass. Stacks of hundreds of putrid human carcasses piled up against the Wall where for two bloody days the Spartans had held the line.

And I climbed the Wall again – this time not in the midst of fierce combat with grunting, shouting, shoving bodies all around me – but alone in the midst of a dusky calm. All I could see was a sea of the dead and the dying.

It should not have been such a shock for a warrior. But it was.

Battle, they say, is everything that manhood is about; the very epitome of glory. But what glory, I asked myself, is there in a spear-point sticking out of a jaw or a mangled headless body rotting on the ground?

And there they all lay before me, the thousands of corpses who were once living beings.

Thermopylae was but an exercise in futility; no bearing upon anything that mattered. The Persians were determined yet to the crush the Greeks. And who on earth could stop them?

Chapter 1

If!

The Agora
Sparta
Autumn, 480 BC

The man was trying to sit very still. He was on horseback, in full armour, facing a throng of mostly unarmed men and women. And yet he was trembling. He seemed too afraid even to dismount his horse.

A man, in front of the crowd, laughed. He was tall, with hair falling well below his shoulder and an equally long moustache-less beard. 'This time they sent us a Greek. Why did the Persians send you and not one of their own? Are they afraid we would stuff them down the well again?'

Laughter roared across the marketplace.

The envoy, still shaking, cleared his throat and said, 'I bring a message from the Great King Xerxes to the King of Sparta.'

A small voice shouted, 'I am he!'

Looking down, the envoy saw a small dark-haired boy of around eight years looking up at him. He waited for someone to laugh at the boy's impertinence or even shout at him. But none did.

'I am Pleistarchus, son of Leonidas,' said the boy.

The messenger plucked up enough courage to say, 'Sparta has two kings. I wish to speak with the older one.'

A young woman had stepped forward. She was long-haired and beautiful. Standing behind the boy, she placed her hands on his small shoulders. 'He is away,' she said. 'You will have to deliver your message to my son.'

'Go on,' said the boy King, his tiny voice carrying authority.

'His Majesty, King Xerxes, says: *I have destroyed your army at*

Thermopylae. My forces have occupied Athens. And your turn will soon come. You are advised to submit without further delay, for if I bring my army into your land, I shall destroy your farms, slaughter your people, and raze your city to the ground.'

There was silence.

The boy King turned around and looked up at his mother. Her eyes blazed as she stared into the eyes of the messenger. Her lips curled mischievously as she gave him her response: *'If!'*

Chapter 2

The Crimson Queen

Royal Compound of the Agiadae
Pitana District
Sparta
Spring, 479 BC

Even though the sun had risen, the morning mist still covered the garden. Beautiful flowers and exotic plants were arranged in neat rows all around the edges of a lawn. Delightful aromas mixed with the dewy smell of the early morning grass. In the centre of the lawn was a huge lone oak with a bench underneath. Close to the tree were rows of comfortable benches fashioned out of single pieces of log. On them sat nine men wearing rich tunics and elegantly embroidered robes. Because of the mist they could not take in the full beauty of the garden; nor did they care to.

'What is taking her so long?' grumbled Cimon, the youngest of the men.

'I told you it was a mistake coming here,' said Xanthippus.

'No one else in Sparta is willing to talk to us. We have no choice but to come here,' retorted the elderly Phaenippus.

'I meant it was a mistake to come here to Sparta,' retorted Xanthippus, mincing his words. 'They have no intention of helping us liberate Athens.'

Cimon, who rarely agreed with Xanthippus, sighed. 'We have been sitting around here in Sparta for over a week now, and all we have are equivocations and half-promises.'

'We fought without the Spartans before,' said a rather tall, pudgy companion of theirs, 'and we can fight without them again.'

'That was eleven years ago, Callias,' said Phaenippus, shaking his head. 'You know better than I that the conditions at Marathon worked to our favour, no matter what we said afterwards. But things are different now. Either the Spartans come to our aid or we surrender to Persia. There is no other choice.'

They did not notice her coming through the mist. Cimon was the first to catch a glimpse of her legs, when she had almost come upon them. She wore sandals, the straps of which ran up her ankles, which was strange because Spartan women rarely wore footwear; nor did their men, unless on campaign. He had hoped to see more of her leg – Spartan women were not called 'thigh flashers' for nothing – but her *peplos* gown reached her ankles.

As she came closer, more of her was revealed to the men. Her loose-fitting white dress could not hide her lithe, athletic body. Unlike the coarse materials ordinary Spartans wore, hers was of the finest linen. Hung over her shoulder was a long *himation* shawl. Its colour was crimson; the colour of Sparta. The colour of war.

As her face emerged from the mist, its beauty mesmerized the men. Her most defining features were her large hazel-green eyes, made more intense and foreboding by kohl. Her long, dark hair was swept up loosely, some falling over her left shoulder.

One by one, the Athenians stood up, in awe of her beauty, enthralled by her presence. Only Phaenippus had seen her before. She looked just as beautiful as she had a decade earlier, yet the expression on her face was now one of authority; her appearance exuding power.

There was a mischievous glint in her eyes as she quietly sat down opposite them on the bench under the oak tree. Normally, a queen waited for her guests to be seated. *But not this time,* she thought to herself. Sparta was the senior partner in this alliance and a queen of Sparta was not bound to stand in ceremony for these representatives of the Athenian rabble.

'Be seated, gentlemen,' she said. The Queen already knew that in a rare display of unity, Athens' democratic Assembly had sent representatives from nearly all their major factions. Their leader was Phaenippus. He had once been *Epynomous Archon* – Athens' Head of State. She smiled at him politely, acknowledging him by name.

Next to him was a handsome-faced man in his late thirties with a trimmed beard but a curiously shaped head; his dishevelled dark blond hair all bunched up at the bottom and rising to a point at the top. *Onion head,* she said to herself, suppressing her laughter with some difficulty. 'Welcome, Xanthippus son of Ariphron, commander of the Athenian Navy.'

Xanthippus was a little flustered, perhaps not expecting her to recognize him without an introduction.

Behind him was a tall heavy-set man with thick lips, a paunchy belly and a pug nose, who was generally quite hairy except on the top of his head. The clothes he wore were made of the most expensive fabrics and his shoes appeared incredibly soft. *Oh yes, that is him; the richest man in Athens,* the Queen said to herself. *How ironic; this ugly man's name is 'Callias'.* But she knew that the irony did not stop there. Behind this façade of a man of affluence, accustomed to luxury, was a hardened veteran; a war hero, who, eleven years ago, had led one of the ten tribal regiments at the Athenian victory at Marathon. She knew that it was as much a mistake to underestimate the Athenians as it was to trust them.

She was about to guess who the person next to Callias was, when the frail Phaenippus spoke. 'Queen Gorgo, where is your army? We have been here a week and have not seen the troops we are promised to liberate Athens.'

'Of course,' she said, 'you are aware that military activity is forbidden during the festival of *Hyacinthia*.'

'Yes, the Regent Pausanias told us as much,' snorted Xanthippus, while the men behind him murmured in discontent.

The youngest of the envoys made his way to the front. A little older than Gorgo, he was a handsome man with curly red hair and a clean-shaven face. His scandalous lifestyle was the subject of gossip right across Greece. They spoke of a string of notorious seductions that included, if rumours were to be believed, his own younger half-sister. And yet, he had a saving grace. The son of one of Athens' greatest heroes, he had recently distinguished himself in battle, against the Persians at Salamis.

'Is this not the very same excuse Leonidas used to avoid Spartan participation in the battle of Marathon eleven years ago? The festival on that occasion was the *Carneia*, now it is the Hyacinthia. The Spartans seem a little too fond of their festivals, don't you think?' said the younger man.

A burst of sarcastic laughter echoed his barb.

'My late husband, Leonidas,' said Gorgo with pride, 'arrived in Marathon to support your troops as soon as the Carneia was over, just as he had promised.'

'Yes,' said the man, 'but only after the battle was over. Where were the Spartans, Queen Gorgo, on the day my father won the great victory at Marathon?'

Some of the envoys began to grumble loudly.

'Cimon, son of Miltiades, tell me how many Athenian warriors were present at the battle of Thermopylae? The Arcadians were there and so were the Phlians. The sons of Corinth fought and died there, as did the Ismenian Band. Those patriots from Thebes fought for us, despite of the treachery of their own government. The Lion Guard of ancient Mycenae fought to the end there. So did the Thespiaeans, and heroically so. Men of high-walled Phocis were present too, as were those of Locris and Malia. Your neighbours, the Megarians, were also there. Even the Mantineans tried to redeem their lost honour by showing up. But not a single Athenian fought at Thermopylae. Where were you, oh men of Athens, on the day our Three Hundred Spartans and their allies fell for the cause of Greece?'

'You know very well, Queen Gorgo, that our fleet was at Artemisium, along with other Greek ships, protecting the naval flank of your land forces. We prevented the Persian fleet from landing troops behind the Spartan lines,' retorted Xanthippus.

'A fat lot of good that did,' she replied. 'For your fleet did not deter the Persians from outflanking the Greek positions and destroying our army at Thermopylae.'

'But, Queen Gorgo,' retorted Callias angrily in his loud voice, 'that is not the point. We have been waiting for your leaders to give us an answer on whether you will support us against the Persians. And today, when we went looking for the Regent, he could not be found, nor could any of your generals. Then we went to the Ephors, and even they refused to speak with us. Instead, they sent us to you. What is going on?'

'Where are your troops, Majesty?' asked Cimon. 'Not a single one can be found in Sparta, and that too in a city supposedly populated by warriors. Don't you think it strange? I am sure your men would not mind a woman answering for them ... for they are not man enough to answer for themselves.' He continued to smile as some of his colleagues shouted in disgust.

'I owe you no explanation, my Lord,' replied Gorgo calmly.

'All right,' said Phaenippus lifting up his hands, silencing his colleagues. 'We understand perfectly, Queen Gorgo. We know that we have outlived our welcome here. You Spartans can stay at home and enjoy your festival. Forget your obligations towards your closest allies. We will have no choice but to surrender to Persia. And once we do so, and when their Great King invades your lands, do not blame us if we join his forces against yours. Only then will you realize the consequences of your inaction.'

'Consequence of our inaction?' she snorted, staring ferociously at the elderly envoy. 'Your Democracy has only survived under the shade of Spartan spears!'

Cimon tried to say something, but she cut him off. 'Ambassadors of Athens,' she began, in a tone matched only by the blazing of her eyes. 'I do not deal with assumptions or presumptions, nor do I make empty threats. The Hyacinthia ended last night. On my recommendation, and in accordance with terms of our alliance, the War Council of Sparta have dispatched an army to liberate Athens. Gentlemen, as we speak, the entire Spartan field army under the command of my cousin, the Regent Pausanias, are already on their way. That is why you could not find even a single warrior in Sparta today ... or a general, for that matter.'

'The entire Spartan field army, Your Majesty? On their way? ... to Athens?' Phaenippus blubbered. 'This ... is ... wonderful ... news!'

'I told you, we made the right decision to come here,' said Xanthippus, smiling. Cimon gave him a stare that combined incredulity with anger. The other ambassadors could not contain their joy.

Gorgo continued, 'This morning, I received a message that they are approaching the Isthmus of Corinth, which means they will arrive at Athens by sunset tomorrow. We have five thousand additional troops, our *Outlander* brigade, waiting outside Sparta to escort you back to your city.'

'But ... why did not anyone inform us?' asked Cimon.

'After all, we are the Ambassadors of Athens, your allies,' said Phaenippus. 'We had a right to be informed the moment you decided to send your troops to aid us.'

'... And tell the entire world that the Spartans were coming?' she replied.

Gorgo knew that many powerful men in Athens had taken the Great King's gold. Nearby Argos was in league with Persia, and she had doubts about the loyalty of Sparta's Arcadian neighbours. Not all the Greeks opposed the Persian presence. Secrecy had to be maintained to ensure the Spartan force would not be intercepted by Greeks loyal to Persia.

'Thank you, Queen Gorgo. You are a true friend of Athens. We never doubted your support for a moment,' said Xanthippus.

'Of course you doubted it,' she said. 'Is that not why you came to see me? To accuse the Spartans of cowardice? Of inaction? ...

Of hiding behind a woman? Lord Cimon, let me tell you why I speak for my menfolk, because it is only we Spartan women who give birth to real men.'

Cimon turned red, a colour matching his flaming hair. But Phaenippus bowed low. 'We apologize, Majesty. Your wisdom has never failed Greece.' Then he raised his head. 'Now, if you would excuse us, we need to hurry home.'

'Not just yet, gentlemen!' Gorgo shouted. 'I have not finished.'

This stopped the Athenians in their tracks.

'The liberation of Athens does not come without its price.'

One by one, the nine Athenians turned to face her. 'Let me ask you, again, why were there no Athenians at Thermopylae?'

There was silence.

'Then let me give you the answer, gentlemen,' she said. 'Did not the democratic Assembly and Council of Athens, under the influence of your great leader, Themistocles, take a decision to disband your army and effectively transform it into a navy? Lord Cimon, did you not march off to the armoury at the Temple of Athena Parthenos on the Acropolis, and exchange your cavalryman's bridle for a marine's shield? As soon as you heard about the Persian victory at Thermopylae, did not your fleet rush back to Athens to evacuate your civilian population to nearby islands? You did not fight on land at Thermopylae because you had made up your minds to resist the Persians by sea.'

Phaenippus retorted, 'But the Oracle of Delphi had told us to place our trust only in the wooden walls that Zeus had given us. Those wooden walls were, after all, our warships.'

'No,' Gorgo corrected him. 'It was because you had no faith in in our strategy – my strategy – to stop the Persians on land. You wanted to confront them at sea. We went along with you against our better judgement. Yes, together we won the great battle of Salamis. But that victory did not get rid of the Persians. They are still in Greece. And once again they have occupied your city, and once again their soldiers gaze across the Straits of Salamis. So we are exactly back to where we were some six months ago.'

She paused to see if the Athenians would react. None did. So she continued, 'For Sparta's help in liberating Athens, I ask a two-fold price.

'The first is that you reconvert a large part of your fleet back into the army so that we can now confront the Persians together on land. We have tried your strategy and it has not worked; now, you must try mine.'

Phaenippus first looked at Xanthippus, the naval commander, who nodded after some hesitation. Then he looked around to see if there were any objections. There were none. 'Done,' he said in a loud decisive voice, 'And what, Your Majesty, is your second condition?'

'That the General who would command these new land forces of Athens,' she said, 'be a man of my choice.'

The Athenians were in uproar. 'We are a sovereign Democracy, Madam,' said an indignant Phaenippus. 'We elect our own leaders. We do not take instructions from a foreign monarch, much less a woman, on who to appoint as our War Archon.'

'Under the circumstances, gentlemen,' she said, curling her lips, 'you have little choice.'

'But the Generals are always elected by the people of Athens,' insisted Xanthippus, 'not selected by us, or anyone else for that matter.'

'And who are the people of Athens, pray tell me, Lord Xanthippus?' Gorgo asked, '–if not you?'

Smiling, she walked towards the Athenians. 'I know how this Democracy of yours works. All of you present here represent the different factions of the Athenian Democracy. If a man wants to be elected in Athens, he needs the support of the majority of your parties. It is thus you, gentlemen, who control the Council and Assembly of Athens, and no War Archon can be elected without your collective consent.'

'So who is this man you would want to lead our armies?' sighed Callias.

'We will not accept that lout, Themistocles,' muttered another Ambassador under his breath, but loud enough for Gorgo to hear.

'Oh, how fickle is this great Democracy of yours,' she said. 'The flesh of the dead Persians that lie at the bottom of the Straits have not even been stripped by fish of their bones that you have become so eager to cast aside that genius who won you your greatest victory? No, gentlemen. It is not Themistocles that I have in mind.'

Cimon breathed a sigh of relief, as did Phaenippus. Themistocles was no longer powerful in Athens; the very Democracy that had once brought him to power was now chasing him away.

Gorgo spoke the name of the man she wanted to command the land forces of Athens. At first, many of those assembled looked a little surprised.

Callias was the first to smile. Xanthippus and Cimon looked at each other for a moment and then nodded simultaneously. Phaenippus again scanned the faces of his colleagues to detect any dissent. And finding none, he concluded, 'so be it.'

The Athenians hurriedly filed out of the garden, leaving Gorgo alone to reflect on the moves to come. The Spartan army was seizing the initiative. The Athenians were on board now. Soon others would be as well. In her head, she was playing out every move.

The Queen did not notice her chambermaid, Agathe, approach.

'Is everything alright, Your Majesty?' the girl asked.

Still lost in thought, Gorgo gently touched Agathe's shoulder as she passed. 'I think we may yet humble a mighty Empire.'

Chapter 3

The Heights Of Cithaeron

The Plataean plain
Boeotia, Greece
Three months later

Dust rose as the rider galloped hard up the hill, his face covered by a visor that resembled a dark skull. The colour of the horsehair plume on the top of his helmet matched that of his light blue cloak. A long-sword hung over the back of his right shoulder.

A thundering sound was following close behind. He looked back and saw them at a distance. A long river of horsemen with their lances upheld, the reflection of their weaponry gleaming beneath the hot sun. These were fresh reinforcements he was bringing to the battlefield – warriors, like him, of Scythian blood – who had come to Greece to fight for Persia.

On reaching its crest, he found his destination ahead. The Persian camp spread out on the reverse slope along the banks of the River Asopus. He took off his helmet and wiped the sweat from his brow, opened his flask of water and poured it down over his head.

As he approached the camp, two riders appeared. They wore artificially curled beards and tall crown-like head-dresses. Fine silk gowns covered their glistening armour. These were officers of the Persian army, and they motioned him to stop. They pointed across the vast plain to the high ridges in the distance. 'All cavalry units have been ordered to attack the Greek positions on the Heights of Cithaeron. Hurry!'

The rider turned to look at his exhausted men, and after some hesitation ordered them forward. As he led his men past the Persian camp, he could not help but wonder at its array of brightly coloured tents, the whole camp giving the impression of a peacock's beautiful splayed wings. In the middle of this long camp, the Persians had erected a wooden stockade – protecting within it the largest and most magnificent tents, made of silk and other fine materials, more colourful and elegant than the rest.

They crossed the Asopos at a nearby ford and galloped across a vast undulating plain. It was randomly pocked by large rocks and the scene presented a pleasant combination of green, yellow and grey. After a long ride, they reached a stream on the side of the plain. The rider ordered his men to dismount and rest, and the horses to be watered, while he rode up ahead towards the Heights of Cithaeron to attain a better view.

As he did so, he heard the thundering of thousands of hooves shaking the slopes. He looked up through the clouds of dust and saw the Persian cavalry charging up the hill in great waves. The majority were horse-archers, armed with powerful bows but little by way of armour. Instead of helmets, they wore felt caps and turbans. The rest of the horsemen were lancers, wearing bronze helmets with cheek-guards and jackets lined with overlapping rows of metal strips – not unlike the scales of a fish. While the horse-archers covered their advance by a volley of endless arrows, the lancers pressed forward up the slopes of Cithaeron to punch a hole in the Greek line.

And where were the Greeks? All he could see was thousands of points of light above the dust clouds thrown up by the Persian horses. These were reflecting from shields and helmets all across the top ridge. And as he rode closer, he began to see them clearly. Tens of thousands of Greek *hoplites*, all packed into a single solid formation – the phalanx – eight rows deep, extending for hundreds of yards along the top of the ridge. These foot-soldiers wore shiny bronze armour and face-covering helmets topped with colourful crests which gave them a fearsome appearance, more like iron monsters than men. In front of their positions, they had set up improvised barricades to protect themselves against cavalry attacks such as these. The Greek army was larger than he had expected; certainly much larger than the Persian cavalry advancing up towards it.

As a seasoned warrior, he knew that attacking up a steep slope was always risky, and taking on superior numbers was always a folly; but cavalry assaulting well-entrenched, disciplined infantry was nothing less than suicidal.

As he rode back to his men, the command came. They were going up in the next wave. He joined his men as they mounted up and formed into battle lines. The horses snorted and shuffled restlessly. He looked at his men and then up the Heights above him.

As he formed up his horsemen at the base of the ridge, he saw a familiar contingent, several hundred strong, ride up alongside his men. Whilst most cavalrymen wore shiny armour with brightly coloured clothes and crests to impress their opponents, these particular horsemen were clad in dark metallic helmets and iron cuirasses worn with dark cloaks and black tunics. There was a menacing air about them. Their helmets were of the Grecian type and each of their shields bore the embossed club of Heracles. These were the dreaded Dark Riders of Thebes; Greeks who had come to fight against other Greeks.

As the Thebans organized themselves, the commander rode up to him. He took off his fearsome iron helmet to reveal a fresh, handsome face. Even his short beard could not hide his youth. This was Asopodorus, commander of the Dark Riders, at twenty-eight already the most feared cavalry commander in all of Greece. 'Prince Sherzada, would you care to join me in partaking of this day's glory?' he asked the rider.

'What glory?' Sherzada scoffed as he watched Persian lancers hit the Greek phalanx, as ineffectual as a wave smashing against a rock, many impaling themselves on their enemy's eight-foot spears.

'Not quite what I had in mind, Highness.' Asopodorus drew his curved *machaera* sword, and pointed it up towards a gentler slope on the right. 'Over there is an enemy contingent, cut off from the main body.'

Sherzada saw a smaller Greek phalanx isolated from the rest of the Greek lines, with its flanks virtually undefended. He studied the emblems on their shields to determine which city-state these warriors belonged to. While most bore the standard designs of Attica, it only took one shield emblem to confirm their identity to Sherzada. 'The Chimera!' he said. 'They are Megarians.'

'Aye,' nodded Asopodorus, 'I would have preferred to attack their neighbours, the Athenians, but for now the Megarians will do.'

Sherzada counted their ranks, estimating their numbers. 'About three thousand of them, and we – your force and mine – are less than two. We cannot defeat a solid phalanx like that.'

'Unless?'

They looked at each other, as if they had read each other's mind.

Sherzada quickly turned his horse around and, approaching his riders, ordered them to change formation; dividing them into three consecutive waves. Asopodorus' Dark Riders formed up behind them. Sherzada told his men to sheath their battle-axes and take out their bows instead. He and his men had practiced this manoeuvre many times with the Thebans but this would be the first time they would put it to use.

Nudging his horse forward, Sherzada ordered his men up the gentle slope towards the Megarian lines. As the distance between his horsemen and the Megarians lessened, he gave a signal and a volley of arrows from the first wave shot high in the air, following a trajectory that came down hard into the centre of the Megarian phalanx. Then he ordered his men to slow down, as he reined in his own horse. And as they did so, the first wave fired their arrows again, this time directly into the massed Megarians, each horse-archer seeking out exposed body parts: arms, thighs, necks and eyes.

Sherzada brought his horse to a halt out of range of any javelins or rocks the Megarians could hurl at him. But the first wave continued forward, increasing their speed. They rode confidently toward the Megarian lines and then at the last moment wheeled around, turning away from the enemy. And as they turned, they fired another direct volley into the Megarian mass. The fire was accurate and deadly.

While Sherzada's horse remained motionless, the second wave repeated exactly what the first wave had done, but causing even greater damage. The Megarian hoplites, however, continued to maintain the cohesion of their phalanx, with the place of each fallen comrade taken by the man behind him. Amid an unrelenting hailstorm of arrows, the Megarians held their ground.

The first two waves kept up a steady fire of arrows from a safe distance, as the third wave came up. And this time, driving his horse at full speed, Sherzada galloped up ahead, leading them sharply to the right, threatening the Megarian left flank. The Megarian shields went up in anticipation of collision. Sherzada could see them bracing for the impact. But there was none; at the last moment, his men swerved away.

The Megarians had been too distracted by Sherzada's feint against their left flank to notice the Dark Riders suddenly appear on their right. Having ridden unnoticed behind Sherzada's first two groups, they now smashed into the Megarian lines. The shock was enough to convulse the phalanx. The Thebans did whatever damage they could and then quickly retreated. Momentum is the ally of every cavalryman; immobility his enemy. Their retreat was covered with a deadly barrage of arrows.

Sherzada halted his force at safe distance and surveyed the Megarian lines. He saw dozens of men dead and the dying. The soldiers in their front rank, if it could still be called so, were literally on their knees, cowering behind their shields. Behind them, the rest of their formation had melted into a mob of men huddling together for protection. And in the rear, he could see increasing numbers of men throwing away their heavy shields, hurrying up the hill for safety. The Megarian phalanx was no more.

'Once more and we'll finish them off,' suggested Asopodorus.

Sherzada agreed. But as he was about give the command, a Persian messenger rode up and addressed them. 'Prince Mashistiyun orders you to retire from the field. He will take over the operations here. His Highness wishes to make an example of these Greeks.'

Asopodorus could understand Persian, even if he could not speak it. He threw up his arms in the air and rode up to the messenger. 'I am a Greek too, you know, if 'His Highness' has not forgotten. Would you like to make an example of me, too?'

The Persian messenger, who had not understood a word Asopodorus had said, chose to ignore the tiresome Greek. He rode away.

Asopodorus muttered, 'We did not take the risk to let the Persians steal our glory.'

Sherzada was about to explain that they had no choice as long as the Persians led them, but then he looked at the Megarian lines, and changed his mind.

Greek reinforcements were coming down the ridge to shore up the Megarians. The first to arrive were some three hundred Athenians. Their officers went over to the Megarian mob and hurriedly reformed them into some semblance of a military formation. The Athenians took up position alongside the Megarian mauled right flank, where the Dark Riders had wrought the most damage.

Meanwhile, four thousand armoured Persian cavalry arrived under the command of an exceptionally large man riding a magnificent, though much suffering, horse. Mashistiyun, wearing a long purple cape over heavy gold-plated armour, had styled himself a 'Prince' even though he was related only by a distant marriage to the royal family. He was, however, a favourite of Mardauniya, the Persian viceroy, and had been appointed by him to command the Persian cavalry. Mashistiyun arrogantly sneered at Sherzada and Asopodorus and then turned to look at the Megarians with equal disdain.

He raised his sword with a mighty roar. 'Let us slaughter these dogs!' Reinforcements thundered down the slopes to the aid of the Megarians, but they were too far. Not even the three hundred Athenians deployed on the Megarian right would make any difference. The pride of the Persian cavalry was about to teach a terrible lesson.

Suddenly the front row of the Athenian infantry went down on one knee. And by doing so, they revealed scores of archers behind them, training their bows directly at their attackers. In a split moment, the arrows flashed into the crowd of oncoming Persian horsemen. Within moments, a second volley followed the first, sparing not even the horses. And then, a third. Mashistiyun and his horse fell with a crash. His cavalrymen were stopped in their tracks; forced to turn back under an unrelenting hail of arrows.

It was not long before the entire Persian cavalry appeared at the scene to gawp at Mashistiyun's corpse. His bloody cape covered most of his corpulent body like a shroud, a dozen arrows protruding from it. Though most of the Persians had no particular love for Mashistiyun, honour demanded his body be recovered.

The ground shook as tens of thousands of Persian horsemen charged up the hill again against the Megarian lines. But Sherzada and Asopodorus held their men back. It was not their fight. By then the Greek formations had come down and formed a gigantic solid phalanx around the Megarians. As the Persian cavalry closed in, the battle-cry *Eleutheria* rang out across the

Heights. With that, the entire Greek army surged forward and charged their enemies. Infantry clashed with cavalry amid a thunderous crash.

Some of Persians' horses panicked and shied away at the last moment, throwing their riders to the ground. Most could not escape being skewered by Greek spears. Screams of men and animals echoed through the valley. The Greeks had smelled blood and pushed through their advantage. As they advanced, injured horses went wild – charging to the rear, crashing into anything that came in their way. The fallen ones flailed their legs wildly in the air. The Persians tried to fight back, but could not. It was not long before they were in full retreat, leaving the bodies of their General and thousands of their comrades littered on the slopes of Cithaeron.

Sherzada shook his head and ordered his men to cover the Persian retreat, sufficiently convincing the Greeks that continuous pursuit was not in their best interests. As they came down to the plain below, Asopodorus began to vent. 'I hate these Persians. And I fight for them only because I hate the Athenians even more.'

Sherzada knew about the age-old rivalry between the two great city-states of central Greece and how over the years Athens had humiliated and overshadowed the Thebans. If it were not for the Athenians fighting on the other side, the Thebans would have just as easily fought against the Persians, as some of them had done at Thermopylae.

They did not notice that they had company. A bare-headed Persian rider had followed them down the slope. He wore a flowing purple robe and armour, similar to Mashistiyun's. Sherzada allowed the others to move ahead, while he lingered to let the Persian catch up to him. The two met and shook hands.

The man was Burbaraz; in his early forties, with long dark wavy hair and a pleasant face. He was a true Prince of Persia, a grandson of no less a man than King Cyrus the Great. Despite his delicate frame, the prince was a hardy warrior, a veteran of many campaigns. He was also the last of a breed; the great thinking generals of the Persian High Command that had once led Persia to great victories. A professional soldier, Burbaraz had fallen foul of royal sycophancies and court conspiracies when Xerxes ascended the throne, ending up commanding far-flung military outposts on the savage frontier along the great river the Greeks called *Istrus*, better known by the locals as the Danube. He had now been called back to fight the Greeks.

'What was all that about him hating Persians?' he asked Sherzada.

Sherzada smiled. 'This might come as a shock to you, Highness, but the Greeks hate you. All of them hate you!'

'Of course they do,' he laughed, 'but the question is, will these particular Greeks continue to fight for us?'

'They will.'

'... Because they hate each other even more?'

The prince knew these Greeks well enough, Sherzada thought. *After all, even his wife claimed to be one.*

Looking back up the slopes of Cithaeron, Burbaraz said, 'This was lunacy. Mardonius simply wanted to prove his point.' Sherzada noted the use of the Greek version of Mardauniya's name; doubtless an insult.

'Which was?'

'That it was not the right time to attack the Greeks, or so he said,' Burbaraz replied.

Sherzada looked incredulously at the Persian prince.

'What have I always told you about Mardonius, son of Gubaruva?' he asked.

'That he is a military disaster waiting to happen,' Sherzada replied.

'And this you have just seen with your own eyes. But I still do not understand why Khashayarshah had to go home in the middle of the campaign, leaving us at the mercy of this jackass.'

Indeed, Khashayarshah – whom the Greeks called Xerxes, the Great King of Persia – had left Greece over two months ago, declaring his invasion of Greece a famous victory and without finishing the job he had started.

Xerxes' sudden decision to depart Greece had been as perplexing as his decision to invade it in the first place. The invasion had been the brainchild of Mardonius. He had convinced Xerxes to avenge the defeat the Persians had earlier suffered at the hands of the Greeks. That particular defeat – in fact, a disaster – took place a little more than a decade ago at a beach called 'Fennel Field' where thousands of those who fought for Persia, Sherzada's father included, had lost their lives. Now the name of that battlefield had become etched in the Greek psyche as a byword for endurance and triumph. The Greeks would never let anyone forget the victory they had won at Marathon.

But in giving his royal assent, Xerxes made it clear he was going to invade Greece his way. Against the advice of the best military minds in Persia, the Great King chose to raise the largest army the world had ever seen and lead to it to trample Greece into submission. Tens of thousands of troops were summoned from all corners of the Persian Empire, and beyond. The greatest army ever known to man was assembled and sent across the Hellespont from Asia into Europe, supported by a large fleet, to bring these troublesome Greeks to heel. Once they saw the mighty armies of Persia pouring down their passes, the Greeks would quickly submit – or so Xerxes had hoped.

Greek tenacity, however, proved much tougher than either Xerxes or Mardonius had anticipated. But in spite of receiving a bloody nose at Thermopylae and suffering humiliation at Salamis, the Persians held the upper hand. Their fleet still outnumbered the enemy at sea, and their army remained undefeated on land, controlling the northern half of Greece. A Persian victory was almost at hand. Still, what baffled Sherzada was why Xerxes suddenly abandoned the campaign, leaving Mardonius to finish what they had started together.

And not only that, Xerxes had taken the lion's share of his best troops with him. Nearly all the regular Persian troops, as well other contingents from the Iranian heartland who were related to the Persians by race and language, had been withdrawn. Except for several Persian cavalry regiments and a hand-picked battalion of veteran 'Invincibles', Mardonius was left behind with mostly non-Persian contingents from nations subject to or allied to Persia – Sherzada's own amongst them. For Xerxes, these foreign troops had come cheap and if they perished, they would not be missed. After all, their loyalty to the Persian Empire had always been in doubt.

Pointing to the neat lines of the Persian camp in front of them, Burbaraz explained how Mardonius' sycophantic commanders spent most of the day drinking and debauching, neglecting their troops. They had acquired scores of captured women for their pleasure. But now, although wine was plentiful, food was running out, while tempers were running high and soldiers were brawling. Internal divisions and ethnic animosities were eating up the army from the inside, while morale was plummeting. 'All this happening on Mardonius' watch,' grunted Burbaraz. 'This is not a camp of the Persian Army I once knew.'

'We still outnumber the Greeks, though only by a slim margin, and we have far more cavalry then they do. Mardonius must have a plan?'

'Oh yes, he has a plan,' replied Burbaraz, 'and it is all about auguries and gold.

'Mardonius has, for the last week or so, been secretly sending gold to some of the Greek commanders in the hope that they will defect to us. In the meantime, he continues to perform elaborate sacrifices to determine the will of Destiny. And each day, he declares the auguries are unfavourable, and then all of us sit around and wait for the universe to rearrange things for us.'

'Surely this is a jest?'

'I have never been more serious,' Burbaraz responded. 'This is only adding to the disaffection in our camp. Many of us are wondering what the enemy have done to receive all that gold while our own side have never seen any of it.'

'This is no way to win a battle.'

'My friend,' replied Burbaraz as he put his hand on Sherzada's shoulder. 'I fear this battle may already be lost.'

Chapter 4

Enemies Of The State

Royal Compound of the Agiadae
Sparta
Two days later

The old man hobbled silently into the main hall. It was just like the living room of any other Spartan home, only far larger; the privilege of royalty. A low fire was burning in the hearth, casting orange light across the room. In the left corner of the room, the man saw the young Queen-mother standing next to two long-haired officers, both in their mid-twenties. He recognized them. Theras, Commander of the *Hippeis* – the Company of Knights – and his deputy, Iason.

The officers acknowledged the presence of the old man with a respectful nod, but the Queen, with her back turned to the entrance, was too preoccupied to have noticed his arrival. She was poring over a large map spread across the main dining table. The old man looked at her with admiration. The precocious little girl he had once known now looked so majestic, in spite of her relative youth and simple dress.

'Theras, you must take the Knights to Plataea immediately,' the Queen ordered, without lifting her eyes from the map.

'We have been through this before, Majesty,' responded Theras. 'I cannot abandon my post. My duty is to remain here and protect the young king, yourself and the family of King Leotychidas while he is away at sea.'

'King Leotychidas' daughter is fully capable of defending herself,' Gorgo retorted with a laugh.

Iason raised his eyebrows and smiled awkwardly. 'I can certainly attest to that,' he said, rubbing his still-throbbing chin. Princess Lampito was something of pugilistic prodigy, albeit with a short temper.

'And I can take care of myself, my son and King Leotychidas' wife. There is no need for you to remain here in Sparta.'

'Do not misunderstand me,' pleaded Theras. 'There is nothing I want more than to fight at Plataea. I did not come first in my class in the Upbringing to stay home in Sparta while my former classmates do battle with the enemy. But as the commander of the Knights, my duty is to protect the Royal Households. That is the Law.'

'In that case, I relieve you of that duty, Theras,' replied Gorgo. 'I shall bear the full responsibility of the consequences. Gentlemen, you must understand. This is a different type of war. It is no longer a question of opposing armies arriving at the battlefield, and having a go at each other until one side gives up and runs away. Logistics can affect a battle's outcome just as easily as strategy and tactics. Right now the biggest threat to our army is the enemy cavalry which is threatening their supply lines, and we simply do not have enough horsemen at Plataea. Yours is the only cavalry unit Sparta has, and it should be up there on the Heights. It is only a matter of time before the enemy cut off food and water to our troops on the Heights of Cithaeron. We must have more cavalry up there to stop them.'

'But what about our internal enemies?'

Gorgo's eyes rolled as she let out a frustrated sigh. Moving away from the map, she straightened her posture, folded her arms and said, 'There are ways of managing these 'internal' enemies. I assure you, gentlemen, we have nothing to worry about for the foreseeable future, excepting the Persians.'

'Majesty, with respect,' replied Iason, 'we simply cannot take that chance. We have no choice but to obey the Law. We are sorry.' The two men bowed low and left the room.

Gorgo's eyes followed them as they left, alighting on the old man. Studying his face, she reflected on the transformation of this once-great warrior. His hair, jet-black in his younger days, was now almost completely white, as was his incredibly long beard. He looked more like a wizened priest then a warrior of Sparta. And like a priest he carried a tall staff, if only to compensate for his much-suffering left leg.

'I trust you are well, *Navarch*?' she asked, addressing him by his official title of Admiral and motioning him to take a seat. He was the first Spartan ever to hold that rank, having served as the commander of the combined Greek fleet at the battle of Salamis. Although the great Athenian Themistocles had been the genius behind that victory, Eurybiadas shared a good part of the glory.

'Tell me, how is your leg?' she asked.

'It is getting better, Majesty.' Eurybiadas' leg, first injured during military training in his youth, had been further damaged the previous year at Salamis when a grappling hook from a Persian warship had torn into his tendons. Although Eurybiadas had been honourably relieved of all further military duties, he continued to serve his Queen in other ways.

'What news of our neighbours to the north?' Gorgo asked as she sat down on a chair beside him.

'The 'gifts' were delivered, as per your instruction, Majesty,' said Eurybiadas, smiling slyly. 'The Tegean oligarchs have come round to our way of thinking. Tomorrow they will send a force of fifteen hundred, along with contingents from other Arcadian cities, to join ours at Plataea. They will also persuade Mantinea and Elis to join our cause. Soon, Argos will be the only pro-Persian state left in the whole of the Peloponnesus. Our gold is doing its work.'

'And to think, that gold was not even ours to start with.'

'It wasn't?'

'The coins are *Darics*, Persian gold. We intercepted a shipment last month on its way to Argos, remember?'

Eurybiadas smiled.

'Even though the current regime in Tegea has been sympathetic to us, some Tegean factions oppose us bitterly. But these 'gifts' will strengthen the government's hand domestically and help them convince other cities to send troops to support us. It was worth every coin.'

'Majesty, I have not had so much fun since the time of your father – may the gods forgive him.'

Gorgo smiled at the compliment. Eurybiadas had always been fond of her father, even though like most Spartans he never quite understood his strange ways.

The Queen looked out through the window as the sun began to set. She saw Agathe and the other servant girl retiring to the small hut where they lived, together with the whole of their extended family. She often felt empathy for these hard-working people, whose only role was to serve their Spartan masters. But for an accident of history, Gorgo could not see the distinction between these 'Helots' and the 'Spartans' they served.

'Have we prepared any contingencies? … In case the battle does not go our way?'

Eurybiadas shook his head. 'We have no more troops to spare. Most of our citizens not with the field army at Plataea are either with King Leotychidas' fleet or on garrison duty in Laconia, Messene and Cythera. The same goes for our *Perioiki* allies. Our border rangers – the *Skiritae* – are manning the fortifications on the Isthmus. I can call up the reserves but, as you know, most of them are young boys or old men and there aren't many of them in any case. Majesty, we do not have enough troops to stop the Persians if we fail at Plataea.'

'What about the Helots? Surely we can raise a few thousand of them, too?'

Eurybiadas thought a moment. 'In theory, we can raise tens of thousands of them, but this is not the point. You know better than I how difficult it is to convince our generals and our politicians to arm the Helots. Majesty, recall the tremendous resistance you faced in arming and training just a thousand Helots as heavy infantry to fight alongside our army at Plataea. Imagine how difficult it would be to arm even more, and that too on Spartan soil.'

'But they are the servants of Sparta,' she said. 'They will be fighting for their homes if the Persians come, just like us.'

Eurybiadas shook his head but said nothing.

'So when will we begin to trust our Helots? When the enemy is on our very doorstep?'

'Not even then,' he answered. 'Spartans will never trust the Helots. That is why we have to maintain our garrisons within the domains of Sparta to keep an eye on them even now, in the middle of war; and that is why we send our secret squads against them year after year. That is why, as you just saw, the Knights will never leave the Royal Families, or indeed Sparta, exposed to Helot threat. They are, after all, the enemies of the State. Spartans fear the day when the Helots will rise up and kill us all.'

Gorgo rose, disgusted. But Eurybiadas was telling her what she already knew. It was not his fault that every Spartan slept with a weapon next to him to protect him against a Helot wanting to slit his throat in the middle of the night. It was not his fault that the Spartans feared their own servants more than their sworn enemies.

She turned and smiled, and coming over to her father's close friend, thanked him. The old Admiral got up and bowed graciously and limped out of the room. After closing the door behind him, Gorgo was about to walk back across the hall towards her bedchamber, when she heard a knock.

Opening the door, she found one of the household Helots standing before her. A small, thin man of barely twenty, dressed in a tunic of coarse cloth, a short cloak made of a patchwork of animal skins, and a dog-skin cap. He was sweaty, he smelled awful, and he was panting hard.

'… Majesty, I have just come from Plataea, with a message for you,' he said.

'From Prince Pausanias?'

'No, Majesty ...' he replied, '... from Prince Euryanax.' He reached into a pouch, and took out a piece of parchment.

'You have run all the way from Plataea?'

The young man nodded. 'I left Plataea two nights ago, Majesty, and I have not ceased to run until now.'

Taking the parchment, Gorgo touched the young man's shoulder. 'Go to your quarters and get some rest. Some food and drink too – and perhaps a wash as well; I shall call you again soon.'

Gorgo closed the door and sat down quietly, unfolding the parchment. What she saw made her smile. *Finally, a coded letter!* she said to herself. *I never thought I would see the day Euro would send me one of these.* Euro had never paid much attention during her father's cryptography lessons when they were children, but she was glad he had finally discovered their value.

Gorgo's father had been fond of solving puzzles, and had developed an unusual interest in cryptography – the only King in Greece with such a hobby. Having a brilliant mathematical mind, his techniques were far more complex that the *Scytale* messages that were routinely used by Spartan field commanders. In any case, Gorgo knew the Scytale code could be cracked by any eleven year old with a little bit of training and a whole lot of patience – at least, she had done so when she was eleven. Her father had taught her and her cousins of the importance of secure communication in all aspects of statecraft; whether war or politics.

Gorgo quickly realized that in spite of his many great qualities, encryption was not one of Euryanax's strongest points. His message was far too long and full of unnecessary errors. She left her chambers and called out to her Helot servants, who quickly brought in more lamps and torches to assist her. It was only after several hours of painstaking work that she finally deciphered his letter:

Our Army is on the verge of chaos. Every single one of the two dozen Greek contingents here wants its own way. Their generals are behaving like unruly children, quarrelling over petty issues. Our own Spartan commanders are not helping matters either, questioning Pausanias' every order and often defying his instructions. Our young cousin does not know how to handle the situation, except to shout and rave, which, believe me, does not help. But I don't envy him. Being the Supreme Allied Commander of the Greek Army is not the easiest job in the world. Pausanias might be a gifted warrior and a capable commander, but he is running out of ideas on how to keep the Greeks together.

Aristeides, the only person who could have sorted us out, is beset with problems of his own. Eight of his ten generals have been arrested after being caught in possession of Persian gold. He does not know what to do with them.

I am still confident that we will beat the Persians once the battle begins; that is, if we don't fall apart first.

These men and their petty egos, thought Gorgo. Quickly, she wrote a coded letter to Euro. Once sealed, Gorgo called for the young Helot who had brought the message. He came running. Confirming he had eaten, bathed and rested a little, she told him to take the message and return to Plataea. Her message to Euro had been short and simple: *Stay on Cithaeron. Make sure the Greeks who really matter fight alongside you, and not against each other. Defeat is not an option.*

Chapter 5

The Spring Of Gargaphia

Plataea
Three nights later

'Did you see him?' asked Asopodorus.

'Yes.'

'Then why did you not shoot at him?'

'He was out of range,' Sherzada replied.

'Who do you think he was?'

'If you didn't know who he was, why did you want me to shoot at him?'

'Shoot first. Ask questions later.' Asopodorus chuckled. 'Is that not the common practice in most armies?'

The distant figure was scampering up to the ridge. 'He seemed to be in a hurry,' Sherzada observed, 'heading for the enemy camp … perhaps a messenger. Looked like he was wearing animal skins; probably a Helot. I wager he was heading for the Spartan lines.'

'If he is,' said Asopodorus, 'it won't be long before this would-be prey of ours informs his comrades. Then we will become the hunted.'

They turned their horses and headed back down the slopes of Cithaeron. With Mashistiyun's death, Burbaraz had taken over command of the cavalry. Sherzada had been helping him mount round-the-clock raids to harass the Greek supply lines. This night he had ridden out with twenty of his horsemen. Asopodorus had joined them, simply for the fun of it. Sherzada had never met a more enthusiastic warrior.

It was a moonlit night and visibility was good, even in the dark. But so far they had not encountered any enemy patrols. They descended into the plain of Plataea and made their way across its rocky, undulating terrain.

'They say you are something of an expert on Sparta?' remarked Asopodorus.

Sherzada nodded. 'I have been studying the Spartans for over ten years.'

'Really? How so?'

'I was in the service of a man called Datis, head of the Persian intelligence network that was gathering information on the Greeks.'

'Was it not Datis the Persian who lost the battle of Marathon?' asked Asopodorus.

'The same, though the defeat was not entirely his fault. And, by the way, he was a Mede, not a Persian,' Sherzada corrected him. 'It is like mistaking you for an Athenian.'

Asopodorus chuckled at the comparison. Thebans hated being mistaken for Athenians.

Soon they came close to the river Asopus and the Persian camp beyond. The party opted for a circuitous route around the side of the camp so as not to alarm the Persian pickets who would have let loose their arrows before bothering to ascertain who they were.

But as they wound around a narrow gully, they heard riders approaching. Sherzada and his men dismounted and took up concealed positions around the gully.

Only Asopodorus did not dismount, signalling his intention to investigate.

Sherzada watched as Asopodorus calmly approached the dozen Greek riders with their shields bearing the insignia of 'the Owl and the Olive'. When challenged, he identified himself as a Plataean cavalryman on a reconnaissance mission. He asked the men who they were.

'We are Athenians, friend,' one of them said in hushed tones, 'on a mission from our War Archon to deliver gold to a Persian commander.'

'Which one?' asked Asopodorus.

'That is none of your business,' replied the Athenian. 'What did you say you were doing here?'

A second Athenian suggested that he might want to accompany them back to camp. 'The War Archon, I am sure, would be interested to hear your report.'

Asopodorus calmly turned his horse, and the Athenians drew their swords. Within seconds, the Athenians went down in a hail of arrows.

Sherzada's men rode over and took charge of the Athenian pack horses, curious to see what they were carrying. Loaded on their backs were dozens of saddlebags full of gold, but all the coins were Darics. Sherzada turned and looked towards Asopodorus.

'The enemy is using the gold Mardonius has sent them to bribe his own commanders.'

'Precisely.'

'So, should we take the gold to Mardonius and tell him his great plan has backfired?'

'From what little I know of Mardonius,' said Aspodorus, 'he will blame us for intercepting his gold and using it ourselves, or even being in the pay of the Athenians. If I were you, I would hide this gold somewhere until after the battle is won.'

As Sherzada's men busied themselves putting the bodies of the dead Athenians on their horses, he began to have a distinct feeling that they were being watched. Hearing a ruffle of leaves and the breaking of twigs, Sherzada sent his men to investigate but they could not find anyone, or anything. It was the second time that night a quarry had eluded them.

* * *

The next morning, Sherzada saw the outcome of their strategy of harassing the Greek supply lines; and still it came as something of a surprise. As the sun rose, the Persian camp saw the entire Greek army come down from Cithaeron and march right up to the Asopus.

The shortage of water, brought on by the cavalry raids, had forced them to come down into the open plain where there was a source of fresh water – the Spring of Gargaphia – in front of which the Greek army now stood.

This new development caused some anxiety amongst the troops in the Persian camp, not only as they saw the entire Greek army present right in front of them, but also at how large it was. Sooner or later, the two armies had to fight. Sherzada was delighted. This was the opportunity to decisively bring the Persian superiority in cavalry to bear on the enemy in these wide open plains of Plataea. For the first time, he felt exhilarated.

Sherzada rode down to Mardonius' headquarters. A conference had already been called to discuss the new situation. On arriving, Sherzada saw a steady stream of commanders and generals entering Mardonius' tent. He could not help but notice one individual standing out amid the throng of men dressed in shining armour and fine silks. This man was alone, pacing up and down as if waiting for someone. His head was shaved as was most of his face, and the only evidence of hair were the thin eyebrows above his intelligent dark eyes and a tiny growth under his lower lip. He wore simple trousers and a metal-studded leather jerkin over a plain military tunic. And yet he appeared more distinguished than all of the well-dressed men around him. This man was not a prince, nor a royal favourite, but a soldier who had risen from the ranks through sheer ability. He was Artabaz.

Sherzada had little respect for the Persian hierarchical system, which was generally viewed as corrupt and nepotistic. In spite of these flaws, the system occasionally recognized and rewarded men of talent.

The first-born son of a humble but brilliant accountant in the

Persian royal treasury, Artabaz ran away from home at an early age and enlisted in the army, much to his father's chagrin, exchanging his family's secure book-keeping profession for the hard and dangerous life of a soldier. Just as his father, Farnaka, eventually rose on the dint of nothing but pure talent to become Darius' trusted Finance Minister, Artabaz rose rapidly, without any help from his father's considerable connections, to be a worthy young general in his own right. His approach to war was logical and clinical, based on calculations, balancing the risks against potential gain. Reducing the art of war to a science gave Artabaz a keen, ruthless edge over many a general.

And so it had been. Over the past ten months of fighting, of all the Persian commanders, only Artabaz could boast victories over the Greeks – minor, but victories, nonetheless. Here was a serious military man who did not suffer fools gladly; and who despised Mardonius and his cronies.

Soon the man Artabaz had been waiting for arrived. Burbaraz wore a simple tunic underneath his long purple robe. He did not want people to forget he was the only blue-blooded prince in Plataea; especially since Mardonius was a commoner, related to the royal family through marriage rather than blood. And like Artabaz, Burbaraz had several victories under his belt, and impressive ones at that. Thirteen years earlier, he had brought all of Macedon to its knees in a lightning campaign that had lasted only thirteen days. Very few Persian commanders could beat such a record.

Entering Mardonius' tent behind the two veteran generals, Sherzada felt the surrealism of it all. The sweltering heat was replaced by cool air and comforts of all sorts. Outside, soldiers were short of food and essential supplies; inside, the opulence of the Persian court was on display. Everything inside this tent, from the silk curtains, plush cushions and rich and intricate carpets, to the fragrance of flowers and perfume everywhere, made it easy to forget there was a war going on outside.

There in the centre of the tent, sitting on a large couch, Sherzada saw Mardonius holding court. Once a handsome man, he had grown fat with royal favours. Once a mover and shaker in the Persian royal court, he was now left behind in Greece to finish the conquest. Sherzada wondered if this man had what it took to deliver a decisive victory for the Great King.

When the conference began, Sherzada stepped forward and urged Mardonius to order a full-scale attack. The Greeks were starving, he argued. Their morale low. This was the moment to strike. The Persian infantry could pin down the Greek phalanx, while the open space would allow the superior cavalry of the Persians and their allies to take their flanks and rear. Victory was thus guaranteed.

When Mardonius hesitated, Artabaz interjected. 'Perhaps, my Lord, there is no need to fight with the Greeks if we wait for our gold to do its work. Perhaps we should retire to the safety and comfort of Thebes and await enemy surrender?'

The Persian viceroy reddened with anger. But then a mischievous calm descended. 'Am I hearing you right, Artabaz?' he asked. 'Is one of our best generals suggesting a withdrawal in the face of the enemy? There will be no retreat. We shall fight and defeat the enemy; but only when the time is right. Do not infect my army with your defeatist talk, Artabaz.'

Amid laughter from Mardonius' sycophants, it was Artabaz's turn to shake with rage. Mardonius' friends began to hurl insults at him, turning his sarcastic words into an example of cowardice. The meeting was over.

For the next three days, Mardonius did nothing except to order his favourite Farandatiya to carry out desultory raids against the Greek supply lines to no effect whatsoever, apart from the occasional slaughter of hapless peasants and their cattle.

On the fourth, once again Sherzada followed Artabaz and Burbaraz into Mardonius' tent. Sherzada smiled as his two comrades grilled their commander-in-chief.

'My Lord, are you shying away from the enemy? Why are you avoiding battle?' asked Artabaz.

'I am not shying away. I am awaiting favourable auguries.'

'Persians have never been led by outlandish superstitions,' Burbaraz chided.

'Actually, it's not the auguries,' Mardonius responded, changing his story. 'I have sent gold to many senior Greek commanders. It is only a matter of days until you will see the Greek lines collapse before your very eyes.'

'Lord Mardauniya,' said Burbaraz, addressing Mardonius by his Persian name, 'we are warriors. We have not come all this way to bribe the enemy. Over the last decade, my meagre frontier forces in Thrace have fought off repeated attacks by hordes of savages across the Danube, many more in number than these Greeks. General Artabaz here has taken city after city with only a handful of troops. And here we are shying away from closing in with an enemy that we still outnumber. In the name of Ahura-Mazda, are we not proud soldiers of Persia? Did we not conquer many kingdoms and extend our empire across three continents? Are we not here to test our courage against those who are considered among the best warriors of Greece? My Lord, you are depriving us of what little honour we have left.

'The other day, Prince Sherzada correctly advised us to attack the enemy with all we have; pin them down with our infantry while we hammer them on the flanks and rear with our cavalry. Why have we not done that? Why do we not attack them even now while they are still vulnerable?'

'If this 'prince' wants to attack the enemy, he can certainly do so. I have just the mission for him. We shall destroy the enemy water supply at the Spring of Gargaphia behind the Greek lines.'

Sherzada stepped forward from the shadows. 'It would be a folly. By destroying their only source of water, we would compel the Greeks to return to Cithaeron. We will have no advantage over the Greeks once they are back on the Heights.'

'Prince Sherzada, it is a rare honour you are being offered. Should you decline my invitation, I shall have no choice but to remove your head from your body.' Two of Mardonius' guards moved their hands to the hilts of their sheathed swords.

* * *

Sherzada arrived with his men at the marshalling grounds, surprised to see several regiments had already formed up. Was Mardonius being unexpectedly generous? But he soon discovered that it was not the case. Mardonius had forbidden native Persian cavalry from joining the raid, preferring to send foreigners to die in such a mission. Nevertheless, the Dahae insisted that they would follow Sherzada. Though Persian-speaking, by blood they were of Scythian stock and they preferred to serve under the command of a Scythian prince than one of Persian blood. Artabaz had added his indomitable Parthian cavalry to Sherzada's force. The Parthian too spoke Persian, but considered themselves a separate tribe. These men were clothed from head to heel in chainmail, even their faces hidden behind a veil of iron; a visage almost as fearsome as that of the Greeks.

And some of the Greeks on the Persian side also came to join the raid. Asopodorus was there with his Dark Riders. The famed lancers from Thessaly joined them too, with their shiny wide *petasos* 'sun helmets', and long capes. They were led by the rather large-framed Thorax, the bravest of the sons of Aleuas, their ruler. Then came the Carian light horsemen – proficient with both the bow and the javelin – led by the dashing and handsome young Dardanus, the favourite of their Queen, and Sherzada's friend, Artemisia. Before returning to Asia with Xerxes, Artemisia had instructed Dardanus to offer his support to Sherzada as and when he needed.

Finally came the troops of Sherzada's own blood – the Scyths.

Among them the Amarygian Sakas – Central Asian Scythians who lived across the Amur River, or the Oxus at it was known to the Greeks. Then there were the Tigrakhaudas, the Scyths of the European steppe – named after their pointed caps. And finally came a single squadron of Sarmatian lancers, European kinsmen of the Scyths, wearing heavy fish-scale armour and round metal helmets. In spite of his misgivings about the whole operation, it was an exhilarating feeling as Sherzada raised his sword to order the advance. He turned and looked the horsemen behind and could not help but swell in pride. He was leading arguably the best cavalrymen from all of Greece and Asia against the finest infantry in the world.

And indeed before him, spread across the plains of Plataea, stood the very pride of Greece – armoured foot soldiers from two dozen cities. The Greek army was a veritable sea of shields and spears all melded into one long solid mass, with beautifully crested helmets and colourful metal-covered circular shields glistening in bright sunshine. With their eight-ranked phalanx stretching right across the valley, their appearance was even more formidable than it had been on the day of Cithaeron.

Sherzada scanned the ocean of shields before him; from the Athenians bearing the letter *Alpha* or the image of *the Owl and the Olive*, deployed on Sherzada's extreme left to the Spartans with the emblazoned *Lambda*s – for 'Lacedaemon,' the official name of the Spartan state – on the extreme right. In between, Sherzada could recognize individual contingents from various city states by their shield insignias – the Greek alphabet *Tau* of Tegea; the winged *Pegasus* of Corinth; the *Far Seeing Eye* of Eretria; the *Flying Eagle* of ancient Sicyon, and the *Flashing Thunderbolt* of Hermione. The Greek army was a magnificent and fearsome sight to behold.

As Sherzada's men began to ride along the river parallel to their lines, the Greek ranks became animated. Men began to shout at the tops of their voices as commands went up and down and across lines. The front ranks of the Greeks brought down their spears towards the enemy while the other ranks in the rear pointed their spears to the sky in increasing angles. Sherzada knew the purpose was to deflect incoming enemy missiles, but this gave the phalanx an appearance not unlike that of a hedgehog – *not very appetizing to cavalry on the hunt,* he thought.

As he approached the river, he saw a small detachment of Greek cavalry ride off in a hurry. However, there were around three hundred Greek *peltasts* – javelin-wielding light infantrymen – blocking their fording point on the Asopos. At Sherzada's signal, a shower of arrows found their targets. His Saka royal guardsmen rode forward and fired at the peltasts at close range. Their high-speed arrows punched through the peltasts' light crescent-shaped shields with deadly effect. Those who survived this barrage tried to throw their javelins at their assailants but were checked by the lancers of Thessaly and Sarmatia, who tore through their ranks. Realizing the danger, some of the peltasts turned and began to run away. It mattered not whether they stood or fled, all were cut down by lances and arrows. In moments, three hundred Greek peltasts lay dead by the Asopos ford, right in front of the entire Greek phalanx. This was a salutary lesson to the Greeks, for none of them now dared to challenge Sherzada's advancing horsemen.

The hoplites in the Greek phalanx began to brace themselves for they must have expected to be the inevitable contact. But, instead, Sherzada ordered his force to make a hard right, and led them in parallel to the Greek phalanx down towards their left flank. Soon the loud human voices, singing battle hymns, began to be drowned out by noises of wind, wood and metal. The shrill blaring of pipes filled the air, as well as mass clashes of the Greek spears against their shields. The cacophony was unbearable. Sherzada recalled how noisy a place a battlefield could be.

At his signal, his force broke from a trot into a gallop. Sherzada's heart started beating faster, at first in time with the hooves of the horses, and then faster still. He had deliberately chosen to go around the Athenians on the Greek left flank, because the Spartan flank was protected by an excessively large number of Helots. The Athenians, by contrast, had only a company of archers and a single regiment of cavalry to protect theirs.

There was a swishing sound as shafts of arrows flew about him. Instinctively, Sherzada raised his shield a split moment before two arrow shafts smashed into it. Sherzada raised his right arm in the air and then pointed to where the arrows were coming from. His horse-archers fired their arrows at full gallop. Athenian archers, unprotected by shields and heavy armour, fell where they stood. And then seeing their opportunity, the armoured Parthians rode down the survivors. The few who tried to escape were cut down by Asopodorus' Dark Riders following up behind. The Thebans were thirsty, as ever, for Athenian blood.

The rest of Sherzada's force poured through the gap created by the Parthians and the Dark Riders, the exact place where the Athenian archers had earlier stood. But then, out of nowhere, came the Athenian cavalry. The Parthians wheeled away to avoid them. But not Asopodorus' Thebans, who took them on with relish. Athenians and Thebans raised battle cries and insults as they charged into each other. Sherzada noticed that the commander of the Athenian cavalry wore no helmet. He was a young man, with his curly red hair waving in the wind. Sherzada suspected this might be the fiery Cimon, son of the famed Miltiades.

The battle hung in the balance until the Royals followed Sherzada against the flank of the Athenian cavalry. Cimon first ordered his men to turn and face them but then he must have seen the Sarmatians and Carians following up behind. He ordered his men to disengage and withdraw. Unlike the Athenian archers who had fallen to a man, Cimon had saved his horsemen to fight another day.

After that, there was not much between Sherzada's force and the Spring of Gargaphia. Most of the defenders fled as they saw the enemy horsemen bearing down on them. The few who tried to make a stand were driven off by a barrage of arrows. The Dahae were first to reach the spring and their horses began to churn up the water and the mud. The Parthians arrived next and quickly dismounted, rolling down rocks to block up the water supply. And just to make doubly sure the Greeks would not make any more use of the water, scores of fully armoured Parthian cavalrymen relieved themselves into the clean spring water.

Sherzada had been keeping an eye on the Greek lines, watching how they would react. The Athenian infantry was closest. He noticed that they were being directed by a lone rider. The Athenian leader was dressed in golden bronze armour and wearing a long black cloak and tunic. The horse-hair crest of his helmet was painted in alternating thick stripes of black and gold – like those on a tiger – matching the colours of his clothing and armour. Because of his helmet, Sherzada could not see his face. But his posture and mannerisms left Sherzada in no doubt that this was Aristeides, the new War Archon of Athens.

Years ago, Sherzada had told Aristeides of the day the two would face each other on the battlefield. Now he watched Aristeides order his foot soldiers to advance against Sherzada's force. Aristeides had made a mistake when he had left his archers unprotected, but Sherzada could not expect him to make another. At Aristeides' command, two battalions of Athenian infantry broke off from the phalanx and started rushing toward Sherzada's men. To slow them down, Sherzada signalled his horse-archers to open fire. But the Athenian foot soldiers merely raised their shields in response as they continued forward. Though some of the arrows found their marks; most fell harmlessly. In all of this, the Athenians lost neither speed nor cohesion. Evidently, Aristeides had trained them well.

So, Sherzada reckoned, it was time to leave.

Chapter 6

Her Father's Daughter

Sparta
Two days later

The Queen settled at the dining table and unfolded a parchment, waiting for everyone to leave before she started to work on it. Again, she found Euro's cryptography atrocious. Though a shorter message, it still took Gorgo a while to decode it.

Afterwards, Gorgo put down the parchment and shook her head. Things were clearly not going to plan. But at that moment, she recalled her father's words: 'It is only in the midst of adversity, that we can test the greatest of our strengths.'

She heard a slight knock on the door, and called out, 'Come in, Agathe.'

A small voice called back. 'It is me, Mother,' and Pleistarchus came in, dressed in his rough grey tunic. His left eye was slightly swollen, and his arms were covered with bruises and scratch-marks, presumably from the day's combat training. Her first instinct was that of alarm. But Gorgo had told herself again and again that she had to accept the brutality of the Upbringing.

The boy seemed fine, and a little excited. He had the same look his father had whenever he won a battle. Gorgo wanted to know what had happened, though like his father, Pleistarchus often kept his victorious feelings to himself.

As Pleistarchus came up to her, Gorgo ran her hand through his hair, clearing it from his big brown eyes. He gave her the same look he always did when he wanted his mother to tell him a story, to inspire him, to encourage him. He wanted to be, tried very hard to be, like his father, the greatest hero Sparta had known.

Usually, Gorgo would tell him a story about his father, about some act of courage, some battle his father had won. Sometimes she told him about true events and sometimes she made up stories. The Queen wanted her son to feel proud of his heritage, of his kingdom, and that one day he would take the place of his glorious ancestors and lead Sparta's armies to great victories. She got up, holding her young son's hand, and led him outside towards the courtyard.

'I suppose you would like me to tell you a story?'

He nodded with a slight smile.

'About the battles your father won?'

The boy shook his head. 'Not today, Mother,' he said, sitting down beside her on the steps. 'I want you to hear about your father, rather than mine.'

It was the first time he had made such a request.

'Today, my team won the competition. I used strategy instead of force. Old Admiral Eurybiadas was there. He laughed until he cried. Apparently, Grandfather had used a similar trick to win a similar competition. He wiped his tears and said I reminded him of Grandfather.'

A smile came across Gorgo's face. Her son had finally asked something she had been dying to tell him all along. But she had refrained. Pleistarchus had so recently lost his father and no one in Sparta wanted him to forget that he was the son of a hero. But though Leonidas was the quintessential warrior, he was not a statesman, and not a politician. Certainly, for Gorgo, her husband was not the king that her own father, Leonidas' half-brother, was.

Gorgo remembered her father, Cleomenes, as the most brilliant king Sparta had ever had – and also the most unconventional.

'Well,' she began, 'your grandfather excelled at everything he did, in war as well as in politics, in everything … except, perhaps, ethics. But he was flawed, as all of us are.'

* * *

It was a day she still vividly remembered. She had been sitting on these very steps by her father's side. She was eight, or maybe nine. There was a pleasant aroma of cinnamon and baking bread wafting out of the house, when Aristagoras, the Tyrant of Miletus, a city-state across the Aegean, came looking for her father. The exiled ruler had been hounding her father for several days; and he now came to their home with an enticing proposition.

Gorgo could tell that Aristagoras did not know what to make of her father's appearance. Unlike the long-haired, bearded Spartans Aristagoras had encountered all over Sparta, King Cleomenes of Sparta was clean shaven. He wore his hair much shorter than most Spartans, simply because he liked being different. Like all his brothers, he was unusually good looking, and had a pleasantly wry, almost mischievous, smile combined with a dry gravelly voice.

Rather than seeing a king on a throne in an opulent palace surrounded by courtiers in glittering attire and fearsome guards, the Tyrant of Miletus found a man in simple clothes sitting on his doorstep, playing with his little daughter. Cleomenes invited his guest to sit beside him – a task Aristagoras clearly found hard, accustomed as he was to sitting on high thrones and luxurious cushions. Ignoring Gorgo's presence – after all, she was only a child and a female one at that – he immediately engaged Cleomenes in conversation. Gorgo continued to sit quietly by her father's lap, pretending to play. But her keen ears were taking in every word.

Aristagoras was one of the leaders of the revolt of the Ionian Greeks against Persia at the time, and the war had not been going well for the rebels. So he had come to Sparta to ask Cleomenes for military support not only to evict the Persians but also to rule Ionia. As the Miletan Tyrant offered immense riches for this endeavour, Gorgo saw her father's eyes glisten. It was no doubt a risky venture, all the way across the sea, but the more

Aristagoras spoke, the more Cleomenes became interested.

And the more interested he became, the more Gorgo became concerned. She pulled at her father's arm. He did not react, and so she rose and tapped him hard on the shoulder. 'Father,' she said.

'Please let our guest finish, my darling,' said Cleomenes, giving her a quick glance.

'But Father,' Gorgo said, trying to regain his attention.

'Shhh ... sweetheart,' Cleomenes responded, motioning Aristagoras to continue.

Frustrated, Gorgo got up, walked over and stood between the two, her back to the guest. 'Can't you see this man is promising you what he does not have ... And his words are making you greedy, Father.'

Aristagoras went red, and then white. 'Surely Your Majesty does not think that. This is a private conversation; would you mind sending the child away?' he asked.

It was a long time before Cleomenes spoke. 'No, my Lord. I shall not send my daughter away. Instead, I must ask you to leave.'

'Surely, Majesty, you do not believe the imaginings of a child?'

'Lord Aristagoras,' Cleomenes responded. 'What you are offering is a very risky proposition and one that might not be in the best interest of Sparta. You are trying to inveigle me with your promises. If you will excuse me, I and my daughter have more important things to do, as do you, my Lord. You will be wasting your time by spending any more of it in Sparta. I wish you a safe onward journey.' That was the end of the audience with the Tyrant of Miletus.

And as he left, somewhat in a huff, Gorgo's father turned to her, kissed her forehead and said, 'You were right, my darling. The greed of kings must never be confused with the interests of the State.'

As an only child, Gorgo was doted upon, but it was not simply indulgence. Even though she was not a boy, her father had decided that he wanted her to be his heir. To Cleomenes, it mattered not that it would be her husband that might one day become king and Gorgo only a queen. He knew from the start that his daughter was much a political animal as he.

For the average Spartan, it was not bad enough that Cleomenes made no effort to look like them – worse, he chose not to think like them either. Spartans resorted to diplomacy and politics as a last resort, and only a poor substitute for the warfare they excelled at. For the Spartans to see their king prefer politics to war was perplexing.

But Cleomenes was, after all, a descendant of Chilon, Sparta's greatest political thinker since Lycurgus, the legendary founder of the state. Long ago, Lycurgus had built Sparta's state and society around security and military survival. But, much later, around a hundred or so years before Gorgo's birth, Chilon came along and challenged this very notion. At a time when Sparta found itself fighting wars along all of its borders, against multiple enemies, Chilon said, 'He who tries to defend everywhere, defends nowhere.' Instead, he urged Sparta to ally itself with friendly neighbours and to use those alliances to contain or dominate potential rivals.

Cleomenes, of course, went a step further by interlinking the defence of Sparta to the politics of Greece. But all of this was lost on most Spartan men, who could not see beyond their own spear-points. They did not understand politics, nor did they want to. But for Gorgo's father, politics was war by other means. He taught Gorgo that Greece was in a constant state of conflict with itself and its neighbours. The only way to save Sparta was through the alliances which ensured Sparta's military superiority and security. That is why King Cleomenes felt the need to intervene politically all over Greece.

Just before her birth, Gorgo's father sent Spartan troops to help Athens liberate it from clutches of cruel tyrants. He also helped Athens expand its influence in central Greece, even at the expense of its rival Thebes. He provided the catalyst that gave birth to Athens' proud Democracy. And still the Athenians hated him.

One evening, Cleomenes arrived in Athens with a small band of armed men, intent on overthrowing yet another regime. The wags in Athens claimed that he was doing it because of a woman, the beautiful young wife of an opposition leader. The Athenians said that he wanted to replace the existing regime in Athens with a friendlier one headed by his lover's husband. But the truth was very different.

The young King Cleomenes had come to overthrow this government not because it was unpopular or because it was unfriendly towards Sparta – it was neither – nor indeed for the sake of any woman. It was because this new Athenian government was trying to negotiate an alliance with Persia. Cleomenes saw the rising power of Persia as a threat to Sparta's existent and he did not want Athens to become its beach-head in Greece. He had arrived in Athens confident that his intervention would have support from the Athenian opposition, if not the Athenian people themselves. In reality, it did not. Nor for that matter did he have any support from Sparta for this Athenian adventure of his. The *Gerousia* refused to authorize a campaign to overthrow an Athenian government that had thus far done nothing hostile to Sparta. But Gorgo's father went in any case, taking with him a small band of armed men, mostly his faithful Helots along with some non-Spartan mercenaries whose wages he paid himself.

The regime was easily overthrown and its leaders expelled. Cleomenes set himself and his followers up on the Acropolis as he went about reconstituting a new government for Athens. The Acropolis was located at the highest point in Athens and it was the home of the sacred complex of the temple of Athena Parthenos, where all the sacred and public business of the city was conducted. The Spartan King invited the citizens of Athens to witness the inauguration of its new leaders. And thus the Athenian people came, and in large numbers, but not in the way Gorgo's father had expected. He had grievously miscalculated.

Angered that a Spartan king would try to impose his will on Athens, the Athenians rose up against Cleomenes and stormed the Acropolis, forcing him and his followers to take refuge in the Temple of Athena. Refused entry by the priestess because he was not of Achaean blood, he told her that all his followers whether Helots or mercenaries were, in fact, of Achaean descent, thus securing their entry into the Temple. Cleomenes then secured his own admittance by confusing history itself and blurring the difference between Dorian and Achaean Greeks.

So, for several days, Cleomenes and his followers remained besieged in the Temple on the Acropolis while an angry crowd frothed outside. Finally, in flagrant violation of their own laws regarding the sanctity of the holiest shrine of their city, the Athenian crowd stormed the Temple complex. The Spartan King, already exhausted and starving, was brought out and put in chains. However, as he was presented before them in this piteous state, the mob threw down their weapons and clubs, remembering him as the man who had earlier rid Athens of tyranny. The people of Athens hastily called to session what was to be their very first Democratic Assembly to try Gorgo's father and his followers. Though the Assembly pardoned him and allowed him to return home in safety along with his Helots, all his non-Spartan followers, including sons of the noblest families of Greece, were executed as a warning against future attempts of this kind. But this did not deter Cleomenes. Upon his return to Sparta, he continued to hound the Athenians until they finally agreed to abrogate the treaty of submission they had concluded with Persia and ally with Sparta.

And that was the crux of it. Half a century earlier, the Persian Empire had appeared on the eastern shores of the Aegean, replacing the Kingdom of Lydia as the overlord of many Greek colonies in Asia. Cleomenes knew that it was only a matter of time before the Persians would cast their gaze across the sea and try to conquer the whole of Greece. Of all the Greek rulers, only Cleomenes had the foresight to see this, and he took action accordingly. All of his interventions throughout Greece were aimed at limiting Persian influence – knowing that Persia's best option would be to try to divide and rule the Greeks. In his view, the best way to defend Greece was for Sparta to establish a web of alliances so that some of the important Greek states stood together alongside Sparta. So he focused on those who had a common distrust, if not hatred, of Persia. 'The enemy of my enemy,' he told the Gerousia, 'will always be my best ally.'

Cleomenes also wanted to address another major threat, this one closer to home. Once the mightiest city in the Peloponnesus, Argos lay only a day's march north of Sparta. The enmity between Argos and Sparta went back centuries, and it was against this state Spartans had fought most of their wars. Seeing it as a potential Persian ally, and a strong one too, Cleomenes attacked the Argive army and completely destroyed it, down to the last man, at the Battle of Sepeia. He then marched on an undefended Argos.

Argive legends claim that the women of the city, encouraged by the poetess Telesilla, mounted such a robust defence that the Spartan army gave up and went home. The Spartans indeed went home, but what the Argives could not explain was why they were made to tear down the walls of their own city. The truth is that as soon as Cleomenes appeared before Argos with his army, the Argives sued for peace. The peace that the Spartan King imposed on them was a humiliating one, without walls, leaving their city defenceless.

Yet this was a victory most Spartans could not comprehend. 'What was the point, Your Majesty,' an Ephor enquired on his return, 'of destroying the entire Argive army at Sepeia, when you had no intention of wiping out Argos itself?'

'Who would the Spartans practice on, if the Argives did not exist?' Cleomenes responded with a smile.

Much later, Gorgo asked him the true reason behind his unwillingness to conquer or destroy Argos. He explained that had he done so other Greek states, especially in the Peloponnese, would have started fearing Sparta even more than Persia, thus undermining Greek unity. 'The balance of power in Greece,' said Cleomenes, 'must be maintained. No state should be allowed to become so strong that it could threaten Greek freedom. Not even Sparta.'

Cleomenes' worst fears, however, were vindicated just a few months before his death when two Persian envoys came to Sparta. They rode into the central market, the Agora, where many were gathered for a festival. Gorgo, who had just turned sixteen, had come with her father and they were watching a dance performance by some of the younger women. This was the first time Gorgo had ever set eyes on a Persian. She had imagined them to be dark skinned, tall, fierce and warlike. Instead, to her surprise, they were men whose hue and height were similar to the Greeks. But everything else about them was strange and alien.

Their hair and beards were long; artificially curled and manicured to the extent that even some twelve years hence, Gorgo thought they could not possibly have been real. The delicate appearance did not end there, but was complemented with eyeliner and kohl, pearl earrings and other forms of cosmetics and jewellery. They looked unmistakably effeminate; faces painted so carefully they could have made a Corinthian harlot jealous, or so she thought. Atop their heads were jewelled turbans. Their clothes were of the finest silk, the type she imagined rich Lydian women wore, and then there were the trousers, exactly like those worn by warrior women in Athenian vase paintings. The Persians held perfumed handkerchiefs to their noses as if to protect their delicate nostrils from unpleasant Spartan odours. While the Spartans watched these strange adorned men with amazement, the Persians in turn sneered in contempt, as if all around them were inferior, dirty creatures.

The Persians laughed at Spartan men for wearing long beards without moustaches, and for covering their bodies with rough cloaks resembling shrouds. They ogled Spartan women who, in their eyes, went about practically nude – especially the dancing girls, whose legs were bare right up to their thighs. But their greatest surprise and loudest laughter was yet to come.

When they asked, through their interpreter, a Greek slave, to be taken to the king, Cleomenes stepped forward and said, 'I am the King of Sparta.'

The Persians paused for a moment, then looked at each other and laughed long and hard. Cleomenes asked the interpreter why they were laughing. He said this was the first place they had visited where they found a king dressed like a beggar. 'To these Persians, Majesty, all you Spartans look like beggars.'

The slave translated as the ambassadors continued to talk to each other. He said that they had heard great stories of Sparta, but they found nothing impressive here, except perhaps the beautiful young women, if one could perhaps look past the slave attire. Despite their mockery, Gorgo watched them stare at the young dancing girls. And then to her disgust, their attention soon turned towards her.

Ignoring their insulting behaviour, Cleomenes calmly invited the envoys to alight from their horses and tell him what they wanted. After some hesitation, they dismounted.

'King of Sparta,' said the thinner of the two, his hooked nose being his most distinguished feature, 'we bring greetings and blessings from the Dariyavush of Persia, King of Lands, King of Kings, the Lord of the East, Conqueror of the North, and Overlord of the West. Our King has sent us here to seek a peaceful conclusion to the cowardly war you have declared on us.'

Cleomenes interrupted. 'Sparta has not declared any war on Persia.'

'You declared war on Persia many years ago at the time of Kurush the Great, when you supported Lydia's aggression against our then peaceful Kingdom,' replied the stouter envoy with a short nose.

Everybody in Greece knew the story of how Croesus, King of Lydia, went to war against Cyrus the Great because of a prophecy. Apparently, the Oracle of the god Apollo at Delphi had advised him that if he crossed the River Halys – the border between Lydia and Persia – he would *destroy a great kingdom*. So he did. After crossing the river and invading Persia, Croesus suffered a crushing defeat at the hands of Cyrus, which led to the destruction of a great kingdom: his own.

'We did not,' Cleomenes exclaimed.

'Were you not allied to Lydia at the time?' said the hooked-nose envoy. 'Did you not warn our King, whom you call Cyrus, not to invade Lydia and not to advance on Ionian Greek colonies who owed allegiance to the Lydian King? Did you not threaten him with war if he did?'

Cleomenes would later tell Gorgo that there was truth to the Persian accusation. But at the time, he said, 'That was long ago and I don't know what this has to do with us. But since you have come here for peace, what does your King propose?'

The stout Persian smiled. 'Our master is very gracious. He abhors senseless bloodshed. And since he wants peace above all else, he asks from you two simple tokens.'

'Tokens of what?'

'Tokens of submission,' the other replied. 'Offer our Great King earth and water, accept him as your ruler, and he will be merciful towards you.'

'And if we refuse?'

They laughed. 'Then you will face certain annihilation,' said hook-nose. 'This hovel of a city will be laid to waste; your temples will be burnt down; all your men put to the sword, and your women will become our concubines,' he said, staring at Gorgo.

'So which of these two options would you prefer, oh King of Sparta?' asked the hooked-nosed one, snickering under his breath.

Cleomenes did not speak. But his signal was enough. The Spartan King's bodyguards seized the Persians and forced them to their knees. Immediately, the Persians' arrogant sneers turned to panic. They began to shout incoherently. They said something about the sacred status of an envoy; the inviolability of his person. To harm an envoy was to bring divine retribution upon oneself. But Cleomenes paid no heed. He ordered them to be tied up and dragged to a disused well behind the marketplace.

The Persians fell to the ground – pleading, crying, begging for mercy. Gorgo thought their behaviour shameful. If these Persians were real men, they would not become so submissive. Spartans preferred to die like men and expected these foreigners to do the same. She spat on the face of the hooked-nose envoy – the one who had threatened to make her his concubine. In broken Greek, upon his knees, he kissed her feet and begged her to spare his life. Gorgo looked into his face and searched her heart but found no compassion.

Cleomenes' voice was calm as he spoke to the Persians through their slave. 'We do things a little differently in Sparta. If you want earth and water, you will find plenty of both at the bottom of this well,' he said, as he signalled his guards to hurl the Persians head-first into the near-empty well.

Gorgo watched her father smile with simple satisfaction when he heard the thuds echo up the well.

'Mischief, do your worst,' she heard him whisper. 'The hounds of hell are baying for blood. From this moment on, we are at war!'

* * *

And indeed, Gorgo thought, *Sparta had been at war ever since.* But her father had not lived to see the coming war, dying unexpectedly just before the first blood was drawn at Marathon. Eleven years on, the conflict was now approaching its conclusion.

Pleistarchus looked at his mother and said, 'So we have no option against the Persian other than victory?'

She nodded.

Gorgo kissed her son on the head as he left the room. She could not help but reflect on his last words. She knew the Greeks had a fighting chance of winning this war. She still had faith in the warriors of Sparta and in the fierce patriotism of the Athenians.

Gorgo sat down on the table and wrote another coded letter, this time using the Athenian method of military cryptography – another technique her father had taught her. Apparently, he had cracked it during his last abortive campaign against the Athenians, before he turned them into his allies. They never knew that he had done it, nor did they know that she, Gorgo, knew the secret. But now they would.

The letter began: *Aristeides, War Archon, from Gorgo, Queen of the Spartans, greetings. If you want to secure victory at Plataea, this is what you must do …*

Chapter 7

Casualties of War

Plataea
That evening

The euphoria of the 'victory' at Gargaphia did not last long. The morning's commanders' conference became something of a shouting match between those who wanted Mardonius to take immediate military action against the Greeks and those who supported his policy of 'wait and see'.

Taking the lead in defending Mardonius was his favourite, Farandatiya – a perfect Persian dandy with long curled hair and a full beard, wearing the finest jewels and perfumes, grown fat on luxury. Once a ruthless field commander, he had realized that life could be infinitely more comfortable and richer through blindly supporting his patron; and there in that tent Farandatiya did everything to earn his keep as Mardonius' chief supporter.

Sherzada smiled as he saw the enormous, hirsute Farandatiya go head to head against the lean and almost hairless Artabaz. The men exchanged insults so elaborate and colourful that no language other than Persian was sophisticated enough to weave, let alone explain, them.

As the meeting grew even more heated, Mardonius offered a compromise. Two more days. He was still confident that his bribes would soon take effect and this would lead to the disintegration of the Greek army. If, however, by the third morning, the situation had not changed, Mardonius promised that he would attack the Greeks and win – or die in the attempt.

'He is just buying time,' Burbaraz whispered to Sherzada. 'Just look at him. He remains locked away in this luxurious tent of his, cut off from the reality outside. And his cronies continue to treat this whole expedition as some sort of a decadent picnic, rather than anything vaguely resembling a military campaign vital to Persia's interests.'

Sure enough, that evening Mardonius' Greek friends organized a dinner party – a *symposion* – very much in the traditional Greek fashion, with the finest wines and delicacies for the Persian generals and their supporters. Sumptuous carpets, couches and cushions had been laid out across a vast tent for the occasion.

The young slaves who had been drafted for service and pleasure were dressed in a peculiar mixture of Greek and Persian attire, with long robes over short tunics. The organizers, probably Boeotians from nearby towns, had the slave girls wear veils, mistaking it for a Persian tradition. In Persia, this veil was only for high-born women, a symbol of dignity and respect. The Persians would have taken exception to this, had they been sober enough to notice.

Burbaraz stayed away, deeming it bad taste to celebrate while the enemy stood ready for battle only a few hundred yards away. Sherzada decided to show up for no other reason than curiosity, though once there he realized Burbaraz had been right all along.

Soon after entering the tent, Sherzada spied Artabaz and Asopodorus reclining on high couches in a secluded corner. They were deep in discussion, and incredibly drunk. As Sherzada approached them, he heard Artabaz say in Greek, 'It's not going to go well, my friend. Look around you. I do not expect many of these clowns to survive the impending battle.'

'How can you be sure, my Lord?' Asopodorus asked.

'All these men are sycophants,' said Artabaz, shouting above the noise. 'Their only purpose is to entertain Mardonius and shield him from the truth. They are not real warriors … And, besides, I have a bad feeling about this battle … It's making me sick … or perhaps it's this wine,' he said, as he retched forth. He struggled to sit up to regain his composure. Then he fell face forward, burying his nose deep inside the thick carpet amid his own bile. The most cool-minded of Persia's generals had just passed out.

Asopodorus looked up with an expression of disgust on his face and saw Sherzada approaching. Raising his goblet, he gave him a broad smile, and in doing so, leaned so far backward that he lost his balance, and fell off his couch headfirst onto the soft carpet below. He too lay unconscious in a drunken stupor.

Sherzada had been looking forward to talking with these two, but they were not in any state for rational discourse, or discourse of any kind for that matter. Looking around the room, he was disgusted by what he saw. Outside, ordinary soldiers were starving for lack of food, thirsting for water, and here their leaders were indulging in the most extravagant gluttony and debauchery.

Sitting atop the couch that Asopodorus had just vacated, Sherzada noticed a young slave girl with long dark hair standing not far away. Something about her was familiar, and she slowly made her way towards him. Coming close, she lowered her veil, revealing a beautiful face, and suddenly he recognized her. Farandatiya's favourite concubine.

The Persians kept their concubines in harems, rarely allowing them the liberty of the camp. But Sherzada had seen this one the day he arrived here, as he was walking through Mardonius' camp. This girl had passed very close to him; near enough for him to get a good look at her face. What had struck him, in addition to her beauty, were her eyes. The colour was rare and unforgettable. He had noticed that her sad face had momentarily lit up to give him a pleasant smile – as if she knew him. It was the same smile and those same bright violet-blue eyes that greeted him now.

Most of the women serving in the Persian camp had only recently been acquired – mostly in the sacking of cities that dared to resist Persian occupation; or, less frequently, taken from their homes simply because a Persian commander liked what he saw.

Now as concubines or slave-girls of Persian nobles, these young women were not meant to leave their tents except to serve their respective masters. Only Persians were allowed to keep concubines during the expedition and these concubines were not supposed to be with other men. They could be killed for such an offense.

The girl walked over and quietly sat down next to him, ignoring the attentions of other men calling for her. She reached her arms around his neck and whispered into his ear. But Sherzada could not understand what she was saying, her soft voice drowning amid the revelry.

Sherzada was about to ask her to repeat what she had said, when a drunken Persian nobleman swaggered towards them and grabbed one of her arms. The girl resisted, stammering in broken Persian, 'I shall be with you soon, Master. I just need to attend to his Lordship first.'

''His Lordship' is nothing but a subject princeling,' sneered the man. 'One of our slaves, just like you.'

Sherzada rose and gripped the soft upper parts of the Persian's hand so tightly that he yelped in pain, forcing his fingers to release the girl. Next, Sherzada plunged his knee into the Persian's groin as hard as he could. The man doubled over in pain, and fell to the ground, where Sherzada quietly but fiercely kicked his head for good measure. The Persian did not get up. He took the girl by the arm and took her outside. 'What do you think you are doing here? Go back to your quarters.'

'But I came here,' she said, 'to see you.'

This he was not expecting.

'I shall explain everything,' said the girl. 'Let us first get away from this place.'

She set off towards a clearing behind a small hill at the rear of the Persian camp. It was a lonely place, where she sat on the stump of a tree while Sherzada stood in front of her waiting to hear her story. She introduced herself as Cleonice, from

Byzantium. Farandatiya had taken her from her family and made her his concubine. Farandatiya, or as the Greeks called him Pharandates, was a vicious lout. He was as brutal as he was sycophantic. Sherzada hated him, but the girl had reason to hate him even more.

'What is it you want me to do?' Sherzada asked.

'You intercepted some gold from the Athenians the other night. I want you to buy my freedom with it and that of the other girls who want to leave Pharandates.'

So this was the person Sherzada had heard that night.

'I was trying to escape, but when I saw your men massacre the Athenians, I got scared and ran back. But before I left, I heard what you were planning to do with the gold. You can put that gold to good use now and free us.'

'What makes you think I don't have better use for it?'

'My Lord, I approached you tonight only because I have heard good things about you. We all witnessed your courage at Gargaphia, but you are also not afraid of speaking your mind, even in front of Mardonius himself. I have heard too that you had a reputation for rescuing women in distress. They say you bought the freedom of the Athenian women and children who were captured when the Persians stormed the Acropolis. So, my Lord, can you not free us also?'

Cleonice got down on her knees before Sherzada. He knew what she intended to do. She wanted to grovel at his knees in the fashion of a Greek supplicant, a practice he had always regarded as humiliating.

He stepped back and motioned her to get up. 'I will do what I can for you and the other girls. But you have to be patient. I expect the battle to take place in a day or two. If the Persians win, I shall use the gold I had captured from the Athenians to buy your freedom.'

Cleonice gathered her long dress and rose to face him. 'And if the Persians don't win?' she asked.

'Well, you will have nothing to worry about. The Greeks, I am sure, would free you.'

'My Lord, all Greeks who are found in the Persian camp will be killed. The Greeks who are fighting against you make no difference between those who fight for the Persians willingly and those who are kept by them against their will. There is even less mercy for Greek women who sleep with Persians.'

'Is there not someone in the Greek camp – some Athenian or Spartan – who could help you?'

Cleonice shook her head. But then she said, 'One of the other concubines is a girl from the nobility of the island of Cos. She told me that her father was a close friend of a man called Cleombrotus, the brother of the late King Leonidas of Sparta.'

'Cleombrotus passed away some months ago,' said Sherzada. 'But his son Pausanias now commands the entire Greek army. Tell the girl from Cos to seek him out when battle is over.'

'But how will she do that?'

Sherzada described the Spartans to her and said that under the custom of his people, Pausanias could not deny protection to the daughter of a *Xenos* – a Guest-Friend. Under the Greek code of hospitality a Guest-Friend was virtually a family member. The girl from Cos could thus win her freedom, he explained, as well that of all the other girls kept by the Persians.

'What if we cannot reach the Spartans?'

'Then seek out the Athenians,' he replied. 'They are led by a general – a good man – called Aristeides the Just. If Pausanias does not help you, Aristeides certainly will. Just mention my name to him. He will protect you.'

Cleonice smiled slyly. 'My Lord, for a commander in the Persian army, you seem to know an awful lot of important Greeks.'

Sherzada smiled back but avoided explanation. 'Now, please return to your quarters,' he said, 'before someone sees you.'

'Stay safe, my Lord. My freedom may well depend on you,'

said Cleonice, before she hurried away.

* * *

Sherzada did not expect what lay in store for him on return to his quarters. As soon as he arrived, two of his officers approached. 'Highness. A Macedonian officer is waiting for you,' one of them said.

'Macedonian?' he repeated. There were no Macedonians in Plataea.

'He says that he has come with an urgent message from Alexander, King of Macedon,' said the second officer. 'We told him you were at a dinner, and it might take a while. But he said he would wait all night if he had to. So we asked him to wait inside your tent.'

The Macedonian king, officially an ally and subject of Persia, was an enigmatic individual. Sherzada had met him some years back, but had no idea what he might want.

'What does this Macedonian look like?'

'We don't know. He did not take off his helmet. But he said he was very hungry, so we sent in some food,' said the first officer.

'He is not tall,' said the other, 'and by his voice he is young, almost a boy.'

As Sherzada walked into his tent, he saw the back of the Macedonian, seated at the table, eating heartily; long russet hair fell down his back right to the waist. Eager to have a look at him, he walked around the table and then let out a gasp. 'Princess Gygaea?'

A dark purple cloak bearing the royal insignia of the blazing sun of Macedon covered much of her body, but the bronze cuirass the Princess wore looked uncomfortably large for her slender frame. The white horse hair-crested helmet that had obscured her face was placed on the table, alongside the food she was feasting on.

'My Lord, it is good to see you again,' she said, with a delightfully exotic Macedonian accent. Most Greeks regarded it very provincial, but Sherzada found it melodic. 'I hope you do not mind me making myself at home.'

'My Lady, you are very welcome here,' he said, 'but I feel a little awkward entertaining the wife of Prince Burbaraz alone. Does your husband know you are here?'

Gygaea shook her head as she finished swallowing her last morsel. 'Burbaraz does not, and must not.'

'I am sure if I were him, I would like to know if my wife were visiting my camp.'

'My brother Alexander is also here at Plataea and he too does not know I am here. With the help of some trusted officers I disguised myself as one of his escort cavalrymen and accompanied him here, without his knowledge. When we arrived, I slipped away to see you. I shall explain everything. But you must promise that what I am going to share is for you alone. Not even my husband can hear of it.'

Sherzada frowned. He walked over to his couch and, deep in thought, sat down opposite his guest. And after a long, awkward silence, he said, 'Very well. I give you my word, my Lady.'

Gygaea got up and walked over to Sherzada across the carpeted floor, sitting down beside him on a broad cushioned chair. Sherzada's tent was not as grand as those that belonged to the senior Persian commanders, but it was tasteful and elegant, with handcrafted furniture and cushions covered with Himalayan silk. Gygaea paused to take in the tent before she spoke. And when she did, leaning over and almost whispering to him, Sherzada felt the gravity of her voice. 'You know that Burbaraz often talked about a traitor on the Persian side, who has been passing vital intelligence to the Greeks?'

Sherzada nodded. He knew that somebody high up was passing sensitive information to the Greeks. Lately, Burbaraz had become increasingly obsessed with uncovering his identity. Of course, Sherzada knew that there were many on both sides spying for the other, and some even passing sensitive information to both sides for profit. But the one Gygaea spoke of was a particularly important man on the Persian side, and the information he was giving to the Greeks was critical.

'I know him well,' she said, slowly. 'For he is my own brother.'

Sherzada had long suspected Alexander, son of Amyntas, the King of Macedon, of having sympathies for the Greek cause. All Macedonian royals claimed Greek descent, even though the Greeks never accepted them as such. For most of the Greeks, Alexander was something of a semi-Barbarian. But then no one was so well placed as Alexander. Through the marriage of his sister to Prince Burbaraz, he was a member of the extended Persian Royal Family. At the same time, he held the title of Friend of the Athenian People. The Macedonian King counted among his personal friends successive kings of Sparta while being hailed by its bitter arch-enemy Argos as its Benefactor. He was the only king of his time to have attended in the same year both the coronation of Xerxes in Susa and the Olympic Games in Greece. He was trusted by both Xerxes and Mardonius, and yet only fourteen years ago he had executed Persian envoys, long before the Spartans and the Athenians followed his example, and still he managed to get a pardon for himself. Gygaea's marriage to Burbaraz – the man who had humbled Macedon – had helped sweeten that particular deal. Alexander of Macedon had literally got away with murder.

'I am not so surprised, my Lady. Your brother has made a career of operating on both sides of the fence.'

'You too are a man of many secrets, my Lord,' she said as she got up and walked about. 'Alexander has come here to Plataea, ostensibly with supplies for Mardonius' army. But the real purpose of his visit was to contact the Athenian, Aristeides, to coordinate his plans with him. A trap is being laid for the Persians, both here in Plataea and on the Macedonian border.

This trap is being sprung as we speak. There is not much anybody can do about it at this stage. The only thing I am certain of is that your army will be defeated here at Plataea.'

'What makes you so sure, my Lady?'

'Are you aware that some Persian commanders are being bribed by the Greeks, with the same gold that Mardonius was sending them?'

'I am, and I believe Aristeides to be behind this.'

'Precisely,' she said. 'If the Greek plan works, many Persians will flee the battlefield once the fighting starts. Some will stand and fight; others will flee. But in the end, it won't matter. All will be killed. My brother will make sure of that. Right now, in Macedon, the entire Persian garrison is being put to the sword. Alexander will ride back tonight to the Macedonian border with Thrace at the crossing of the river Strymon. It is there he intends to ambush and massacre the defeated Persian army fleeing Plataea. After that, Macedon will once again be free of Persian control, and my brother will become king of an independent state.

'This brings me to the reason I have come to you. You and my husband are among those who will not flee. You will fight and die bravely. But you can save yourself and my husband too. All I ask is that if the battle turns against you, run away. And when you flee, do not take the shortest and easiest route to Thrace across the Strymon. Take any other route; just avoid that crossing. You must convince my husband to do the same, but without betraying my brother's plan.

'My Lord,' continued Gygaea, 'you see me as a Macedonian princess. But in my heart I am Greek as well as Persian. For me, it matters not who wins. I am caught between the sin of betraying my brother and the land of my birth and that of abandoning my husband and being disloyal to the blood of my children. Either way, one side or the other will call me traitor. But I do not care. I love Macedon and Greece but I cannot hate Persia either. My own children have been brought up as Persians. The blood of Cyrus the Great runs through their veins. I cannot stop this useless war, but I can try to save my family. Of all the men here in Plataea, you are the only one I trust – not because you are neither Greek nor Persian but because you have a reputation of being a man of honour.'

It was a reputation that was lately becoming very difficult to live up to. 'My Lady, I promise that I shall do what I can to save your husband,' he said.

'That is all I can ask of you.' She rose and put on her ill-fitting crested helmet. 'Stay safe, my Lord.'

Afterwards, Sherzada paced his quarters. Was a Persian defeat really a foregone conclusion, or was there yet a possibility of Mardonius awakening from his torpor?

Chapter 8

The Hero's Dilemma

Sparta
The following morning

'How glorious fall the valiant, sword in hand, in front of battle for their native land!'

Standing in the middle of the vast courtyard, Pleistarchus recited the lines of the war-poet Tyrtaeus under the strict but satisfied gaze of his instructor.

Gorgo sat on a bench alone in the corner watching her son go through his lessons, but her mind was on Plataea. She felt dismayed that Pausanias was making needless blunders when he ought to have been taking control of the situation. While anxiously waiting for more news to arrive, she also dreaded what it might be. Whether for good or for ill, Gorgo knew the decisive moment was approaching.

Her thoughts drifted to the past, eleven years ago to the very day – the day the Persians first arrived in Greece.

* * *

It was the first night of the Carneia Festival. People were in the streets, dancing and celebrating. But something made them stop and turn around. Dressed only in a loin-cloth, a young herald had come running into town. His lean bronzed body and curly dark hair caused much excitement as people tried to speculate who he was. Was it really him?

Instinctively, the crowd got out of his way, allowing the man to run up to the Agora, where Gorgo and Leonidas were holding court. On reaching it, he all but collapsed at Leonidas' feet. Kneeling before the king, the young man produced a golden laurel wreath – the Olympic Crown – from his satchel and placed it upon his head. The crowd gasped. Spartans were not easily impressed, but in this they were; for the man was Pheidippides, the greatest athlete in all of Greece. The Athenians could not have sent a better envoy.

Gorgo's father had died less than a month earlier, shortly after her marriage. She was only sixteen then, and Leonidas forty-four. He was her father's younger half-brother. Like him, he was unusually good-looking. In his tall muscular frame and long combed hair, he appeared the very epitome of a Spartan warrior. None could match his courage in battle. He was the darling of Sparta. The marriage had been the idea of her father to ensure the solidarity of the clan Agiadae, though Gorgo had long been infatuated with her handsome half-uncle.

'The Barbarians have landed at Fennel Field. Athens needs Sparta to stand by its side. How soon can you send troops, Majesty?' Pheidippides asked, still panting.

By the terms of the alliance that Gorgo's father had crafted shortly before his death, they were bound to come to Athens' aid. Yet Sparta's leaders were unsure. Some feared they might be sucked into a trap, even more so if the Persian army was as large as reports claimed; even more so when intelligence was coming in that Athenian traitors were planning to deliver their city to the invaders. Others argued, however, that no self-respecting Spartan warrior would pass up such a glorious opportunity to repulse a hated enemy.

Leonidas was caught in a bind. Though a warrior of Sparta, he was also her king. 'Thank you for your message, good Pheidippides. You shall have your answer shortly. I must consult the Ephors and the Generals, and perhaps also seek the will of the Heavens. In the meantime, you must rest.'

Leonidas had bought himself some time, but still he did not know what to do. That night, he spent hours arguing with the Ephors and the Generals. So perplexed was he, he returned home and sought his wife. He found her with their Helot servants helping them to sew clothes for their children for the approaching winter. While her husband did not exactly approve of Gorgo's compassion for the Helots, he tolerated it, seeing it merely as a sentimental quirk she had inherited from her father. Like him, she too was viewed as a little strange.

When she saw him, Gorgo followed him into their bedchamber, where he sat down upon the bed. He held his head in his hands. They said Leonidas knew no fear. And indeed, he feared nothing, except confusion. 'I don't know what do. Cleomenes would have known exactly how to handle this,' he said. 'Tell me, what would you do if you were in your father's place right now?'

In battle, Leonidas was a lion among men. As a commander, he was skilful and decisive. He was everything Spartans could admire in a king, but in politics, he was completely at a loss. She gave him the most honest advice she could. 'Sparta does not have a large army. If the invading Persian force is as strong as the reports suggest, then it does not matter whether Athens fights alone or with Spartan help, the Greeks will be defeated. If Spartans lose this battle and the Persians decide to move against Sparta, we will have no one to protect us. Is it wise, my Lord, to take such a risk?'

After a long silence, Leonidas got up and walked over to the hearth in the centre of the room. 'But how can I refuse the Athenians' request without violating the terms of our alliance, and without being seen a coward?'

'My Lord,' she said calmly. 'The Carneia festival begins tonight, and our laws forbid any military activity during this period. All you need to tell Pheiddipides is that Sparta will send a force to support the Athenians as soon as the Carneia is over.'

'And after that?'

'If the Persians defeat the Athenians by then, it will have meant the Barbarian army is much stronger and our absence from Fennel Field has been prudent. But if they are weaker than the Athenians, they will delay battle and if you lead our army after the Carneia, you and the Athenians will have a good chance of gaining victory.'

Leonidas continued to frown; this strategy went against the very grain of the warrior in him. He was dying to go and fight at Fennel Field.

Next morning, he told Pheidippides that military activity was forbidden during the period of the Carneia. As soon as the festival was over, he would personally lead a Spartan force to help the Athenians. 'And we shall come running,' Leonidas promised.

Disappointment appeared on the face of the young Pheidippides. He bowed and said, 'I shall convey your decision to the Assembly and Council of Athens.' And then he sprinted away.

Most Spartans, being religious, accepted Leonidas' decision without question. They did not want to invite the wrath of the gods against by violating the laws of the Carneia.

And so it was that under the guidance of the red-haired Miltiades, the Athenian army destroyed the Persian force at Marathon. Even though much was made of this spectacular victory, rumours persisted that the Persians never saw this to be more than a scoping mission and their army was not as large as the Athenians claimed.

True to his word, Leonidas arrived at Marathon with a strong Spartan force as soon as the Carneia was over. And they had come *running,* as he had promised. Still, they arrived a day after the battle was over. The Spartan army was shown the aftermath of Marathon and the amazing extent of the Athenian victory. Athens had triumphed without Sparta. Sparta's ego was bruised but her army had been preserved. Even though there was much grumbling by the troops for letting the Athenians win such spectacular victory on their own, the army accepted Leonidas' appeal to their piety; it was the will of the gods.

But after Marathon, Leonidas wanted to restore the army's confidence in itself. An opportunity soon presented itself when the Mantineans began to raid Perioiki settlements and Spartan farmsteads in Messene. Leonidas marched a force of three thousand troops to check the Mantinean incursions. He wanted to show off his military talents to his young wife, and so invited Gorgo to come along with the expedition. It was her first experience on a military campaign, and she felt just like the warriors, eager to see the enemy and repel their aggression.

As the troops approached the border, the Mantineans reacted by sending their entire citizen army – seven thousand strong – and dug them in on a high ridge near the village of Gortys, just inside Spartan-controlled territory. No self-respecting Spartan king could tolerate foreign occupation of Spartan soil and Leonidas had every intention of driving out these invaders, no matter what the odds.

The Spartans arrived at Gortys as the sun was setting and found the enemy force camped in strength just outside the village. The Mantinean army was impressively arrayed on an imposing ridge. Gorgo was not sure how three thousand Spartans could dislodge them.

Later that night, Leonidas' commanders debated alternative strategies of how to defeat the enemy. Growing impatient with the discussion, Leonidas interrupted them. 'Gentlemen, you can discuss your plans all night if you wish, but all of us know that any plan we make is shot to Hades the very moment we make contact with the enemy. Must I remind you that Spartan military strategy consists of two simple steps? The first step is to locate the enemy; the second to destroy it. Today we have found the enemy force; tomorrow, we shall finish it off.' With that, he dismissed the officers and went to bed.

And so it was with a degree of anticipation that Gorgo watched the events unfold from a safe distance of an opposing hillside that calm spring morning. Marshalling his men, Leonidas took them to the bottom of the ridge as the sun rose above the horizon. There he addressed them in his loudest voice, loud enough for even the enemy to hear.

'Spartan kings do not normally address their troops before battle, because Spartans warriors need not be told how to fight. And, comrades, that is not what I am going to do. I just wanted to share an observation with you.

'I have taken a good look at our enemy above us, and do you know what I see? I see farmers, shepherds, and masons; potters, carpenters, and even fishmongers; and smiths of all kinds. Given the increasing influence of the Athenians on our Mantinean neighbours, I am sure there must be a playwright or two up there; a philosopher too … perhaps even an architect …'

Laughter convulsed the Spartan ranks.

'… and somewhere in that rabble above this hill, without a doubt, is also the village idiot!'

More laughter.

'But what I don't see up there,' he continued, 'even after searching again and again through this crowd of Mantineans … is a single warrior. The Mantineans have brought here all sorts of men of all sorts of professions, but they forgot to bring their soldiers.

'Brothers!' he continued, 'Look at us! There is not a single potter among us, no beekeeper, no ironsmith, not even a part-time plumber. We are all soldiers. So what, I ask myself, stands between us and the top of that ridge today … if anything at all?'

The Spartan warriors responded with a loud collective grunt. For some moments, Gorgo's gaze had rested at the Mantinea force arrayed across the ridge, looking quite formidable. But at the point the Spartans grunted, she saw something strange happen to those troops on the ridge. She saw the knees of some begin to quake. Some vomited and she could clearly see others defecating where they stood.

She was so busy observing the Mantineans that she did not realize the Spartans had started charging up the steep slope. Having grown up in a warrior society, and often instructed by her father on matters military, Gorgo knew it was generally considered a folly to attack your enemies uphill, especially if they were well dug in as these Mantineans were. And it was an even greater folly to do so if the enemy outnumbered you, as on this occasion. And so her first instinct was to think that her husband had lost his mind.

A deafening crash shook the valley as metal and wood collided in fury. The Spartans had struck the enemy lines. The night before, Leonidas had chided his generals that no plan survives first contact with the enemy. On that serene spring morning, it was the Mantinean army that did not survive first contact. It simply collapsed under the weight of the Spartan onslaught. The battle of Gortys, if it could be called a battle, was over in no time. The few Mantineans who had the courage to resist were cut down as swiftly as blades of grass before a slicing scythe. The vast majority of them, however, turned and fled. Their shields were the first things they threw away, and then their helmets. Some kept their spears for comfort, others simply let them go. It soon became a chase by the victorious Spartans after their Mantinean prey – the latter trying to run as fast as they could away from their pursuers. For reasons no one could explain, all the Mantineans raced down the other side of the ridge and sought refuge in a wooded grove nearby, where the Spartans quickly surrounded them.

Leonidas shouted to the Mantineans, 'We will burn you alive in there if you do not come out,' and quickly ordered the outer trees to be set on fire. First in dribs and drabs – one soldier and then two, and then as the fire spread through the grove a huddle of men and then a mob – emerged from the smoking woodland, until finally the entire Mantinean army had surrendered.

Leonidas had them strip almost naked and bade them sit in

neat rows on the very ridge the troops had charged up.

'Worthless maggots,' he said as he walked among them, 'you are a disgrace to the good name of Greece.

'If my late brother, King Cleomenes, may the gods forgive him, were alive today he would have personally slit your throats. His daughter, my Queen,' Leonidas pointed as she walked towards him, 'I am sure would love to do us the honour in his stead.'

Of course, Leonidas was joking, but Gorgo saw the entire Mantinea army shudder in horror as she approached. One or two, she noticed, began to vomit uncontrollably.

'... But killing you would be an insult to our weapons,' continued Leonidas. 'The lambs we slaughter have more courage than you ever will. Why did you don your helmets and carry your spears if had no intention of fighting? Why did you not fight and die like men? Why did you run so quickly from this field of honour?' He looked searchingly at the defeated mob. 'Is there any among you who has the decency to answer?'

A boy of around eighteen got up and said, 'We were afraid of you, Majesty. We were afraid to fight the Spartans.'

'Then you should not have invaded our land.'

'We had no intention of truly fighting you. We thought you would look at how strong our army was and start to negotiate with us. We didn't expect you to attack us.'

'I never understood this business of negotiations,' said Leonidas, shaking his head. Then he looked at the boy. 'Lad, at least, you had the courage to speak up. Perhaps there is someone in this lily-livered rabble of yours worthy of slaughter, after all.'

The boy's face went white and he immediately sat down again and buried his head in his chest so that he would not be recognized. The Spartans roared with laughter. But Leonidas' expression became serious.

He walked up the hill alongside the prisoners and said, 'Do not go to war, if you do not expect to die. Nothing becomes a man more than courage in battle. It is better to die a hero's death than to live a thousand years.' He sneered at the Mantineans as he walked through their ranks; the prisoners gaping in awe at this angry Spartan King. 'Thousands of years from now, people will honour the brave of our time in ways we cannot even begin to imagine. But no one will remember the Mantineans, or even care. And why should they? You are disgraceful, the lot of you. Let me never see you again, unless you have any intention of skewering your miserable carcasses on this,' he said, drawing his sword and pointing it at the nearest prisoner. The man cringed with terror and all of the prisoners around him stared in horror at the glinting sword.

'Go home! The lot of you,' he said turning away from them. 'You will rue the day that you were not killed by the Spartans. You will never join the company of the glorious. You will never dine in Hades with heroes. You will always cower in the shadows. Go home, and live forever!'

Thus Leonidas sent home the Mantinean army, almost naked and in shackles. Along with them he sent a bill to the leaders of Mantinea claiming the cost of the shackles themselves. 'Let it not be said that the King of Sparta does not have a sense of humour,' Leonidas told Gorgo afterwards, as he roared with laughter.

* * *

As Pleistarchus finished his poetry lesson, Gorgo heard him recite another verse from Tyrtaeus. It was Leonidas' favourite. '*... learn to love death's ink-black shadow as much as you love the light of dawn.*' And so Leonidas had heroically embraced his fate.

But now the final battle was about to begin.

Chapter 9

The Wax Tablet

Mess of the Kynosoura Regiment
Sparta
The same night

In their younger days, they had instilled fear into the hearts of their enemies; leading Spartan armies to great victories. These five grey-bearded warriors grimly stood around the hearth fire. Sitting in front of them was their young Queen. After a long silence, Gorgo got up and walked up to them, looking each man in the eye. She knew them well – most had granddaughters around her own age. None of these wizened former generals was younger than sixty-five. They had now been called back from retirement to lead men into battle for one last time. And yet she hoped it would not come to that.

'Gentlemen,' said Gorgo, 'I am confident that our troops will prevail at Plataea.'

The men grunted in approval.

'But you know better than I the fog of war,' she continued. 'And should the tide turn against us there, be prepared to defend Sparta with all you have.'

The oldest commander rose. He bowed deeply to her and said, 'Under your guidance, Gorgo 'Bright Eyes', victory is assured.'

Gorgo acknowledged the old soldier's words with a polite nod. Sparta's soldiers and politicians saw her as their guiding light in this war. But this had not always been the case. And it would not have been, had it not been for a curious incident three years earlier.

* * *

It was late afternoon and Gorgo was playing in the courtyard with little Pleistarchus. They were playing a version of Olympic hockey along with children of the household Helots, using sticks and a soft ball of leather.

Thus absorbed, she did not notice that an officer of the Company of Knights was standing waiting on her until he cleared his throat and said, 'Majesty, your presence is requested in the Gerousia this very instant. Please accompany me.'

She soon arrived at the Hall to see it full of commotion. Whereas Spartan men always looked so calm in battle, in the Gerousia they were in complete disarray. As she walked silently to the centre, she felt some of the men turn in surprise, for they had never seen a woman among them.

Gorgo could not help a flutter of excitement inside this hallowed Hall. Even kings were not above the laws made here.

She quickly saw Leonidas was looking very pensive and not a little frustrated. Next to him sat a tall lean man, his Eurypontid co-King, Leotychidas, a dull man by all accounts. Gorgo's father had made him co-King after removing his predecessor. He had seen Leotychidas as nothing more than a pliable tool and had treated him as such. But the fact that he was reluctant even to command armies caused Leonidas to despise him. Fearing Leonidas' temper, Leotychidas had the sense to keep his mouth shut on most occasions, letting Leonidas do the talking, and even the thinking – not to mentioning the doing – for him.

But on this day, both were looking equally glum.

'Your Majesties, you have summoned me here?'

'No,' said a tired but respectful voice. 'It is the Gerousia that has summoned you here, Majesty.'

Gorgo turned to see it was the Senior Ephor who had spoken.

'We have a problem,' he said, 'and we were wondering if you could help us solve it.'

'I would be most honoured,' she had said, a little too eagerly – a young Queen, after all.

At the Ephor's signal, a slave presented her with a folding writing-tablet. It was an ordinary writing-tablet, covered with wax on which words or characters could be written and then easily erased. But the tablet was covered with several inscriptions in different languages, including Greek. And none of them made any sense, especially the Greek.

'This slave claims that his master is an adviser to Great King Xerxes, but sympathetic to the Greeks. He has sent a message for the leaders of Sparta. We have tried everything but we cannot find the message. The slave swears his master did not tell him anything about the message or what it is. We are having a problem trying to find the message in all the inscriptions scribbled on this tablet.'

Gorgo could have roared with laughter. 'Have you tried scraping the wax off?' she asked the Ephor.

'What?' he said, 'And destroy all this writing? The message is somewhere in these inscriptions.'

'This writing can easily be erased and re-written. The message is not here. Has it occurred to you that it may be underneath the wax?'

'Underneath the wax?'

'Yes.'

'A hidden message?'

'Yes.'

'You want us to scrape the wax off?'

'All of it!' she insisted.

The Ephor looked around the Hall and then he looked at the kings. Leotychidas regarded him blankly, but after a moment's thought, Leonidas nodded. Still hesitating, the Ephor gave the attendants orders to scrape off the wax. Carved into the wood underneath the wax was the message. Of course, it was in code. A quick examination told Gorgo that the words had been arranged in a repetitive sequence.

'A pen and a parchment, if you please?' she asked the Ephor, who promptly gave her his.

It did not take her long to decipher and when she was done, she read out the message:

King Xerxes, the new Persian king, is preparing a mighty army to wreak vengeance on the Greeks. The destruction of Sparta is one of his objectives.

Thirty-seven pairs of eyes looked on in amazement.

'Majesty, how did you know that the message was underneath the wax?' asked one of the Gerousia members.

It was obvious, you idiot, she thought to herself. However what she said was, 'Since in your wisdom, you gentlemen had eliminated all other possibilities, I thought we might try this. Perhaps it was a lucky guess.'

She humbly bowed to the Hall and quietly left, leaving behind thirty Gerousia members, the five Ephors, and the two kings. Since that day she had been invited to every single session of the Gerousia. However, what intrigued her was the identity of the man who had sent that secret message.

* * *

The news of the impending invasion had plunged Sparta and the rest of Greece into a state of panic. This was the largest army anybody had ever seen, its strength estimated at almost two million men. Some put the numbers even higher. Later they heard stories of this army drinking rivers dry. It was less of an army, and more of a pestilence descending on Greece.

Strangely enough, Gorgo was pleased. This was a vindication of her father's fears and thus it finally provided her with the opportunity to put her father's vision into practice. She suggested to Leonidas that they create the Hellenic League – a patriotic alliance to resist the invaders.

Furthermore, she asked him to establish its headquarters at Corinth, one of Sparta's strongest allies. This would help to keep the Peloponnesian states together, and by proximity make it easier for the Spartans to manipulate, if not control, the League.

But not all the Greek states joined the League. As the Persian threat started to materialize, many Greek states decided that they would give in to the invaders. Others prevaricated, delaying the 'when' but not the 'if' of submitting to the Persians. In contrast, those states which came over to the Spartan side were actually a minority, and sometimes joined for no better reasons that their local rivals were planning to go over to the enemy. At the heart of this disunity lay the hatreds and rivalries many Greek states and cities had for each other.

Gorgo's concerns, however, lay closer to home. She was afraid that in spite of her best efforts all their plans could fail if the leadership of the Spartan army refused to follow her plans. This was because the *Boule* – or War Council – that governed it had a mind of its own. But so did Gorgo. She started pestering Leonidas to let her attend the meetings. Ever the stickler to Spartan tradition, he repeated that women were not allowed there. But then one day she confronted him and said, 'If the Gerousia can benefit from my help, so can the Boule.'

Leonidas snorted. 'The Boule is not like the Gerousia. Soldiers do not like women telling them what they should do.'

'Nor did the members of the Gerousia,' she retorted, 'until they had no other choice. Do not come to me, my Lord, after you lose your first battle.'

'Very well,' sighed Leonidas. 'You can attend the meetings, as long as you listen and don't speak.'

So Gorgo went to her first meeting of the Boule. It was full of tough, no-nonsense men, eager to make a name for themselves, and ambitious for victories. She soon knew the company was not exactly comfortable with her presence. This they showed by completely ignoring her, expecting her to sit quietly at the rear-most table.

The meeting was always held in one of the regimental messes, with the two kings sitting on the high table, while the Captain of the Knights stood behind them. The six generals of Sparta were seated, in order of seniority, from right to left around the mess-table, facing their kings. Leonidas often conducted these meetings alone, with Leotychidas absent on one excuse or another.

Gorgo listened in horror as the War Council authorized the dispatch of virtually the entire army to join the Athenians at a pass called Tempe in the north near the Greek border with Thrace. The Spartan 'no show' at Marathon was still pricking the sensibility of these generals. They did not want to allow the Athenians to beat the Persians again on their own.

Gorgo could not maintain her silence. 'Why do Spartan men prefer to lose reason before losing face?' she asked as the Generals seated in the rows in front turned to look at her. 'Gentlemen, tell me. How will a few thousand Greeks stop millions of Persians?'

While others tried to restrain themselves, one of the younger generals blurted out, 'We Spartans do not ask how many are the enemy, but where they are. The Persians will enter Greece from the north, and it is in the north that we shall defeat them.'

The other generals nodded forcefully. She wanted to reason with them, but decided to keep her views to herself, at least for the time being.

And sure enough, a large Spartan force was sent to Tempe to join the Athenians. Soon afterwards, everything descended into a farce. The Spartan commander Evaeneutus took an immediate dislike to his Athenian counterpart – none other than the brilliant, if arrogant, Themistocles. Both spent more time quarrelling with each other than trying to find the best way to stop the enemy. And when they finally got around to it, they realized that they had picked the wrong place to block the Persians. The pass could easily be outflanked and turned, by land as well as sea. The Persians could even bypass it completely and avoid confronting their troops at all, and thus cut them off from the rest of Greece, rendering both Athens and Sparta virtually defenceless. And when the local rulers of the area began to defect to the Persians, the two allied armies beat a hurried retreat. So the Spartan army returned home without a fight. Tempe was a narrowly avoided disaster.

As soon as the army returned, Gorgo went without invitation to the Boule.

'Gentlemen, you consider yourself the best warriors in Greece, as you should. You consider our troops superior to the enemy, which indeed they are. But the fact is no army, no matter how good, can overcome an immensely larger one without a strategy. To defeat the enemy, we have to think differently; plan differently; and act differently. Remember, gentlemen, what we are up against now is a monster of great size and strength. We have all heard, since our childhood, stories of how our great heroes fought and overcame powerful enemies. Of our own ancestor, Heracles, who slew the Hydra, not by brute force, but by logic. Of Odysseus, who killed the Cyclops using deceit and trickery. And then there was Perseus, who used his wits and the reflection of light to slay Medusa, that fearsome, ugly Gorgo.'

There was gentle laughter at the deliberate pun on her own name.

'Our heroes defeated mightier adversaries through skill and cunning. Xerxes' army cannot be beaten in a single battle. We have to defeat it by shrewd strategy. We need to wear it down, sap its strength and undermine its morale. At the same time, we need to strengthen our alliances, build up our defences, and raise more troops so that in the end we can have the upper hand.'

She turned her gaze to Leonidas, who said, 'Tempe has shown our carelessness. We do need a strategy.' Then he smiled. 'And perhaps we may have to turn to a Gorgo to win this war.'

A single knuckle knocked loudly on the surface of a table. This was Evaeneutus, and it was followed by another rapping of the knuckles, and then more. Soon, all the generals, the entire War Council, were doing the same.

But soon enough, another problem appeared. The Athenians, led by the very same Themistocles, came up with a different idea about how to fight the war. In the years running up to the invasion, they had built up a powerful navy, thanks in part to the discovery of silver at the mines of Laurium and in part to Themistocles' brilliant vision. The Athenians not only demanded that the defence of Greece should be based around a naval strategy, they also wanted to command the combined fleets of the Hellenic League. This was not acceptable to the Spartans nor to many of their allies. No one trusted the Athenians.

As the Persian army slowly made its way into Greece, it took the better part of Gorgo's diplomatic skills to help Leonidas achieve a compromise with the Athenians, under which the Greeks would have dual, and mutually supportive, land and sea strategies. While the Spartans commanded both the land and sea forces, their admiral Eurybiadas would defer operational command of the Allied Fleet to the Athenians, who had more sea-borne experience.

Gorgo's strategy soon faced its toughest test at Thermopylae, which had cost the life of her husband. And even the Athenian-led victory at Salamis failed to stop the Persians. Now the fate of Greece was to be decided at Plataea.

* * *

The elderly commanders followed Gorgo outside the mess into the parade ground where their troops were waiting. Amid scores of flickering torches, she saw the reservists, only two thousand strong. Their orders were to man the fortifications on the Isthmus of Corinth, where they would make their final stand. She looked at these warriors and felt sad; all at extreme ages: either fresh-faced youths between sixteen and nineteen or grizzled veterans from sixty to eighty.

Most of the elderly men looked grim, knowing the heavy responsibility on their shoulders, for if Plataea was lost the only thing between the enemy and Sparta would be their spears. But almost all the boys were beaming. Gorgo's gaze went from boy to boy. It pained her heart for she knew the parents of too many of them, and had watched them grow from babyhood. But they were now on the verge of manhood. Many of them had signs of facial hair, while others still looked like the young boys that they were. Some were excited to be going to war, oblivious of the dangers ahead; others simply proud to be considered men at all.

Gorgo addressed them in her loudest voice. 'My uncles and my nephews, Sparta has no walls because you, her warriors, are her walls. Sparta's boundaries are undefined because these, your spear-points, define her borders. So when the Barbarians come, let them find nothing but death on the frontiers of Sparta!'

The men, young and old, grunted in unison.

Then orders rang out for the formation to face left. Immediately, the two thousand warriors did so with brilliant precision. As they marched off in the darkness towards the north, Gorgo could not help wondering how many of these would return alive, if any at all.

If they did not, Sparta's fate would be sealed forever.

Chapter 10

The Dancing Floor Of War

Plataea

The following morning

Sherzada was awakened at dawn. 'Rise, Highness, the Greeks are fleeing.'

Strange thoughts raced through his mind. Was it possible that Mardonius' gold had bought off the Greeks?

Outside, the sun was rising behind him. From his vantage point on the hill above the Asopus, Sherzada could view the entire Plataean plain. The Greeks were in full retreat.

When he had first arrived here, Asopodorus of Thebes had made a prediction. 'Leonidas of Sparta tried to stop the Persians in the northern passes but perished there,' he said. 'The Athenians tried to end it by sea, at Salamis, but failed for the Persians are still here. The Persians thought that burning down Athens and a few other cities would bring their enemies to heel, but that did not happen either. The war will not end in the mountains of the north nor in the Peloponnesian Peninsula in the south, nor at sea. It will end here in these broad plains between Athens and Thebes. For centuries, the fate of Greece has been decided here, the place we call the Dancing Floor of War. This is where this war will end.'

And now the dance was on. The Greek army had broken into three separate formations heading in different directions. On the extreme left, the Spartan force, along with their Tegean and Arcadian allies, headed for their original position on Mount Cithaeron. A small Spartan detachment had been trailing behind as if to cover their withdrawal. But that too had started to fall back towards the main body.

On the other flank, the Athenians were heading in a direction further to the right, but they seemed to be moving slower than the others, though in a cohesive and disciplined manner. In the Greek centre, however, was confusion. This was the largest of the three groups the Greek army had broken into and this one seemed to be in a hurry to fall back to the town of Plataea at the base of mountainous Cithaeron. They seemed to be in a state of panic and utter disarray.

Sherzada could sum up the entire scene in a single word – Chaos!

'My horse,' Sherzada ordered. And as soon as it was brought, he rode hard to Mardonius' tent. On arriving inside his tent, he saw Mardonius raving, 'Did I not tell you that the Greek army will collapse before your very eyes. See, what did I tell you?'

There was much commotion, with messengers and officers running in and out of the tent. Initially, Sherzada was pleased that a general assault had been ordered. But instead of smelling victory, all he saw was confusion. Mardonius had ordered an attack on the enemy without any sort of battle plan. He had not even bothered to deploy units in a proper line of battle. Wasting time with such tedious details was not Mardonius' style. He wanted his men to close in with the Greeks and kill as many of them as possible, before they got to higher ground. Mardonius was too busy barking orders to listen to anyone.

As he left, Sherzada met Burbaraz and Asopodorus. Both were returning to their respective commands. Asopodorus told him that he would be taking his Dark Riders to support the Boeotian infantry who were already chasing the hated Athenians on the right flank.

Burbaraz announced that Mardonius had asked him to lead the Persian cavalry to support his Invincibles on the left.

As he was about to leave, Sherzada grabbed Burbaraz by the arm and said, 'Before you go, Highness, there is something important I need to tell you. We do not know the outcome of this battle, even though it seems to be going in our favour now.'

'Quite,' replied Burbaraz, 'with Mardonius you are never sure. He is quite capable of extracting defeat from the jaws of victory.'

Sherzada nodded. 'So if the battle does not go our way, leave this battlefield immediately. And when you do, do not to take the shortest road to Strymon river-crossing between Macedonia and Thrace. Find another way.'

Burbaraz looked confused. 'What do you mean? That territory belongs to Alexander, my brother-in-law. I don't think he will fail to provide us safe passage. He was here last night, bringing supplies and intelligence.'

'So he was, but I have received very credible intelligence that our enemies are preparing an ambush at the Strymon crossing for any Persian force returning from Plataea. It might be prudent to take an alternative route rather than fall into an ambush. Be careful in battle today. I know you love your wife. For her sake and the sake of your children, you must survive this battle.'

Sherzada could see confusion on Burbaraz's face followed by a slight smile. 'I thank you for your concern for my safety,' he murmured, before riding off.

Sherzada turned to Asopodorus, who had been listening in silence. 'My friend, I don't know whether I will live to see the end of this battle or not. All I ask of you is to ensure that those of my men who survive are guided back to Asia in safety.'

'Rest assured, I shall make certain they reach Thrace safely. And then they can return home once they cross the Euxine Sea,' replied Asopodorus.

He smiled warmly. They shook hands and parted company.

Sherzada rode to where his troops were preparing for battle. The sun was now above the horizon but the morning air was still cool. The Dahae horsemen were the first to arrive, dressed magnificently in colourful tunics and light armour, riding their famed white horses. They were followed by the war-bands from the Indus kingdoms. Their warriors wore long cotton tunics, cloth wound around their upper legs like improvised trousers, and carried short swords, spears and long bows made of cane. But they wore very little armour; for they regarded wearing any form of protection as a sign of cowardice.

Then the remnants of the Pactyans, Arachosians and Gandharan troops arrived. They had been decimated by dysentery and disease, but those left were as eager as ever to fight. Soon the others, the Amyrgian Sakas and the Tigrakhaudas Scyths also arrived, as well as the lancers from Sarmatia. All of these arrivals told Sherzada that the Persian nobles who commanded them had not been seen since the party of the previous night. Rumour was that many of them had left Plataea altogether. Sherzada could not help recalling what Gygaea had told him the night before.

He addressed the men gathered before him: 'Warriors, comrades, kinsmen! Today we fight for Persia for the last time. If they win, Greece will fall on its knees and we will not be needed here anymore. If they lose, Persia will not persist in this war and there will be no reason for us to stay here any longer. We have been fighting in a war that was never ours. After today, we owe them nothing. For today, we have to fight, and fight we shall. But if the battle turns against us, make an orderly retreat towards the north-west. Do not take the direct route towards the Strymon crossing. Go instead to Thrace over the hard road and then head east for the Euxine coast. There, Scythian merchant ships will take you to the Sarmatian coast on the other end of the Sea where you can take the overland route to your homelands. But, before that, let us fight this one last time together.'

The answer was a resounding battle-cry in half a dozen tongues. As Sherzada led his troops forward, he tried to survey the battlefield ahead. On the left, he could see clouds of dusts and the long spears of both the Persian infantry and cavalry. Mardonius and Burbaraz were pursuing the enemy. On the far right, he could see one phalanx chasing another; the Boeotians,

Thessalians and the Phocians trying to close in on the Athenians – Greeks pursing Greeks.

And in the centre, there was a mad rush of various contingents of the Persian army as they charged, in an unformed mass, the retreating Greeks in front of them. These Greeks stepped up their pace and then realizing that the Persians were too close, changed course and headed up a steep hill towards a large temple.

But the pursuing Persians seemed in equal disarray. There was no one to orchestrate the action, the Persian army looking more like a disjointed mob than a unified force with a single objective.

Sherzada had been too busy watching the enemy's movements. He had not noticed that his own force was being followed. As one of his officers pointed to the rear, Sherzada turned and saw a Persian force behind them advancing slowly, in neatly arrayed ranks and in good order but in no hurry to engage the enemy. Artabaz's contingent. He had a reputation of being a cautious commander. He would never commit troops to a battle he could not win. 'He is using us as a shield,' Sherzada thought.

Chanting their war-cries, Sherzada's warriors crossed the Asopus and headed for the Spartans towards their left. Up ahead, Sherzada could see that Burbaraz had already reached close to the Spartan lines with his cavalry, but he was wise enough not to charge his horsemen into their phalanx. Instead, he ordered his men to launch their arrows at them, while waiting for Mardonius' Invincibles to catch up.

Burbaraz's horsemen fired their arrows in the air with such accuracy that they came down directly on the Spartan phalanx. But the long spears of the phalanx, held up at varying angles, deflected some of the arrows while others fell harmlessly to the Spartans' upheld shields. Still, the odd arrow found its mark through the helmet eye-slot or the unprotected neck of a Spartan warrior. Soon casualties began to mount as arrows continued to rain down, but the Spartans stood motionless. Sherzada had heard stories that the Spartans often paused before battle to carry out ritual pre-battle sacrifices to determine whether their gods would grant them victory. Even so, he was perplexed at why they were refusing to react to the enemy, under the constant hailstorm of arrows from Burbaraz's horse-archers.

The first inkling Sherzada had that something was not quite right was when he saw reflections of bright sunlight flashing at the extreme left flank of the enemy. He could see dozens of their shields organized in a rectangular array, deliberately angled so that the entire Greek force could see the sun's reflection. *A heliogram,* Sherzada said to himself. *The Athenians are sending a signal to the entire Greek army.*

The various Greek contingents started flashing similar signals to each other. Then the Greeks, at least most of them, turned around and went into action, right across the plain.

The Athenians were the first to do so. They calmly about-faced and lowered their spears at the Greeks on the Persian side who had been chasing them thus far. Then they attacked. Almost simultaneously, the Spartans in front of them charged the Invincibles, who were about to crash into them anyway. Greeks on both flanks turned and attacked the Persian units closest to them.

The Greek counter-attack took the Persians by surprise. It was a disciplined manoeuvre, beautifully executed. The lack of cohesion of the Persian army and the piecemeal nature of its advance began to take its toll as the Greeks started to encircle and destroy each individual unit.

However, in the Greek centre, confusion reigned. While most Greek contingents turned and charged the enemy, some continued to flee towards the temple complex at the base of Mount Cithaeron. Sherzada could see that among these fleeing Greeks were the Megarians who had suffered so heavily on the day of Cithaeron.

As the Greeks ferociously attacked their enemy, many of the contingents who fought for Persia turned and ran. And as their front-line units fled the charging Greeks, they collided with troops behind them who were trying to join the fight. A bizarre scene ensued as troops from the Persian army became entangled with each other, spreading even more chaos and confusion. This only helped the Greeks to press home their advantage. From his increasingly restricted vantage point, Sherzada could see some troops in the Persian centre putting up the best possible resistance but being overwhelmed by numerical superiority of their enemies. The Persian centre had fallen apart.

On the Persian right, the Athenian counter-attack also began to take effect. The Phocians were the first to flee. In any case, their loyalty to the Persian cause had always been in doubt. After all, their city had been subject to a brutal sacking by the Persians and they had been brought to Plataea to fight against their will, alongside their local enemies, the Thessalians. But it was not long before the Thessalians too followed suit. This left only the Thebans and their Boeotian allies to confront the Athenians on their own. For a while, they managed to keep the Athenians at bay, even though they were outnumbered; with Asopodorus' cavalry wreaking havoc, as usual. But gradually the outnumbered Boeotian infantry began to give way and they too broke and ran.

As Sherzada's force continued to make progress towards the Spartans, he wondered about the Persian cavalry. Yes, the Dark Riders of Thebes were covering the retreat of the infantry of their Boeotian allies. Burbaraz's veteran horse-archers were protecting the flanks of the Invincibles. Parthian heavy cavalry and Khorasmian lancers were marching alongside Artabaz's infantry behind him. Sherzada's horsemen were doing exactly the same. But these were only a tiny remnant of the once great host of horse-borne forces the Persians had gathered in Plataea.

'Where is the Persian cavalry?' Sherzada asked. Their

appearance could make all the difference.

Mardonius had recently put the bulk of the Persian horse-archers and lancers plus other allied cavalry under the command of his favourite, Farandatiya. Twenty-four regiments of cavalry could not just suddenly disappear into thin air. But they had.

One of Sherzada's officers answered, 'Highness, they were seen leaving the camp at first light, heading north on the main road, away from the battlefield.'

Sherzada sighed as he saw the Persian army implode on itself. Within moments, it seemed as if most decided to leave the battlefield without order or instruction. Many units were leaderless; their commanders nowhere to be found. Some of the fleeing troops ran and took refuge inside the fortified camp Mardonius had constructed for his personal use. Others took the same main road north; the one that headed directly for the Strymon.

The remnants were left to face the full might of the enemy. Sherzada was now in an undulating part of the Plataean plain, the rest of the battlefield obscured from sight. A heavy battle was waging in front of him, as Mardonius' men, backed up by Burbaraz's cavalry, engaged the Spartans and their allies. The outnumbered Invincibles continued to fight, with Mardonius leading them in person. But then a flying rock knocked him off his horse, as the Invincibles were forced to give way to superior numbers. They fell back, still in good order, carrying an injured Mardonius with them as they slowly backtracked to the river.

Burbaraz continued to harass the Greeks with his horse-archers, but the enemy numbers were too much for him to offer Mardonius any effective support.

With Mardonius and Burbaraz in retreat, it was now Sherzada's turn to take on the Spartans. He told the infantry – the Indus warriors, Arachosians, Pactyans and Gandharans – to charge Sparta's allies, the Tegeans and the Arcadians, while he led his cavalry against the Spartans themselves. His force first ploughed through a disorganized rabble of Helots, easily sending them into full retreat. And then he saw the unbroken line of gold and crimson – the Spartan phalanx advancing. It is usually suicide for any cavalry to take on good infantry in a frontal attack – even worse when the infantry happened to be the Spartans. But Sherzada had based his attack on an idea – albeit a risky one.

He shouted at his cavalrymen to charge the Spartans 'in the way that we are accustomed,' and his men raced their horses towards the Spartans. The Spartans responded by charging full speed against them. The best cavalry in the world was about to collide with the best infantry on earth. But as the Spartans increased their speed, Sherzada signalled his cavalrymen to start decelerating. And as they did so, they armed their bows as they came right up to the Spartans. As the distance between the two lessened, the charging Spartan infantry was lunging towards Sherzada's men, who were reining in their horses. The horsemen slowed to almost a standstill, seconds short of making contact with Spartan spear-points. Then, virtually at the last moment, Sherzada and his men turned and rode in the opposite direction.

And as they retreated, the Tigrakhaudas, the Amyrgians and the Dahae turned in the saddle and unleashed a terrible barrage of arrows, catching many of the Spartan front ranks in their eyes and in their necks, arrowheads piercing between the unprotected areas of the Spartan helmets. The Spartan line faltered as the injured and dying fell. Sherzada's horsemen withdrew another few dozen paces, unleashing another volley; their archery flawless. This was doubly unkind to the Spartans, for Sherzada knew that of all things, they despised archery.

Sherzada wheeled around and led his mounted Royals around the enemy's right flank. With battle-axes in hand, they followed him as he attacked the Spartan rear. Being in the lead, Sherzada was the first to strike. He struck the Spartan warrior in the rear-most rank in the exposed back of his neck with his long-sword. The man crumbled to the ground, blood spraying from his neck. The Royals followed suit and likewise slashed into the rear of the Spartan hoplites, whose heavy armour hampered them from turning fast enough to face their foes. Confusion spread. The Spartan phalanx stood paralyzed for a moment or two while Sherzada's axe-men tore through their rear. It was then that orders rang out, probably from their Regent, Pausanias, or some other commander, and the Spartans rose into action from their apparent torpor, like a monster rudely awakened.

Ignoring the arrows of his horse-archers, they turned and charged Sherzada's axe-wielding horsemen, raising their blood-curdling battle cries. It was a terrifying sight, and this was not the first time Sherzada had seen it. He had no choice but to fall back.

Sherzada's infantry, who had managed to push back the Tegeans and other Greek contingents, withdrew in good order as well. Artabaz's Parthian armoured cavalry and the Khorasmian lancers came forward to support them and to cover their retreat. The Spartans too halted to regroup and organize themselves.

As they made their way back to the river, Sherzada's force saw the remaining units of the Persian army crossing it. These remnants accounted for less than a fifth of the original strength of the Persian army at Plataea. Once they reached their destination, Artabaz's cavalry rejoined his main force, which was already across the river. Sherzada saw them preparing to leave the battle-field without a fight. Artabaz's heart had never been in this battle from the start.

Soon, the Invincibles also arrived to cross to the other side of the river. Mardonius appeared to have somewhat recovered from his injury, although blood was oozing down his forehead. He ordered some cavalry officers ahead to rally the remnants of the Persian army outside the stockade in the centre of the Persian camp. That was where he was going to make his last stand.

As soon as Mardonius' eyes met Sherzada's, he motioned him to approach. When Sherzada rode up to him, he said, 'I, and only I am to blame for what is unfolding here today. Perhaps I still can stop the Greeks across the ford. I would like to make one last request, Highness. Hold the Asopus crossing as long as you can so I can reorganize the survivors on the other side. Perhaps I can still turn the battle against them. And if not, I will show the Greeks what it is like to die a Persian.'

'Lord Mardauniya,' Sherzada said to him in his best Persian, 'I will guard this river crossing as long as it will take for those under my command to reach safety, then I also will leave the field. Our debt to your King has been paid in full.'

'And so it has!' Mardonius nodded. He turned his horse and rode across the ford towards his camp.

Sherzada turned to his troops and started to organize their crossing in an orderly manner. He kept back his Royals only to cover the retreat of the others, ordering them to dismount and give their horses' reins to those going across. He formed them up as infantry. The Amyrgians volunteered to stay behind also. They too dismounted and formed their lines alongside the Royals.

'Remember the Iron Gates,' their senior-most officer said, raising his battle-axe, recalling the famous battle a generation earlier in which the various Saka tribes had fought side-by-side, ironically against the Persians. The Dahae and the Tigrakhaudas crossed to the other side but only to take up position to give them supporting fire from a safe distance.

Then the Spartans appeared, with other Greek troops not too far behind them. As they came closer, Sherzada realized how easy it had been to face a phalanx on horseback, where safe flight was always a possibility. But it was an entirely different matter to fight it on foot. And it was all the more terrifying if the phalanx was a Spartan one. And he had seen all this before – nine months ago at Thermopylae.

The Spartan phalanx advanced like a giant bristling monster. The frightening sound of the Spartan pipes kept time with its slow but dreadful progress. As it came closer, the spears of the front ranks came down to face Sherzada and his men. The heat was becoming unbearable now. Removing his helmet, baring his head, he told his men to protect the river crossing until most of their troops were safely across. Then they would also cross – even if they had to do it while fighting.

The Spartans were by now very close – a veritable mass of bronze and crimson behind a storm of spears. It was a sight at once awesome and terrifying. Sherzada knew that a Spartan warrior was a ferocious individual. But a phalanx of Spartan warriors was greater than the sum of its parts. It was one of the most efficient killing machines he had ever seen. He began to recall what a terrible thing it was to fight the Spartans. And he also realized how small his own force was compared to theirs. The only way to defeat the phalanx was to break it up. Sherzada knew that his men would not be able to, but the terrain just might.

A cry went through the Spartan ranks. It was the *paean* – the war-cry. Drawing his long-sword from over his shoulder, Sherzada moved forward. With the battle-cry *Yavanae Marayna!* – 'death to the Greeks!' – he led the counter-charge against the Spartans. But it was the Spartan phalanx that crashed against the Saka lines like a hammer coming down on a sheet of metal. Though they reeled at the impact, the Sakas were able to keep their lines relatively straight. Unlike the weak shields of the Persians which could not prevent Greek spears from punching through, the stronger Saka shields were able to push back the enemy spears. Both sides began to push and shove. The confined space was too tight for Sherzada to use his long-sword, though he tried to use its length to strike through any gaps he could find in the enemies' lines. But there were none. There was no crack in the Spartan line protected by interlocking shields. Instead, it was the Spartans who were creating a crack in the Saka lines.

But the Sakas fought back. Sherzada's axe-men lopped off, in turn, the Spartan spear-points and butt-spikes, forcing them to draw their swords. Yet the Spartans had the upper hand. They continued to push back their foes, relying as much on skill as on superior numbers. The very ground under the feet of Sherzada's men seemed to move forward. The forces of nature were on the side of the Spartans as they pushed Sherzada's men down a gentle slope that descended towards the ford. The terrain was becoming rocky and uneven. The Sakas were driven back across this broken ground right down to the river. And then it happened.

As the Spartans shoved ahead, the integrity of their phalanx began to crumble over broken ground. Gaps began to appear in their front ranks. Immediately, crying out to his men to follow him, Sherzada pushed through the gaps. Cracks had emerged in the Spartan ranks which were wide enough for Sherzada to use his sword to full effect, and his axe-wielding warriors followed him.

With neat battle lines disappearing, the Sakas battled the Spartans as equals. But the Spartans fought back with equal ferocity. The two sides tore through each other's lines as the battle raged to feverish intensity. Sherzada reckoned he must have killed at least three Spartans, but it had not been easy. Each Spartan had died fighting to the last breath, inflicting on Sherzada his fair share of cuts and bruises. But now finally the Sakas were gaining ground.

Through the din of battle, Sherzada heard the sounds and clatter of movements behind the crest of a small hill to his right. At first, he thought it was reinforcements coming to his rescue. But then it struck him ... a haunting sound ... a beautiful sound – music mixed with song. He had heard it before ... on the mist-covered field of Eleusis on the very eve before Salamis; as terrifying as it was melodic. A chill must have gone down the spine of every one of those older men who had fought and survived the slaughter at Marathon eleven years ago. It was the Battle Hymn of the Democracy.

Sherzada turned to the right and saw the Athenians attacking his flank.

Chapter 11

The Winds Of Salamis

Sparta
The same day

Gorgo pulled her shawl over her shoulder. She could not help but recall that she had felt the same unseasonable cold breeze before, on the very day her husband fell at Thermopylae. Gorgo was on her way back from the Agora. The marketplace had been buzzing with speculation. There were rumours of a great battle in the offing, or even being fought, at Plataea. But she knew that no news would arrive until after it was over.

As she came over a rise, Gorgo noticed a lone figure hurrying up the road. It was a young woman walking silently and fast, trying not to notice the world, and hoping the world would not notice her. Gorgo called out to her, but she did not respond. Gorgo knew why.

The girl was an outcast and reviled throughout Sparta. Her crime: she had dared to defend her father, Aristodemus. Just before the battle of Thermopylae, Aristodemus contracted an eye disease that impeded his functions. Seeing no use for him in the battle line, Leonidas had sent him home.

Gorgo still remembered the day Aristodemus returned to Sparta; sick and blind in one eye, being guided by his faithful Helot. Rather than sympathy, all he found back home was censure and abuse. He was branded a coward – a 'Trembler' – who ran away from the fight where his comrades perished. His situation became all the more embarrassing when news came that two other Spartans who had also been sent away by Leonidas chose not to return alive. Both chose to die – one went back to Thermopylae and died in battle and the other had committed suicide rather than return home in ignominy.

Aristodemus was drummed out of his regiment, and a yellow patch was stitched to his cloak indicating his 'cowardly' status. No one wanted to talk to him, let alone take meals with him. At all public places he had to make way for other Spartans, even younger men. He was no longer thought to be a Spartan.

Having caught the girl's attention, Gorgo approached her and asked, 'How are you today, Ione?'

'I am well, Majesty,' responded Ione, after a little bemused hesitation.

Gorgo understood Ione's bewilderment. Why was the Queen being civil to her when the whole of Sparta heaped abuse on her? 'I just wanted to know how you were keeping up. I hope you do not miss your father too much.'

Ione's own brother had disowned Aristodemus. Her mother had retired to her country home because she could not bear to show her face in Sparta. But it was young Ione who had borne the brunt of the humiliation and abuse on his behalf. While he had been shunned, she had been despised. Ione was a pretty girl, but in spite of her beauty, no man would marry her. Who would wed such a woman and produce more Tremblers?

On the night before Pausanias set off to face the Persians, Aristodemus had come to Gorgo to plead that he be given a second chance. She knew that this would mean that he would not return alive, but for Aristodemus, death in battle was infinitely more attractive to the life that he was leading. So it was with some difficulty that Gorgo had convinced a sceptical Pausanias to take him with him to Plataea.

Ione shrugged and said, 'I miss him. But I'm not sure if he is coming back.' Then she stared at Gorgo. 'I am not like you, Majesty. I am not like most Spartan women who can rejoice at the loss of a loved one in battle.'

Gorgo walked over and gently embraced her and told her to be strong. This did nothing to soothe the young Ione. 'How do you do it, Majesty? How did you remain strong when your husband died?'

From the girl's face Gorgo knew that Ione had asked that question a hundred times before of other Spartan women and each time she had been given the same answer. She had to do what was expected of her. This was the Spartan way. Ione had no choice but to conform. But this was not what Gorgo told her.

'It was not easy. It is never easy. We still have to be strong,' said Gorgo, her thoughts flickering to ten months earlier.

* * *

'Majesty, the King and the Three Hundred have perished,' reported the young naval officer.

It was not that Gorgo had not been expecting this news. Of course, no other outcome could have been possible. Leonidas and his men could not have survived the odds. They were not meant to. But what surprised her was her own reaction to the news. She had not anticipated it.

Pangs of all kinds of pain shot through Gorgo's body. She felt the strength seep out of her legs as her heart-beat accelerated at a reckless pace. All types of emotions, none of them pleasant, began to take hold of her. She was on the verge of a breakdown. But she could not let it happen. So, summoning all the strength she could muster, Gorgo did what every Spartan woman was expected to do in such a situation. She smiled.

'The prophecy has been fulfilled. King Leonidas has saved Sparta by sacrificing himself,' she told the Spartan officer.

He nodded, satisfied with Gorgo's response.

'Through pain comes wisdom,' murmured the Athenian softly to himself. Gorgo did not know what to make of him. The two officers had just arrived from Artemesium where the allied Greek fleet was facing the Persian navy, bringing her the news of the battle at Thermopylae which had ended three days earlier. Though devastated, she put on a façade of complete calm.

Focusing on the matter at hand might help, she thought. And it did. For there was something very strange about her Athenian guest.

In his mid-forties, he was short and plump, with a balding head, thick eyebrows and a scruffy brown beard. His expression was of a man lost in another world; his eyes constantly staring out into empty space. He was dressed like a civilian, in a simple tunic, partially covered by a robe. There was nothing remotely military about him.

'Where are my manners, *Trierarch*,' she said, addressing him by his proper naval rank – that of a warship Captain. 'Welcome to Sparta. I trust an Athenian mariner like yourself had no trouble tackling last night's storm.'

'I am not afraid of storms, Madam,' said the Athenian, 'for I'm still learning to sail my ship.'

His response caused a frown to appear Gorgo's face, as she wondered what type of captain the Athenian navy produced.

Perhaps reading her thoughts, the Spartan officer intervened. 'The Trierarch fought with the Athenian army at Marathon, with distinction.'

The Athenian smirked. 'The long-haired Persian remembers and can speak of it too.'

Gorgo gasped at the man's conceit. She looked at him from top to bottom and found any of it hard to believe; she was not sure if this man even knew which end of a sword he was supposed to use.

'So, Pericleidas,' Gorgo said, turning to the Spartan officer, who was everything the Athenian was not; tall, handsome, and muscular. 'What does Admiral Eurybiadas suggest we do now?'

'We fought the Persian fleet at Artemisium,' said Pericleidas, 'for three consecutive days in running sea battles, inflicting heavy casualties on the enemy in each engagement ...'

'... Except for the time we fought the squadron of Queen Artemisia of Caria,' interrupted the Athenian, his eyes lighting up, 'who almost turned tables on us. But nobody wants to talk about that. As I have always said, in war, truth is the first casualty. The plain fact is that the Persian fleet still outnumbers ours and we cannot hold our position at Artemisium.'

Gorgo allowed herself the shadow of a smile, pleased that a woman had given these warlike men a headache. She had always admired the warrior Queen of Caria, even though she fought on the other side. But her face quickly became sterner. 'Hence my question. What do we do next?'

The two men looked at each other and hesitated. Pericleidas decided to go first. 'Admiral Eurybiadas and most of our allies want to fall back to the Isthmus of Corinth to stop the Persians at the narrow entrance of the Peloponnesus, but ...'

'But ...' the Athenian interrupted again, 'our admiral, Themistocles, has requested the allied fleet to redeploy to Salamis instead, where we can try to hold off the Persians fleet ...'

'And do what?' Pericleidas retorted. 'If we go to Salamis, their fleet can simply bypass ours, and even support an amphibious landing in the Peloponnesus. The only reason you prefer Salamis is that it is close to Athens and you want us all to come and protect your city.'

As the Athenian resumed his gaze into the distant unknown, Pericleidas turned to Gorgo. 'We are at an impasse. That is why we have come here to seek your guidance, Majesty.'

Gorgo gave the Athenian a harsh stare. 'Perhaps our Three Hundred would not have perished so easily if the Athenians had bothered to send an army to support my husband at Thermopylae. Now you want us to support this hare-brained strategy of your Admiral, Themistocles.'

The Athenian turned to Gorgo and smiled. 'Not so hare-brained, Madam. Our combined fleet is less than four hundred ships and we face an enemy almost twice our strength. The Isthmus offers no protection to an outnumbered fleet, whereas the Persians will be unable to exploit their numerical superiority in the tight Straits of Salamis.'

'But that depends on the premise that you can somehow lure the Persian navy into a battle in the Straits,' said Gorgo. 'Why would they want to fight us there? But the bigger question is why I should follow Themistocles' strategy when he has no interest in supporting mine.'

'I suppose,' said the Athenian, 'that if you don't agree with our strategy, we can always take our two hundred ships and our citizens and relocate to Italy or some other place. But then, without the Athenians, the Greeks won't have much of a navy.'

'You are not as dull as you look,' said Gorgo drily.

'It is a profitable thing, if one is wise, to seem foolish.'

'But you do make foolish threats. I know enough about you Athenians to know when you are bluffing. And indeed, Trierarch, I have no qualms about calling your bluff and you will surely regret it when I do.'

'No … no, Madam. Forgive me. Allow me to start again.' The Athenian swallowed hard, cleared his throat and said, 'King Leonidas' sacrifice at Thermopylae has taught us that it is better to die on your feet than to live on your knees. We Athenians want our Spartan allies and other patriotic Greeks to stand by us. Together, we will fight for freedom. Together, we shall avenge the Three Hundred. Together, we shall bring the Persians to justice. The cold breeze of sorrow will turn into an angry wind of retribution in those narrow Straits of Salamis. That is what Themistocles promises.'

Gorgo turned from the window and looked at the man a little suspiciously. Squinting her eyes, she asked him his name.

'Aeschylus,' came the response.

'What is your trade? I mean, when you are not learning how to sail your ship?'

His eyes lit up again. 'I am a playwright, of course.'

'Of course,' Gorgo said to herself, rolling her eyes. 'Why am I not surprised?'

'He is famous in Athens for his tragedies,' Pericleidas added.

'In that case, good Aeschylus, may you live long enough to write one about the Persians.' Then she sighed. 'Very well! Tell Themistocles that he has my support, provided he is able to trap the Persians in the Straits at Salamis and defeat them. But tell him too that even though he can beat the Persians in a thousand battles at sea, it is all for nought unless we defeat them decisively on land. That is the only way we can end this war.'

* * *

And so it had been. Salamis was won but did not end the war. And right now, Gorgo had no way of knowing which way the winds were blowing on the Plains of Plataea.

Chapter 12

Supplication

Plataea

Later that afternoon

When Sherzada awoke, the terrible throbbing in his head was still there; in fact, it was worse. The rest of his body was aching too, which was not surprising given he was shackled hand and foot.

He looked around the unfamiliar tent, and tried to recall how he had ended up here. All he remembered was the ferocity of the Athenian charge. As he ordered his troops to fall back across the river, he had suddenly felt his head swaying. The noises of battle were replaced by a deafening silence, and the last thing he recalled was the enemy pressing his men from all sides. And then everything went dark. Someone, he realized, must have hit him over the head, and hard.

Outside, Sherzada could hear voices being raised. But he could only recognize one; the elegant and eloquent elocution of the War Archon of the Athenians, Aristeides. He shuffled himself closer to the entrance.

'He is your prisoner, Aristeides. Why don't you keep him?' asked a young voice in Attic Greek, but with a thick Dorian Spartan accent.

'After all, he burnt down the Acropolis, Pausanias. I do not think his life expectancy in Athens would be terribly long,' came the reply from a voice Sherzada knew only too well.

'Then do the merciful thing. Slit his throat while he is still unconscious,' was Pausanias' comeback.

'This man is one of the enemy's bravest and best commanders,' replied Aristeides. 'He will be of more use to you alive than dead. Take him to the Queen. She will know what to do with him.'

'She will probably kill him, if I don't first …' muttered Pausanias. 'But what's this?'

Sherzada managed to find a tiny chink in the tent's entrance. He saw a line of weary girls led by a determined-looking Cleonice.

'They had asked me to lead them to you, Regent,' said the Spartan warrior who accompanied the women.

As they approached Pausanias, one by one each girl went down on her knees, except Cleonice and the girl next to her. Then Cleonice nudged her neighbour forward. The girl, with a little hesitancy, slowly walked forward, fumbling as she did so. Once directly in front of Pausanias, she too went down on her knees. Even though Sherzada could not see it, he knew the Greek custom. She would have bowed low and clasped his knees in supplication.

'Lord, my name is Hieronyma. I am … I am the daughter of Hegetorides, son of Antagoras of Cos,' said the girl, her voice trembling.

'My father had a close friend called Hegetorides of Cos,' responded Pausanias.

Sherzada glimpsed the girl tug something from her neck and present it to Pausanias. 'This necklace was sent by your father to my mother through my father.' Sherzada guessed it carried the emblem of Sparta.

'Then under the code of *Xenia*, you are as close to me as a sister.'

Gasping a sigh of relief, Hieronyma cleared her throat and spoke, 'Lord, these girls here with me are all of Greek blood. They were forcibly taken from their families by the Persians. All I ask of you is to ensure that all of us are returned to our homes in safety.'

'Granted. I shall make arrangements.'

Then Sherzada saw Cleonice's face redden as she lowered her

gaze.

'What is your name?' he heard Pausanias ask her.

'Cleonice of Byzantium,' she responded with a hint of defiance.

There was silence for a moment.

'Correct me if I am wrong, Euro,' Sherzada heard Pausanias say to someone next to him in a low tone. 'Byzantines are not exactly Greek, are they?'

Cleonice spoke up. 'My father's father came from Megara and a part of my mother's family are of Mycenaean origin. I was raised as a Greek, my Lord, and regard myself as one.'

Pausanias spoke again to the man beside him. 'I shall let all the girls go except that one. I want her.'

An exasperated voice responded, 'You have already given your word. Let her go, Pausanias.'

'I shall treat her well ...'

'As well as you can treat any war concubine, that is,' corrected Euro. 'If you take her to Sparta, her status will be that of a slave – a Helot. Sparta is not kind to love matches between Spartans and non-Spartans. With those in bondage it is even worse. Have you not learnt from my example?'

'If it's not too much trouble, I would like to get back to the fate of our prisoner,' said Aristeides. 'He you must take to Sparta, Pausanias.'

'Like Hades I will,' said Pausanias. 'I shall end it now. Bring him here.'

Chapter 13

A Trembler No More

Sparta
Two days later

It was still dark outside as Gorgo opened her tired eyes. Still in bed, she saw Agathe hovering over her, trying desperately to wake her. *If Agathe wanted to wake her before dawn*, Gorgo thought, *she must have very good reason.*

'Majesty, two messengers have arrived from Plataea, one after the other. One sent from the Regent Pausanias and the other from Prince Euryanax.'

Gorgo got up as calmly as she could and demanded to see the messages. After weeks of preparation, planning, and anticipation, all had come to this point.

Before they had left Sparta, she had made it clear to her cousins that she should be the first to hear of the battle's outcome – before the War Council, before the Ephors, even before the Gerousia. If someone was to break the news to Sparta, it should be her.

Only now, Gorgo was not sure what news there was to break. She went outside into the courtyard and sat down on the steps. She decided to start with Euro's letter. It was long and not in code, which surprised her a little. This was all the more reason to read it first, and so she did:

Dearest Cousin, from Euro,
Love and greetings.
I wish I can say that the battle of Plataea was won by Pausanias' leadership skills, but that would be laughably incorrect. I wish I could take the credit for winning the battle through my tactical brilliance, but that would be an even greater exaggeration. The day was won for

Greece, but sadly not by the Spartans, nor for that matter any other contingent; certainly not by some of the cowards on our side who fled the field of battle. It was won solely by Aristeides the Just – the man you rightly convinced the Athenians to elect as War Archon. And in spite of this, Aristeides refuses credit, giving all the glory instead to Pausanias.

It was his stratagem to use Persian gold against the Persians that first shifted the odds in our favour. He had bribed many Persian commanders to leave the field, which they did when battle began. And even after the debacle at Gargaphia, when we had decided to withdraw, it was Aristeides who told us that we should use this to our advantage – to lure the enemy into a trap. He said that we should continue our withdrawal until he gave us a signal to turn the tables on our foes. The words that I heard were his, but I suspect the ideas were yours.

Of course, things did not go exactly as planned. When it came to withdrawing, confusion reigned. The entire Greek army inadvertently broke into three groups, retreating in separate directions – rather than to the agreed point. Even within our ranks, there were Spartan commanders who considered any form of withdrawal as cowardice. Other Greeks took the retreat for a general flight, even though they had been told it was only a stratagem. We had not counted on this cowardice, especially from the contingents of Corinth and Megara. But the two contingents had suffered badly that day when the Persian cavalry tried to storm the Heights of Cithaeron, and their morale had not completely recovered. These contingents, a total of nearly ten thousand men, took refuge like scared children inside the fortified precincts of the Temple of Hera at the foot of Mt. Cithaeron, only to emerge from their hiding place in the middle of the night. And then the Dark Riders of Thebes ambushed them, leaving them brutally mauled. Even in defeat, these Thebans showed greater courage than most.

And, indeed, courage was not the monopoly of the Greeks – on either side. Indeed, those of the enemy who did not run away fought with admirable bravery and skill. Had all the Persians fought like those valiant few, they would have surely beaten us. I was later told that most of those we confronted were largely non-Persian subjects or allies of the Great King. Whoever they were, they were among the best warriors I have yet seen. Until Plataea, I thought the Spartans the best warriors in all of Greece and all Greeks superior to all Barbarians. I am not so sure I believe this now.

And it was not just these brave enemies of ours who demonstrated great courage. Even those among us whom we considered cowards proved us wrong. Aristodemus, whom we had labelled 'Trembler' proved his heroism by charging the entire Persian army single-handedly. He plunged deep into their lines with his spear and thus died a painful death, but only after making the enemy pay dearly. While most of us felt that he had redeemed his honour by this act, Cousin Pausanias refused to grant him any battle honours afterwards because he had broken ranks and charged the enemy against orders. This is rich coming from Pausanias, who has spent a lifetime defying discipline.

Towards the end of the battle, the bravest of the enemy made the last stand by the river near Mardonius' fortified camp. They almost routed us at the Asopus River crossing, had not Aristeides and his Athenians come to our aid. And after that, at the front of his camp, Mardonius and his troops also died, fighting bravely to a man. It was only after Mardonius' death that all resistance ended.

During the battle, one of the enemy commanders, in my reckoning their best, was taken prisoner. Aristeides asked Pausanias to take him to Sparta, suggesting you 'would know how to use him.'

Gorgo could not think of any possible use for the Persian, other than target practice.

Today the Mantineans arrived, a day after the battle was over. They were shown the battlefield and marvelled at the enormity of our victory. Many hung their heads, saying they had very much wanted to share this victory with the Spartans. They remembered the curse uncle Leonidas had placed on them of being cowards forever. Indeed, theirs was the first Greek contingent to abandon the Thermopylae Pass when the Persians outflanked it. Of course, Pausanias rubbed salt into their wounds by suggesting that they had deliberately delayed their arrival at Plataea to avoid the battle.

However, what the Mantineans were shown was a cover up. We told them, like we are telling everyone else, that the Greeks suffered very few casualties, less than 200. We are also telling everyone that our 70,000-strong force faced a Persian army of at least 300,000, though the fact is that their army outnumbered ours by a very thin margin. In reality, if you multiply the number of 'our dead' by twenty you will not come close to the true number we lost. I, myself, buried hundreds of those under my command. Plataea could have easily have been a defeat rather than the resounding victory we are claiming it to be. But the truth, as an Athenian recently put it to me, is war's first casualty.

And then finally, at the bottom of the parchment was a postscript, clearly written more hurriedly than the rest:

News has just reached us that the majority of the Persian Army that fled Plataea has been ambushed and destroyed by Alexander of Macedon's army at the Strymon River.

This is the account of the battle as I saw it.

Beneath these words, her cousin's familiar seal.

Gorgo got up and walked out of her room into the living quarters. Agathe and the girls had lit the fire and she sat down by the hearth and unfolded Pausanias' missive. It read simply:

I, Pausanias, Regent of Sparta and Hegemon of the allied Armies of Greece, have crushed the Barbarian hordes on the Plains of Plataea. Greece has been saved.

Gorgo laughed aloud at Pausanias' conceit. But, surely, he could have done a lot worse.

She asked Agathe to fetch Pleistarchus. Though the people of Sparta regarded him as their king, Gorgo could still guide him for a few more years.

Soon enough, Agathe returned with the little king, dressed in his tunic, the crimson slightly darker than the average fare, indicating his superiority over other Spartans.

As Gorgo took him by the hand, he asked her, 'What is it, Mother?'

'I have got some good news, my darling, but we need to share it with everyone.'

His eyes flashed. 'You mean we've …!'

She put her finger on his lips. 'Shhhh … Let us not spoil the surprise. But we also have to do something else.'

Gorgo took Pleistarchus to the Agora. It was early morning still and the market was full of people buying and selling. Fresh produce, meat and fish had been brought into town by the Perioiki merchants, and people were gathering to buy them. The stalls were neatly arranged alongside a path which led to a platform at the centre of the Agora. Even though there were a lot of people there, no one thought it strange for the King and his mother to visit the marketplace. But when Gorgo started climbing the platform with Pleistarchus, people stopped their business and began to gather around. The banter of trade was replaced by a commotion of speculation, as the citizens of Sparta waited to hear what news their Queen brought.

Gorgo waited a little to let the people settle. But more and more people slowly started to come around. She cleared her throat and said, 'Is Ione, daughter of Aristodemus, present here?'

There was silence.

'Is Ione here, daughter of Aristodemus?' she repeated.

'You mean Aristodemus the Trembler, Majesty,' someone shouted from the crowd. There was mocking laughter.

After a moment's pause, she shouted again, 'Are you here among us, Ione, daughter of Aristodemus *Monophthalmus*?'

She had deliberately called him *Monophthalmus* – 'One-eyed' – in reference to the infected eye that had prevented him from fighting and dying at Thermopylae, the eye he later gouged out in anger over his plight.

A timid voice blurted out, 'I am here, Your Majesty.'

'Then would Ione, daughter of Aristodemus *Monophthalmus*, do the honour of joining His Majesty and myself on this platform?'

Seeing the shocked look on the girl's face as she reached her, Gorgo hugged her warmly as disapproving shouts rang out from the crowd. She locked Ione in a tight embrace and whispered in her ear, 'Ione, I only ask you to do one thing for me. Be strong. As long as you are up here, with me, be strong and proud. You will have ample time to shed your tears later. Keep yourself together, Ione ... just for a little while. Just smile ... Remember that you are still a woman of Sparta.'

The Queen took the girl's left hand in her right hand and placed her other hand in that of her little son's. And then, clasping their hands, she wheeled them around to face the crowd.

As Gorgo looked through the crowd, she saw disapproving faces; even anger in some. Most, if not all, were visibly hostile to see the daughter of the Trembler stand next to their young King.

All this time, Gorgo was trying to work out how she should break the news to these good citizens of Sparta. Should she tell them that Pausanias had won a famous victory? That would be a lie. Or should she tell them Plataea had been won through trickery and deceit, not by courage and skill? That the enemy was brave as the Spartans? That the Greeks came very close to losing? But then she remembered that it did not matter to the people of Sparta how the battle had been fought or even indeed where it had been fought. They only wanted to know its outcome. Whatever she had to say, it should be brief and to the point. That is all they expected.

So at the top of her voice, she shouted, 'Citizens of Sparta, the Persian army has been destroyed. Thermopylae has been avenged. He whom we called a coward has died a hero.'

Deafening silence descended on the packed Agora. Gorgo scanned the crowd and slowly saw smiles light up every face. There were no cheers, no catcalls, no clapping like elsewhere in Greece. There were only satisfied faces. This was because victory was the only expectation Spartans had. They would have settled for nothing less and nor would have Gorgo.

As she slowly came down from the platform, Pleistarchus' hand still in her own, the people bowed and made way. Ione followed them with a slight if somewhat contrived smile on her face. There were no more angry looks towards her; only smiles.

And just as they cleared the crowd, Gorgo heard an old woman say something to Ione. A loud sob burst out of the girl. She ran from the marketplace, tears streaming down her eyes. All the old woman had done was to warmly greet Ione, and call her the daughter of Aristodemus *Monophthalmus.*

Aristodemus the Trembler was no more!

A tear slid down Gorgo's eye. Pleistarchus noticed it and asked, 'What is wrong, Mother?'

She wiped it away and kissed his head. 'Nothing, my darling. You father did not die in vain. We finally have our victory!'

Chapter 14

'Bright Eyes'

Sparta
A week later

The first time he saw it was at a distance – nestled at the foot of the forbidding snow-topped Mount Taygetus. It was not what he had imagined.

For all its fame, Sparta was like no other city. No great walls; no grand boulevards; no impressive buildings; and no monuments of any kind. And yet, Sherzada had to remind himself, this city had just humbled a great empire.

As he was dragged through its winding streets, he recalled that Sparta was less a city; more a collection of villages loosely connected to each other. And yes, their names came back to him – *Pitana, Mesoa, Limnae, Kynosoura,* and *Amylcae* – which were also the home bases of the standing regiments of the Spartan army. Each of these settlements had simple houses interspersed with longer barrack-like structures. These villages, marked by low hills, were separated by pleasant clumps of oak, fig and cypress trees and olive groves. The haphazard streets and the disorganized nature of the settlements meant that no one had actually bothered to plan this city. And yet, order was what Sherzada saw all around him. But the order was not in its streets or buildings; it was in its people.

Sparta, he recalled, was, after all, its people – the so-called *Spartiates* or the *Homioi* – the 'similar ones'. Though it was its male citizens that made up its fearsome army, all Spartans, whether male or female, child or adult, were in one way or another a part of the war machine that made Sparta so awesome. It was no wonder a city like this had no need for walls.

As the crowds lined the streets to quietly welcome their

troops home, Sherzada could not help noticing how strange the Spartans looked to outsiders.

Most of the men wore long hair and long beards – down at least to their chests – but without moustaches. They almost reminded him of the wild savages he had encountered in his travels. But the Spartans considered themselves the most civilized of Greeks. While every Spartan male wore a long crimson cloak, covering most of his body, their women had much less cloth covering theirs. The married ones had cut their hair short – very short – and a few were completely shaved. For a foreigner like Sherzada, this reversal in clothing and hair-length was indeed shocking. But to the Spartans this was perfectly normal.

All he had learnt about Sparta in the preceding years raced through his mind as he was taken through its streets. The throbbing pain in his head was replaced by the pounding of his heart, as the excitement of being in Sparta temporarily numbed his pain. But soon enough a sharp pull on his chains rudely brought him back to reality. His Spartan guards pushed him into an open field behind a very modest marketplace – the *Agora* – which stood at the centre of the city.

Soon people began to file into the field, almost as if in a military drill. Although none spoke, there was a sense of pride everywhere. An occasional smile, a beaming face – Spartans could not have been marking a happier event. Their young Regent-General had scored a spectacular victory; their army had avenged the death of a much-loved king; and they had driven out an invading army. Greece had been liberated. And he, Sherzada, was being displayed as a trophy of war.

As the people gathered, two simple chairs were placed under an oak tree. Five distinguished looking men stood behind them. *The Ephors,* Sherzada thought. Then a young boy – not yet ten – walked up and sat on one of the chairs. From the moment he saw him, Sherzada knew who he was. Despite himself, Sherzada couldn't help smiling at how much he resembled his father.

The second chair was left empty, and while Sherzada was wondering to whom it belonged, he overheard talk of a victory King Leotychidas had won at sea. The King had, as reports suggested, destroyed the Persian fleet in a battle on land, rather than at sea – *a fittingly bizarre end to a strange and pointless war,* thought Sherzada.

He did not see her at first, even though she stood there right in front of him, invisible in plain sight. It was only when the child-King looked nervously over his right shoulder that Sherzada noticed her. She was standing alone, at a distance, separate from the crowd. In her appearance too, she stood apart from the rest. She wore a simple peplos dress, creamish-white in colour, as opposed to the drab dark colours worn by other women. Over her shoulders, she wore a light beige *himation* shawl. Her long hair fell gracefully on her shoulders; there was pride in her poise and determination in her eyes. Like Sparta, she too had surprised Sherzada.

For all the stories he had heard about this woman, he had never expected her to look so youthful and so beautiful. Being the legendary birthplace of Helen of Troy, Sparta was famous for its stunning women. Even so, her beauty was exceptional. He could not help but stare. What was more incredible was that he could not believe that someone so young could be so wise.

For the briefest of moments, a look came over face which told him she was uncomfortable at being stared at. But then she stared back, her hazel-green eyes blazing in anger. 'Bright Eyes,' Sherzada recalled. So apt. And her stare was indeed dreadful, like that of her namesake – the mythical Gorgon who turned men to stone. But what perplexed him most of all was why, on the day Sparta was celebrating its greatest victory, the person who deserved most of the credit was standing at a distance, aloof among the shadows.

Then Pausanias walked into the centre of the field. He looked even younger than his twenty-some years, in spite of his long beard. Handsome and cocky; this young man clearly loved being centre-stage. Silence spread through the crowd as he began to speak.

The young Regent-General addressed the child-King Pleistarchus and spoke glowingly of his father, the late King Leonidas and his heroic death at the battle of Thermopylae. He dedicated the victory of Plataea to the two reigning kings, neither of whom was present at the battle. Then Pausanias went on to praise his warriors – and then himself.

Pausanias' self-eulogy was, however, interrupted when a Spartan warrior stepped up behind him. A little older than Pausanias, this man looked the perfect Spartan specimen – muscular, slim, and tall, with his curly long black tresses hanging down his crimson cloak, and a long beard that came down to his chest. The man's alert green eyes seemed to Sherzada to betray a rare intelligence. This was Euryanax, the deputy-commander of the Spartan army.

Whatever Euryanax had said made Pausanias turn towards Sherzada. He motioned to the guards, who dragged Sherzada into the middle of the field. There, Pausanias told the crowd that the prisoner was a 'Persian' commander captured at Plataea and brought to Sparta as a trophy of his victory. The crowd nodded its approval.

A voice rang out, 'Well done, Pausanias. Now can we get rid of him?'

'He should be in Hades with the rest of his comrades,' someone else chimed in. 'Let us put this poor creature out of his misery.'

Pausanias shouted back, 'Not so fast! He can be useful to us. I want him alive. For now, at least.'

The Queen walked slowly to the centre of the field, towards Pausanias. She stared angrily into Sherzada's eyes. 'This man's fate, dear cousin, is not your decision,' she said. 'It is that of the

Gerousia. You can petition our highest body to show clemency towards this prisoner. But the decision will be theirs, not yours.' Giving Sherzada a contemptuous look, she added, 'We are nothing if not slaves of our laws ...'

And still with her stare fixed on him, she said, '... But if it were left to me, I would take a sword right now, and thrust it through his heart. As far as I am concerned, this Persian deserves the same mercy his comrades showed my husband at Thermopylae.'

There was a muted, but prolonged, cheer from the crowd. This was the closest a Spartan crowd came to going wild ... and they were going wild, thirsting for Sherzada's blood.

Gorgo's lips curled up slightly as she waited for the cheer to die down, as if satisfied with the crowd's reaction. When silence returned, she said calmly, 'But then again, the decision is not mine, either.'

'Very well,' Pausanias responded. 'If it pleases the King and the Ephors, may we discuss the fate of the prisoner at the next session of the Gerousia? King Leotychidas will be among us also, back from his victory at Mycale. Until then, I suggest the prisoner be kept in the royal residential compound of the Agiadae, under my protection and responsibility.'

The Ephors nodded in approval. Following their lead, and after looking over his shoulder at his mother again, the child-King nodded too.

* * *

Surrounded by pleasant groves, the compound comprised two rows of simple-looking houses connected to each other as though they were one long building. Made of strong dark wood, they had the distinct look of a barracks rather than a set of homes.

Next to these was a small hut. This hut was dark, dank and cold, with only one small window, barred by iron rods. It had a faint musky smell, slightly on the pungent side. The room was square shaped, with each side being roughly the length of a Persian long-spear, two hands longer than a Spartan one.

Sherzada looked around the room and found it – unlike the dungeons in other lands – surprisingly clean. A stool was placed at the centre of the room; and there was a bed of reeds on the floor covered with a faded cloak. One small bucket of water, with a jar-like earthen cup and another larger empty one, were placed close by. His 'prison' was very basic; containing nothing more than the bare essentials … so typical of the Spartans.

The window was also close by and he could smell something very pleasant – it took a few moments for him to realise this was the fragrance of flowers. He looked outside towards a cobbled path leading to a pleasant garden nearby. It was spectacular, with Mount Taygetus in the background. He knew that the Persians prided themselves on their gardens but he never imagined Spartans as being horticulturalists.

Much later, a servant, a Helot no doubt, brought him a bowl with a dark thick liquid inside, along with a piece of stale bread. This black broth, he had been told years ago, contained some form of meat, combined with pulverized vegetables, fruit and herbs, cooked in milk, vinegar and blood. Sherzada was famished, but just as quickly as the broth went into his mouth, it came out again. The Spartan black broth was a triumph of practicality over gastronomy.

Chapter 15

Language Of The Enemy

Royal Compound of the Agiadae
Sparta
That evening

Gorgo stood staring at him, dumbfounded. She could not believe her ears.

'An interpreter will not be necessary, my Queen,' is what Sherzada had said.

What amazed her was that these words were not spoken in a Barbarian language, but in Greek. In fact, not only in perfect Doric Greek, not only in the Spartan dialect, but in the accent that only Spartans of the two Royal Spartan families normally spoke in.

Gorgo began to study her prisoner as he squatted on the floor. His face was not painted like those of the Persian envoys they had killed some twelve years ago. Instead, it was adorned by battle scars across his forehead and his left cheek. This Barbarian was much taller than the average Spartan and as swarthy as she expected an Asiatic to be. His dark brown eyes belied curiosity and intelligence. He did not seem like those Persians.

'Persian,' she asked, coming closer to him, 'tell me, who taught you our language?'

'Demaratus taught me,' said Sherzada, adding, '... And I am not a Persian.'

Gorgo gasped at the mention of that name. This man surely knew too much. All the more reason he must not see her afraid. So she snapped back at him, 'Like Hades you're not! You're a Persian right down to those disgusting trousers.'

She waited for him to respond; he did not, except to look down at his trousers and shrug.

'I don't care who you say you are,' she said. 'You came to this land uninvited, to kill our people, burn our cities, defile our temples and to make us your slaves. You cannot expect pity.'

There was defiance in his sullen eyes. 'I am quite familiar with your Spartan hospitality. The Persian envoys who came here were no doubt given special treatment. Oh yes, a drink of water at the bottom of a deep well. No, my Queen, I do not expect mercy. Nor will I ask it.'

He was certainly not like those Persians they had killed.

'You seemed to recognize me this afternoon at the mustering field,' she said, pacing about. 'Tell me, how did you know who I was?'

'Your hair is much longer than that of any other woman I have seen in Sparta.' It was true – married Spartan women cut their hair very short, but Spartan widows would grow it long again. 'Second, even a Spartan child-King looks towards his mother for comfort. Finally, your exceptional beauty. A gift from none other than the spirit of Helen of Troy, as Demaratus often said.'

Ignoring the compliment, Gorgo continued, 'Why did you smile at my son?'

'He resembled his father, your late husband.'

'You have seen my husband? Where?'

'At Thermopylae.'

'You could not have seen his face. He always wore his helmet in battle.'

'No, my Queen. He was not wearing his helmet when he died.'

'But that is impossible,' she said, after a moment's thought. 'I have heard that he died fighting. He was decapitated afterwards and his body mutilated.'

'King Leonidas' head remained very much attached to his body, even after his death. The man whose body was mutilated was another Spartan, whose corpse was mistaken by King Xerxes for that of your husband's.'

Gorgo took a step back and walked around the room a little

nervously. Thermopylae had never been an easy topic for her to discuss. She wanted to know more, but perhaps that would come later. So she decided to raise another matter. 'Barbarian, you mentioned the fate of the two envoys your King sent to us demanding earth and water. We killed them because they threatened to enslave us, to do unspeakable things to our women. And you did to our women exactly as they had foretold. Oh, how brutally your men raped the Greek women of Phocis. Women refugees from the Aegean islands also told of the horrors the Persian soldiers visited on them, of infants smashed against walls.'

'My Lady,' he said. 'I have never knowingly killed or harmed an innocent person, whether man, woman or child. The brutalities you speak about indeed occurred. And I will not defend them. But please tell me, my Queen, do Greek slave-raiders treat 'Barbarian' women and children with any less brutality? What about the women captured by your forces at Plataea? Tell me, did they fare any better than the women of Phocis? And do not tell me that none of your brave Spartan warriors has ever raped a Helot woman, or that none of your *Crypteia* squads have ever slit the throat of a Helot infant. Do not be quick, my Lady, to accuse others of crimes that your men commit themselves. You Greeks are no different, and you have no right to consider yourselves superior.'

At last, he was displaying some emotion. 'We are indeed superior to your kind, because we value something that you don't have …'

Before he could react, Gorgo continued, '… do you know, Barbarian, what we Greeks hold most dear? *Eleutheria*!'

From the look in his eyes, she knew he understood the meaning. It was the oldest word in the Greek language, and the most sacred. 'We will sacrifice everything for *Eleutheria*. This is the one thing that unites all Greeks; that binds us together. It is what defines Greece. Both my father and my husband died for this. You, who are slaves of the Persian King, can never truly appreciate what it means, for you have no notion of liberty!'

'... Nor, my Queen, do the Helots of Sparta,' interjected Sherzada. 'What rights do they have in your paradise of freedom? You also suppress the Perioiki, forcing them to die in wars over which they have no say. You have built your freedom around the slavery of others. You Greeks think you invented the whole notion of freedom, but freedom, my Queen, is not the preserve of the Greeks. Every nation on earth values its freedom just as you do.'

This Barbarian seemed to know a lot of about Sparta. But Gorgo did not want the last word to be his. 'So, prisoner, did the Great King lead a million men into Greece just to free the Helots from Spartan oppression?'

'A million men?' laughed Sherzada. 'Oh, how you Greeks love to exaggerate! ... But it is you Spartans whom the Persians blame for starting the war in the first place, not them.'

'Two generations ago, a Lydian King went to war with Persia after misinterpreting a prophecy from the Oracle of Delphi, and so the Persians blame us for starting a war!'

'Sparta not only had considerable influence over Lydia at that time, but also over the Delphic Oracle. And there are those who believe Sparta has considerable influence over the Oracle even now.'

This was a secret. How could he possibly know this? No one else in the whole of Greece knew this. Perhaps he was bluffing. 'How can the Persians possibly justify invading and conquering other people's lands?'

'Now that you have won the war, my Queen,' he said, 'you can say that right was on your side all along. History is written by the victors. But all sides in any conflict believe their cause is just. You and your *Eleutheria* and the Persians their *Arta*.'

She did not know the word.

'Just as you hold your *Eleutheria* dear,' he explained, noticing her confusion, 'the Persians value Truth – *Arta* – above all else. Every Persian must learn three things from childhood: to ride well, to shoot straight, and to tell the truth. But the kings of Persia have become skilful in manipulating the Truth for political ends. They are masters of propaganda. It was Darius, one of Cyrus' successors, who first declared war on the Lie, to justify his illegal seizure of the throne. Everything he did, he claimed, was to preserve the Truth and to damn the Lie. So much for a man who had seized power by killing the rightful heir and covering up his crime with piety. The Persians claim to fight for the Truth against the Lie, just like you Greeks fight for freedom against oppression, and yet all I see is hypocrisy on both sides.'

This strange Barbarian was turning out to be as fascinating as he was annoying. 'Tell me about Demaratus, who was once our king,' she demanded. 'How did you come to know him?'

'I first met Demaratus in Sardis, the centre of Persian rule in Western Asia, some ten years ago. An exiled former King of Sparta, coming all that way to offer his services against his own people, was something the Persians could not refuse. At the time, I was working for a man who was head of Persia's intelligence apparatus responsible gathering information on Greece. He instructed me to befriend Demaratus in order to learn as much I could from him. And indeed, Demaratus taught me your dialect with your distinct royal accent, and almost everything I know about Sparta.'

'So, Barbarian,' she said, 'all this time, I had thought you a warrior; you are actually a spy.'

'I have been both and a lot more, my Queen. But that is not important.'

Gorgo was amused by his modesty, but also alarmed at what he had revealed. She wanted to know more about the secrets Demaratus had shared with him. But to her own surprise, instead she asked the one question that she had longed to ask Demaratus. 'I suppose Demaratus still hates my father?'

'My Queen, you know better than I about the enmity between your father and Demaratus. But he never said a disrespectful word about King Cleomenes to me. He admitted that only he, himself, was to blame for tearing their friendship apart. Though he was obviously bitter about the way your father had had him dethroned, he admitted that he had brought it all upon himself, by repeatedly undermining your father's plans. Demaratus could not comprehend why King Cleomenes had to interfere in the affairs of other Greek states. Of course, only after Demaratus had defected to the Persians, did he realize what your father had been trying to do. That he had been attempting to unite the Greeks against a common threat – the Persians.'

How strange, she thought, *that it took a Barbarian to truly appreciate her father's genius.*

'Demaratus told me that once he and your father fell out, King Cleomenes accused him of being an illegitimate child and not the true heir of the Eurypontid King. An oracle from Delphi backed up your father's accusations. The Ephors met and deposed Demaratus, replacing him with his rival, Leotychidas.

'But Demaratus has always maintained that he was the legitimate child of King Ariston. He was born prematurely – seven months instead of nine, and King Ariston really was his father. Surely you don't believe your god Apollo lies?' he asked.

Gorgo smiled and said to herself, *Ah ... but that is politics!* Then she addressed Sherzada. 'Have you forgotten yourself, prisoner? *I* shall be the one to ask questions. So, what happened once Demaratus defected to your side?'

'... the Persian side,' he tried to correct her.

'Your side!' she asserted.

'Demaratus thought the Persians would help him regain his crown. But he soon realized they were not interested in restoring him. Afterwards, he felt guilty about what he done and later did his best to undermine the Persian war effort. Did he not warn you about the Persian invasion, my Queen?'

How could the Barbarian possibly know all of this?

'The wax tablet containing the warning of the Persian invasion?' he prompted. 'Demaratus was certain that no one would know how to decipher the secret of the wax tablet. No one, that is, except you, my Queen.'

Gorgo, once again, ignored his compliment. She needed to know more. 'They say Demaratus was close to Xerxes. How did he convince the Persians he was loyal to their cause?'

'Demaratus is a likable man. Xerxes found his company agreeable from the start. So he made Demaratus his advisor on all things Greek. When the invasion began, Xerxes regularly turned to him for advice. While he was ingratiating himself to the Persian King, Demaratus was playing a double game, as you know better than I.'

'So, where is he now?' Gorgo asked. 'Surely he must have been executed.'

'For what?'

'Their defeats, of course, and his role in aiding the Greeks,' she responded.

'Only if they had known … or cared. The Persians do not see the Greek adventure as a complete defeat. Had they not killed a Spartan King and burned Athens – twice?'

'So, what happened to Demaratus?' she asked, with too heavy an impatience for someone in her position, she realized too late.

'For his loyal service, the Great King has made Demaratus ruler of Pergamum and two other neighbouring cities.'

'Not bad for a traitor, and a two-timing one at that. I am happy for him. But still, all the thrones of Asia are not worth half a kingship of Sparta.'

'Spoken with true arrogance, my Lady,' he said, 'just like a Persian.'

Chapter 16

The Gorgon's Mask

Sparta
The following evening

The sun set on the second day of Sherzada's captivity in Sparta. It was not yet completely dark when he heard steps outside. Looking out of his cell window, he could see a torch-lit path leading to the garden and the now familiar figure of Gorgo walking towards his prison. Three figures appeared from the opposite direction, all dressed in long crimson cloaks. He could not make out the figures, other than that the men were dressed in typical Spartan garb. One of them was limping, walking only with a help of a tall staff. Gorgo's face was lit up by the torchlight, as the dark blue sky began to vanish into darkness behind her.

The three men bowed slightly, even though there was an air of panic about them. The oldest of the three, the one with the staff, spoke first. 'There is disturbing news, Majesty. We need your advice.'

'Would not my cousins, Pausanias and Euryanax, be better to guide you on military matters?' Gorgo responded quietly.

'They have already left for Corinth to attend the League's conference,' said the tallest of three, 'And, in any case, we have always sought your opinion before anyone else's.'

Sherzada saw a satisfied expression alight on Gorgo's torch-lit face. 'So, gentlemen, what seems to be the problem?' she asked, her voice ringing clear in the night.

'We have heard that our allies, the rulers of Tegea, have been overthrown,' responded the tallest. 'A faction known for its sympathies towards Persia and hatred for Sparta has replaced it. We now have enemies on our very doorstep. Tegea is less than a day's march away. They can attack us whenever they want. We must pre-empt them.'

'However, our dilemma, Majesty,' interrupted oldest general, 'is, as you might recall, the services the Tegeans rendered for Greece at Plataea. Is it wise to strike at a people who only a few days earlier were among our strongest and staunchest allies?'

The youngest disagreed. 'The only reason they fought with loyalty at Plataea was that their leadership was loyal to us. But the situation has changed. Must we take chances?'

'Gentlemen,' said Gorgo, 'Do you have proof that even if they are unfriendly towards us, they will attack us?'

The oldest general shook his head, and once again the youngest disagreed. 'They have not disbanded their army,' he said, 'while we have demobilized ours. Many of our warriors have left Sparta for their country estates. If the new Tegean leadership is hostile to us, they would want to attack us now, catching us completely unprepared. We do not have the luxury of waiting.'

'But if you are wrong?' asked Gorgo. 'What if the new rulers of Tegea, no matter how pro-Persian or anti-Spartan, are not going to doing anything hostile against us? If we attack them, even pre-emptively, would we not be attacking our own allies? ... and without provocation? What kind of message would that send throughout Greece? That we are just as bad as the Persians, if not worse! They will turn to our old rival, Argos. Thus, in one fell swoop we shall give the Argives everything that we have spent the last two decades taking from them.'

'Surely,' said the youngest, 'Your Majesty doesn't expect us to sit around and wait for the situation to become any clearer?'

'Act we must,' she said and then added, 'but with subtlety and finesse.'

The three men turned and looked at each other, obviously not quite sure of what Gorgo had just said.

'Have the Argives rebuilt their walls?' she asked.

The youngest became impatient. 'What has that got to do with all of this?' he complained. 'We are talking about Tegea, not Argos.'

'The two are linked, Arimnestus,' said Gorgo, 'at least in how we must resolve this crisis.' After a moment's silence, she continued, 'Once again, I ask you gentlemen, have the Argives rebuilt the walls that my father made them tear down fifteen years ago?'

The tallest general chimed in. 'There are persistent rumours that they want to rebuild them … but we have no proof that they have done so.'

'Well, someone ought to go and find out, don't you think?' she asked. 'And what about the Crypteia?'

The Crypteia, comprising the best of Sparta's military graduates, was sent out each year to assassinate potential Helot troublemakers as a test of skill.

'I wonder if sending the Crypteia to kill recalcitrant Helots is the best way to utilize their talents,' she continued. 'Where is it now … in Laconia or Messene?'

'The Crypteia is to leave for Laconia tonight,' responded the tallest.

'Strange,' she mused, 'all the evidence we have suggests that the troublesome Helots are in Messene and yet we send our secret squad against the loyal ones in Laconia. I think the Crypteia needs a lesson in geography … as do their generals!'

The generals shifted nervously, apparently stung by Gorgo's criticism.

'The Crypteia is wasting its time,' she continued. 'It should be recalled immediately.'

'But why?' asked the tallest. 'And what has this got to do with the present crisis in Tegea?'

'Absolutely nothing, Evaeneutus, and that is precisely the problem. They should not be preying on innocent Helots in Laconia. They should be in Tegea spying on the new leadership there. Send the Crypteia to Tegea, tonight. Have them report back to you soon as possible. We need to have accurate information of the intention of the new Tegean leadership. And we need that information now.'

The one called Evaeneutus nodded and hurried away.

Arimnestus spoke again. 'But that may be too late. What if the Tegeans attack us tonight?'

'You know the terrain. There are only two ways the Tegeans could attack us. Over the mountains from the north-west or by following the River Eurotas from the north-east. Either way, they would have to cross difficult ground. It would take them more than a day. And our border rangers, the Skiritae, would see them coming. But I do not think they are foolish enough to take on the Spartan army without thinking twice.'

'What shall happen in the morning?' asked Arimnestus.

'We shall prepare for war.'

It was the turn of the oldest general to become nervous. 'Officially, the Tegeans are still our friends and allies. How can you justify going to war against them, Majesty?'

'Who said we are preparing for war against Tegea, Eurybiadas?' she smiled.

The two generals looked at each other, utterly confused.

'Send the word out tonight,' she continued, 'to the *syssitionoi* that by daylight they should have an expeditionary force ready to march out. We do not need the whole army. As Arimnestus pointed out, most of them are away. But we can easily mobilize three battalions from the Homioi and a similar number from the Perioiki overnight. And, just to be on the safe side, send instructions to the Skiritae to watch the mountain passes as well as the Eurotas crossings. That ought to do the trick, don't you think?'

'But, Majesty,' asked the eldest. 'What will be the objective of this expeditionary force?'

'Their mission, good Eurybiadas, will be to see if the Argives have continued to obey our instructions not to build their fortifications, as they are required under the treaty that ended our last war with them. Our troops shall remind the Argives, in no uncertain terms, that if they put even a brick in place, we shall level Argos.'

A broad smile appeared on Eurybiadas' lips, but Arimnestus asked plaintively, 'But Majesty, what has this to do with Tegea?'

Gorgo spoke slowly and patiently to the young general. 'Your troops, dear Arimnestus, will march through Tegean territory on their way to Argos. Once there, you will inform our Tegean friends about the objective of your expedition and request their assistance. If they are still our allies, their army will join ours in this expedition. If they are not, then they, and not the Argives, will have to answer to you. The entire Tegean army is less than three thousand men, and they will be facing over four thousand of ours. Once they see your big battalions, Arimnestus, I am sure the Tegeans will do the right thing.'

The two generals stared at Gorgo in silence, before Eurybiadas responded. 'This is brilliant, Majesty.'

'Remember what Father used to say.' Gorgo seemed to smile modestly. 'When in doubt, march on Argos!'

The two generals roared aloud. But Gorgo quickly hushed them up. 'Shhhh … Quiet, gentlemen. We must be discreet.'

Eurybiadas smiled. 'Of course, Majesty,' he said. They bowed and quietly left. As they did so, Gorgo looked over her shoulder, almost as if she knew Sherzada had been listening in on the conversation.

The word '*Metis*' was going through his head; a Greek word that was difficult to translate. *Metis* encompassed clearheaded wisdom, skilful intelligence, cunning, and above all, subtlety. And this word so perfectly defined Gorgo. The Queen liked to play the bright-eyed Gorgon with her terrible stare but it was the woman behind that mask that intrigued Sherzada.

Within moments, she swept into his cell, sat down on the stool in front of him, and motioned him to sit on the floor in front of her. Sherzada had been expecting some form of torture and brutal interrogation, but all he got were questions. Of course, he was fine with that, for he had nothing to hide – except one detail; and revealing *that* would lead to certain death.

Gorgo was methodical in her interview, looking directly into Sherzada's eyes before each question. 'Even though you have fought for the Persians, you have been trying to have me believe that you are not a Persian. Is that not so?' she asked.

He nodded.

'Then what are you?' she asked.

'I am a Saka,' he replied.

'A what?'

Sherzada laughed. 'You are so like the Persians, in your ignorance and your arrogance.'

Gorgo's eyes burned with rage. 'Why do you take so much pleasure in likening us to the Persians?'

'Well, you are! Not least, in your claim of being superior to others. The first time Cyrus the Great encountered Spartan ambassadors, he asked the question, 'Who are the Spartans?' Your Spartan envoys were outraged. How could anyone not know about the Spartans? This was long before the Persians felt the sharp end of your spears. Today, you ask me a similar question. You ask me who my people are, even though your troops have fallen to the battle-axes of my warriors. Are you then not unlike the Persians, my Queen?'

'Careful, Barbarian, you test my patience,' she snapped.

'I hail from the Asiatic branch of the Scythian people. We call ourselves the Sakas. I am from the Sindhic tribal group. Though we speak a language that is in some ways similar to Persian, we are not Persians. We, the Scyths, once roamed the great Eurasian plains from eastern edges of Europe to deep into northern Asia. But now we are divided into clans, tribes and confederacies, spread out across the two continents.'

Gorgo mused for a moment and then said, 'My father had a Scythian friend, an ambassador, from across the Euxine Sea. But he looked nothing like you.'

'True,' he said, 'our culture is similar to the European Scyths, even though my appearance is not. But all Scythians were originally nomadic. As the Scyths have dispersed into different lands, they have assimilated with the peoples they live among, often intermarrying with native populations. Thus, my ancestors are both Scyths and locals and hence my dark skin.'

'But you Scyths are supposed to hate the Persians,' said Gorgo. 'Was it not your people who killed Cyrus? Was it not to avenge that death that Darius invaded Scythian lands?'

Sherzada's right eyebrow went up. He was impressed at her knowledge. 'Those who killed Cyrus were the Massagatae, distantly related to us. And yes, Darius sought to avenge his predecessor's death by invading Scythian lands. But the Persians have been at war with Scyths and other northern tribes for generations. You are right, indeed. Little love is lost between the Scyths and the Persians.'

'Then why have such ancient enemies of the Persians fought on their side against us?'

'A long story, my Queen.'

'Which I would like to hear,' she insisted.

'Many generations ago, my people migrated from the northern Asiatic plains, to a land you call India. My ancestors occupied the northern half of the valley of the River Indus, including a fertile land irrigated by the five main tributaries of the Indus – the Land of the Five Rivers – *Punj-Aab.* This is my homeland, just across the eastern edges of the Persian Empire. Even though I may look like an Indian, I consider myself a Saka.'

Gorgo gave him a quizzical look and said, 'My father told me it takes three months to travel to the Persepolis. How far is your land from there?'

'The furthest end of the Persian Empire is another two months' journey from Persepolis, and my home is less than a week's ride beyond that.'

Gorgo's eyes widened as her beautiful chin dropped. It was clear that she was unable to comprehend the distances involved. Sherzada could not help smiling at her amazement.

But he continued nonetheless. 'Darius first avenged the death of Cyrus by subjugating the Massagatae. Then he went to war against the northern Scyth, but they humiliated him badly. Then he went to war against us across the great mountain ranges. My grandfather, who was then the High King of the Sakas of the Indus, decided to stop the Persians in the north-western mountains, before they could reach the plains where our homesteads lay. Our warriors rode up to a high mountain pass, known as the Iron Gates, and there they blocked the Persian advance. In spite of their best attempts, the Persians could not force the pass. After thirty days of hard, ceaseless fighting, the two armies were exhausted. Though the Persians had suffered severe casualties, our army was even more dangerously depleted. Our warriors could not continue the struggle for very much longer. My grandfather also knew that once his army fell back, nothing could stop the Persians from ravaging the Indus Valley and seizing our homesteads and despoiling our lands. He was forced to accept a compromise. He offered Darius earth and water as tokens for their submission to the Persian King as long as the Persians agreed not to cross into the Saka lands. But Darius was reluctant to accept this compromise. He believed that victory was at hand and wanted to continue the fight. However, his generals told him that pursuing such a victory might be their undoing. They said the army was exhausted and could not continue the struggle any longer. So finally Darius agreed to accept the offer of earth and water, provided the Saka gave him the best of their warriors to fight his wars in the West.

'My grandfather agreed. And, ever since, he has provided the Persians with our best troops, our Royal Guardsmen always led by a royal Prince, as long as they were not used for Persia's wars in the East.'

'So in other words, you came all the way from Asia to help the Persians attack us so that the Persians would not attack you?'

Sherzada could not refute her logic.

'A Spartan would never do such a thing. You are no better than mercenaries!'

'My Queen, have Spartans not waged wars in alliance with other states? Have not Spartan mercenaries fought for Cumae in Italy, for Syracuse in Sicily, for Cyrene in Libya and elsewhere? Have not Spartan warriors made private fortunes fighting in foreign lands?'

Gorgo allowed herself to smile a little at his sparring. Then she added with a little seriousness in her voice, 'Have you always been this vexatious? I wonder how the Persians put up with you all this time.'

'I did not make many friends among them, it is true.'

'So if I have you killed, they will not miss you?' she asked.

'No, and perhaps you might even be doing me a favour, my Queen.'

'How so?'

'I was the eldest son of the heir apparent to my grandfather's throne. I came out here to replace my father when he died at Marathon. A year ago my grandfather also died, and according to our tradition I should have gone back to claim my throne. But at that time Xerxes' invasion plans were well advanced and he would not allow me to return to my native land. If I go now, I return in shame, without my men. To come back alone and without glory is to come back as a dead man.'

'As in Sparta!' she whispered.

'Moreover,' he continued, 'I know of men here in Sparta, who have over the years taken the Great King's gold. If they knew what I know, they would never allow me to leave here alive.'

'Is that so?' she asked, with a sly smile.

Her smile worried Sherzada, for he was not sure what this woman of *Metis* was planning.

Chapter 17

The Trail Of The Fox

Sparta
The following evening

Gorgo had spent the whole day considering the prisoner's revelation. Was it true that there were traitors in Sparta? Or was he just making that up? Certainly, he knew much. But how much?

So preoccupied was she with this that even Pleistarchus had to ask her at dinner if she was feeling all right. 'Of course I am, little Majesty,' she said, patting her head as she took off to see the prisoner, leaving her meal unfinished.

The strategy she opted for was the direct attack. Entering his cell, ignoring his respectful habit of standing for her, Gorgo looked Sherzada in the eye and asked him to tell her about his career as a spy.

Sherzada stood silently until she had settled down on the stool. Gorgo noticed his eye brighten as he slowly sat down on the floor and crossed his legs. For a change he looked at ease, which only made Gorgo even tense.

'Well?' she demanded.

He smiled, and, to her surprise, began to tell her everything.

* * *

Eleven years ago, I was summoned to Sardis, where I was informed about the debacle of Marathon and the death of my father. As part of our treaty I was to take up command of the Sakas who survived the battle. But seeing their wretched condition I persuaded the Persians to repatriate them, on the condition that they would be recalled to service if the Persians went to war in Greece again. In return for this, I was to remain behind as a guarantee – a hostage – to ensure our end of the bargain. The Persians treated me well – more like an honoured guest than a hostage. I was allowed to do as I pleased as long as I remained under their supervision. The man whose responsibility I became was a man called Datiya, or Datis, as he is known in Greece.

He had commanded the Persian forces at Marathon alongside Prince Artafarna, Darius' nephew. But Datis was a Mede, not a Persian. The Persians sought men of exceptional talent among their Median cousins to serve them, and Datis was one of them.

In spite of the humiliating defeat at Marathon, King Darius had forgiven Datis. He knew that Marathon had been one beachhead too far and that the blame did not entirely lie with Datis. The Great King had already asked Datis to set up an intelligence network focusing solely on Greece. Datis had studied Greek and understood the Greeks like no other. He secretly recruited a number of 'operatives' and made each of them specialize in a different aspect of Greece. He made sure that all information was sent to him and him alone. No one knew for sure, but there was a widespread belief that in spite of Marathon Datis was winning the war of shadows – as the spying game was called – with an increasing number of Greek states offering earth and water to the Great King.

Datis held my father in high regard. In the closing stages of the battle of Marathon, troops from the Persian force were retreating to their ships as the pursuing Athenians bore down on them. My father, having been gravely injured, decided to sacrifice his life to ensure the safe evacuation of his Sakas. To do that, he made Datis exchange clothes and armour with him and then with a handful of volunteers he created a diversion, drawing the Athenians away from the sea. This enabled his Sakas to embark the ships unharmed. Of course, he did not survive. However, Datis flattered himself by believing my father had given his life for him and felt obliged to take me under his wing. He invited me to join his intelligence network. He needed someone to focus on Sparta at the time, and given my propensities for languages and learning, I agreed.

When I asked him what his strategy was, he replied in Greek: *Diaírei kaì basíleue* – 'divide and rule'. Datis believed that the Greeks were their own worst enemies and all the Persians had to do was to exploit their mutual differences and encourage them to tear each other apart. Persia could only conquer the Greeks by dividing them. However, to do that he needed to find out more about each individual state. And it was around that time that Demaratus turned up. Datis asked me to befriend him and find out as much as I could about Sparta, especially its military strength and its politics.

I had expected to find a haughty, embittered old former king, but instead I found in Demaratus a charming and affable man, always willing to oblige. And so he did: teaching me everything I know about Sparta, including your royal dialect.

But Demaratus had a price, explaining, 'One day I shall ask you to do something for me in return for all I am about to teach you.'

When I asked him what it was, he said he did not know it yet. But as everything must have its price, he said that one day he would hold me to this and I must not refuse. Given that Datis had given me this task to do, I thought I would pass on the price to Datis, who would surely pay it.

Thus began an unlikely friendship between a hostage and a traitor both held in a gilded cage by the Persians.

Around that time, I also learnt the fate of my father's body. The Athenians, of course, believed they had killed Datis. Soon after the battle they sent heralds to the Persians, offering to return the bodies of their dead – all, excepting that of Datis. Refusing to hand it back, the Athenians placed it in a vault in the Acropolis until they had decided what to do with it.

I wanted to go to Athens to recover my father's body, to give him a proper burial. But Datis refused for I was not allowed to leave territories controlled by Persia. But soon enough, everything changed.

When Xerxes, the son of Darius, ascended the throne, he made Mardonius, his cousin, his Viceroy in the West. Mardonius not only forced Datis into retirement but he also completely dismantled his spy network. When the Persians later invaded Greece, they did so without the vital intelligence that Mardonius' team had painstakingly gathered. This was a grave mistake the Great King made under the influence of Mardonius, the son of Gobryas.

And soon enough the preparations for the invasion began. My grandfather sent his Royal Saka Guardsmen to fight under my command. My status changed to that of an allied commander.

Not long afterwards, Demaratus came to me with an offer I could not refuse. 'Do you remember the price I asked of you when I began to divulge everything I knew about Sparta?'

When I told him I did, he told me that I had to go to Athens for him on a discreet personal matter. I could not believe my ears. I told Demaratus about my father's body and how I wanted to recover it.

Demaratus gave me a brooch, a simple but elegant piece which did not look very expensive. 'I would like you to deliver this to a man in Athens,' he said. 'It is a gift of immense personal value. Once you deliver this item, he will be more than happy to help you.'

All Demaratus told me about this Athenian was that he was nicknamed the Fox. And all I had to do was to send word once I arrived in Athens that a foreign merchant was looking to do business with the Fox; he would come and find me. In addition, Demaratus gave me two things he said would be useful in my journey. The first one was the Royal Seal of the Great King – the seal which would protect me throughout the Persian Empire. The second was a document – a certificate – approved by the Athenian Democratic Assembly, giving protection to its bearer. Affixed was the seal of the Archons of Athens.

And so I disguised myself as a Western Scythian merchant and boarded a ship at the port of Sinope on the Euxine Sea bound for Greece. The ship crossed the Hellespont and set its course to Delium, where I was supposed to change to another ship headed for Athens. But that night, while I was sleeping in the lower deck, the ship began to rock violently. Sensing something was wrong, I reached for my most precious possessions, including the two articles Demaratus had given me, which were in a waterproof pouch. I slung the pouch over my shoulder, stuck my dagger in my belt, and climbed to the upper deck. A violent storm was blowing the ship dangerously out of control. Seeing the ship was about to hit massive rocks, I jumped overboard. As I plunged into the cold water, my body went into shock, as my lungs began to gasp for breath. But I managed to swim back up to the surface and saw the ship had broken into pieces. As I grabbed a floating plank for support, I heard a man crying for help. He shouted that his legs were caught and he was being dragged underwater. Realizing he was not a good swimmer, I dove into the water and cut the ropes that bound his legs. Freeing him, I helped him to the plank I had been hanging on to earlier.

In the morning, we found ourselves washed up on a beach. I now got a good look of the man whom I had saved. He was in his fifties, lean, with a short grey unkempt beard. He got up and walked towards me and thanked me profusely for saving his life. I had never heard more beautiful, elegant and eloquent Greek. He asked me who I was and I told him I was a Scythian merchant bound for Athens. The man said that he was an Athenian. His name was Aristeides, son of Lysimachus.

I told him that the only Aristeides I had heard of was the famous Athenian, Aristeides the Just. A veteran of Marathon, he was famous all over Greece and beyond for his statesmanship, honesty and fair dealings. The man smiled and thanked me for my kind words, and told me that he was the same Aristeides. When I asked him what he what been doing on the ship, he told me that he had been exiled by his fellow citizens.

Aristeides then explained to me the novel Athenian practice of *ostracism* – under which unpopular Athenian politicians were sent into exile for several years. It was a civilized alternative, Aristeides claimed, to political assassination and in spite of being one of its earliest victims he supported this method. He then explained how it worked. It was something like a negative election. Each citizen would pick up a shard – *ostracon* – of broken pottery and write the name of the candidate he wanted to go into exile on it and cast it as his vote. At the end of the voting, the shards would be collected and the politician who got the most votes would be given ten days to go into exile.

When Aristeides discovered he was nominated for ostracism, he came to see the voting. An illiterate peasant came up to him and not knowing who he was, asked him to write down Aristeides' name. Aristeides asked the peasant what he had against the man. The peasant told him that he had nothing against Aristeides but he was fed with hearing about Aristeides 'the Just' all the time. Aristeides complied with the peasant's request, and beat his nearest rival by one vote. The very vote he had written got him ostracized.

Guessing we were in the badlands between Macedon and Thessaly, Aristeides asked me if I did not mind traveling north-westwards with him towards Aegae, one of the two capitals of Macedon. I was surprised. Macedon was a Persian vassal and ally. Its king, Alexander, had marriage alliances with Persian royalty. Persian troops were also stationed on Macedonian soil. An Athenian leader of his stature would not be safe there, I argued, even in exile. But Aristeides said there was at least one man in Macedon he could trust, which was more than he could say for the whole of Thessaly. Once we reached Macedon, he said, he would help me get to Athens safely and help me with whatever I wanted there. He still had influence in his native city, even though it had exiled him.

It was a hard journey over mountainous terrain, and by dusk I was exhausted. We had scarcely started a fire when I dozed off, without even touching dinner. It was a blissful sleep, until I was rudely awoken. The man whose life I had saved was on top of me, pointing my very own dagger at my throat. In his other hand, he held the certificate of protection from the Athenian Democratic Assembly. Trembling, he asked what my business was in Athens. I told him that I had to meet a person called the Fox. He grew angrier, demanding to know what I wanted from the Fox. I told him that I would rather die, that the only person I could discuss this matter with was the Fox himself. Looking confused at first, Aristeides relented. He let out a deep sigh, got off me, dropped my dagger and sat down by the fire.

'I am the Fox.'

He said that he came from the district of Alopeke outside Athens. He used to represent that district in the Athenian Democratic Assembly. The Greek word for fox – *alopex* – is similar to Alopeke. Some of his closest friends, those who knew him well, gave him that nickname. It was a private joke, he said. Very few people outside his close circle of friends knew that he was called 'the Fox,' the majority knew him by his other nickname, 'the Just'. Only two foreigners knew of it; both were Spartan kings. One, Cleomenes, was dead and other, Demaratus, was in exile. 'This must be Demaratus' certificate, I presume?' he asked.

I nodded. 'This is the item Demaratus asked me to give to the Fox,' I said, passing Aristeides the brooch.

Aristeides thanked me. He looked at the brooch and swiftly hid it under his clothes. Then he asked me why I was going to Athens. 'Surely there is more to it than delivering Demaratus' gift?'

I told him that the man whose body the Athenians had taken to the vault in the Acropolis was not that of Datis but of my father, the leader of the warriors the Athenians called the 'Axemen'.

Aristeides smiled. 'You know, your father very nearly killed me at Marathon. After he struck down poor Callimachus, our War Archon, he came directly towards me. So powerful was his first blow that it nearly cleaved my shield apart. His repeated blows made it useless and I was knocked back to the ground. He would have surely finished me off had not my comrades come to my aid and formed a shield wall around me. Your father then turned his attention to Themistocles, my rival. He too came within an inch of losing his life and was also saved when other hoplites came to his assistance. I have often wondered whether Athens would have been the same had both I and Themistocles perished at Marathon.'

Then he shook his head. 'Your father's body had been brought to Athens, and kept in the vault beneath the Temple of Athena Parthenos on the Acropolis because my fellow citizens were convinced that it was Datis' body. They were sure that the Persians would offer a pretty price for it. But as soon as they found out that Datis was alive and well, living in Sardis, a mob took your father's body out of the Acropolis and threw it into the sea.'

Seeing the anger and sadness in my eyes, Aristeides patted my shoulder and left me to my pain. By the following morning, I had decided there was no need to proceed to Athens. As we walked towards Aegae through the rugged, mountainous terrain, Aristeides was clearly in an upbeat mood. He started propounding the glories of Athenian Democracy. I called it an exercise in hypocrisy where the rich could hold on to power by manipulating the poor. He was appalled. We continued to argue for hours. Then he changed the subject and turned to the battle of

Marathon, exaggerating Athenian glory. He smiled broadly as he remembered the day 'they ran' – referring to the Athenian claim that they had charged for a mile before crashing into enemy lines at Marathon, forcing the massive Persian army into headlong retreat.

There was no way, I told him, that hoplites weighed down by armour and weaponry could have charged such a distance and still maintained the cohesion of their phalanx. Nor could they have defeated the Persian force, unless it was actually far smaller than the Athenians claimed.

Needless to say, I called Aristeides' version rubbish and much worse, while he continued harping on about how well the Athenians had fought. I'd had just about enough of his Athenian aristocratic arrogance and said, 'I wish someone would come along and shut your pompous mouth.'

Just then, four armed riders appeared; all of them Persian. I told them my cover story and said the Greek was a business partner. We had been shipwrecked and were heading to Macedonia. The Persians asked proof of our story and, unfortunately, we had none.

The Persian soldiers said that they were under instructions to arrest any travellers on this road and to execute all Greeks, for only spies dared enter Macedon through this route. They forced Aristeides down on his knees. One held him down, another pulled his hair in order to bare his neck, and a third drew his sword to decapitate him. The fourth held me back.

Even then in the face of certain death, Aristeides quipped, 'I suppose, my Scythian friend, that this is your idea of someone shutting my pompous mouth.'

At that moment I showed the Persian soldiers the Great King's Royal Seal. I told them my identity as a commander in the Persian Army and said that I had been on a secret mission on behalf of Xerxes. I told them I was under orders to help this Greek get to the Macedonian capital, Aegae, urgently and in safety. The Persians immediately kneeled before me, or rather before the Seal of the Great King, and begged forgiveness.

Aristeides asked if it was not ironic for the son of a man who tried to kill him many years before to save his life, not once but twice. I said in the field of battle, I would not hesitate to finish off what my father had begun, but as long as I was not at war, I bore no ill will towards him or any other man. I told him that I had arranged for a horse to take him to Aegae. I wanted to return to Sardis, so I would take another route.

Though he expressed the hope of us meeting again as friends, I said it was unlikely, given the impending conflict. I predicted that the next time we would see each other again, it would most likely be across a battlefield.

'In that case,' said Aristeides, shaking my hand, 'let us part now as friends.'

He got on his horse and rode off to Aegae. I later heard that when the war started, the Athenians not only asked Aristeides to return from exile but also made him a military commander. I was told that he served at Salamis under the command of his rival Themistocles. And, of course, he commanded the Athenian forces in Plataea.

What I never understood, though, is what he was up to in Persian-controlled Macedon.

* * *

Gorgo smiled to herself. It was time she put the Barbarian out of his misery. She got up and slipped her long shawl off her shoulders. The reaction was as she had expected. The Barbarian's eyes bulged with disbelief as he pointed a finger at her shoulder.

Chapter 18

The Madness Of King Cleomenes

'My Queen, that brooch ... it resembles the one I gave to Aristeides.'

'It is the same.' Gorgo took off the brooch and with her thumb pressed a small lever which opened, revealing a small hollow chamber inside. 'You see, at the time I had also begun to play my games, contacting potential allies among the Greeks, including those on the Persian side. Demaratus and I were passing secret messages to one another. He had asked me which Athenian was worth trusting. And since I did not trust many Athenians, I sent this brooch to Demaratus, containing the coded word for 'the Fox'. Demaratus sent it to Aristeides, through you, warning him about the Persian threat and urging him to work closely with the Spartans. Also, I believe, the message contained an appeal to bring more allies to our cause. The fact that the two of you accidentally ended up in Macedon proved very convenient. Aristeides used that opportunity to make contact with King Alexander – the one man in Macedon whom he could trust – to recruit him for our cause. Alexander, in turn, sent it to Leonidas, confirming he was on our side. The brooch had travelled full circle and you, my Barbarian friend, were an unwitting instrument in my game to unite the Greeks.'

Realising he had been tricked, Sherzada flew into a rage.

'Barbarian, I thought you owed the Persians no loyalty. So why are you angry at having betrayed them, albeit unwittingly?'

Sherzada, finally spent, sat and rested his head in his hands. 'It is not betraying the Persians I regret. That fact that I helped you create an alliance that led to the deaths of those under my command in Plataea is what hurts me.'

'Blame the Persians for that,' retorted Gorgo. 'We did not invite them or you to invade our land. This was war, and many awful things happen in war.'

Then she gathered her red gown, rose and started walking around him, as though she too were angry. 'Barbarian, did you love your father?'

He nodded.

'Were you angry at what the Athenians did to his body?'

He nodded again and told her that he had taken his revenge. Gorgo's eyes widened as she asked him how he did so.

'After the Persians stormed the Acropolis, after rescuing the women and children who had taken refuge there, I burnt down the Temple of Athena Parthenos and the vaults below which housed his body.'

'My father spent three days in that Temple surrounded by an Athenian mob baying for his blood. But tell me, Barbarian, do you know how he died; my father?'

'From what I have heard, my Queen, your father died a few months before the battle of Marathon. People say he went mad and killed himself,' said Sherzada, his eyes following her movements.

Gorgo sighed. 'People say that his madness was punishment for his blasphemies. People say he had broken promises, committed sacrilege, bribed oracles and above all, he had committed the sin of *hubris,* regarding himself above even the divine. But it is not the truth.'

'So, he did not bribe the Oracle of Delphi in the case of Demaratus' alleged illegitimacy?'

'Of course he bribed the Oracle,' said Gorgo, 'but they used false evidence against him. It was fabricated because no one ever found the real proof.

'The *Pythioi,* the Spartan ambassadors to the Delphi Oracle, accused him of using them to bribe the priests. But that was not true. My father had certainly bribed the Oracle, but he did it in a manner that left no trail.'

Seeing Sherzada sitting there looking even more bewildered,

Gorgo explained. 'To bribe the Oracle, rather than using Spartan intermediaries, he relied on an old and trusted friend to act as his secret courier to the Priests of Apollo. The man's name was Gorgus. He was a prominent Delphian merchant. There is a tradition in Sparta and elsewhere in Greece that children are sometimes named after very close friends of their parents. So close was he to my father that he had in fact named me after him.'

Sherzada gasped. 'So what about your father's massacre of the Argive soldiers who had surrendered at Sepeia and the murder of the two Persian envoys? Are you saying, my Queen, that he did not commit these crimes?'

'On the contrary,' she let out an exasperated breath. 'He did all of it and more, but only to preserve Sparta and protect her interests. Yet, people saw things differently. They said when a person commits *hubris,* the gods make him go mad. Not long after that, people started seeing evidence of his madness. They said that the gods led him to his own destruction. And so the story goes that they made him commit suicide by slicing himself in thin strips from the ankle upwards.'

'So he *did* go mad?'

'No, Barbarian,' said Gorgo, her eyes brightening with rage, 'he most certainly did not! I saw my father just a few days before he died … and there was nothing irrational about him. Of course, he was bitter. Blamed everything on Spartan short-sightedness and pig-headedness. Said the Spartan leadership was blind to the threats around them. That no one was willing to admit the threat from Persia and no one understood why the Greeks should stand united. He said that Sparta, with its military prowess, needed to lead the Greeks in their resistance against the Persians. But he feared most Greeks would either remain neutral or give in to Persia, leaving Sparta isolated and vulnerable.

'Father insisted Sparta could not save Greece alone. To do that, an alliance of strong Greek states was needed. Though he did not care much for the vagaries of Athenian 'Democracy', he strongly believed that the secret to defeating Persia lay in the Spartans and Athenians standing side by side, something it seems Datis was also wise enough to understand.

'Two days after this meeting, my father was declared insane and locked in a cell. The very next day, his body was found. Suicide, they said. He had cut himself into slices from ankle to chest. How could he have inflicted these wounds upon himself, and with a knife that was never meant to be in his cell to start with?'

'You suspect he was murdered.'

'I know it, Barbarian. Someone paid a Helot to slice my father up.'

'But who?' asked Sherzada. 'I doubt it was the Persians.'

'So sure, Barbarian?'

'The Persians never took an interest in your father's exploits until … well … I started working on Sparta. And that was at least a year after your father's death. And had they done such a deed, I who worked among them, would have picked up even the faintest of rumours. No, my Queen, I do not think the Persians had a hand in his death.'

'No, Barbarian, the men who had my father killed were not foreigners. They were Spartans.'

Chapter 19

The Huntress

Sparta
The following afternoon

Sherzada had not known that his request, though a simple one, would bring him to the Queen's own apartment. He stood there, in chains, waiting on Gorgo.

Sherzada was struck by what he saw. Instead of a Great Hall of a Spartan king, what he found was a simple hearth room with sparse but very tasteful decorations; with a distinct feminine touch. He reminded himself not be surprised by what he found in Sparta.

Gorgo was sitting at the dining table by the hearth reading a parchment. On the table next to her was a small wooden chest containing documents. Without looking up at him, she motioned him to sit down on one of the chairs beside her, which he did.

'You wanted to see me?' she asked, still focusing her attention on the document.

'Forgive me, my Queen,' said Sherzada, 'there is much I would like to know ...'

Gorgo cut him off. 'Must I remind you *again* that is I who asks the questions around here?' And then her tone softened. 'I shall, however, make an exception today. I shall only answer one of your questions you sent me ... the one about Artemisia?'

'Was she also somehow involved in this ... plan ...of yours, my Queen?'

Gorgo's eyes widened. She looked up at him with a half-smile and asked Sherzada how he knew her.

He replied, 'She was ... is ... a friend.'

Gorgo's eye glinted mischievously. 'A little coincidental, don't you think, that the two of us would share the same circle of friends?'

* * *

Gorgo still remembered the first day she had laid eyes on Artemisia; the day she came to visit Sparta along with her father the King of Halicarnassus. She was a queen in her own right having married the King of Caria when she was only fifteen, her husband thirty-five years her senior.

Gorgo, who was thirteen, was in awe of the glamorous young Carian Queen, then in her early twenties, full of beauty and energy. No sooner had she arrived in Sparta than Artemisia wanted to go out on a hunt and asked Gorgo to join her. This was most irregular, for Spartans never hunted. It was a distraction from soldiering, so they left the hunting and gathering to the Helots.

'Are you coming or not?' Artemisia asked Gorgo.

For Gorgo there could have only been one answer.

A little while later, the Spartan princess accompanied her guest and a score of servants and slaves into the forests south of Sparta. Whereas Gorgo wore one of her father's worn-out military tunics, Artemisia was elegantly dressed. She wore a long slim dress with the sides slit at the bottom to allow her more movement and a pair of high deer-skin boots which came up to her knees. Her hair was neatly tied up in tail above her head. Carrying a powerful composite bow, the Carian Queen looked every bit her namesake; the Greek deity called Artemis – 'the Huntress'.

Seeing that Gorgo only carried a spear, Artemisia remarked, 'You won't be able to catch much game with that, little sister.'

Spartan women were trained, just like their men, to use the short sword and the spear. Though they were not taught to hunt, they knew how to protect their homes and hearths against invaders.

Patting her bow, Artemisia said, 'This can kill anything within five hundred paces.'

It was not long before the Helots became animated, having sighted wild boars. Artemisia ordered the servants to harass the boars and drive them into the clearing where she and Gorgo stood. But things did not work out as planned. At the last moment, the wild boars changed course, forcing Gorgo and Artemisia to give chase. Gorgo ran up ahead but it was not long before she realized something was wrong.

The ground shook beneath her as she turned, and on the path that had already been cleared by the other wild boars, she saw a huge beast charging her. It was she who was being chased, and Artemisia was nowhere in sight.

There was no time to panic. She did exactly what her military training had taught her. Gorgo pushed the butt-spike at the rear end of the spear into the ground at a low angle. Then she went down on one knee, levelling her spear, like a stake, at the oncoming animal. Holding the spear with both her hands, and aiming it between the boar's eyes, Gorgo waited for impact. She shut her eyes as she braced herself for the jolt.

But it never came. All she heard were three successive 'twangs' in rapid succession, each followed by a 'thud'. Gorgo opened her eyes to see the boar lying dead just in front of her spear, three arrow shafts protruding from its body.

'I am sorry to have stolen your kill, little sister,' came a voice above her, 'but I had a clean shot and I could not resist.' Artemisia was perched on a strong tree branch above Gorgo.

Before the end of the day, Artemisia had also bagged three deer and several quails. By late afternoon, they returned to Sparta amid the silent adulation of Artemisia's hosts. The Spartans were beaming when they saw the Carian Queen return with her prey. For Spartan warriors, it was conclusive proof, if one was ever needed, that the bow was after all a weapon for women.

Later, over dinner, Artemisia walked over to Gorgo and sat down with her. 'So, do you consider me a Barbarian, little sister?'

'No. You speak Dorian Greek. So by definition you are not a Barbarian.'

'Aye.' Artemisia nodded. 'I am only one-quarter Carian and three-quarters Greek. My mother was a princess from Crete. And among my ancestors are Spartan princes and princesses of the House of Agiadae.'

'So we are related?' asked Gorgo, her eyes widening.

'More than you think, little sister.'

'But are you not the slave of the Persians?'

Artemisia took her time swallowing her morsel and then replied, 'Yes, the Greeks of Asia live under the Persian yoke, but like all Greeks we yearn to be free. Freedom will not come to us for a while, but there might come a day when we shall have to fight together for *Eleutheria*.'

'And on that day, big sister, I shall be with you!'

* * *

Sherzada wondered if they were talking about the same woman. He recalled the beautiful Artemisia, now in her late thirties, though she looked ten years younger, if not more. A woman of ageless beauty, sensuality and rare intelligence, who charmed everyone she met.

She was a warrior queen, the only woman who led troops and ships in the Persian army that invaded Greece. Artemisia, he told Gorgo, was one of Xerxes' closest advisors. It was said that that the Great King had many eyes, but only one ear. And it was she, Artemisia, who had that ear. Xerxes liked to call her *Arta-Masia* – 'The Bearer of Truth'.

'You know she had correctly advised Xerxes not to risk a sea battle, insisting that continuing to fight on land would be the best option,' said Sherzada.

'She did so knowing that all the other naval commanders would vote her down,' replied Gorgo, 'and indeed the Persian defeat at Salamis eventually proved her right.'

'My Queen, Artemisia fought valiantly for the Persians at the battle of Salamis, braver than any Persian admiral. After the battle, King Xerxes summoned her and said, 'Today, my men became women ...'

'... And my women, men,' finished Gorgo.

Sherzada was flabbergasted. 'So, she was a part of your conspiracy?'

'I would prefer to call it strategy, Barbarian,' Gorgo corrected him. 'And, yes, for the reasons you have just given, she was my most important asset in the Persian camp. She pretended to be the most loyal of Persian subjects just to get as close as she did to Xerxes. No one knew about my contacts with her; not Demaratus, not even Aristeides.'

Gorgo explained how she had used a Greek traitor in Persia pay to deliver messages to Artemisia. He was a resident of Sicyon and believed he was carrying letters from Spartan traitors and would personally deliver them to Artemisia. The letters were in code, but the code could be broken, though not easily. And even if he did break it he would have found the message inside quite innocuous. But in these letters there was another code, a code within a code, a message within the message. This was a secret which Gorgo and Artemisia had agreed on during the latter's last visit to Sparta, just before Xerxes' invasion.

Gorgo dug up a sheaf of parchment from inside the little chest in front of her. 'These pages contain the deciphered version of her last message to me,' she said, collecting them together. 'On the eve of Salamis, I sent Artemisia a message with a specific question. And this was her reply.'

Gorgo explained that the message, in the form of a long letter, had not been delivered in the usual way though the Greek traitor from Sicyon. Instead, it had come from a trusted source in Crete.

This was how she had her most important messages delivered to the Spartan Queen.

Handing the letter over to Sherzada, Gorgo said, 'This may answer some of your questions, and I think you might have answered one of mine.'

Sherzada began to read.

I had indeed sunk an Athenian ship during the battle, but I did not have the heart to tell Xerxes that I had also sunk an allied vessel in an attempt to escape the Athenian warships that were bearing down on mine.

Xerxes complained that the invasion of Greece had not been as easy as his cousin, Mardonius, had led him to believe. Thermopylae had been painful but Salamis was an unmitigated disaster.

'My Generals are divided,' he said. 'Some of them think victory is still in hand; we still outnumber the Greeks by land and sea and we can beat them. Others are disheartened. We have conquered half of the Greek mainland and we have burnt down Athens; still the Greeks continue to resist us. Indeed, all is not well back home. My ministers urge me to return, saying that my Empire is suffering in my absence. But Mardonius wants to continue the fight. He says either I stay and lead it, or I go home and leave him in charge. Either way, he assures me, a Persian victory is within reach.'

I told the Great King that it was not an easy choice. Certainly, Xerxes had been away from his Empire for too long and his people were yearning for his return. And the cost of this campaign had all but emptied his treasury. I explained to him that it was not the conquest of Greece that concerned me, but the stability of the Empire. Was the conquest of Greece so important that it would cause the Empire to go bankrupt and deplete the numbers of Persian troops so vital for the security of the homeland?

'You have achieved your objectives,' I said to him. 'Let Mardonius now finish the task. But to ensure the empire's security, take all your best troops with you.' I reminded him that revolts were breaking out in Upper Egypt and Babylon was burning. Xerxes needed his best troops

to secure his empire. They would be no use to him in this far-flung corner of his Empire. 'If Mardonius wins, the glory is yours; if he fails, the fault will be his.'

Xerxes went so far as to ask me which troops he should leave behind with Mardonius.

I suggested that Mardonius be allowed to keep only the reserve cavalry regiments. He could keep a small force of veteran Invincibles to act as his bodyguards, but the bulk of the troops remaining should be those from the foreign subject nations of Persia. After all, some of these troops came from rebellious corners of his Empire. Better they died serving the Empire than returned home to raise the banner of revolt. Other subject contingents could prove their loyalty to Persia. I myself would gladly leave behind my famed light horsemen to support Mardonius. They were led by my best commander, the young General Dardanus.

The handsome Dardanus and I had been lovers for a while, but he had recently taken a younger mistress. When I learned of it, my first reaction was to kill myself. But on reflection, I felt if one of us was to die, better it were he.

Among those who would remain behind with Mardonius were Bubares the husband of my dear friend Gygaea, Princess of Macedon, and the brilliant Artabazus. Persia's most capable generals. If they survived the war, they would find a way to save the Persian Empire from further collapse and thus prevent the Greeks of Asia from becoming free.

Initially, Mardonius complained about Xerxes' decision, but in the end he had to accept it, given that he had been long pestering the Great King to allow him to take over the invasion.

So now, I am escorting Xerxes back from Greece to Sardis – Thus I have succeeded, little sister, in achieving what you had asked of me. I have split the Persian army into two!

'So, it was you, my Queen,' whispered Sherzada, 'who split the entire Persian army.'

'Well, Artemisia did that. I only gave her the idea. But the letter is not finished,' smiled Gorgo as she passed him the last parchment to read.

Among those I asked Xerxes to leave behind to support Mardonius is a Scythian prince from a land beyond the Persian Empire. He is a good man and a friend. He fights only for the Persians because honour demands it. He too is to be sacrificed for the cause of our liberty. The meaning of his name, incidentally, is similar to that of your husband.

Looking up to Sherzada, Gorgo asked, 'What is your name?'

'Sherzada,' he replied curtly. 'Son of the lion,' he admitted.

'Lion-cub,' she said, 'just like *Leonidas*. So you do have something in common with my late husband. This, at least, clears up a little curiosity I've had. And now there is another besides Aristeides who can vouch for you at your trial.'

But Sherzada knew that if the Queen of Sparta knew the truth, she more than anyone would want him dead.

Chapter 20

The End Of A War?

Sparta
The following morning

'Is our guest still alive?' came a voice from the hall.

Gorgo came out to find Euro standing with his helmet cradled in his arm.

'He is,' she answered, offering him a chair.

'In one piece, I hope?'

'Go and see it for yourself, if you doubt me,' she said, sitting down in front of him.

'I do not doubt you, cousin. But Pausanias wanted to make sure the prisoner had not met some unfortunate accident in our absence.'

'True. He could have easily ended up at a bottom of an empty well,' said Gorgo, with a mischievous glint in her eye. 'But tell me, how was Corinth?'

Euro sat down beside her. 'It appears we are becoming unpopular throughout Greece, not least because of our instructions to all cities to dismantle their fortifications and build no new walls. They are all angry about that.'

It had originally seemed a good idea to encourage the Greek states to resist the Persians together in the open battlefield rather behind their respective walls, but Gorgo now realized the resentment it could have caused.

'And that was not all,' Euro continued. 'A number of delegations questioned Sparta's right to lead both the land and naval forces of the Hellenic League. They insisted on a shared command. When Pausanias told them to go to Hades, some of the delegates told him to stop treating them like his Helots.'

Gorgo could quite imagine the scene.

'Pausanias' temper did not help,' Euro went on. 'He called the Megarians spineless for running away from battle at Plataea, and cast similar aspersions against our Corinthian hosts. But what really annoyed the delegates was that he had invited a Theban delegation, led by Asopodorus, son of Timander, who had commanded their cavalry at Plataea, to the Conference, and without consulting anyone. Most of our allies regard the Thebans as traitors who fought for the enemy. But Pausanias believed the Theban presence at the Conference would encourage other pro-Persian Greeks to join the League also. The Plataeans told Pausanias that if Thebans could come to this conference, the Argives should be invited to the next one, which infuriated Pausanias no end. But tell me, what of our prisoner?'

'He is a strange one, indeed. Even though he has fought against us, I do not think he is our enemy. And sometimes I forget I am talking to a foreigner. There is absolutely nothing Barbaric about him.'

'So you don't want him dead, after all?' Euro laughed.

'I don't know, but perhaps I can get one last bit of useful information out of him,' she said, gathering her things to leave.

'You and your scheming!' Euro continued to laugh.

* * *

For the first time, she acknowledged Sherzada's courtesy in rising for her with a smile. Agathe placed a small table in front of the stool. Then she fetched some parchment, some ink and a writing instrument and placed them all on the table.

'If you would be so kind, my Prince, to write down the names of all the Spartans who were bribed by the Persians?'

Agathe brought the torch closer and Gorgo hovered over Sherzada's shoulder. The very first name he wrote caused her to gasp, but she told him to go on, and so he did.

Afterwards, Gorgo gave the parchment to Agathe, who

quickly disappeared outside. The door slammed shut behind her.

'So, what is to be my fate?' he asked. 'Now that I have given you all you could want?'

'You will soon find out soon enough. The Gerousia meets tomorrow.' She searched for a reaction in Sherzada's expression or body language, but found none.

Agathe quickly returned along with the other servants, carrying trays of bread and meat, cheese, fruits and honey-cakes.

Sherzada had eaten nothing but stale bread since his capture. Gorgo continued to study him as he ate without hurry. She was not without admiration. Here was a man unconcerned with his fate.

Just then, the door opened again and this time it was Euro, with Sherzada's list in his hand. Gorgo introduced Euro to Sherzada. Euro was surprised at Sherzada's excellent command of Greek and soon they were talking of Plataea.

'The moment you fell, your men went crazy,' Euro was saying. 'They fought like demons despite being woefully outnumbered. So strong was their fury that we were forced back. This does not usually happen to us Spartans. But as soon as we regrouped, Scythian cavalry charged us from across the river, allowing your men to extricate themselves.'

'So my men survived?'

'Aye.'

At last, a smile appeared on Sherzada's face.

The door opened and a weary-looking Pausanias entered the room. He looked at Sherzada and then to Gorgo and said, 'Is this not the man in whose heart you wanted to bury a sword? So what are you trying to do now, cousin? Feed him to death?'

With that, Pausanias sat down on the floor next to Gorgo and started to devour the soft olive bread and tenderly roasted lamb that was placed before him. 'I am pleased you are giving our guest a proper meal and not the tasteless gruel we Spartans pass for food.'

'You mock our Spartan ways, Regent?' asked Gorgo.

'I am afraid,' he replied, 'I have recently discovered I am not a typical Spartan after all – at least, where food is concerned. And as for our cousin Euryanax here, he is the only true Spartan among us ... even though many in Sparta won't consider him as one.'

It was a sensitive matter; so much so that Gorgo changed the subject. 'Euro told me what happened at Corinth.'

Pausanias let out a sigh of frustration. 'The less said about Corinth the better. This is the last time I'm going to that mad house. I hate those upstarts. Sparta did not save these Greeks to have them lord it over us.'

Then he turned to Sherzada and said, 'I don't know what will happen in the Gerousia tomorrow, but I need some urgent information. Persian survivors from Plataea were massacred at the Strymon crossing and their fleet was destroyed at Mycale. Tell me, what do you think the Persians will do next?'

Sherzada cleared his throat. 'The main Persian fleet withdrew months ago. All the bigger squadrons from Phoenicia and Egypt returned to their home ports as soon as Xerxes left Greece. The naval force your fleet encountered at Mycale, I believe, was one of two Persian naval squadrons left behind to protect the Western Asiatic shores. From what I understand, your Eurypontid King Leotychidas caught the crews asleep on shore and destroyed them with overwhelming force. But the second squadron is still out there, and it is led by the Phoenician admiral, Hanni, nicknamed *Barqa* – the Thunderbolt – one of Persia's best naval commanders.

'And even though Alexander of Macedon may have killed a large number of survivors from Plataea, I am sure a Persian column under Artabaz and Burbaraz has escaped to Asia. They will be rallying what Persian forces that remain across the Aegean. Burbaraz is a veteran campaigner, having beaten off countless incursions of Celts, Getae and other tribes along the

Danube with only a small force. And Artabaz is also among the ablest of Persia's generals; a little unconventional, yet very dangerous. He will be difficult to defeat.

'Another Persian commander, Bogesh, still holds the stronghold of Eion in Thrace. He is a fanatic, and would destroy Eion before he surrenders it to you. Then there is Doriscus, not very important strategically, but the Persians will not give it up easily, either.'

Pausanias smiled and said, 'Your information about the second squadron is corroborated by the latest news we have received. The Persians, it appears, have raided Didyma by sea, and burnt down Apollo's temple there, one of the holiest of the Greek shrines, in retaliation for Mycale. There have been other sightings as well, even closer to our shores.

'So, what will the Persians do next?'

'What, indeed?' Sherzada replied. 'The Persians have had enough of Greece for the time being. Mardonius, the driving force behind their invasion, is dead. Neither Artabaz nor Burbaraz nor even Bogesh have the will or the means to take the war back into Greece. And King Xerxes has more pressing matters to worry about. So, you should not expect the Persians to hurry back.

'The war is over. Of course, you can try and start a new war across the sea – in Ionia, Aeolia, Caria and elsewhere, but that would be a mistake. You might liberate some Greek cities, but others, as in Greece, will side with the Persians. And they will certainly make sure you get bogged down there. The Persians have all the advantages in Asia.'

Pausanias thought for a moment. 'If I understand you correctly, there is no Persian fleet between here and the eastern coast of the Mediterranean, excepting the one squadron you mentioned?'

Sherzada nodded.

'And what about Byzantium? I heard the Persians no longer

control it.'

Sherzada shook his head. 'I do not know. As you can appreciate, I have been tied up lately.'

Euro chuckled.

'But you should check,' Sherzada suggested.

Pausanias nodded, got up and left the room, munching on a leg of lamb. Euro followed him, still smirking.

Gorgo leaned closer to Sherzada. 'He will check all right. Pausanias has been infatuated by this Byzantine girl, this Cleonice. Do you know her?'

'She is beautiful, my Queen, and charming too!'

Gorgo asked him whether she and Sherzada had been lovers. 'Apparently, it was she and Aristeides who convinced Pausanias not to kill you at Plataea after you had been captured.'

'She is a friend,' he shrugged, 'nothing else.'

Gorgo could not keep it inside her. She burst out, 'You realise you might be executed tomorrow? You are so calm ... unafraid ... just ... just like a ...'

'... like a Spartan warrior facing certain death?'

'Yes,' replied Gorgo. 'But you are not a Spartan. Why are you so unafraid?'

'My Queen, I have lost practically everyone I have ever loved. So I am not afraid of dying. But I also have my faith and I know that my God often works in mysterious ways. So whatever the outcome of this Gerousia of yours, my Queen, I shall embrace it – and happily.'

Chapter 21

Gerousia

Sparta
The following morning

The door suddenly opened wide. Two guards entered and began unshackling Sherzada. Gorgo and Euro followed, trailing a small group of Helots.

'We need to clean you up,' Gorgo said to Sherzada.

Euro took Sherzada to a pool by the courtyard. It was not that he avoided taking baths. On the contrary, he enjoyed them. Of course, he preferred a warm bath any day to a plunge in the river. But it appeared heating a bath was a luxury below the dignity of Spartan warriors.

As Sherzada entered the freezing water in nothing but his loincloth, Euro sniggered. 'Not cold enough for you? This bath is warmer than the Eurotas this time of year. We bathe there in the river every morning.'

Two young male Helots entered the pool and gave him a quick scrub. Then, after he had dried himself, they helped him put on his new clothes. Full Persian military dress complete with golden fish-scale armour and armbands in addition to a dark blue silk cloak with etchings in gold. These had belonged to Mardonius, Sherzada recalled. The Spartans must have taken them from his tent after storming his camp.

With Sherzada looking once more like a warrior, Euro ordered the guards to escort him, unchained, to the Gerousia. Euro, Gorgo and Pleistarchus followed close behind. Sherzada marched in step with his guards; it was easy to get back into character. The distance from the Agiadae compound to the Gerousia hall was a short one. Soldiers marching through the city must have been quite a routine sight, for it was not until they reached the crowded Agora that people started to notice him. It would have been a strange sight – a foreign warrior, not in chains – marching among Spartan soldiers.

Just beyond the Agora, Sherzada noticed a dark, forbidding structure. It was the Temple of Athena of the Brazen House. Standing on top of a hill in the city centre, this structure was the most defining feature of the Spartan Acropolis. And next to it was a building that looked rather like a theatre. This was the meeting hall of the Gerousia. Once inside the massive hall, Sherzada found his first impression confirmed. In the centre was a stage and around it were rows of seats arranged in the form of a co-centric semi-circle. Sitting in two consecutive rows of seats were around thirty men. Most of them were similarly attired, in long crimson cloaks. The similarities did not end there. All were grey-bearded and, in the case where they had any hair, grey-haired. None was below sixty. These were the men after whom the Gerousia – the Council of Elders – was named.

In the front row sat five men who wore white cloaks bordered with crimson. Except for one, they were all a little younger than the crimson-cloaked Elders. These were the Ephors, the elected magistrates whom Sherzada had seen in the Agora on his first day in Sparta, all sitting in the front row.

The Elders and the Ephors sat patiently, as if waiting to see a performance. He wondered at the irony of Spartans, who did not appreciate the dramatic arts and yet played out the drama of high politics in such a theatre.

Sherzada was escorted on to the stage and made to stand next to two large throne-like chairs. Little Pleistarchus sat on the chair closest to him; Gorgo took her position by his side. Pausanias soon arrived and sat on a low chair brought out for him and placed beside Pleistarchus. On the other chair sat a man with shifty eyes, a scrawny grey beard and a demeanour that managed to convey both a flickering impatience and a steadfast arrogance. Sherzada guessed this was Leotychidas, the Eurypontid King of

Sparta.

Beside Leotychidas stood a young man in his late teens. He had long wavy brown hair and deep-set dark blue eyes, betraying both intelligence and malice. Sherzada guessed this must be Archidamus, Leotychidas' grandson and heir apparent. When everyone was seated, Leotychidas requested the senior Ephor to open the session of the Gerousia. The man rose and began to read the case against 'Scirzadus, a Persian general captured at Plataea whose life or death was now to be determined by the Gerousia.'

The explanation was lengthy, and Leotychidas cut it short, 'The prisoner deserves to die. All we have to decide is how. I think the customary method is decapitation … or is it disembowelment? But first, I would like to report on the victory at Mycale. After that, we can decide on how to execute the prisoner.'

'Your Majesty,' said the Ephor, 'the prisoner has to be tried before he can be executed. That is the Law. Moreover, I need not remind you that it is not customary among Spartans to gloat over victories. If you might recall, your predecessor, King Demaratus, was fined for boasting of his success at the Olympic Games.'

'I am not going to gloat about Mycale,' said Leotychidas, 'at least not in the way the Regent Pausanias praised his little triumph at Plataea last week … or so I have been told.'

Pausanias turned red with rage, as Leotychidas proceeded to present the Mycale campaign as the greatest of Greek victories, overshadowing Plataea in every respect.

When Leotychidas stopped, the senior Ephor got up and asked if anyone had any questions.

Pausanias spoke at last. 'Thank you, Your Majesty, for that very enlightening report. So, I take it you have destroyed the entire Persian Aegean Fleet?'

'That is correct.'

'So, there are no Persian ships operating in the Aegean anymore?'

'None!'

'Then how does Your Majesty explain the sightings of a large number of Persian warships in southern Aegean a few days after the battle of Mycale? These ships attacked the shrine of Apollo at Didyma. Four days ago, they sank an Aeginetan squadron off Hermione. And last night, Persian warships were seen off the island of Cythera, close to our own coast. If the Persian fleet perished at Mycale, what are Persian ships doing roaming the Aegean and attacking at will? Are these the ghosts of the ships you destroyed, Your Majesty?'

Leotychidas shifted uncomfortably. 'Perhaps they are reinforcements. I tell you, I destroyed the main Persian naval force at Mycale.'

'What you destroyed, Your Majesty,' said Pausanias, 'was a Persian naval squadron whose crews had beached their ships and gone to bed. You slaughtered them in their sleep. That is not a victory worthy of Sparta. And if I am not mistaken, your mission was not to destroy the Persian fleet but to support the Greek uprising in the cities of Samos and Chios. Instead of helping to liberate them, you went after an easier target. Your failure to come to their support compelled these cities to submit once more to the Persians. Samos is close to Mycale, and one of our oldest allies. You could easily have gone to its rescue. But you chose not to. Can Your Majesty give the Gerousia a reasonable explanation as to why you failed to liberate Samos and Chios?'

It sounded peculiar to Sherzada that a king could be challenged thus, but this was the Spartan way. He looked at the Gerousia members and noticed many approving Pausanias' exposition, several of them nodding vehemently, while Leotychidas fought to control his embarrassment and rage.

'My dear Pausanias,' said Leotychidas, 'if you are so keen on proving me wrong, why don't you go and chase away these mysterious Persian ships? And while you are at it, why don't you liberate some of these enslaved Greek colonies you accuse me of ignoring?'

'It would be a great honour,' said Pausanias. 'And one I would not take lightly.'

That concluded, the senior Ephor rose once more and laid down the general arguments for and against Sherzada's execution. Afterwards, he asked if anyone had anything to add.

Gorgo drew herself to her full height and spoke with the regal authority Sherzada had forgotten she carried. 'I have a few things to say, with the permission of the Gerousia, of course.'

The Ephor nodded.

'Prince Sherzada is not Persian. He is a Saka Prince, heir to the throne of a Scythian kingdom which lies beyond the eastern borders of Persia. He fought for the Persians at Plataea as well as at Thermopylae and his father died fighting against the Athenians at Marathon. In that sense you can regard him as an enemy. But he did not fight for the Persians willingly, rather the only reason he and his father fought in Greece was that they were obliged to do so. He did not fight us because he wanted to enslave us. He fought only for the freedom of his homeland.'

There were angry grumblings across the hall.

'Since his arrival in Sparta,' Gorgo continued, 'Prince Sherzada has been helping us with vital military and political intelligence. He has helped us in the past also, though unwittingly. Since he is not a Persian, he owes them no loyalty. If we can forgive the Thebans even after they sided with Persia, why can we not forgive those like Prince Sherzada who are trying to help us even now?'

Pandemonium broke out throughout the hall, and Gorgo was obliged to wait for the angry shouts to die down before continuing. 'Prince Sherzada has worked with Persian military intelligence, and has known much about Sparta, and what has been going on here. This list he has given us,' she said, raising a scrolled parchment in her hands, 'has been corroborated by independent enquiries carried out by our own army, to which

General Evaeneutus and Navarch Eurybiadas can attest. It is also backed up with evidence provided to us recently by the Athenian Archons, Aristeides and Xanthippus, that emerged while they were investigating their own traitors. I have no reason to doubt this list.'

The senior Ephor rose and asked Gorgo to share the list with the Ephors.

'If my understanding is correct,' Gorgo replied, 'the Ephors have precedence in all legal matters, but on issues of security, it is the Kings who have precedence in their capacities as Supreme Commanders of the Army. A sensitive matter such as this must first be discussed among the Kings and their representatives. Then it will be brought to the attention of our Ephors who can initiate necessary legal action. With the Gerousia's permission, I shall now show the list to the Kings.'

There were nods of approval. First, Gorgo gave the list to her son. Little Pleistarchus took one look at the list and his young face betrayed his shock. He looked at the list and then towards Leotychidas and then back to the list again, and once more towards Leotychidas. Before he could say anything, Gorgo took the list from him and gave it to Leotychidas. The Eurypontid King's face turned white as he read it. His grandson reading over his shoulder also began to shudder.

Gorgo turned to the Gerousia again. 'While His Majesty examines the list, I will ask Prince Sherzada to speak in his own defence.'

'Will there be a translator?' asked one of the elders of Gerousia rising from his chair. 'How will we be able to understand him otherwise? All these Barbarians seem to say is Bar-bar-bar!'

Laughter echoed through the hall.

Gorgo smiled. 'Good Heracleidas, I assure you an interpreter will not be necessary.' Then she nudged Sherzada forward.

Sherzada was at a loss, not knowing what he should say. So he said the first things that came to his mind in the best Dorian

Greek he could muster.

Sherzada was prepared to die. But he also wanted the Spartans to know that he was a warrior just like them. He told the Gerousia about his origins and that of his people. He told them that they were also a great warrior nation. He told them of his admiration for Spartan warriors as well the wise politics of their kings. He praised both Cleomenes and Leonidas and said a kind word for Pleistarchus as well. He told them he had fought against the Spartans and knew how terrible a thing it was to face them in battle. So if the Gerousia wanted to approve his execution, he concluded, all he asked for was a warrior's death. He said that Germanic warriors in the wild North of Europe preferred to die with swords in their hands. That was all he asked for.

When Sherzada stopped speaking, there was utter silence. He looked at the thirty or so faces in front of him, with thirty or so jaws dropped as far as they could possibly be.

It took Sherzada more than a moment to realize, but what had rendered them speechless was not exactly what he had said, but the manner in which he had said it. The last thing the Gerousia was expecting was a Barbarian prisoner addressing them not only in perfect Greek and in their own dialect but in an accent spoken only by Spartan kings.

Amid this confusion, Gorgo took the list back from Leotychidas. Sherzada heard her whisper in his ear, 'Surely Your Majesty knows what to say now.'

The King arose, cleared his throat and addressed the Gerousia. 'Queen Gorgo has presented a compelling case. If the prisoner speaks to us in our language, like a Spartan, can he really be called a Barbarian? If he is passing vital information about the Persians to us, he is helping us and not them. If he is helping us uncover traitors in our midst, he is bolstering our own security. I see no reason to execute this prisoner, seeing how valuable he is to the interests of Sparta.'

For a moment more, there was silence.

Sherzada could see the stunned expressions of the elders and he could tell that some were not happy with Leotychidas' words. As they rose to protest, a single clap was heard from the back – Euro. It was followed by another, this one from the corner of the retired generals, who still wore their armour in the Gerousia. He saw an old man with a long grey beard and a tall walking stick clapping loudly. Sherzada recognized him from the night he and the other generals had come to visit Gorgo. It was the legendary lame Admiral Eurybiadas, who had led the combined forces of Greece at the battles of Artemisium and Salamis. Other generals joined in. And then the clapping became pervasive, accompanied by shouts of approval, drowning out those voices that sought to protest the King's verdict.

Leotychidas continued, 'The prisoner is hereby freed and will be kept under the protection and supervision of the clan Agiadae – particularly Regent Pausanias and Queen Gorgo. He will remain in Sparta as long as is deemed useful.'

A smattering of applause, instigated once more by Euro. Gorgo looked stonily ahead, displaying no pleasure at the Gerousia's decision.

'And as for the list,' said Leotychidas when the applause died out, 'I would like to confer immediately with the Regent Pausanias and Queen Gorgo and thereafter we shall consult the Ephors. I hope this is acceptable?'

There were nods of approval. The meeting was adjourned.

Leotychidas, Pausanias and Gorgo hurried out of the hall. Across the courtyard was a small hut-like structure in which direction they headed. Euro took Pleistarchus by the hand and motioned Sherzada and the guards to follow. Halfway across the courtyard, the guards noticed that Leotychidas' grandson, Archidamus, was shadowing them. Euro gave him an angry scowl, and young Archidamus quickly scampered in the opposite direction. Euro instructed the guards to block the courtyard entrance and let no one in. Then he, Sherzada, and little Pleistarchus headed for the hut.

Leotychidas, Pausanias and Gorgo had bolted the door behind them. But this did not stop Euryanax from putting his ears against the door and listening in. The door was not thick and there was a small window above, so the conversation could be easily heard by those standing outside. Something made Sherzada look to the ground. There he saw Pleistarchus sitting on the floor, looking at him and Euro, quite amused. Sherzada smiled as he realized how silly he and Euro must appear to the boy – two grown men eavesdropping like little children.

Through the door, they could hear a heated argument.

'How come my name is on the top of this list? There must be some mistake, or else this is a conspiracy against me.'

'There is no mistake in your case, Your Majesty,' said Pausanias. 'There is overwhelming evidence against you. We have testimonies from your closest associates.'

'Liars all!'

'We found your gold exactly where they said you had hidden it. We also found more in your private chambers, even inside your clothes. The Knights raided your house as soon as you left home this morning. All the coins are Persian Darics.'

'Let's not be hasty, shall we?' said Leotychidas, changing his tone. 'I have always been a friend to the Agiadae, haven't I? This morning I helped you free your Barbarian friend. I too have been useful to your family in the past. Without my help, Gorgo, your father could not have got rid of that clown, Demaratus. Without me, your father would not have got away with the murder of the Persian envoys. I supported him in all his mad schemes. Without my support in the courts, your *mothax* of a cousin would still be an outcast. Turn me in now, and you will lose your best ally.'

Gorgo's voice was steadfast. 'You only supported my family when it served your interests. Your Majesty did not free our prisoner for my sake; you did it save your own skin.'

'Leotychidas,' spat Pausanias, 'you are no better than your predecessor, that filthy traitor Demaratus. You Eurypontids are all the same. You collaborated with the enemy and now you have the gall to ask for our help.'

'Turn me in and I shall tell everyone the truth about King Cleomenes and how he died. There will be hell to pay.'

Gorgo responded in a measured tone. 'I grow tired of remaining silent. I want the truth known and I want those who were involved punished. I would be very pleased indeed, if Your Majesty could tell the world what really happened.'

'Now, now, my child. No need to get worked up. It was but a jest. I will do nothing to damage your family's good name. All I ask is to have my name removed from this list. I will do anything.'

'How dare you ask such a thing,' growled Pausanias. 'You betrayed Sparta and expect us to cover it up just like that!'

'Perhaps,' said Gorgo, 'King Leotychidas is right. We should not be too hasty. I am sure we can reach an accommodation with His Majesty. Remember at Plataea, when Aristeides discovered that some of his generals had taken Persian bribes; rather than punishing them, he forgave them. Consequently, those same generals fought with exceptional bravery in the battle that followed. I must believe that people deserve second chances. Not only him, but others also. We will expunge King Leotychidas' name from the list. We will present the remainder of the names to the Ephors with a recommendation to pardon most of them. Only a token few would be chosen for punishment.'

'I don't believe what I am hearing,' said Pausanias. 'What would be the criteria for choosing those who will be punished?'

'It is simple,' Gorgo replied, 'only those deserve to be punished who have held the highest elected office in Sparta. The office of Ephor is a powerful one. They have powers to prosecute, punish and even execute kings. We have to send a message that even the Ephors are not above the law. So any individual who has ever held the office of the Ephor and received Persian gold must not be allowed to escape the severest of punishments.

'Is that acceptable, Pausanias?' she asked, after a pause.

After a moment of silence, she continued, 'Good. I expect both you, Pausanias, on behalf of my son, and King Leotychidas, to work with our Ephors to ensure that what we have agreed is enforced.'

'It shall be done,' said Leotychidas.

As the three came out, Sherzada studied their expressions. Pausanias seemed confused, Leotychidas relieved, and Gorgo triumphant. *Something was not quite right*, he thought.

Chapter 22

The Half-Caste Prince

Sparta
The following morning

The rising sun shone on a grisly sight in the centre of Sparta. Five bodies were strung up in front of the Temple of Athena of the Brazen House. They had been executed in the traditional Spartan way, just before dawn with the sword. But breaking from tradition, the bodies of these former Ephors were publicly displayed for the first time as a sign that treason would not be tolerated.

Gorgo was staring at the hanging corpses when she saw Leotychidas approach accompanied by his tall, long-haired daughter, Lampito. Though very attractive, there was something quite masculine about her. Gorgo always felt uneasy in the company of this often aggressive young woman.

'So it is done,' Leotychidas whispered to Gorgo. 'As you had wished.'

'I did not wish it. They brought it upon themselves.'

The Senior Ephor walked over to where Gorgo, Leotychidas and his daughter were standing. 'So perish all traitors,' he said. 'No one is above the law. Not Ephors; not even kings.'

'Wouldn't you agree, King Leotychidas?' Gorgo asked mischievously.

Leotychidas mumbled something but realizing that no one understood him, simply nodded.

Gorgo smiled and bid the company good day. As she began to walk away, Sherzada came up behind her and said, 'I know what you have done. These men you have had executed. They were a part of the conspiracy to kill your father. Were they not?'

'You think too much, my Prince,' she responded evasively. 'At times it can be dangerous.'

They walked across the training area next to the mustering field; the place where Sherzada had first seen Gorgo. In the centre of the training area was a sandpit where seven young Spartan men stood in a circle. Each wore the grey tunics of recent graduates of the Upbringing. They stood in a circle, their swords drawn.

As the sun rose behind him, a lone warrior entered the pit. Though he too wore no armour, except for his face-covering helmet, his tunic was dark crimson. The horse-hair crest was traversed sideways rather than back to front; an indication that he was a Spartan General. He carried no weapon except a tall staff. As soon as he reached the centre of the ring, the other seven men attacked him.

With amazing agility and dexterity, he evaded some of his attackers while striking others down with his staff. But the young men did not stay down for long. They got up as fast as they could and again lunged at the helmeted officer. He countered each of them by his skilful use of his staff. Yet, in spite of having their limbs shattered and noses broken, they kept on coming; for this was the Spartan way.

Gorgo left Sherzada alone to watch the spectacle; and he did so with considerable interest. A Greek helmet may be the ideal protection in a phalanx like formation, but it is a hindrance in single combat. The vision is restricted and the hearing impaired, forcing the warrior to rely on his instincts and his training.

And yet, the helmeted General continued to dominate the struggle in spite of being outnumbered. It was as if he could anticipate their every move – all seven of them. He repeatedly whirled his staff over his head and brought it down on his attackers with devastating effect. In the end, the youths were exhausted, lying on the sand with faces, bloodied. The General remained standing, unscathed.

Once it was over, he helped each young man back on his feet.

'Next time, *Strategos*,' said one of them, smiling as he wiped the blood from his mouth and limped off the field.

Even before he had taken off his helmet, Sherzada already knew who this *Strategos* – this General – was. There could not be a better specimen of the perfect Spartan warrior – not only in skill and discipline but also in outwards appearance, for he was tall, lean and muscular with tresses of long hair hanging down to his chest. Dropping his bloodied staff on to the ground, the man took off his helmet and greeted Sherzada with a nod. 'Gorgo said you wanted to ask me something?'

'Yes, Prince Euryanax.'

'My friends call me Euro,' he said as he came over and sat beside Sherzada. 'It is less of a mouthful.'

Indeed, Euro was a curiosity to Sherzada. In all his years of gathering information on Sparta, Sherzada had never encountered his name or any information about him. And yet he was the deputy commander of Sparta's land forces and a cousin of the Queen. He said, 'I have extensively studied your family's history, but I can't seem to place you in it. I know of the names of all of the male members of Agiad family but not yours.'

'Have you heard of Dorieus?'

Sherzada nodded. He was the elder brother of Leonidas and also the younger half-brother of Cleomenes; the brother who lost the claim to throne after their father King Anaxandridas died. He was the brother who died in exile, in battle against the Carthaginians in Sicily.

'I am his son,' said Euro.

'If you don't mind me prying, Prince Euryanax, if you are the son of Dorieus, the second son of King Anaxandridas, under Spartan Law it is you who should have succeeded King Cleomenes, not Leonidas. Is that not so?'

'Under normal circumstances, I would have indeed been King Cleomenes' successor. But my circumstances are anything but normal. I am the son of a Spartan Prince and a Helot woman. Do you think the Spartans will ever accept the son of a Helot as their king?'

Sherzada was taken aback by this revelation. Spartans usually considered offspring of such unions as *mothoi* – 'illegitimates'; who were treated as outcasts, often forced into exile. Yes, Euro was right that no *mothax* could ever become king. But making one a general, even if he was the son of a royal Prince, was just as unusual.

'You see,' continued Euro, 'my mother was from Messene. Its proud Achaean kingdom was destroyed by the Dorian invaders who were my ancestors from my father's side. These invaders became the Spartans – the rulers – and made the original inhabitants of Sparta, Laconia and Messene their slaves – their Helots. Ever since that time the Helots have been kept in their place by the Spartans. When the Spartans are not coercing the Helots themselves, they send in *Perioiki* to keep the Helots in their place. The Helots know no existence other than subservience to the Spartans. This was the culture into which my mother was born.

'The Messenian Helots, in particular, have always been recalcitrant. The Spartans have never tolerated that. They have repeatedly gone into Messene to crush the Helots. It was during one of these expeditions that my father found my mother among the captives. He immediately fell in love with her. He not only freed her but he also married her. She was not his Helot slave–concubine, which some Spartan men are known to keep; my mother was his wife.

'So when my father claimed the Spartan throne on my grandfather's death, the weakness of his claim compared to that of my uncle Cleomenes became less of a concern in Sparta than his marriage to my mother. My father's attempts to legalize his marriage to my mother were blocked by the Ephors. The only solution for the Spartan elite was to get rid of him – which they did. They effectively exiled him by sending him away on colonizing expeditions, first to the Libyan coast of Africa, and when that expedition failed, they packed him off to Sicily. There must have been sighs of relief when news came that he had died fighting there.'

'And what of your mother?' asked Sherzada.

'She wanted to accompany my father abroad, but was forbidden to do so by the Ephors. In any case, she died from some sickness when I was four. At the time, my father was in exile, and the most unlikely person came to my aid – my uncle Cleomenes, King of Sparta; the same uncle who had fallen out with my father. It was he who took me in and raised me as his own son. Gorgo was born much later. Cleomenes, who did not have a child then, used all his political clout to have me adopted as his son.

'While there have been precedents of half-Helots being adopted as *Hypomeiones* – Spartans of an inferior status – provided their fathers were full Spartans, most Spartans were concerned about the legal implications of giving Spartan citizenship to someone who was a son of a Helot and could conceivably become their king one day. After a great legal battle in which Cleomenes had to expend much of his personal and political capital, the Ephors finally agreed to give me full status as a Spartan citizen – with all rights, except one. I had to relinquish my claim on the throne. It was, and still is, forbidden for a son of a Helot to become a Spartan king.'

* * *

Sherzada was sitting on the floor of his new accommodation. It was a larger room in the same building as Gorgo's, only two doors down from hers. To Sherzada, the room did not look very different from the cell he had been in. Only it was larger, it had a large window – without bars – and a proper bed rather than a damp reed mattress. The rest was the same.

He was lost in thought when he heard a gentle knock on the door. Moments later, Gorgo entered. As always, he rose for her, but he did not smile as he usually did.

'You seem pensive, my Prince. What is on your mind?'

He offered her the single chair, which she took. 'I have travelled through many lands,' he said, sitting back down on the floor, 'and I did not find a single place where slavery did not exist in one form or another. Sparta is no different in that regard, and yet there is still something savage about this society of yours.'

'The Spartan system,' she explained with some indignation, 'is designed to protect Sparta from enemies foreign and domestic. Had it not been for this, Sparta would have been overrun long ago by our enemies and the Peloponnesus would have remained in perpetual chaos. Sparta's supremacy has provided a degree of peace and stability to this region that is missing in many other parts of Greece.

'Most Spartans fear that if we do not suppress the Helots, they will rise up and wipe us out, as they have tried to do in the past. And while we oppress our Helots, we are brutal to ourselves also, as you saw on the training ground today. Our military education is incredibly harsh and many do not survive it. The system demands our citizens be tough and disciplined. If we cannot even do that, we might not survive – and we might not deserve to survive. We even kill our weak babies so that only the strong survive.'

Gorgo bowed her head. 'Why do you think I did not have a second child? I knew that my first baby, if it was a male, would not be that closely examined, even if it was weak … and Pleistarchus was certainly the frailest of babies. Being the first-born son of a king, the Ephor gave him the benefit of the doubt, and thus his life. But I knew my second child would not survive a similar inspection. It is one thing to lose a grown-up son on the field of battle, it is quite another to lose a child before he or she has even started to live. You are right, my Prince, there are aspects of our culture which are truly savage.'

Sherzada got up and looked back at Gorgo. 'Well, change this savage behaviour of yours,' he urged. 'For a start, stop killing your infants.'

Gorgo shook her head. 'Survival of the fittest babies is part of the Code of Lycurgus – our ancient Lawgiver. Spartans would never accept any change in the Code.'

'Then, at least, change those practice that are outside the Code,' he suggested. 'I too have studied the Code. It says nothing about killing Helots. This measure was instituted much later, only after the great Helot rebellions, if memory serves me right.'

Gorgo again shook her head. 'Any leniency towards the Helots will be interpreted as weakness on our part. We will be seen to be compromising on our security.'

Sherzada began to pace about impatiently. 'Security,' he scoffed. 'Do you think your outnumbered Spartans can continue to control this multitude of Helots forever? There will come a day when your enemies will use your Helots against you. Spartans must find a way to accommodate the Helots before that happens. Not for their sake, but for your own.'

Sherzada waited for Gorgo's reaction but none came. It was a rare moment to see her at a loss for words. But then, after the longest pause, Gorgo's lips began to curl in a sly way. Sherzada knew she had come up with an idea.

A moment later, the two young Helots, who had scrubbed Sherzada on the day of the Gerousia arrived, carrying a large wooden chest. They placed it before Gorgo and Sherzada.

'There is something I want to ask you,' she said, as she opened it.

Sherzada got up and looked inside the chest, recognizing his satchel and his dagger. The chest was full of his belongings.

Gorgo explained that Euro had recovered these from Plataea.

'But I am curious about something,' she mused. 'You told me that after the battle of the Iron Gates the Sakas selected the battle-axe as their weapon of choice. But according to Euro, at Plataea you were the only Saka who fought with a sword rather than a battle-axe.' She reached inside the chest and brought out Sherzada's long-sword, sheathed in its scabbard. 'I have indeed found this long-sword in your belongings ... but I found no axe; none, whatsoever.'

Gorgo took the sword out of its scabbard, and slashed it through the air as she moved nimbly around the room. 'This is a very strong and sturdy sword,' she said, 'yet very light; so light that I could use it easily. If I am not mistaken, it seemed as if this sword were made for a woman.'

Sherzada sat down on his bed with a wistful smile on his face. He saw Gorgo looking at him, expecting an explanation. 'It belonged to my late wife,' he said simply.

'Your wife? A warrior woman? An Amazon?' Seeing him nod, she continued. 'We Greeks have many stories about the Amazons, including the time they invaded Greece and besieged Athens in order to recover their kidnapped queen. I have also heard stories about their relationships with Scythian men. Perhaps yours was a similar story?'

Sherzada laughed. 'The truth is that the warrior women you call the Amazons are in fact also Scythians. Scythian women have a tradition of fighting alongside their men. In fact, the Greek word *Amazon* comes directly from the Iranic word *Hamazan*, which in our language means 'warrior'. Amazons are merely Scythian women warriors, not a separate tribe.

'It is true that Scythian women have formed separate communities at times. But that had more to do with wars or pestilence, where the menfolk had been wiped out or somehow separated from them. I encountered one such community of women in the extreme north of your continent. And that is where the story of this sword starts,' he said, taking it from her gently.

Sherzada rose and walked to the window, gazing upon the compound's beautiful garden; in his mind's eye, travelling back in time. 'It was springtime, some fifteen years ago, and I was traveling through the vast North-western plains of Scythia. I had been inflicted by this wonderful condition that Germanic tribes call *Wanderlust* – a love for travel and adventure. I wanted to explore the earth and see as much of it as I could …'

Chapter 23

The Sword Of The Valkyrie

European Scythia
Spring, 494 BC

I had joined a group of intrepid Scyths, taking a caravan north-west in search of a rare stone called amber. Although not as precious as gold or diamond, amber is very much in demand throughout the Mediterranean, in Greece as much in Phoenicia and Egypt. Most of it comes from the extreme north of Europe by a sea called the Baltic.

When I set off with the expedition, I had no idea what I was getting myself into.

The winter snows had begun to melt as we set out into uncharted territory. After only a few days of riding, we encountered a tribe of fierce warriors, wearing black cloaks and hoods. They attacked us near one of their settlements, but we easily beat them off. Not wanting to meet a larger force of 'Black Cloaks' up ahead, we changed course and began to skirt westwards around their territory.

Once we thought we had put some distance between ourselves and these warriors, we lowered our guard. We had entered an area of great beauty, mysterious and yet completely desolate. That night, we made camp on a high hill above a vale. However, we were attacked by a considerable force. These creatures wore skins and covered their bodies in war-paint, their faces painted like human skulls. No matter how many we killed, more kept on piling in. In the midst of battle, they dragged away two of our party and withdrew. I, and some of the others, wanted to rescue our friends immediately. But our leader forbade us.

He said that our attackers were the *Androphogoi* – 'the eaters of men'. It would be a mistake to pursue them in the dark in their own territory. If we followed them, they would certainly have us for dinner, if not breakfast. In spite of my conscience urging me otherwise, I obeyed. The next morning, when we moved out, we found the remains of our two companions on a nearby hill. We decided to move north-west this time and at speed to avoid further attacks. We soon came across a large river flowing through a deep gorge. We continued to ride northwards along the river as fast as we could, looking for a place to cross it. But all the time we had the feeling we were being watched and followed.

We finally reached a point where the river could be forded. But many of my party were afraid of what might lie across it. The dense forest beyond the river did not look too hospitable. I volunteered to go across and take a look. I crossed the river and rode into the forest, careful to glance back every now and then over my shoulder, in case danger lurked.

Finding nothing, I turned my horse to tell my party all was clear. However, when I approached the fording point, I saw my companions across the river being attacked by a large force of Androphogoi. Those of my companions who tried to cross the river were brutally cut down and their bodies dragged away. I wanted to join the fray, but my instincts of self-preservation kept me hidden under cover of the forest.

I decided to ride up along the gorge, and follow the river northward to see if I could make contact with the survivors of my party further upstream. After riding for several miles, I heard shouting and screaming down below. I climbed to the tallest spot above the river to get a better vantage point. Downriver, I saw a group of riders trying to cross the river and the Androphogoi pursuing them. I started to descend towards the river, firing my arrows at the pursuers. I killed several during my descent. But when I came down to the river bank, I saw some Androphogoi on horseback crossing the river, closing in on the riders they had been chasing. As the Androphogoi closed in, the riders turned in their saddles and fired volleys of arrows at them in true Scythian fashion. Many of the attackers fell, but a few continued the chase. At that point, I fell upon them from behind and dispatched them with a few blows from my battle-axe. Yes – I had an axe then. The remaining Androphogoi rode back across the river.

I tried to catch up with the riders in the hope of finding who they were and hearing news of my companions. As I approached, the lead rider swung around, knocked me off my horse and lassoed me. I lay helpless on the ground, trying to make out who the riders were. They wore fur-lined clothing and cloaks and their faces were covered by the masks and the iron visors of their helmets. As I managed to sit up, the leader of the horsemen dismounted and began to question me. What surprised me was not the questions or the language they were asked in, but the voice of my interrogator. And soon enough, as the leader's helmet came off, everything became clear. She was a young woman with long blonde hair that dropped most of the way down her back.

She spoke to me in heavily accented, broken Greek, asking who I was. I told her I was a Saka. She reacted angrily, saying I did not look like a Saka. She turned to her companions to ask what to do with me, speaking in a dialect of Scythian which I could make out with some difficulty. At that point, all the riders removed their helmets and masks. The riders – nine of them in all – were all young women, and amongst the most beautiful I had ever seen. One of the women responded to their leader by saying that they had a choice of either killing me or setting me free.

'We cannot let him ride with us,' the leader said.

'But I am one of you,' I shouted back in Scythian. 'I am also a Scyth.'

'Like hell you are,' the leader said, as she rubbed her hands roughly across my face. 'This dark colour of your skin does not come off. You are not a Scyth.' Turning to her companions she said, 'I think we should just kill him.'

One of the riders, who seemed to be the youngest and was by far the prettiest of them, said, 'I don't think any of us would have made it this far without his help. And he does fire arrows like a Scyth. He is even dressed like one. And he does speak our language ... well, sort of.'

The leader thought for a moment, and looked at me. 'Very well. Ride with us, but one wrong move and I shall kill you myself. I have a feeling you will bring us nothing but trouble.'

As I rode with them, the leader, who called herself Hild, asked why I was travelling across these lands. I told her of the amber expedition. 'I don't know what people see in that stone,' she said, 'but we can take you to a place where there is plenty of it.'

I thanked her for that.

'But you must leave us as soon as you have collected the amber,' she instructed me. I told her I wanted nothing more.

Then it was my turn to ask Hild what she and her party were doing in the area. She said that she and her companions had been separated from their tribe while chasing a herd of wild white horses. While they were trying to return north, they came across the Androphogoi. The Androphogoi were attacking a party, dressed similar to me. But then they turned their attention to Hild and her party, so they rode across the river to escape them. It was there that I had met them.

That night, we set up camp under the light of a bright full moon. Once again, I began to have a feeling that we were being watched. I told them we should find a more defensible site to make camp.

Hild responded contemptuously. 'You worry like an old woman. There is nothing I and my girls cannot take care of. Now, go to sleep.'

Sure enough, we were attacked in the middle of the night, this time by men wearing wolf skins and dark leather. The attackers were tougher than the Androphogoi, and they fought with considerable skill. But still we beat them off.

I thought it was over, when one of the women cried out, 'they have taken Rán.' She was the pretty one who had earlier urged Hild to spare my life.

Hild said it would not be wise to go after the attackers, whom she called the *Neuri*. They might have set up an ambush for us, she insisted. We had to at least wait until first light. I told her that if we waited until then, Rán would be dead. I was going after her, even if I had to go alone. As I took off in search of Rán, I looked behind and saw the women silently following me. The bright moonlight and fresh footprints on the muddy ground helped me track the *Neuri* to the place where they had taken Rán. When we arrived, we saw Rán lying tied up on an altar outside a cave, being prepared for some sort of sacrifice. Growling noises were coming from inside the cave. As they grew louder, the wolf-skinned men moved away, leaving Rán alone and struggling to free herself from her bonds. A tall man emerged out of the cave, wearing the head of a large wolf. As he began to move towards Rán, I charged at him. At that instance, the other warrior women let loose a volley of arrows, killing several of the wolf-skinned men, and then they followed me towards Rán.

Before the wolf-headed man could touch Rán, I struck him a violent blow in the chest with my battle-axe, leaving a considerable gap in his chest. He fell down but continued to groan. The wolf-skinned men were terrified to see what had happened. But one of them, dressed as a sort of priest, said something that caused the men to calm down and turn once again towards us in a menacing manner.

As we tried to untie Rán, the priest shouted at me, this time in Greek, 'you have not killed our lord, the Werewolf. Only a weapon of silver can destroy him.'

At that, I smiled. I struck the Werewolf another piercing blow in the chest, and with my hand, ripped out his still-beating heart. I raised his heart and my battle-axe above my head and shouted, 'behold the heart of the Werewolf and my axe with blades of silver!' The silver of my axe gleamed brightly in the moonlight as I sliced open the Werewolf's heart.

Pandemonium broke out as all the men, including the priest, fled in panic. I took off the wolf's head to find underneath it the face of a man with unusual hair growth, seemingly sharp teeth, and a terrifying appearance. His breath had a revolting but familiar smell. Hild ordered her women to burn the 'monster'. Even though I told her that he was a man and I wanted to examine him more, his body was set alight.

The smell on 'the Werewolf's' breath was similar to that of a powerful intoxicant drink the Amyrgian Sakas consume before battle. It makes them think that they are invincible and immortal. And in battle, they go berserk. This hallucinogenic concoction also sometimes causes a rare condition that temporarily effects a change in appearance, giving a horrifying aspect. To me, the 'Werewolves' were mortals who used fear to control their *Neuri* war-bands, terrorize neighbouring communities and carry out extortion of every kind.

The following day, Rán came to thank me for saving her life from the 'monster.' And when I told her what I thought about the 'Werewolf,' she laughed. 'Must you always try to rationalize everything? I suppose you are also going to tell me that Androphogoi don't eat humans.'

I told her perhaps they were using their cannibalistic reputation to scare off potentially hostile strangers.

Rán also asked me if my battle-axe really was made out of silver. I told her it had been specially ordered for me by my grandfather, and its blade was an alloy of iron and pure silver. In part to protect the axe against rust and give it a stainless quality and in part to appear as shiny and impressive as it had that moonlit night.

As we rode together, I asked her about her companions and why they spoke Scythian though they looked Germanic. She said that five generations before her, a Scythian tribe had become separated from its confederation. Hostile tribes had forced them to continue to travel north. During this time, their menfolk died off, mostly in battle, but also from disease. Many of the old and the weak did not survive the bitter cold. The tribe and its security were in the hands of the young warrior women who had guided it to the lands of the north. There they met a tribe of a Germanic people who lived in the lands and islands called Scandia, across the Baltic Sea and beyond, but often came across to the mainland for war and trade. The women agreed to marry the men of the Scandians as long as they were allowed to keep their warrior traditions.

The Scandians knew nothing of horses or archery and were only too happy to have women warriors protecting their flanks and provide supporting fire in battle. In return for this service, the warrior women demanded that all their female offspring and even the female offspring of their sons and grandsons be allowed to serve in their *Skyle* – the war squadrons. Additionally, it was the Scythian women who would choose their men, not the reverse. The final condition was that these women would preserve their mother tongue from generation to generation, which they use as part of their military communications. The Scandians readily agreed to all these conditions. However, the Scandian warriors also asked the women to carry out an additional task.

Germanic tribes ritually mutilated the bodies of their enemies after battle and collected their skulls as trophies. At the same time, it was equally important for the bravest of their warriors to enter their paradise – *Valhalla* – in one piece. What was the point of turning up at the feast of their chief god Odin at Valhalla, Rán asked, 'without one's head?'

So the Scandians asked the Scythian women to observe the battle closely and to pick out the bravest among their warriors. Once these warriors fell, the Scythian women would charge into battle and recover their bodies. These Scandians were later given a heroic funeral. When the Scythian women started carrying out these tasks in battle they were given a new name – *Valkyries* – 'the choosers of the slain'. This was the name Rán and the other warrior women shared.

We travelled many more weeks and had further adventures in which I proved of much use to the Valkyries. But every day I found myself drawn to this young northern beauty. Her face was of incomparable exquisiteness and her body of mesmerizing perfection. She had a smile that could melt my heart and a soft melodic voice that my ears constantly longed for. Above all, her outer beauty was matched by an attractive personality that drew me helplessly towards her just like a lodestone cannot help but point at the North. Named after a sea-goddess, Rán, in the Norse dialect of the Scandians, also meant robbery. This could not have more appropriate, for I soon realized she was stealing my heart.

We finally reached the shores of a sea named after a local tribe, called the Balts. It was here the Valkyries were reunited with their menfolk, who had been searching for them. The following morning, I participated in one last battle with the Valkyries, when the Scandian camp was attacked at dawn by a war-band from a rival Germanic tribe, the Bastarnae. I was woken by their wild battle-cries and immediately reached for my weapons. I saw the Valkyries running to mount their horses, but the Scandian men took their time, calmly strapping their swords to their hands. They believed that those who did not die with a sword in their hand would not be allowed to enter Valhalla.

But I could not wait, for the attackers were already upon us. With my battle-axe in my right hand and a short sword in my left, I fell among the enemy with ferocity. Blocking with one weapon and striking with the other, I kept on advancing, slaying all those before me. Still, I did not go unscathed, receiving several blows, cuts and slashes in turn – including the scars that still adorn my face.

I was later told that I had single-handedly beaten off the

attackers. By the time the rest of the Scandian men had joined battle, the enemy were already on their heels. When I saw the enemy flee, I raised my arms in triumph amid the cheers of the Scandian warriors. And as I turned around to face them, I saw her. And the sight of her made me oblivious to everything going on around me: oblivious to the pain; oblivious to the blood drenching my face and body. All I saw was Rán's beautiful face, radiantly lit by the rays of the rising sun. That was all the succour I needed, before I passed out.

Over the next days, Rán healed me with great care, but though I could sense her strong desire for me, I detected some reticence also. Because of that, I did not initiate any advance towards her, though I badly wanted to.

As I soon as I was well enough to ride, Hild, as she promised, led me to a deposit of amber. I had never before seen so much of the stone. Her tribesmen even gave me a pack of a dozen horses to carry it. Guides and porters were also hired to help me on my journey. Hild seemed to be in a hurry to see me off. She even told me of a relatively quicker and safer route back to Scythia. I would have no difficulty returning this time.

But it was then I realized that I did not want to leave. I was deeply in love with Rán and I did not know what to do. Hild knew it only too well. She had told me right from the start that I would bring trouble to her womenfolk. She said that each Valkyrie was required to select a man for herself before she could go on an expedition. This was to give them a longing for their men and a reason to live – so they wouldn't take needless risks. Each girl in the squadron had a husband or a male partner of some sort. Rán was no exception. Hild told me to forget about her, because Rán had already chosen her man; a man whom she would soon marry. 'If you press this issue you will create problems for yourself and for all of us women with whom you claim a bond of kinship,' she said. 'If you are truly our kinsman, you will put the interests of your tribeswomen before yourself.'

I was devastated, but I saw logic in what she said. So I quietly collected my amber and had it packed and ready for travel on the horses the Scandians had given me. As I was about to leave, Rán came to me. I asked her about what Hild had told me. She answered that she was indeed in love with the man who would soon be her husband. Rán said that in all probability she would not see me again, but she wanted me to give her something she could remember our adventures with. I told her she could have anything she asked for. She said she wanted my battle-axe, the one with which I had rescued her from the Werewolf. I gave it to her and started to leave.

Then she told me to stop. 'I don't want to send you off defenceless,' she said.

I still had a sword, I said. She laughed, 'you call that sorry piece of metal you have with you a sword! Take mine.' She gave me the long-sword slung over her shoulder. 'This was made for my mother,' she said, 'who was a great warrior.'

I bade Rán farewell and soon returned to the Scythian lands with my sacks of amber. I have been a rich man ever since. But as far as my heart was concerned, I had never felt poorer.

Ten years later, a man came to see me at my military camp outside Sardis. I was in Persian service then. He was an elderly Scandian *Jarl* – chieftain – called Gunnarr. I knew the name meant 'warrior' in the Norse tongue of the Scandians and the man certainly looked it, with impressive broad muscles and battle scars, and great rings of gold and silver around his arms; evidence of his courage in battle. He explained he was Rán's father. I asked him if Rán was well and why he had come to me. He told me a sad tale. Some months earlier, in battle with an invading tribe, Rán had broken the Valkyrie code. Her husband was about to be killed by the enemy when Rán rode out to save him rather than wait until he was dead. In saving her husband, she suffered serious injuries.

After the battle, Rán was tried for her crime in breaking the

Valkyrie code. Even her husband bore witness against her. He repudiated her and renounced their marriage. Among the charges levelled against her was infertility. After many years of marriage, she had not borne him a child. In fact, he had already taken another woman as his 'hand-fast' wife, as Scandian men often do. Rán had not known about that and was devastated when she found out. The man she had loved, the man for whom she had even risked her life, had betrayed her in such a callous manner. She did not want anything more to do with him. It was then she began to speak of me.

Later, she went back to the tribal council and made two requests. First, that she would be allowed to choose her next husband. Gunnarr told me she had chosen me. The council told her that was her right since she no longer had one. Second, since she could no longer bear children or ride, she was of no more use to the tribe. She wanted permission to leave the tribe.

While the council gave her permission to do as she wished, Gunnarr told me that as her father, he could not let her marry without knowing for sure that I would not treat her badly. He said that his daughter had already suffered too much. I assured him that I still loved his daughter exactly as I had when I first met her. I even showed him her sword, which was constantly strapped over my shoulder. And I told him that nothing could make me happier than marrying Rán.

After a few days, he returned with Rán. That was the first time I had seen Rán in nearly ten years. She looked just as beautiful as the last time I had seen her and on her face was the expression I had seen the day I fought the Bastarnae.

I smiled and said, 'So, you have come to return my axe?'

'The axe is mine,' she said. 'Remember, you gave it to me. Now I have come to take you as well.'

We were soon married.

At the time, I was still in Datis' service. He gave me one of King Croesus' former palaces as a residence and summoned physicians from all over the empire and beyond. Under their care, Rán's health began to improve dramatically. Her scars began to heal and she even started walking and running. Riding a horse was still difficult but occasionally against their advice and my pleas she would disguise herself as a Saka cavalryman, and wearing my spare armour and helmet, sneak into the exercise grounds on a horse and train with my men. She longed to be in battle again. But she also knew that was not to be.

Then she became pregnant. A little after our marriage, she had converted to my belief in one God. One day, she started to talk to me about death. She said that if she ever died before me, the only thing she wanted to take with her to the grave was my battle-axe. She said she wanted to see me again in the afterlife. It would be easier for me to find her there if she took my axe with her, she said.

* * *

Sherzada's story came to an abrupt end, but Gorgo felt no need to probe him further. There was no child, she was sure of it, and now she knew why he showed fear of death neither on the battlefield nor before the Gerousia.

She wished to touch him, to offer comfort of some kind, but did not.

Chapter 24

The Curse Of Battle

Training grounds
Sparta
Autumn, 479 BC

A fifth warrior stepped into the sand, and Gorgo gave a small gasp. 'Is that not Pericleidas?' she asked, remembering the young naval officer who had visited her with the eccentric Athenian playwright-turned-captain, Aeschylus.

Euro nodded. 'Fought with distinction at Salamis and commanded an elite marine detachment at Mycale.'

Gorgo watched as Pericleidas walked up to Sherzada and aggressively lunged his sword at his chest. This forced the Saka Prince to move to the right, only to have Pericleidas smash Sherzada's face with his shield. Though stunned for a moment, Sherzada recovered fast enough to avoid Pericleidas' second sword thrust, this time aimed at his face. Pericleidas kept the initiative and the pressure on Sherzada. Though Sherzada countered every move, he seemed to be on the back foot. The Spartans cheered, and at that moment Sherzada left his chest open for Pericleidas to strike at. Gorgo's heart was in her mouth, but as Pericleidas threw his entire body weight into the attack, Sherzada elegantly sidestepped him, tripping his opponent in the process. The tall young Spartan fell face first on the ground. Sherzada walked over and put his foot on the man's back. Pericleidas tried to rise but Sherzada pinned him down, pointing his sword at the back of the prone Pericleidas' neck. It was over.

Gorgo walked over to the scene of combat. 'Tell me, my Prince, how come you can best our warriors individually, and yet lose to these very same men in battle?'

'Ah, but battle is different,' he responded, as Euro led the defeated Pericleidas away, and the crowd dispersed. 'I am merely better at single combat than most. But these warriors of yours, when these men fight in the line, fight and move as one, fight as if they don't know the meaning of fear, they are unbeatable. It is terrible thing to fight Spartans. I would never want to face these gentlemen across the battlefield again.'

For a moment, Gorgo scanned the scars on Sherzada's face, arms and neck – so much a part of him, and quite beautiful too. For a moment, too, she felt giddy, and when she remembered the parchment and went to take it from her bag, she brushed his arm with hers, feeling the smooth surface of his knot of scars. She picked up the crumpled piece of parchment. 'Recognize this, my Prince? I found it among your personal effects,' she said. 'For a long time, I have been trying to teach myself how to write and read Persian, but without much success. All I can make out is that this is some sort of poem, and it has to do with the Spartans in battle.'

'It is indeed poetry, written by a young Persian Prince – Khorrem, son of Mashista. This father and son are amongst the noblest and bravest I have met. This poem describes a part of the action on the first day of the battle of Thermopylae, when Khorrem led the charge of the first wave of the *Anusiya* – the elite Persian regiment whom you call the 'Immortals' – against your husband's Spartans. He was wounded thrice before he was ordered to withdraw. I shall translate, if you'd like? Forgive me if the verse does not sound quite as it should.'

I watched them raise their shields
Against an endless hail of arrows
They played their haunting pipes
And they sang their chilling hymns
Their shouts rose like thunder
As they tore our ranks asunder
On the day the Spartans stood strong.

So many brave men fell beside me on that cursed day
Would I have fought or run away?
Yes, fear lies in the soul of every warrior
I wonder if the Spartans have felt this too
In every battle they have been in,
In every victory they have won:
That cowards lurk inside heroes even when they are standing strong?

Gorgo gave Sherzada a dubious look. 'So, this 'brave' Persian Prince implies that deep down Spartans are cowards?'

'Do not underestimate the courage of the Persians, my Queen. They have fought and won battles on three continents. But what the Prince is conveying here is a simple universal truth which every combat veteran knows. Battle, they say, is governed by fear – *phobos* – the greatest enemy of a warrior. And when fear becomes infectious, it turns into sheer terror – *diemos* – the destroyer of armies.

'And yet fear is but a natural emotion, like love. And for the best of warriors, the fear of showing fear is often worse than the fear of death itself. Against that the warrior must be armed with courage – *andreia*. As long as his courage holds, the warrior has every chance of prevailing – or at least dying in the attempt.

'The advantage of your Spartan military education is that it teaches your young men not only to develop their *andreia*, but also to manage their *phobos*. The iron discipline of your training ensures that the only thing your warriors fear is fear. And only those who know how to control their fear can defeat it. Your warriors are taught to hold ground against the enemy, dying where they stand rather than running away. And so your men prefer to die heroically than face any form of disgrace. That is the one thing that makes your men, of all the Greeks, so feared in battle.

'But, my Queen, the Spartans have no monopoly over

courage. In all the battles I have fought, I have seen ordinary men turn into heroes; just as I have seen brave warriors flee the field, merely because they showed fear before their opponents did. Courage is not the absence of fear; courage exists in spite of it. Show me a brave man and I shall show you one not willing to admit he is afraid.

'The warrior in battle, my Queen, is a part of a fraternity; a bizarre, mysterious brotherhood born out of violence and the nearness of death. Warriors go to battle for many reasons; for the love of their country, for the glory of their nation, to defend their families, or for the sake of their religion. Some go into battle for the right reasons, and others for the wrong ones, and some for no reason at all. But when battle begins, what binds warriors together is neither love, nor glory, nor greed; neither king, nor country. They fight to hold the line. They fight to hold their ground and force the enemy back. Once the line breaks, once panic spreads, when men begin to flee, the battle is lost; all is lost. So the best of warriors will risk pain or death rather than the possibility of flight and the probability of disgrace. No other creature courts pain and self-destruction in such a way as man.

'They call battle the quintessence of glory; I call it slaughter. At the end of every battle, there the corpses lie. I have been in many battles, my Queen, and no doubt will see many more. But given the choice, I would prefer peace, any time, over war.'

Despite years of trying to understand it, no one had explained the essence of battle to Gorgo more vividly. But there was something else she yearned to know. 'So, this poem is about Thermopylae? Tell me what happened there. Tell me about the battle.'

Sherzada shivered. 'It is time we went in, my Queen. Thermopylae is not for now. You lost your husband, and I my younger brother, to that battle. I shall tell you everything, I promise. But not now.'

Though Gorgo wanted to press him, she relented.

Thermopylae made her uncomfortable, too. 'Very well, though there is one more thing I wished to discuss today. I have been through your letters and am struck by your faith in one God.'

'It is the only faith that makes any sense to me.'

'And you seem to have gone to extreme lengths to acquire it?'

Sherzada explained how, in his youth, he travelled across different lands to find those who preached the Word of God, in the monotheistic monasteries of Lake Tana, one of the sources of the River Nile in Africa; in the Temple of Solomon in the ancient city of Yerushalaim; and at the Sacred Precinct of Abraham in the desert of Faran in Arabia. Afterwards, he looked at Gorgo curiously. 'Why are you fascinated by my faith? Do you not believe in your gods, as most Greeks do?'

'Our gods are a strange lot, who like to play tricks on mankind and use us to score points against each other. I do not believe that the cosmos is governed by so many fallible, quarrelling, selfish, idiotic deities. If this was the case, the universe would be in chaos. I am not convinced by these superstitions.'

'So you don't believe in any god, then?'

'I am not sure,' said Gorgo. 'But there are times I want to believe in something.' As they began to leave, she turned to ask him, 'Tell me, do you believe in a forgiving god?'

'As long as His forgiveness is sought, not taken for granted.'

'Then pray to your God to forgive me, for I have committed a horrible crime.'

Chapter 25

Then Everything Changed

Sparta
Three days later

There was a knock on the door. It was Agathe. She was wearing a white dress instead of her customary dark gown, and had flowers in her hair.

'Highness,' she said, bowing low. 'Her Majesty desires the pleasure of your company at her table.'

Sherzada was curious, for he knew the dates of all the Spartan festivals, and none fell on this day. Despite the late hour he followed Agathe into the grounds of the compound, where he found scores of Helots all dressed in white; the men wearing improvised laurels on their heads, and the women, like Agathe, flowers in their hair. They all seemed to be busy preparing food – barbequing slaughtered sheep, cooking great batches of soup and baking what smelled to be some kind of spinach bread. There was music and laughter, and an extraordinary feeling of possibility and freedom in the air.

Upon entering Gorgo's apartment, Sherzada found the hearth room full of people, mostly Helots with only a few Spartans. Some of the Helots were dancing; others were clapping, sitting nearby on the bare floor. Gorgo sat in the centre listening to a harp playing, flanked by her cousins. Euro was beaming, but Pausanias looked bored. Pausanias' younger brother, Nicomedes, was there too. And the bewildered expression on the youth's face summed it all. Sherzada was not the only one confused. But not Gorgo. She smiled triumphantly as her eyes met Sherzada's.

'I'm glad you could join our celebrations, my Prince,' she said, motioning him to sit.

He came and sat down on a chair next to her and asked her

what she was celebrating.

'Taking your advice, my Prince.'

Seeing Sherzada's muddled expression, Gorgo asked him if he remembered their discussion about the ancient Law Code of Lycurgus. 'Every year,' she said, 'around this time, the Ephors declare war on the Helots. This is a tradition that goes back nearly two centuries, when the last Helot revolt was crushed. But it is not part of the Lycurgan Code. This declaration of war gives Spartans the legal right, if they so wish, to kill Helots. It is under this legal cover that the Crypteia squads of the best of Sparta's young military graduates go out on their assassination missions. Well, I have begun to change all that.'

Sherzada's eyes widened and a smile broke out on his face. 'How did you manage that?'

Gorgo described how she had convinced the Elders to pass a law forbidding the Ephors from making this declaration this year. 'It was not easy but they relented in the end,' she said. As soon as the law was passed, she explained, the War Council forbade all Crypteia missions against the Helots. Instead, the Crypteia would be send across Sparta's border to collect intelligence and provide early warning against possible threats to Sparta. 'Something they ought to have been doing from the start,' she concluded.

'But this is only for one year,' Sherzada pointed out.

'Indeed. Still, it is a start. If we can manage to repeat it every year, Spartans will get used to it.'

Euro leaned over and said, 'This is not the only thing my royal cousin is celebrating.'

Sherzada looked at Gorgo and found a mischievous glint in her eyes. She explained that Athens' former leader Themistocles was trying to make another bid for power in the run up to their elections. This time he was building his political campaign around xenophobia, particularly playing on suspicions about Sparta. He was trying to blame all Athens' ills on Spartan conspiracies.

'And you really think your plan will work?' asked Pausanias.

'It is already working.' Gorgo said that Themistocles had been behind the Athenians' push to take over the command of the Hellenic Fleet from the Spartans. 'Because this issue is so close to his heart, I have invited Themistocles here to discuss the possible division of the command of the Fleet. Today, I received confirmation that he is on his way.'

'Of course, when he comes he will not get everything he wants, but just enough to save his sorry face. The victor of Salamis, however, will be feted like a god here; showered with honours and gifts. And hints will be sent back to Athens that he has also been given a hefty bribe, which he will indeed be offered. Even if he refuses, I will see to it that all his enemies in Athens believe that he accepted it under the table.'

'You want to shut him up?' asked Sherzada, smiling.

Gorgo laughed. 'No one will believe him after that. They will see him every bit a part of the very conspiracies he is construing. Our alliance with Athens has to be maintained at all costs. And if it is comes at the cost of muzzling an irritating spoiler like Themistocles, so be it.'

Pausanias shook his head. 'I still do not trust the Athenians. Sooner or later they will challenge us for the control of Greece.'

'The solution, dear cousin,' replied Gorgo, 'lies in neither of us controlling Greece but both Athens and Sparta working together to ensure its security. All we need do is prevent mavericks like Themistocles from rocking the boat.'

Pausanias got up, shaking his head. 'You are too trusting, cousin, when it comes to the Athenians.' He gave her a fleeting kiss on the forehead, and left.

'Oh dear Pausanias,' she said. 'How easily you are ruled by the heart.'

Turning to Sherzada, she said, 'So, my Prince, what do you think about the changes I have begun to make around here? This is only the beginning. Will you stay and assist me? You see things differently, and that helps me no end.'

Sherzada did not know how to respond.

But Gorgo continued to explain all the plans she had in mind not only to stop the brutalities against the Helots, but also to win some privileges for the 'inferiors' – *Hypomeiones* and the 'illegitimates' – *Mothoi*. 'These people should live a life of dignity and have a stake in the betterment of Sparta.'

She moved closer and continued to tell him her plans. She was feverish with enthusiasm, plotting to change Sparta's course forever and soliciting Sherzada's help in doing so. He too felt her infectious enthusiasm, though he warned her to be cautious. 'Remember the fate of your father.'

Late into the night, Agathe went out to fetch more food. She returned with a tray of honey-cakes and accompanied by an older Helot. In his late forties, he was short and thin, with a shaggy and uneven stubble across his face. He approached Gorgo in a submissive posture, his eyes fixed to the ground. Then he fell on his knees and kissed the Queen's hands.

Gorgo smiled. 'I am glad you could make it, Menander.' Turning to Sherzada she said, 'My Prince, I would like you to meet my most trusted servant. He accompanied my husband to Thermopylae.'

Sherzada smiled politely as the man's eyes met his. But he was not prepared for what followed.

Chapter 26

The Hot Gates

A few moments later

'If you ever wished for reason to kill me, my Queen, you have it now,' he said.

'Tell me about Thermopylae. I want to know everything!' Gorgo voice was restrained, though not without a touch of menace.

Moments earlier, when Menander had made his accusation, Gorgo told him and Sherzada to quietly get up and follow her. And so Sherzada had followed her, out of her apartment, past the revelling Helots, right back to Sherzada's old prison cell.

* * *

'Molon Labe!'

This had been his reply to Xerxes' command for the Greeks to lay down their arms. When he asked me translate what the Spartan warrior had said, I told the Great King to 'come and get them'.

Xerxes swore with rage in his eyes, 'For that, I shall take his head.'

There was no doubt in my mind that the Spartan warrior who had said those words was King Leonidas. He was dressed in his long dark crimson cloak, the colour of which matched the sideways crest on his helmet.

Xerxes had taken the better part of five days to deploy his troops at the front of the narrow Pass of Thermopylae – the 'Hot Gates', so the Greeks could see what they were up against. There might have been only three hundred Spartans there, but they were backed up by 2,000 Helots and perhaps a few hundred

Perioiki and a contingent of over a dozen Greek cities. All in all, around 8,000 Greeks faced a hundred thousand Persians – not the million men you Greeks talk of, but still the odds were formidable.

So on that first day of battle, Xerxes ordered some of his best troops – the Medes of Western Iran and the Persian-speaking Cissians of Elam – to force their way through Thermopylae. The Pass was well chosen by King Leonidas because its mouth on one side was a steep ridge and on the other a deep cliff. Within the Pass itself, the narrow spaces meant that the numerical superiority of Persia's forces counted for nothing. Leonidas had prepared his positions well. He had constructed a broad wall inside the entrance of the Pass, behind which the Greeks waited to repulse the enemy attacks. The lightly armoured Medes and Cissians carried shields of wicker which could not protect them against the powerful spear thrusts of the Greeks. And in that narrow pass, the Persian numerical advantage was for nought. The result was a massacre. Scores dead within minutes. But these men of Iran had preferred to die than to retreat.

As the Medes and the Cissians fell, the Persian King sent in more men – and then even more – under a constant barrage of arrows from tens of thousands of Persian bows. A Greek warrior was heard to complain that there were so many arrows that they were blocking out the sun. A Spartan warrior responded, 'so much the better; then we can fight in the shade.' Yet the waves upon waves of Persians could not make any dent in the Greek defences.

Successive contingents of the Persian army went through that narrow space towards the Greeks, like lambs to slaughter. They paid dearly for Xerxes' folly. Panic began to take hold of the Persian front lines, and many started to flee. Xerxes ordered his personal guards to whip the troops running from the fight and force them to return. And heroically, the Greeks beat off one attack after another.

Throughout the day, King Leonidas had been rotating his troops at the wall, so that they would not tire. He had let the allied Greeks fight for most of the day, keeping his Spartans in reserve. But as the sun began its descent, he ordered his Spartans to the front lines. I watched as the Three Hundred took up their positions, wearing their crimson cloaks, carrying their bronze-covered shields with the *Lambda* insignia of Lacedaemon, their magnificent horse-hair crests above their helmets making them appear taller and even more impressive. On their flanks were the Helots, in animal skins, armed only with javelins and slingshots. Against these men, Xerxes decided to send the very best of his troops; his elite bodyguard the Anusiya, whom the Greeks call the 'Immortals'.

Demaratus warned Xerxes not to underestimate the discipline and training of the Spartans. He said that the Persians were facing the best warriors in Greece, but the Great King paid no heed. And so he watched as his proud Anusiya fell victim to Leonidas' many stratagems, including luring them into believing they had the upper hand, only to turn the tables when they least expected it. Needless to say, the Anusiya were mercilessly mauled by the Spartans; the cream of the Persian Army falling in their scores, though not without courage.

And the Spartans fought with confidence and exceptional skill in that cramped crevice of Thermopylae. As they gained the upper hand they charged into the Persian ranks, pushing some of the Persian troops off the cliffs, down into the Gulf of Malia below. With the battle-line of the Anusiya on the verge of collapse, I was ordered to lead my Sakas to help stabilize the Persian line. We managed to push your warriors back behind their defensive wall, losing many of our best men in the process. And still the Spartans fought back. If their spearheads were hacked off, they reversed the spears and fought with metal spikes which were just as lethal as the iron spear-points. Any wounded enemy unlucky enough to fall under their feet would be butt-spiked to death – I believe the term your warriors use for that is *lizarding*. And when their weapons failed, the Spartans would scratch, kick, and bite. Even at the point of death, a Spartan could take several enemy warriors with him to Hades.

Thus, in spite of the heavy odds against them, the Spartans continued to deal death to their enemies. In the midst of battle, they sang their haunting hymns. Had the battle continued, I was not sure my Sakas could hold the line. But, to my relief, as the sun went down, and the dead lay in piles before Leonidas' wall, a retreat was called on the Persian side.

Later that night, many of Xerxes' advisors and generals tried to convince him to take an alternative route south, through Aetolia, avoiding the Spartans altogether. But Xerxes called it cowardice. He would not rest until he had killed Leonidas. He commanded me to pick my troops and seize the wall from the Spartans.

At first light, I went through all the regiments to choose my force. Since most of the 'Persian army' was lightly armed, I looked for those more heavily equipped, and especially those who were proficient with certain types of weapons. Virtually all of these were found in the 'foreign' contingents. From Africa, I selected the Cushites who fought with the heavy spear and the Libyans, wielding their double-handed *khopesh* sickle-swords. I also chose the warlike tribesmen from the hills of Assur – the last of the Assyrians – who carried huge clubs studded with iron spikes; and a small band of the long-haired Cimmerians – also the last of their kind – who fought with metal-cleaving broadswords. I selected men from amongst my distant kin from the north the Amyrgians Sakas, carrying their large war-axes – the *mahasigareis*. And to them I added our neighbours to the West of the Indus: the warriors of Gandhara, the fierce Pactiyans as well as the hardy Dadicans who carried sledge hammers into battle. Needless to say, my own Royal Sakas followed me. I told these men to take up their heavy weapons and literally smash their way through the Greek lines.

First, though, we had to negotiate the stacks of bodies of the Persian dead piled up against the wall. The stench was unbearable; a macabre testament to the deadly skill of the Spartans. Still, the momentum of our attack was strong, and tactics of fighting like the Greeks in close order, using our heavy weapons to snap the Spartan spears and cleave apart their shields, carried us over the wall, pushing the Spartans back. It seemed we were beating the invincible Spartans.

Suddenly, the Spartans broke off the engagement and began to flee. Shouts of encouragement and war-cries from my men echoed across the narrow walls of the pass as we chased after them, thirsty for blood. But this was Leonidas' ploy to lure us deep into the narrow pass, where, ironically, the Greeks, and not us, would have numerical superiority. It was also a place where the Persian archers could not see, let alone hit, their targets. So, as we reached that point, the fleeing Spartans turned and charged us. They were joined by other Greeks who fell on us without mercy. The space was so narrow that there was not enough room for us to wield our doubled-handed weapons, nor did we have any shields to protect ourselves. Many were cut down by the efficient short-swords – the *Xiphé* – of your Spartans. Thus, the Greeks forced us back to the wall.

I sent a runner back to Xerxes to request reinforcements. But none came. So I rallied my troops and led them in another charge against the Spartans. Once more we forced them to retreat, at terrible cost to ourselves. But this time we did not follow them into their killing zone. We stopped, instead, and awaited their counter-assault. It was not long before it came, but not in the manner I had expected.

First, we found ourselves subject to missile attacks – sling-shots, rocks, light javelins; though no arrows. Hurling things at the enemy, rather than fighting them hand to hand, was not the Spartan way, I knew. But it was effective, inflicting casualties on those who were not so well-protected. After a while, the rain of projectiles stopped.

Then I heard a war-cry: *Messene, Hellas, Eleutheria* – 'Messene, Greece, Liberty' – and I saw them come. I understood, at last, that those who were attacking us were not Spartans at all. Hundreds of Messenian Helots charged us, in a disorganized mob. Some had picked up the spears, swords, and shields of fallen Greeks but most had no protection whatsoever and many were armed only with rocks and sticks. I told my men to close ranks. These Helots lacked the skill and discipline of the Spartans, but they did not want for courage. They attacked us knowing they would be cut down like corn before a scythe. And fall they did under our merciless blows.

These young Messenian slaves died for freedom, just as bravely as free-born Spartans, with honour, without hesitation, as our equals, and thus bought for themselves in death what they could never have won in life. Magnificent; glorious, but alas, it was nothing but slaughter; and I took no pleasure in it.

But the suicidal charge of the Helots gave the Spartans and their allies a pause to recover and reform. No sooner had we stopped massacring the Messenians than the Greeks were already upon us. We were in no position to resist. I was hoping that Xerxes would send us reinforcements so we could hold on to the wall. But none came. Since Xerxes was not interested in supporting us, I ordered my troops to fall back.

The Persians, however, renewed their attempt to take the wall, but well after my men had withdrawn. It seemed they did not want risk their troops to save the lives of mine. The Persians, in their turn, failed even to take the wall. I was furious at their incompetence and arrogance. We had lost good men and still had nothing to show for it. Xerxes, by contrast, was delighted. He called me to his tent and congratulated me for proving that the wall could be taken and the Spartans could be pushed back. He said that in return for my impressive feat, he would give my

Sakas the honour of defending the King's tent for the rest of the battle. He was sending his Anusiya on a special mission, or so he told me. He seemed very pleased with himself. I found out later what had happened. The Pass had been betrayed. A local shepherd had showed a way to other side of the Pass.

Once King Leonidas had learnt that the Persians had found a way to attack his rear, he urged all non-Spartan contingents to leave in order to preserve most of the Greek force. It was said the Mantineans were the first to leave, and then the rest followed; many reluctantly. Only the few hundred Thespieans and Thebans stayed behind to fight alongside the Spartan; as did some eighty Mycenaean Knights – men who guarded their city's famed Lion Gate. Thus far the Greeks had been fighting from behind the wall. But as soon as most of his allies began to withdraw, Leonidas led those who remained in a mighty charge from the wall, of all places, against the Great King's own tent – where my Sakas stood guard.

It was an awesome sight as the Spartans came along with their remaining allies, crushing all in their path. Yet, in spite of its glory, it was also a sad sight. For it was clear that these outnumbered Greeks were coming to die. But even then, they made the Persians pay dearly. Two younger half-brothers of Xerxes were amongst the first to fall as the Spartans smashed through the Persian lines, like a hammer smashing down upon a vase. Once again, many Persians were pushed to their deaths over the cliffs on the edge of the Pass.

Even though Xerxes knew that his Anusiya were on their way to attack the Greeks from the rear and the Spartan collapse was only a matter of time, he still wanted Leonidas' head. The irony, however, was that it was Leonidas who came looking for Xerxes before his tent. But Xerxes was not there. He was busy preparing his troops for the final counter-assault. But when he saw the Spartans moving towards his tent, he rushed back to defend it himself. For all his faults, Xerxes can never be called a coward.

However, Xerxes' brother, Prince Mashista, who was nearby, asked me to come with him to stop his brother. The King, like his two half-brothers, would have easily been killed had he reached his tent.

Leaving my younger brother, Mauga, in charge of the Sakas outside the tent, I ran towards the King, a lone figure riding towards the Greeks. Mashista and I wrestled him away from the fray. In the end, he only relented after I told him that there was no glory in killing men who were already dead.

I rushed back to the mêlée outside the tent, only to see my brother, Mauga, die at the hands of the Spartan warrior leading the charge. Full of hatred and overwhelmed with a desire for vengeance, I began to slash my way towards the Spartan. In the grip of my emotions, I forgot that this man was the same man who had shouted *molon labe* to the Great King. So blinded was I with rage that I did not care who he was. All I knew was that this man had just killed my only brother and he had to die. In the heat of the battle he got separated from his men, who were pushed back under the axe blows of my Sakas.

The warrior kept fighting bravely, even though he had been cut off and was left all alone. His spear had snapped, so he had drawn his *Xiphos*. One by one, he killed all those who went for him. Soon enough, it was my turn. He had grown weary from fighting so many men, his movements becoming slower and more predictable. I easily avoided his thrusts and slashes. In frustration, he lunged at me with full force. I stepped sideways, avoiding his blow as he went past me. But as he did so, I plunged my sword into his exposed thigh, wounding him deeply. As he winced with pain and fell on his knee, I raised my sword with both hands high in the air and brought it down forcefully through the opening above his breastplate between his chest and throat, penetrating his lungs, and probably heart, wounding him mortally.

One of my men came over to me and said, 'Sire, you have just killed the Spartan King.' Another examined him and said, 'He is still alive, but barely.'

Just then a Persian officer on horseback galloped to me and said that the Great King had ordered my men to withdraw to make way for his Persian troops to finish the job. I also saw the Spartans regrouping and about to attack us to recover Leonidas' body.

I quickly asked my men to gather round so as to hide what I was about to do. I took off Leonidas' helmet and put in on the head of a dead Spartan lying beside him. I also took off Leonidas' armour so that no one would recognize him. I wrapped Leonidas' cloak and gave it to one of my men to hide in his satchel. I then ordered my men to carry my brother's body and Leonidas', covered with my cloak, away from the fighting.

I met Xerxes on the way and asked his permission to bury my dead. So flushed with success was he that he assented without giving me or my men another look. 'The time has come to make an end of this,' he said, with an air of confidence. He then ordered his Persian troops to recover the body of Leonidas. 'I want to see that insolent man's body in pieces,' he thundered. The Persians and the Spartans fought bitterly over what they thought was Leonidas' body. In the end, the Persian numbers prevailed. They seized the body and mutilated it beyond recognition. But it was not that of Leonidas.

We took his and my brother's body away from the Persian camp, behind a hill completely out of its view. I had always respected Leonidas, and had it not been for his killing my brother, I might not even have let him die. But such things happen in war. I decided to give them both funerals worthy of their station, although at the time Leonidas was not yet dead. He was delirious, and I don't think he could see clearly. So I knelt and put his head on my lap. I heard him groan. I did not want to alarm him, so I spoke in Attic, not Doric, Greek.

I asked him who he was and he answered, 'I am Leonidas son

of Anaxandridas, King of the Spartans.' Then he asked me, 'How goes the battle?'

When I told him that it was going badly for the Greeks, he asked, 'What of the Spartans?' I told him that they were still fighting but would not last very long. I assured him that they were about to die bravely – all of them.

On hearing my words, Leonidas moved about agitatedly, and tried to reach for his sword, but none was there. I told him that he had done all he could and could do no more. 'You must let it go now. You must make peace with yourself,' I said to him.

The King was in extreme pain. He sighed and gently touched my shoulder. After a long silence, he said: 'Stranger, go and tell my people ... Go tell the Spartans ... that here ... at the Hot Gates ... obedient to their laws ... we have fallen.'

I had my men place Leonidas' body on a pile of olive leaves and cover his body with his crimson cloak as is, I believe, the Spartan custom. Then I said a few words praising him in Doric Greek. However, I soon realized my men did not understand a word I had said. I wanted to tell them about Leonidas and the Spartans. So I reverted to the Saka language. I told my men that the King of Sparta was a noble leader of a great nation. Like us, the Spartans were famous warriors. Like us, they deserved respect. They were here fighting to defend their homeland against the Persians as we had done not long ago. I drew the parallels between our battle of the Iron Gates and the Spartans' last stand at the Hot Gates. Like our warriors before, Leonidas and his men had died for liberty. According to our custom, my Sakas sang a funeral hymn sung in praise of a fallen hero as they buried your King.

* * *

'He is right, Majesty,' Menander confirmed. 'I secretly followed him and witnessed the respect and dignity with which he buried

King Leonidas.'

'Would you please excuse us, Menander,' said Gorgo, her voice breaking a little.

As Menander left, she turned to Sherzada. 'I suppose I am not a very good Spartan wife. I am supposed to be happy when I am told that husband died fighting bravely in battle.'

She approached him and was about to say something when the cell door was forcefully thrown open. Euro and young Nicomedes barged in. Nicomedes' face belied incredulity and Euro's usually calm demeanour was panicked as he said, 'The traitors' bodies are being removed from the temple complex by a group of armed men.'

Without a word, Gorgo got up and hurried out of the door followed by her kinsmen.

Sherzada was left alone in the cell, contemplating what he should do. Then he rose and ran to his room to fetch his sword.

Chapter 27

Brazen Dawn

The Spartan Acropolis
Shortly afterwards

Sherzada arrived in open ground outside the Temple of Athena of the Brazen House. He was out of breath, having run as fast as he could to catch up with Gorgo and Euro. He found them standing in front of the temple, which looked even more sinister in the dark. Dawn was breaking and the twilight enabled them to assess the situation more clearly. The bodies of the five former Ephors had been removed from the poles they had hung from. A group of armed men, wearing crimson cloaks, their faces covered by dark masks, were wrapping one of the bodies in a shroud to carry it away.

'What do you think you are doing here?' Gorgo asked the men.

'Striking a blow for freedom,' responded the man closest to her.

'These are the bodies of traitors,' Gorgo said, as she moved closer to the figures in front of her. Sherzada and Euro stepped forward and flanked her on both sides, drawn swords protecting her body. But Gorgo gently pushed aside their blades and moved even closer to armed men.

'You are the traitor, daughter of Cleomenes,' said the man, 'like your father before you.'

'Damon, son of Eurysthenes,' she fumed. 'Is that you?'

The man stepped back in confusion and almost tripped over the body on the ground. 'You are the son of a traïtor, Damon,' she said. 'How dare you remove your father's body, without permission?'

One of Damon's companions stepped forward. 'We do not

need your permission. There is no law against sons giving their fathers a decent burial.'

'There is one against defying authority.'

'You have no authority here,' shouted the man. 'You have made a mockery of our laws. Now we cannot even defend ourselves against the Helots. And you … you prefer the company of bastards and barbarians, to those of your own kind. How can you call yourself our Queen?'

'You are a coward, Magnas, son of Antinuous, and always have been,' she struck back. 'You hide your face because you are not man enough to show it. Then again, you weren't man enough to show your face at any of the battles where real Spartans fought and died for our freedom. By what right do you call yourself a Spartan?'

'By what right can you?' Magnas retorted. 'We Spartans always say: "Not by caring for my fields but by caring for ourselves did we acquire those fields." And now you want us to return those spear-won fields to those we took them from. You are the traitor.'

Meanwhile, the other masked men were exchanging quizzical gestures. They seemed to be wondering how the Queen knew who they were without seeing their faces.

Euro stepped forward. It seemed he wanted to take a closer look at the men. 'Stay back, *Mothax*,' said one of the men with a squeaky voice, drawing his sword, 'or I'll run you through.'

'Oh, put that thing away, Cleandridas,' shouted Gorgo, 'before you hurt yourself.' She pointed to a deep scar on his thigh. 'Remember what happened the last time you tried to handle a weapon? The butt spike of the spear is meant for the ground, not your thigh. And besides it's rich calling my cousin a bastard when both of us know about your secret Helot sweetheart and that she is with child.'

'There is no truth to this!' Cleandridas protested, turning to his comrades.

A quarrel broke out among them. The tallest, standing at the back, shouted at the rest to be quiet. He addressed Gorgo. 'Behold this new dawn. This is when we begin to take back our dignity.'

The sun was rising behind the Temple of Athena, its golden ray reflecting off its columns. A mist was rising where the bodies lay. The masked men cheered.

'We Spartans are guardians of liberty,' another added. 'We are destined to rule all of Greece. Tegea, Argos and Athens have no choice. Either they submit or they will be destroyed.'

'You know nothing of liberty, Sthenelaidas, you idiot!' said Gorgo.

Behind him, Sherzada heard footsteps. Many footsteps. He turned to see it was Nicomedes, Pausanias and a detachment of the Knights led by Theras, their commander. They were running down towards the Temple.

Their arrival caused much consternation among the five men. Four of the men hurriedly gathered the body and ran away. The tallest man was the last to leave. 'Gorgo, Queen,' he said, 'as long as you prefer this Barbarian over Spartans, you are not safe in Sparta.'

He disappeared into the mist, like the four men before him and the body of the traitor Eurysthenes, father of Damon.

* * *

'How did you know who those men were?' asked Euro.

Gorgo was sitting at the table in her hearth room next to her cousin, Pausanias. Behind them stood Euro. Sherzada was sitting cross-legged on the floor opposite the Spartans. The morning sun was now clear above the horizon. It had all become so awkward since the conversation in the cell. But it was not just what he had confessed to which made her so uneasy. It was also what she had not said.

'We Spartan women spend a large part of our lives seeing men's faces hidden behind those bronze helmets,' replied Gorgo. 'We have become used to identifying you men in other ways; by the shape and size of your bodies, by your gait, by your voice, and by your various peculiarities. All these men revealed themselves to me in one way or another.

'Oh yes, I recognized all of them. Magnas stayed behind in Sparta during the Persian war citing some vague prophesy in support of this, the violation of which would be construed as blasphemy. Damon conveniently disappeared to our colony Taras in Italy, on the excuse that he had urgent family business to attend to – only to return now, after the Persians have left. Sthenelaidas, son of Alcemenes, was in Corcyra during that period on a similar pretext. Cleandridas opted for garrison duty in Messene to avoid being sent to front lines. That is where he met his young Helot concubine. All of these men stayed behind during the war while braver men fell on the battlefield. To me, they are all Tremblers, and ought to be treated as such.

'All except one, that is,' she continued, 'and that exception worries me. He was the tall one standing in the back. I am certain it was Pericleidas, veteran of Salamis. Why would a war hero join this bumbling crew of cowards?'

Euro and Pausanias looked at each other; neither could offer an explanation.

The night had been long and eventful. Sherzada could feel his eyes drooping with exhaustion. He did not know if he was wanted here, or even why he was here at all. Perhaps she had meant him to remain in his cell.

'They have not broken any law, technically speaking; taking down the bodies was not an offence, after all. But I do not want them to spoil my party for Themistocles,' Gorgo was saying.

Pausanias suggested sending them all to do garrison duty at the far-flung fort in a remote corner of Messene.

'But our problem is still Pericleidas,' countered Euro. 'He is close to Leotychidas and we cannot move against him without further complicating our relationship with the Eurypontidae.'

Gorgo nodded. 'Though we cannot touch Pericleidas, we can split up the rest. Do not send them all to Messene. Young Cleandridas, I am sure, can cool off on the island of Cythera, away from his Helot woman. Perhaps that will teach him to appreciate her even more.'

Euro smiled and got up to leave.

Pausanias also rose. At the door, he turned and said, 'Do not underestimate the threat these men pose. They oppose change and thrive on hatred.'

Gorgo nodded. 'They fear change more than fear itself. But we cannot let them win. Change is the only option if Sparta is to maintain its pre-eminence amongst the Greeks.'

'My Queen ...' began Sherzada, now the two of them were once again alone. 'About Thermopylae ...' he said, his voice croaking with emotion.

'Prince Sherzada,' she said quickly, 'I want to thank you for this morning. Coming down to the Temple to protect me, though as you saw yourself it was not necessary.

'I also want to thank you for Thermopylae,' she said quite calmly.

'Woman, why are you thanking me?' Sherzada scoffed. 'I killed your husband, the father of your child. If you ever lacked a reason for wanting me dead, I have just presented it.'

Gorgo got up and moved closer to Sherzada. 'I thank you for giving him the funeral he deserved. It is of great comfort to me that he was not mutilated but buried with great respect by warriors as brave as ours. And as for his death, I don't think he would have preferred it any other way, than at the hands of a noble warrior like yourself. I do not think he died a disappointed man.'

'Are you not listening to me?' he protested. 'I killed Leonidas!'

'You have an interesting death wish, my Prince,' said Gorgo.

'You might have your reasons, but must also suffer to live with the consequences of your actions, just like the rest of us.'

She walked over to him then, and said to him in a low tone, 'And besides, you did not murder my husband. You killed him in a fair fight. If you hadn't killed him, he most certainly would have killed you. He would not have hesitated a moment.'

She turned away so he almost could not hear her whisper: 'And anyway, Leonidas was not meant to return alive from Thermopylae.'

Chapter 28

Departure

Agiadae Compound
Sparta
A week later

The sun was setting as Sherzada returned to the Agiadae compound, after a stroll through the main streets of Sparta. He had seen enthusiastic preparations underway to welcome one of the great heroes of the Greek resistance against the Persians, Themistocles of Athens. Soldiers were practicing impressive drills and young girls were rehearsing their dance moves. The entire city was alive with activity. Sherzada remembered how this man, Themistocles, had risen from humble beginnings to become a redoubtable leader of the Athenian Democracy and the genius behind the Greek naval victories over the Persians. All of Sparta was preparing to receive their famous guest the following day.

But it was Gorgo and not Themistocles who had been on his mind all this time. What did she mean by saying that Leonidas was 'not meant to return alive from Thermopylae'? On more than one occasion Sherzada had tried to draw Gorgo back to the question of Thermopylae, but the Queen simply changed the subject each time.

Two days earlier, Gorgo had introduced her son Pleistarchus and asked Sherzada to share his experiences with the young King, 'so that he would learn that there is a whole world outside Sparta.' The meeting had been awkward for Sherzada, but not, it seemed, for the boy. 'Perhaps he sees in you something of what I have already seen,' Gorgo later explained.

But despite spending an ever-increasing amount of time with the Queen, Sherzada was beginning to feel restless. He was no longer a prisoner, and yet he had remained in Sparta for some time now. And he could not forget what she knew, nor the insinuation that his presence in Sparta was a threat to her.

Sherzada had lately struck another friendship, an unusual one, with Menander. The Helot said he had changed his view about Sherzada even though he had killed his beloved King. 'If the Queen trusts you, Highness, so can I.' But Sherzada felt there was more to it than that. Though obsequious in front of most Spartans, Menander was allowed by Sherzada to freely speak his mind, giving him a kind of freedom he had not been used to. So he visited Sherzada frequently to speak to him of matters he could not discuss with others, even fellow Helots.

Returning from his walk that day, Sherzada found Menander waiting at his porch. Sitting on the ground, the Helot gave him a grim look. It was the same look Sherzada had seen in the eyes of the Messenian Helots who had charged his positions at Thermopylae.

'Helots are meant to be seen, not heard. And so I hear a lot of things,' began Menander.

Sherzada invited him into his room and sat down on the floor cross-legged, motioning Menander to do the same.

With a little reticence, Menander sat down next to Sherzada. 'There are those in Sparta who doubt Her Majesty,' he said. 'They say she has made too many concessions to us Helots – concessions that are dangerous for Sparta. These people also say that Her Majesty has been seduced by you, Highness, and your outlandish ideas. That you possess an evil influence over her.

'But these are the very people who took Persian gold. Those who once tried to betray Sparta now hide behind the mask of patriotism. They promise a new dawn but all they will do is pull Sparta into the depths of darkness.'

Menander got up and looked down at Sherzada. 'Tell me, Highness, why does the Queen refuse to take a husband?'

It was true that Gorgo was a woman under pressure –

pressure to remarry. Had she been just another young widow, a Spartan warrior would either propose to her, or simply carry her off. But she was a Queen and not an ordinary one at that. Out of respect for her father and her late husband, no Spartan warrior dared propose to her. Carrying her off was simply out of the question. And while Spartans were reluctant to approach Gorgo with a marriage suit, it did not stop other Greeks.

Sherzada had witnessed how Gorgo treated her suitors. A Cretan prince, a famous warrior and a champion wrestler, was reduced to tears when Gorgo told him his flirting was effeminate. She went on to compare this, the most masculine of men, with the most vulnerable of women. The man left in a state of shock.

Menander left soon afterwards, and Sherzada spent the night thinking over what the Helot had said to him. By early morning, he had made up his mind.

Chapter 29

Heads Of The Hydra

Velathri (Volterrae)
Tuscany, Northern Italy
Early summer, 478 BC

Perched high above the most charming Tuscan countryside, Sherzada saw neatly marked fields of olives and vines in a perfect patchwork covering the landscape. Directly below him was a valley centred around a gentle hill, Cyprus trees dotting its periphery. Squinting into the distance, he could see rolling hills bordered by lush trees. He felt cradled in beauty and serenity. Sherzada had spent the past months travelling through this truly bewildering land. And certainly, he had not met a stranger people. The Etruscans, or rather the *Ra'senna,* as they called themselves, were an enigmatic lot. While Sherzada found strong similarities between most Italian languages, especially Latin, with that spoken by the Persians, the Indians and his own people, he could not link the Etruscan language to any other linguistic group that he knew. There were a few odd Etruscan words in common with Sanskrit and the Saka dialect – but nothing else. And yet, the Etruscans claimed to hail from Asia. And interestingly, the name *Ra'senna* reminded him of the Persian name for his own homeland, *Paruparaseanna.*

He found the religion of the Etruscan equally bizarre. Although it claimed to have been a revealed religion, it bore little resemblance to revealed religions elsewhere. His impression was that the Etruscan religion may have originally been a monotheistic one, but had been changed over the course of time. The religion now placed more emphasis on auguries and prophecies than a moral code. And indeed the Etruscans were criticized by their neighbours, sometimes unjustly, for having no morals or ethics whatsoever.

And yet the Etruscans were an enterprising and ingenious people, who had devised fascinating ways of transporting water and oil across mountainous terrain using structures called aqueducts and had developed irrigation systems that could drain marshes and at the same time make arid soil fertile. Etruscan influence extended all over northern Italy. But they were ever casting covetous glances at central Italy, particularly the lush plains of Campania in the south, and even beyond the high mountain ranges in the north called the Alps. They sought to strengthen their control over Sardinia and their sea-raiders plundered the lands on the northern end of the Mediterranean Sea. Their greed for gold, slaves and lands was boundless.

The Etruscans had all the makings of a great nation, and yet their land, once a proud confederation of twelve cities, was no more. Now even though more Etruscan city-states had emerged, the land itself was descending into chaos. Tuscany was hard at war with its neighbours and even more fiercely with itself. Not so long ago, their cities had been run in a manner which was similar to Greek democracies; now each city was ruled by a warlord or tyrant. Although the city-state of Velathri, by far the most remarkable of them, existed in relative peace and harmony, mutual jealousies and rivalries among the Etruscans continued to weaken the Ra'senna as a nation.

Velathri was ruled by an elderly woman, the wisest of all Etruscan rulers. Long ago, she had tried to keep the Ra'senna united as a nation; now she was struggling to protect Velathri against the threats from Etruscan tyrants who were ever eager to expand their territory and power. Lady Velia, the Zilath, or ruler, of Velathri had been kind to Sherzada, hosting him during his stay. But he knew it was only a matter of time until the strife that was spreading across Tuscany would engulf beautiful Velathri as well.

Velathri's lucrative northern trading post, Florentia, across the Arno bridge, had already fallen to the ambitious ruler of an emerging city-state of Viesul. Armies of other warlords were inching ever closer, reducing Velathri's once extensive domains by fire and sword. As Sherzada sat on the ramparts of Velathri, reflecting on this sad state of affairs, a slave came with a message forwarded by the Spartan ambassador Timaeus, Gorgo's trusted envoy in Taras.

Sherzada had been writing to Gorgo each month, and this was the first time he had received any correspondence in return. But his forehead frowned in disappointment as he began to read the letter. It was not from Gorgo.

Prince Sherzada from Euro, Greetings

Pausanias has just returned from his naval expedition which took him all the way to Cyprus. Of course, if you ask him what happened, he will give you a glorious account of how he chased what was left of the Persian fleet all the way to the eastern edges of the Mediterranean Sea and gave the Barbarians a bloody nose. What a piece of horse manure! It was our side that got beaten up pretty badly. While he did make it all the way to Cyprus, he did not quite succeed in liberating it. And on his way back his fleet was ambushed and almost destroyed by the second Persian naval squadron – the one you had spoken about. Like the thunderbolt he is, Admiral Barqa appeared out of nowhere and inflicted severe damage on our fleet. It would have been completely destroyed, had it not been for an unexpected thunderstorm which enabled our ships to disengage and escape.

I wish I could say that everything is going well for the Greeks, but it is not. Now that the Persians have left our old rivalries are coming back – between Thebes and Athens, Doris and Plataea, between Chalcis and Eretria, Thessaly and Phocis, the list goes on and on. Greece, once again, is a land divided.

And so is Sparta. There are certainly people who would support Gorgo in bringing change, though without compromising on our principles. Others, however, want to return to the closed society of more than three generations ago.

You must have heard the legend of the Hydra? It is one of those stories we Greeks love to tell. The Hydra is a monster with several heads. Every time you cut off one of the heads, another two will grow in its place. The problems of Greece are like a Hydra. The moment you solve one, two more immediately present themselves. There is no end to it.

Enough of our politics. I am sure you want to hear about other things. So I should mention the real reason I wrote this letter to you. Gorgo tries not to show it, but she eagerly awaits your missives. She rushes into the privacy of her bedroom and does not come out until she has read each new arrival many times over. But she refuses to write back, saying what if her writing were intercepted by our enemies – an inconvenience we both know she could avoid.

In the last letter that you sent us, you included a sketch on a piece of parchment of an exceptionally beautiful young woman, who you called the Zilath of Velathri. Gorgo flew into a jealous rage. It was towards the end of your letter that you had clarified that this sketch had been made over half a century earlier, and this lady, your current hostess – the ruler of Velathri – as you explained, was in her dotage and in poor health.

Putting aside the letter, Sherzada did not know how to react. A part of him wanted to rush back to Sparta, but he knew that he had to await Gorgo's word. He could not go back until she called him.

Looking over the troubled land before him, he did not know what he would do in the meantime.

Chapter 30

The Walls Of Athens

Royal Compound of the Agiadae
Sparta
Summer, 478 BC

'Where is Prince Euryanax?' Gorgo asked Theras, the Captain of the Knights.

Theras pointed towards the garden below.

Noticing that he had a black eye, Gorgo asked him what had happened. When Theras refused to discuss it, she smiled. 'Oh, you had a disagreement with Princess Lampito again.'

The young long-haired Captain sheepishly nodded. 'She refused our offer to escort her to her father, King Leotychidas' country estate. We then paid the price of insisting – all six of us. But it was only for her protection. We were just doing our duty.'

'When it comes to Lampito, it is not her protection I am ever concerned about,' Gorgo said, barely holding back her laughter, 'but yours. Don't worry, Theras, your secret is safe with me.'

Theras managed to pull a slight smile onto his otherwise serious face.

Gorgo lifted her gown and raced down to find Euro. She found him sitting on her favourite bench writing on a parchment. 'What are you doing?'

'Writing back to our Barbarian friend,' he replied. 'He has been writing letters to you consistently and you have not answered a single one. So whenever I have a chance, which is not very often, I reply on your behalf. Sitting on this bench of yours gives me great inspiration,' he chuckled.

'Put that letter away,' chided Gorgo. 'We have more pressing matters at hand.'

They looked across the garden and saw Pausanias

approaching, accompanied by the five Ephors and Sparta's leading generals. They were all of a similar appearance, with long flowing hair, long beards, and crimson cloaks. Only Pausanias, with his shorter hair and moustached beard, looked a little out of place. Gorgo noted that King Leotychidas had not come. 'Shall we wait for him?' she asked.

Then Theras came down and made an uncomfortable gesture, pointing to a newcomer who had entered the garden. It was the long-haired Lampito. She wore a crimson Spartan cloak, with a tunic made from coarse material underneath, slit up to the thighs in typical Spartan fashion. Lampito gave the suffering Theras a mischievous, mocking look. However, as she came up to Gorgo, she addressed her in a serious tone. 'If the Agiadae can be represented here by a woman, so can the Eurypontidae. My father has sent me here on his behalf.'

Gorgo welcomed the girl with a warm smile and a gentle hug.

It was not long afterwards that a lone man strolled into the garden. He was dressed in a white robe, edged with purple, made of the finest linen. His hair was a bit dishevelled, and his beard a little scruffy. A heavy-set man with a prominent bull neck, his forehead was large, his nose small and his lips thin. His demeanour was that of a thug, were it not for his winning smile that had not very long ago made him so popular back in his home city. Almost a year ago this man had been welcomed in Sparta like a hero, but the Spartan eyes that now beheld him did so with suspicion.

'Welcome, former Archon Themistocles,' said Gorgo. 'How nice of you to visit Sparta again.'

'Majesty,' said Themistocles, bowing to Gorgo and presenting her with the most charming of his smiles. 'I am but a mere citizen of Athens, sent by our Assembly and Council to consult with our Spartan allies – seeing that I am, at least amongst my countrymen, the most honoured in Sparta. My task is to clear up a little misunderstanding.'

'Misunderstanding?' retorted Pausanias. 'You have repaired the walls of Athens against our express instructions and you are building additional fortifications. How can you dismiss this gross violation of trust as a 'little misunderstanding'?'

'Spartans,' replied Themistocles in a testy voice, 'were our friends and allies, Regent, the last time I checked; not our masters. You have the right to make requests, but not to hand down instructions. You did indeed ask us not rebuild our walls and I assure you we have not. As you know, Athens was twice burnt down by the Persians during their recent invasion. There is a lot of reconstruction work going on in the city, some of which can easily be confused with rebuilding our walls. But nothing of the sort is happening.'

'He is lying,' whispered Pausanias into Gorgo's ear.

Lampito nodded. 'Remember what they say about the Athenians,' she said under her breath. 'After shaking hands with them, be sure to count your fingers.'

Themistocles smiled again. 'I know there are many of you who don't believe me. I have been here several days now, trying to convince both your Gerousia and your War Council that the rumours are untrue. So I have asked to be joined by another colleague, whose words might carry more weight in Sparta than mine. Perhaps you would listen to him.'

'I trust that pompous lout Cimon even less than yourself, Themistocles,' replied Pausanias.

'Oh … It is not Cimon I speak of,' said Themistocles, using his silver tongue. 'And by the way, Regent, we do have something in common, after all. I share your sentiments about Miltiades' haughty son. However, the man I speak of has already arrived in Sparta. He will join us here momentarily.'

The Spartans began to speculate among themselves.

Please let it not be Aristeides. Aristeides hates Themistocles. Let him not be his accomplice in this farce, said Gorgo to herself.

And sure enough, Aristeides arrived a few minutes later and

was warmly welcomed by everyone. No Athenian was more loved in Sparta than he. Gorgo had not seen him in years, and while the Athenian had aged considerably, he had lost none of his elegance and charm. He greeted each Spartan with great affection, embracing everyone, shaking every hand and asking after each man's health. He then spent a considerably long time with Lampito, asking kindly about her parents, recalling fond memories of the last time he had seen her when she was but a small child. The Princess appeared genuinely enchanted. And then he walked over to Gorgo and hailed her, '*Megisto-Anassa*, the Greatest of Queens.' Then he went down on his knees before her and kissed both her hands, calling her, 'Our saviour.'

Gorgo wondered whether the man humbling himself before her was one they called the Just, or the Fox.

Finally, Aristeides got up and addressed the gathering. He began by describing his fondness for Sparta and its proud martial traditions. He extolled Spartan leadership in the war against Persia, which he said could not have been won if Sparta had not led the Greeks. He spoke of Spartan courage at Thermopylae, Salamis and Plataea, giving individual examples in each case. He spoke of an alliance between Sparta and Athens that had saved Greece; an alliance that had survived many storms since it was first formed by King Cleomenes.

Then he said, 'I had come here to tell you that the walls being erected are part of our reconstruction work for buildings destroyed by the Persians on the edge of our city. And that they would be pulled down as soon as the renovation work was completed. That is no doubt what Themistocles has already told you.'

Some of the Spartans nodded.

'But that is a lie,' Aristeides admitted. 'You are my friends,' he continued. 'I cannot lie to you. Athens has indeed constructed its walls. But our army is not as strong as yours. And Athens is vulnerable to attacks by land as well as by sea. Had Athens not had its walls, the Persians would have surely sacked Athens twelve years ago instead of landing at Marathon. We need the walls to protect ourselves and our fleet in case the Persians return. It is merely a measure for our own protection. However, we will fight alongside you wherever you wish us to. We are your allies, after all. Whenever you need us, we will come to your aid, as you have always come to ours. This is a solemn pledge I make on behalf of the Democratic Assembly and Council of Athens. We need the walls but we also need Sparta. Let us not choose between the two.'

The Spartans turned to Gorgo, expecting her to come up with a challenge. She looked around, and then she nodded. 'Our alliance is far too important for a matter of masonry to get in the way. We would require certain assurances from Athens, of course. But let us not sour our relations at a time when our two great cities can unite all of Greece behind us.'

Later that evening, Gorgo sought out Aristeides. The Queen found him alone in the courtyard of the city's official guesthouse. Fittingly, it had been designed by an Athenian architect. The building made extensive use of marble and contained several comfortable quarters. This was the closest thing Sparta had to a palace. But only foreign dignitaries stayed here. This was a preferred alternative for them, sparing the discomfort of hard Spartan living. Greeting him, she asked, 'Why did you build your walls without telling us? And why are you doing this for Themistocles? I know this is his idea; but you hate him.'

'Despise Themistocles,' replied Aristeides, 'I most certainly do. However, while Your Majesty has always hastened to put Greece's interests before Sparta's, we Athenians always put Athens' interests before anyone else's.'

'But surely the interests of Athens lie in a united Greece?'

'Majesty,' said Aristeides. 'Times are changing. Each city must now look after its own interests. But this does not mean we cannot continue as partners.'

Gorgo sighed. 'Having all Greek cities tear down their walls was my idea. I issued the instruction at the height of the Persian invasion, when it made more sense for all of us to fight the Persians together at one place rather than allow them to besiege us and take each city separately. But I am no longer in favour of these instructions. However, though your walls do not directly threaten us, they will do so indirectly. If Athens rebuilds its walls, then Megara will do the same. Corinth will not be left behind, nor Mycenae, nor Sicyon. And then nothing will stop our arch-enemy Argos from refortifying and rearming itself. Thus by increasing the security of Athens, you are undermining ours.'

'Forgive me, Queen Gorgo,' responded Aristeides, 'but that is the least of our problems. There are increasing numbers of Spartans who view all outsiders with suspicion – even fellow Greeks. They think they are superior to all other Greeks and that is not helping Sparta's relations with other Greek states, not least Athens. It was not long ago that all of us together fought more or less on the same side. But listening to people here in Sparta, sometimes I think it is almost as if the Persian invasion had never happened. At least then we had something noble to fight for.'

'How wistful your words, *Alopex*,' said Gorgo, calling him by his nickname – the Fox. 'You seem to suggest that the Persian invasion was the best thing that ever happened to Greece.'

'Well, it kept us together for a while, rather than at each other's throats. And I believe you also found someone because of that very invasion. Where is he these days?'

'Relaxing on some Italian hillside, I imagine. I forgot to thank you for saving Sherzada's life and sending him to me. You have always been a good judge of character.'

Gorgo bade farewell to Aristeides and returned to her compound. Then she went looking for Euro and found him in his lodgings, where she uttered a request that was not without pain to her. Complying, Euro wrote down her words: *My Prince, I must ask you to remain away a little longer. You will hear from me before long. In the meantime, I trust that you have found in Italy the peace you have been longing for.*

Chapter 31

Rome

The Fields of Fidenae
Roman–Etruscan border
Italy
Summer, 477 BC

Sherzada sat by the side of the hill with his sword arm covered up to his elbow in blood, surveying the carnage before him. He had left Greece to escape conflict, only to find a worse one in Italy. All around him were bodies of men strewn as far as the eye could see – a testament to the cruelty of man against man.

He was still not sure how he ended up fighting in this war, and against the Etruscans too – the very people he had originally come here to live among.

Who would have thought that the mighty Etruscans would meet their match in a relatively unknown city-state called Rome? Now the tide would begin to turn decisively in Rome's favour. Rome would no longer be a bounded, embattled and threatened little republic. This victory could well mark the beginning of Rome's martial greatness. Yet the truth was that this great victory was in reality a defeat, so narrowly averted.

The Etruscans had been an enigma to him; the Romans even more so. The strangest thing about Rome was that it was an artificial state. The majority of its population was not native. In addition to the Latins who claimed to be its founders, the people of Rome originated from all over Italy, some even from Greece. Rome was a state created out of nothing – supposedly by two brothers, one of whom killed the other – not a good omen as founding myths go, felt Sherzada. And yet the idea of a Roman nation was not a myth at all. Its citizens were willing to make sacrifices to defend and preserve it. It was not a city, nor a state;

it was a country – what the Romans call *Patria*. And for the Romans, the notion of freedom – *Libertas* – was as sacred as *Eleutheria* was to the Greeks.

Yet the Romans had borrowed much from the Greeks. Like the Athenians, they divided themselves into tribes for political and military purposes, and their officials were also elected. But in some other aspects, the Romans were more similar to the Spartans. Like the Spartans, they had two rulers, called Consuls. But they were not kings. In fact, power was divided among the Consuls so that they neither of them could be kings. The Romans had expelled their kings and no longer trusted the concentration of power in a single individual. Thus the Consuls were elected to rule for a year only. Like the Spartans, the Romans took pride in calling themselves true warriors. But they also took pride in other professions like farming, craftsmanship, trade and even the law. Being warriors, though, was what truly defined Romans – just like the Spartans. And also like the Spartans, the Romans tended to expose their weak babies to the elements after birth. Only the strongest children could survive to be a defender of Rome – yet another example of outright savagery, thought Sherzada.

However, what really differentiated the Romans from the Spartans was pragmatism. Romans were nothing if not practical. They liked new ideas. The fact that their population comprised of so many communities invited innovation. The Romans were always likely to try out new things. The Romans' tendency to adapt to changing circumstances had been one of the causes of their success thus far.

The other was their army. The area under Rome's control was not very large, and it was surrounded by hostile expansionist powers. Romans realized very early on that relying on a small standing army would be disastrous, especially if they had to fight on multiple fronts. So they decided to expand the pool from which soldiers could be recruited, extending it to the poorest citizens. In return for serving in the army the poorer classes –

called the Plebs – were given rights and prospects for economic, though not social, advancement. These even included the right to vote, although not on par with the upper classes. The elections had always been skewed in favour of the latter. Still, it meant that even the poorest of the Romans had some sort of say in the government, as well as access to wealth. This also gave them an incentive to protect Rome – even to fight and die for it. They had a stake in the state's survival just as the rich did.

The Romans extended the same formula beyond their borders. When they fought and defeated neighbouring communities, rather than destroying or enslaving them, they made them their partners. In return for certain privileges, Rome's new allies fought to defend Rome and themselves against common enemies – which more often than not meant Rome's enemies.

Sherzada knew that the Romans had the best trained army in all of Italy; though not always the best led. Fond of military innovation, they were constantly changing their style of warfare. If one technique did not work, they would try another. Still, the Romans might lose more battles than they would win, and yet somehow they would invariably end up winning the war. Defeat was a concept alien to the Roman mind. If they lost one battle, they prepared to fight another and they continued to raise more and more armies and fight more and more battles until they finally won, even if it took years, or even decades, to do it. Sherzada had not met a more stubborn and determined people than the Romans, except perhaps the Spartans.

However, the Roman system was not without flaws. The poorer citizens were not completely satisfied with the rights they had been given. They constantly demanded more. At the same time, the ruling class was jealous of its powers and privileges and reluctant to share more of them with the poor. The Roman classes spent as much time fighting each other in the assemblies and the courts as they did fighting their external enemies on the battlefield. And there were occasions when one type of conflict overspilt into the arena of the other. It was not unheard of for the Plebs to refuse to fight during a military campaign until their demands were met. And likewise, there were persistent cases of Roman Patricians who preferred to defect to the enemy rather than compromise on sharing power with their own Plebs.

Not long before Sherzada arrived, a Patrician called Gaius Marcius Coriolanus, a brilliant military commander, defected to one of Rome's enemies, the Volsci, rather than give in to the democratic demands of the Plebs. In his new identity as a Volscian commander, Coriolanus did great damage to Rome. It was only the pleas of his wife and mother that made him stop his onslaught against his former homeland. The Volscians later killed him for what they saw as his betrayal.

The Romans indeed had the makings of a great nation, but only if they could solve their internal problems first. If they could not, no matter how many wars they won, no matter how innovative they were, they would never become what they aspired to be. Instead, the Roman state would become a prize for any ambitious general who could manipulate its politics and seize it by force. And then Rome would become just another ruthless empire seeking to enslave others. For while the Romans were good at absorbing great ideas, they are equally good at adopting the worst. This was Sherzada's biggest concern about Rome's future.

Sherzada had not come to Italy to take sides, let alone to fight. He had come here to observe and study. In spite of the beauty of Tuscany and the mysterious culture of the Etruscans, he was disappointed with them and their mercurial warlords; their cruelty, and their avarice. The Etruscans, like the Romans, could have aspired to greatness, but the only quality their leaders really worshipped was power.

In Rome, Sherzada was warmly welcomed by Patrician and Plebeian alike. They admired the Greeks and the fact that he had spent some time in Sparta impressed them even more. He did not tell them about his time with the Persians; their love of everything Greek easily translated itself into scorn for anything Persian. But Rome and its openness to foreign ideas fascinated him. After all, most Romans themselves had alien roots. It was a refreshing change from the close-mindedness of the Etruscans, as well as the Spartans.

Still, Sherzada missed Gorgo. He had left Velathri just before it fell to the armies of neighbouring warlords, having escorted his aging hostess and what was left of her family to safety, just as winter was setting in. At the time, he wanted to return to Sparta, but it was around then he finally received the message. It was the first time he had actually received one from her. But it was not what he expected.

So Sherzada went to Rome. And every week or so, he would sit by the banks of Rome's Tiber river and write a letter to Gorgo. He used the trusted Ambassador, Timaeus in Taras, to pass these letters on, and Sherzada always got confirmation from Sparta that his letters were delivered.

One pleasant spring evening, Sherzada was invited to dine with the leaders of the Fabian clan and other Roman aristocrats at their farmland estates at Cremera, a little distance north of Rome close to the Etruscan border. It was while they were dining that night, that a large band of Etruscan raiders from the nearby town of Veii decided to attack Cremera. Their assault was ferocious. They left no human or animal alive in their path. Being a guest of the Romans, Sherzada knew he would not have been spared. However, Sherzada had no intention of fighting until he saw the Etruscans attack women and children. It was then that he took out Rán's long-sword and went to work. He fought off the Etruscans while the Roman women escaped with their children. Soon, the Fabii men, including his host Marcus Fabius Vibulanus, came to his aid. The Etruscans were driven out after a fierce fight. One of the guests, a Patrician called Lucius Quinctius, nicknamed *Cincinnatus* or 'curly', told Sherzada that by drawing his sword, he had chosen Rome over the Etruscans.

Sherzada later found out that Cincinnatus' own family had made the very same choice not very long ago. The uncomfortable truth about the Roman aristocracy was that nearly all of them had some form of ties with the Etruscans; indeed, many of them were of Etruscan blood, including both Cincinnatus and Fabius.

Still, Sherzada tried to remain impartial. He told a group of Senators the following day, when he returned to Rome, that he wanted to help end the dispute with the Etruscans. During the attack on the estates at Cremera, the Veii raiders had carried off some men and women to be sold as slaves. Sherzada offered to go and ransom them and to use his visit to mediate peace between the Romans and the Etruscans.

Though his Roman friends thought it was an exercise in futility, Sherzada remained adamant. So he got the Senate's permission to negotiate the release of the hostages on behalf of Rome. He immediately set off for Veii and sought an audience with Aranth Telumnas, the self-styled King of Veii. Sherzada had met him earlier in his travels and thought he might be able to reason with him.

On arriving at Telumnas' palace in Veii, Sherzada found him at court playing dice with some companions. Telumnas asked him what he wanted.

'*Laukhme mi*,' said Sherzada, greeting the King in the Etruscan tongue, 'I have come to ask for the freedom of the people whom your men recently captured at Cremera.'

Telumnas listened as Sherzada made an impassioned speech, pleading with him to release them because they were only civilians. And if he had any grievances with the Romans, Sherzada could try to help him resolve them.

Telumnas looked at him and smiled. 'So you want to deprive us of our hard-won slaves?'

'I just want you to release them, my King,' he said, 'as a gesture of goodwill to Rome.'

'Is Rome in need of goodwill?' he asked as he ordered the prisoners to be brought up from the dungeons. There were at least forty of them – their clothing tattered, their skin betraying marks of beatings and whippings. Sherzada was greatly moved by their plight.

When the prisoners were assembled before him, Telumnas turned to Sherzada and said, 'I gave you leave to have your say, now it is for the gods to have theirs.' He rolled the dice and smiled at its outcome. Then he raised his fist in the air and shouted, 'The gods have spoken!' He inverted his clenched fist and brought it down with his thumb sticking out, pointing to the ground.

In a single movement, the Etruscan guards slit the throats of their prisoners. Sherzada watched in horror as dozens of men and women fell lifeless to the ground and their blood flooded across the shiny marble floor. Sherzada shuddered at the horrible sight.

'Scythian, go tell the Romans, I do not want their gold; I want their blood.'

A couple of months later, Telumnas managed to rouse most of the other Etruscan cities against Rome. A large army began to gather outside Veii. Rather than wait for them to attack Rome, the Romans decided to meet them head on, at the border town of Fidenae.

Sherzada had just been given his Roman citizenship, even though he had made it clear to the Senate that his stay in Rome was only temporary. It was difficult for him to refuse to serve in their army, especially when the city was threatened by an enemy like Telumnas. Sherzada was elected a military tribune and he accompanied Marcus Fabius, now a Consul, to confront the Etruscans. But the circumstances were not the most auspicious. That entire month had seen great social conflict in Rome. The Plebs had been agitating for their rights even more vociferously than usual, and the Patricians resisting their demands with equal determination. So when the news of the Etruscan war preparations reached Rome, the Patricians were certain that the Plebs would use this crisis to extract more concessions from them.

Two Roman legions, the Third and the Fourth – each four thousand strong – marched out of Rome. The Third Legion was nicknamed the *Sublician* after the bridge in Rome where a generation before, a handful of its soldiers under the command of a legendary officer, Horatius, tried to check the advance of forces of the invading Etruscan warlord, Laris Pu-ra'senna. The Fourth Legion was called the *Caelian* after one of Rome's seven hills. Ironically, this was where Etruscan settlers had made their home. Now the descendants of these immigrants were marching out to defend Rome against the compatriots of their fathers.

On the way, the Romans were joined, near Cremera, by two *Alae* – or brigades – of allied Latin infantry – each roughly the same size as a Roman legion. The Romans always demanded that their allies sent an equivalent force of troops whenever they went to war and the Latins invariably complied. But what Sherzada had not been expecting was the squadron of Lucanian cavalry which also arrived at Cremera. Lucanians were by far the best cavalrymen in all Italy, but they were very far from their homelands in the south. He wondered what business they had this far north. Marcus Fabius, Sherzada soon learnt, had hired them as mercenaries. A large force of retainers from Cremera loyal only to the Fabian clan – effectively, their private militia – also appeared. Many of them were relatives of those killed by Telumnas in cold blood. They were spoiling for revenge. Still, he did not know the significance of these new arrivals until they reached the battlefield at Fidenae.

That night the senior centurion of the Third Legion, a Plebeian by the name of Publius Decius, came to see Marcus Fabius in his tent with a complaint. Sherzada was there, along with some of the other officers – Patricians all – to plan the battle ahead. Decius was a thin little man with facial features not unlike those of a rodent; and that, together with his unusually squeaky voice, earned him the nickname *Mus* or Mouse. But Mus was respected among the rank and file to be a courageous man and competent leader. The complaint that Mus brought with him was that the legionaries had been issued with defective spears.

As part of Rome's obsession with innovation, a new type of spear had been experimented with. It was supposed to have a powerful sharp iron head and an elongated metal neck to ensure deeper penetration. The Etruscans were famous for their shield wall; a formation very similar to the Greek phalanx which was practically impossible to breach or dislodge. The spear had been designed to pierce right through their shields, rendering them useless. If there were no shields, there could not be a shield wall; so ran the logic.

What seemed like a very good idea did not quite work in practice. Publius Decius Mus said that though the spearhead was strong enough to pierce the shield, the long neck could not aid any further penetration as it tended to bend under pressure. To prove his point, Mus asked Sherzada to hold up a shield while he tried to punch one of the defective spears through it.

For a small man he had considerable strength and thrust the spear into the shield Sherzada was holding. He was right. While the spearhead lodged itself firmly into the shield, the neck of the spear bent, making further penetration impossible.

Leaving Sherzada holding a shield with an awkward spear hanging down from it, Mus turned to the Consul, Marcus Fabius, and said, 'Sir, with respect, the men cannot be expected to face the enemy with a weapon like this. If you want them to fight tomorrow, you will have to give them something better.'

Mus did not wait for an answer. He saluted Marcus and smartly turning about face, marched out of the tent. While he struggled to remove the bent spear from the shield, Sherzada overheard some of the officers whispering to each other.

'See, I told you. The Plebeians will come up with any excuse not to fight,' said one officer.

'All the soldiers have been issued with swords. If the spears don't work they can always use those,' said another.

'I bet, if we ask them to use their swords, they will tell us that they won't work either. The Plebeians have no intention of fighting the enemy tomorrow, unless we give in to their demands and those of their demagogues back in Rome.'

Even though Sherzada tried to make the point that Mus was right about the spear being defective, it seemed that the Patricians had made up their minds.

In the morning, as the sun rose, the Roman legionaries formed up on the parade ground in the stockade, awaiting orders for battle. Instead, Marcus Fabius ordered them to lay down their swords, shields and spears. He said that new equipment would soon be issued to the soldiers. They did as they were told and the equipment was collected by the officers and taken outside.

Once outside the stockade, Fabius had the gates of the stockade barred from the outside, thus imprisoning the entire – now disarmed – rank and file of the two Roman legions, comprising entirely of the Plebeian class. From behind the gate, the soldiers shouted out their entreaties. They pleaded that they wanted nothing more than to fight for Rome. They said while they had concerns about the spears, it did not mean that they did not want to fight the Etruscans. They even swore by their gods that they would fight until victory or death. Publius Decius Mus in particular vowed to sacrifice his life, if he were given a chance to win the day.

Finally, a young military tribune from the Fourth Legion, Aulus Antonius, stepped forward and demanded that the Fourth Legion be released. He said the *Caelians* had fought loyally for Rome and with distinction in every battle. He vouched for their discipline and courage. But Marcus Fabius Vibullanus remained unmoved. Throwing down his weapons, Antonius insisted that he too be incarcerated with his men.

'You are a coward just like the rest of them,' said Marcus. 'I will deal with you later.'

As Aulus Antonius was taken away to the stockade, he fixed his gaze on Sherzada. It was a reproachful look, demanding that he do something. Sherzada had befriended Antonius during the march and knew he was a man of principle. And his look made Sherzada feel guilty. His act was neither that of cowardice or treachery; it was one of courage, equal to any other on the field of battle.

Marcus Fabius, however, did not see it that way. Like the other Patrician officers he was convinced that the Plebs were bent on political agitation; to cause trouble, as they had done in every previous campaign. 'Better to lock them up right now than risk having to deal with them in front of the enemy,' Marcus said.

Thus a large part of the Roman army was incarcerated by their fellow Romans and their own allies as the enemy looked on.

Had I been on the Etruscan side, thought Sherzada, *nothing would have been so exhilarating and assuring of victory than such a sight.* In any case, the Etruscans already outnumbered the Roman-led force by three to one.

So when the battle began, the Etruscans had no problem dislodging the Roman-led army, or at least the part of it not imprisoned, from the steep hill on which it was deployed. Marcus Fabius did not see this as anything more than a temporary setback and immediately launched an attack to retake the hill. In spite of the fierce attack, the Romans and their allies were repulsed with heavy casualties. The Etruscan shield wall remained undented. Among those who fell was Marcus' brother Quintus; the other serving Consul Gnaeus Manlius; as well as Gavius Hostilius, commander of the Roman cavalry. Marcus Fabius told Sherzada to take the latter's place. And, yet again, Marcus ordered his men to take back the hill. But his Lucanian and Latin allies had had enough. They said that charging up a hill to face an enemy several times their number was suicide.

They simply refused to attack.

It was at that point Sherzada asked Marcus to allow the Plebs to fight.

'Are you out of your mind?' he said.

'You have no choice, Marcus,' said Sherzada, 'and by the way, I think that defective spear might well be the key to our victory.'

'You really have lost your mind, haven't you?'

'It is you who have lost your mind. Your brother lies dead along with some of your best commanders. So will you and I if we continue this course of action. This battle is as good as lost; unless we let the Plebs fight. If we don't, there will be nothing between this Etruscan army and Rome.'

'Let them out,' spat Fabius. Then he turned to Sherzada. 'What did you say about the defective spear being the key to our victory?'

The Plebs were freed and given back their arms. But they refused to serve under the command of those who had interred them. The Third Legion wanted Decius Mus to lead them, and the Fourth, Aulus Antonius. And so it was decided. Sherzada went over to both of them and suggested what might win the battle for them.

'You mean you want us to attack the Etruscan shield wall with those useless spears?' asked a shocked Mus.

Marcus formed up the two Latin infantry *Alae* and his militiamen once again and led them up the steep hill against the Etruscan shield wall. The attack failed and his force fell back in panic. The Etruscans, sensing victory, chased after them down the hill. The wall of shields began to lose a little cohesion as they ran down.

As the Etruscan warriors came crashing down the hill, the two Roman legions charged their left flank from concealed positions with the war-cry *Victoria aut mors* – 'victory or death'. The Etruscan left turned to meet the new threat. The Romans, instead of charging with their spears, hurled them at the Etruscan shields, which surprised the Etruscans no end. The spears, piercing the metallic boss, harmlessly transfixed themselves into their shields. The long twisted necks of the spears became bent, and the shafts began to hang down from the front of the Etruscan shields. They became heavy and awkward to carry. The Etruscans tried to remove the spears in vain as the Romans rapidly began to close in on them. The Etruscan warriors were struggling to keep their shields up when Mus' men attacked them with their swords. Their Etruscan shields, being pulled down by the spear shaft, became useless. Unable to use their shields, the Etruscans' shield wall began to crumble under the weight of the Roman onslaught.

So ferocious was Mus' attack that the Etruscan army's neat lines were severely convulsed. Mus, as he had vowed, died leading that charge. His last words were *Pro gloria Romae* – 'for the glory of Rome', as he led his men into a breach in the Etruscan line. The Mouse fell fighting like a lion. Following up, the Fourth Legion managed to puncture the Etruscan left flank and drive deep into its ranks. As this was happening on the Etruscan left flank, Marcus attacked the Etruscan right with his Cremeran militiamen and Latin allies.

In the meantime, concealed behind the woods, Sherzada had taken the Roman and Lucanian cavalry squadrons around to the rear of the Etruscans and rode up the hill behind their lines. He had just reached the summit when the Roman legions made contact with the Etruscan left flank down below. From the top of the hill, Sherzada charged the Etruscans. As he rode down the steep hill, he aimed his lance at the weakest part of the Etruscan formation. Hundreds of Roman and Lucanian lances followed his.

The Etruscans, already in disarray, were taken by complete surprise. Even though some turned to face the onslaught of Sherzada's cavalry, they did not stand a chance. His lance found its mark in chest of an unprepared Etruscan warrior. A moment later, he heard the clash of arms. The shield wall had now been breached. Earlier that very day, every Etruscan warrior had been assured of victory; but now everything had changed.

The momentum of Sherzada's downhill charge drove his lance deep into the Etruscan warrior's chest; and pierced through his back. With his lance irretrievably stuck inside the enemy's body, Sherzada let it go. He took out his sword and started slashing through the Etruscan ranks. But the shock of the Roman attack was already reverberating through the Etruscan lines, sowing fear in even their bravest warriors. Chaos was spreading. And as panic turned to terror, the Etruscans started to flee. Those who were away from the fighting peeled off first and then little by little, other sections of the Etruscan line followed, running away as fast as they could. Their army was rapidly losing strength as more and more Etruscans fled the field. By the time those in the Etruscan front lines in the thick of the fight realized no one was covering their backs, it was already too late. Their enemies were upon them and there was no escape.

The Romans were now in battle frenzy. Drunk with victory, lusting for blood, they had no room for mercy in their hearts. Rome's legions had triumphed. The day belonged to the *Sublicians* and the *Caelians* – the heroes of the Republic. Yet Marcus knew, as did Sherzada, that they had come close to defeat that day.

As he sat on that hill near Fidenae deep in thought, Sherzada heard a familiar voice.

'Highness, these Romans should know that were it not for you, they could never have won.' It was Menander. He bowed low.

'It's about time, Menander,' Sherzada replied, 'I should stop fighting other people's wars.'

But then it occurred to him that if Menander was here, Gorgo must have sent him. 'What news of Sparta?' he asked.

Menander gave a sigh and lowered his head. 'Things are not

going well in Sparta, Highness. The Eurypontid faction is becoming stronger. They are being led by young Archidamus, the grandson of Leotychidas. He has always been jealous of the Agiadae and wants to ensure that his branch of the royal family becomes dominant. Archidamus is attracting all kinds of reactionaries.

'But, Highness, the reason why I have been sent to you concerns Prince Pausanias. The Prince has resigned his regency and gone off to Byzantium, where he is preparing for battle against the Athenians, and not the Persians. Queen Gorgo is worried about him. She believes he is in real danger.'

Sherzada asked him why all this had happened.

'Highness,' Menander replied. 'It all started when Prince Pausanias captured Byzantium. After that, the Athenians turned against him. They accused him of all sorts of things – above all, of taking bribes from the Persians. The Prince was recalled to Sparta to stand trial at the Gerousia. But no evidence was found against him. Still, he was very angry. He announced he was no longer a regent of Sparta and returned to Byzantium to become its ruler. But once he returned, he got into more trouble with the Athenians, who now control a large part of Thrace and many of the nearby islands. They are determined to remove him from Byzantium, one way or another. That is why the Queen is concerned.

'She asks you to go to Byzantium, Highness, and see what you can do to help Prince Pausanias. She wants you to convince him to return to Sparta. If he insists on not returning, she asks you to see to his safety. You are her only hope.'

'What about Euryanax?' said Sherzada. 'Surely he would be a better person to see to Pausanias than myself.'

'He is still in Thessaly leading a column of troops to support King Leotychidas' expedition against the House of Aleuas. I don't have any details, except that it is not going well there. In any case, Queen Gorgo says you are better equipped than Prince

Euryanax to help Prince Pausanias.'

'I am not sure about that, my friend,' said Sherzada, 'but go to Pausanias, I shall. I just need a few days to conclude some business in Rome. And I shall to go to Athens before I go to Byzantium, to find out what the Athenians want to do to Pausanias.'

'But you once told me that you were not welcome there,' said Menander, with a look of concern. 'They might kill you for burning down their Acropolis.'

Sherzada laughed. 'On the contrary, my friend. This time they will welcome me with open arms.'

Chapter 32

The Sins Of Our Heroes

Piraeus Harbour, Athens
Three weeks later
Summer, 477 BC

'Marcus Fabianus Scirzadus Ferratus,' a voice thundered. 'Quite a mouthful, don't you think? Nice toga, by the way!'

Sherzada recognized that pompous voice. It was unmistakably Aristeides. Sherzada had barely debarked from his ship at Athens' busy Piraeus Harbour and had not expected to run into someone he knew so soon. But it appeared Aristeides had been waiting for him. The man seemed to have aged a good deal in the last years. His hair was greyer than before. His eyes and his gait reflected a weariness that could only have been brought on by fatigue and age, though he had lost none of his high spirits.

'How did you know I was coming?'

Aristeides was a bad liar. His eyes innocently looked towards the sky as he said, 'Some of our spies … I mean, sources … in Italy got wind of a Roman delegation heading towards Athens, led by an ambassador with a familiar name ... speaking of which … how on earth did you acquire such an outlandish name?'

'My first name is that of my host-friend; the second after the Fabian clan that adopted me; and my last is the surname, *Ferratus*, which derives from the Latin word for iron and refers to the chainmail armour I wear in battle.'

'I heard about your great battle,' Aristeides responded. 'Not an easy victory, I take it. Mind you, the Etruscans will not take it lying down. This war is not over by a long shot. These Italians are very stubborn. All of them … and not very civilized, either.'

Sherzada laughed at Aristeides' haughtiness.

A cool breeze blew through the busy harbour amid the

swearing of sailors, the haggling of merchants and the cackling of seagulls. He had not seen a busier port; this was perhaps the busiest in the world. Yet only a little over two years ago, when Sherzada had stood at this very spot – on the day after the Persian debacle at Salamis – this place had been deserted.

Sherzada introduced his Roman colleagues to Aristeides, among them Aulus Antonius, the former military tribune of the Fourth Legion, who had now been charged by the Roman Senate to carry out a study of the Athenian democratic constitution. He hoped that this constitution would provide some answers to Rome's perennial conflict between the Patricians and the Plebeians. The other was Lucius Quinctius Cincinnatus, with instructions to purchase an Athenian warship. Rome did not have a navy but wanted to consider the possibility. The rest were commerce officials charged with reaching a trade agreement with Athens.

Soon Aristeides guided Sherzada and his delegation to the city centre. It was quite a walk, and Aristeides told Sherzada there were plans to build fortifications all along the way. These would be called the 'Long Walls,' extending to the sea, protecting the route between Athens and the harbour and naval base at Piraeus. Another set of long walls would also be built along the route to Phalerum, Athens' other port.

'I thought the Spartans did not want you to build these walls?' Sherzada asked.

'They most certainly did not,' replied Aristeides. 'But our interests dictate otherwise. You see, my friend, Athens now has the strongest navy in the Aegean and no one can beat us at sea. However, anyone can destroy our naval might on land by taking Athens, burning down our shipyards, damaging our harbours, and seizing the silver at Laurium. I am sorry that this upsets our Spartan friends, but we have to protect our assets.'

Although almost two years had passed, there were plenty of signs of the destruction that had been inflicted on the city. But thanks to the industrious nature of the Athenians, the city was slowly rising again, above the ashes, like the mythical phoenix.

'Speaking of burning ...!' Aristeides began, 'I would not have thought I would ever see you in Athens.' Then he whispered, 'There are rumours that you burnt down our Acropolis.'

Sherzada whispered back, 'Shhh ... the less said about that, the better.'

'Well,' Aristeides responded, 'in that case, I would keep it to myself if I were you. By the way, coming here as an ambassador is quite impressive ... a stroke of genius, in fact. This way you are guaranteed protection under the law. But, then again, this did not stop us Athenians from executing one or two in the past. The privilege of being civilized, my friend is that we can call everyone else a Barbarian, while overlooking our own barbarity.'

Aristeides then spoke loudly, winking at Sherzada, 'So, Ambassador Fabianus, what brings you to Athens at the head of this Roman delegation?'

'Rome is interested in trade with Athens,' Sherzada replied. 'We have grain, salt and timber to offer, in return for the silver of Laurium. In addition, in my delegation there are lawyers who want to study your constitution and see if we can replicate some of its clauses in our republican constitution. I also have military experts in my delegation who would like a closer look at your warships. We have heard that you the largest dockyards in Greece, which are producing these vessels on a massive scale. Though Rome is still far from having a navy, our experts want to learn from your considerable experience. The Romans have always been impressed by Greeks.'

'Yes, they like to mimic us, don't they?' whispered Aristeides. 'The Romans think they are democratic also but somehow their votes always end up benefitting their richest classes.'

'As if all the elected officials in Athens are from the poorer class!' Sherzada interrupted. 'When was the last time anyone not from the aristocracy was elected as Archon in Athens?'

Ignoring his remark, Aristeides went on, 'At least the Roman system is better than the Spartan one. There, the one who gets elected is the one who gets the loudest shouts – not necessarily the most votes. But here in Athens we are truly democratic. One man; one vote.'

'Certainly,' Sherzada said, 'it is very democratic of you to allow half of your population to vote.'

'What do you mean, half our population?'

'Well, you have not extended the right of voting to your women.'

'Talk to me about women's rights in Athens the day you give the right of franchise to Saka women.'

Sherzada laughed. 'That might take a while, I am afraid. You see, we haven't yet got around to giving voting rights even to our men yet.'

They continued to walk among the devastated buildings and through debris-filled streets, until Aristeides brought the delegation to a halt at a reasonably intact and well-furnished inn. After his Roman colleagues had settled in, Sherzada accompanied Aristeides to his house for a private dinner. Sherzada wanted to talk to him alone.

The two men walked south towards the sea again, but this time a little to the east, to Aristeides' home in the Alopeke district. It was getting dark and Sherzada could not make out much of the city except the rubble the Persians had left behind or that the new construction work was creating. It was hard to tell which.

Aristeides asked him what the real reason was for his visit to Athens.

'Pausanias!' Sherzada replied. 'What do you intend to do to him?'

'I thought that might be it.'

'I also want to see Themistocles. Surely he still has some influence here?'

Aristeides shook his head. 'Themistocles is not here. In any case, I don't think there is much he can do now.' After thinking for a moment, he continued, 'Imagine a man … a charismatic leader … who wins for Greece an unlikely victory … A victory so spectacular that it goes to his head. He begins to think he is the only one who knows best. He starts to make enemies among those who were previously his friends and he begins to seek friends among his former enemies. But in his arrogance, he continues to believe that he is still right and everyone else wrong. He is the only one who knows where the dangers lie. Only he can lead his people to greatness. He thinks he is their saviour, but others think him cursed … and a man out of touch with reality.'

'So this is what you think happened to Pausanias?'

'I was actually talking about Themistocles. But you are right. The same can also be said of Pausanias. These two men are amongst the most renowned of all the Greeks. They are our heroes. But now they are fallen, no longer in favour with men or the gods.

'Themistocles is becoming unpopular due to his overbearing attitude – throwing his considerable weight around everywhere. His enemies in the city are increasing by the day. Now he has stormed off somewhere in a fit of pique and there is talk of ostracizing him … not that it hasn't been tried before … every year votes are cast to exile him, but each year there is always one person in Athens more unpopular than Themistocles. But it is only a matter of time before he is ostracized. He is accused of many things, including taking bribes from the Persians.'

'Surely not the victor of Salamis?' said Sherzada.

Aristeides shrugged. 'It was never beneath him or, for that matter, most Athenian politicians, to take bribes from anyone. Moreover, Themistocles has been dealing with the Persians in secret for a long time. He would have never been able to lure them into our trap at Salamis had he not contacted them personally. After that, I thought the Persians would never trust him again. But now there are persistent rumours that they are in touch with him again. I really don't know what he is up to. What I do know is that he is still an Athenian patriot and he will always put Athens' interests first, even though his methods are, and have always been, questionable.'

'Aren't you being a little too kind to your former foe?'

Aristeides smiled. 'I am no longer a politician and so Themistocles is no longer my rival. But he is not my friend, either. And still, I was proud to have served under him at Salamis. We Greeks could not have won that battle without him. But that victory and this naval reconstruction programme have made him big-headed and now he is getting out of control.'

When Sherzada asked him where Themistocles was, Aristeides shrugged. 'I don't know but he likes disappearing to the Peloponnesus. I suppose he enjoys baiting the Spartans. Themistocles' dislike for them is well-known ... much like Pausanias does not like Athenians anymore. The two have gone completely mad.'

'If Themistocles is away, who is the most influential man in Athens?'

'Cimon, the son of Miltiades,' replied Aristeides as he led Sherzada up a winding street, 'is the rising star here. His father's fame as the victor of Marathon has helped his career. Still, he has no shortage of talent, nor of important people willing to back him. He replaced me as the commander of Athenian forces in the northern Aegean. But I received a message from him last night that he wants me to return to assist him in the North. Cimon is trying to reduce Eion, one of the last remaining Persian strongholds in Europe.'

Sherzada knew the Persian commander at Eion, a fanatical officer who would rather burn down the city than hand it over to the enemy.

'While I am not at liberty to tell you everything,' Aristeides continued, 'suffice it to say that Thrace is rich in timber and silver, and nearby islands are rich in gold. Athens needs to secure these resources for future military operations.'

By this time they had reached Aristeides' house, or of what remained of it. It was only a shell of the magnificent residence it had once been. But it was being renovated, and in spite of its poor state of repair, some of its quarters were still inhabitable.

'So, will you go?' Sherzada asked.

Aristeides nodded, a little gravely. 'These past few years have not been particularly kind to me. I am no longer the rich man I once was. Politics and the war effort against Persia sucked up a considerable part of my wealth. What was left of it was completely destroyed by the Persians when they occupied Athens. Had it not been for some rich and influential friends – rich and influential friends of Cimon to be precise – I would have become a pauper. I'll take you to meet one of them tomorrow – a person who also has considerable influence over politics in Athens, and on Cimon himself. It is the generosity of people like these that keeps me fed, keeps a roof on top of my head – especially one that does not leak – and helps me to keep up appearances. So, you see, I cannot very well bite the hand that feeds me. Now that Cimon has asked me to come to him, I shall almost certainly go.'

They sat down for dinner on a comfortable terrace that opened up towards the sea. A pleasant breeze was blowing amid the flickering night lights of the nearby harbour. Servants brought in the famous Athenian charred fish with warm bread, olive oil, cheese, and salad.

As he tucked into the food, Aristeides muttered, 'Cimon wants me to come and help him solve our "Pausanias problem", while he busies himself with the siege of Eion.'

'Aha,' said Sherzada. 'Tell me about your "Pausanias problem." How did your once greatest ally become your worst enemy, all in the span of a year?'

'That, my friend, is still something of a mystery to me, but I shall tell you all I know,' said Aristeides. 'On his return from

Cyprus, Pausanias took command of the combined forces of the Hellenic League in the Aegean. It was Plataea all over again. Even though he was the overall commander, he regularly deferred to me. We worked together very closely and effectively. Island after island fell to us. We liberated many cities and won many engagements both on land and sea.'

'However,' he continued, 'it was not long before Pausanias gave up the fight and retired to Byzantium. He took with him a small force and set up himself up in the city. I was left in charge of the Greek forces to continue the struggle. To his credit, Pausanias continued to send ships and supplies to support our forces. But it was not long before all sorts of stories started emerging about him.

'According to these stories, he abducted a woman and forced her to become his concubine. He later killed her. Now they say he is being driven mad by her ghost. Her spirit, they say, demands vengeance. Then there were complaints that he had abused people living in the city. His haughtiness alienated some of our other Greek allies ... many have left the Hellenic League as a result. And last but not least, stories suggest that he is talking to Persians. They have offered him the hand of a Persian princess in return for his support of another Persian invasion of Greece.'

'And you believe all of that?'

'Not all of it. Not even most of it. But you know us Athenians. We like intrigue and propaganda. Now that Pausanias has replaced Xerxes as the most hated man in Athens, it's easy to spread virtually any gossip about him.'

'But why has he become the most hated man in Athens?'

'Pausanias did something Athens cannot tolerate. He is using his tiny fleet supported by a battery of catapults on shore to block the narrow straits of the Dardanelles and intercept shipping bringing grain and other supplies to us from the northern coast of the Euxine Sea. He is choking off our food supplies. It's tantamount to war!

'Pausanias sees us, the Athenians, as his enemies. He has not forgiven us for lying to the Spartans about our walls. We had no choice, you know. We needed to keep the construction secret as long as we could. But he sees an Athenian conspiracy everywhere. He accuses us of breaking up the Hellenic League and undermining the authority of Sparta in Greece. He says we are in league with Argos against Sparta and are poisoning relations between Spartan and other Peloponnesian states.

'Of course, Pausanias forgets that he himself did something similar against us, when he refused to punish Thebes after Plataea. Instead, he made peace with them and brought them into the Hellenic League without our consent. I suspect he thinks that by intercepting our grain at Byzantium, he can cow us into submission. Perhaps he could have, had he had the backing of Sparta. But the Spartans have forsaken him and so has practically everyone else.

'It will not be long before our forces strike at Byzantium. Leading them will be my unpleasant duty. We'll leave within the week, as soon as the transport ships arrive from Cimon's base in Thrace.'

After dinner, Aristeides accompanied Sherzada back to his inn and on the way gave him a guided tour of the glories of Athens. Sherzada could not help but wonder what glory his companion could see in his mind's eyes of the burnt-out city.,

The next morning, Sherzada and his delegation were taken by Aristeides to meet with the Trade Commission of Athens. There was not much negotiation; the Athenians simply agreed to almost everything that was asked. Not only was the trade agreement swiftly concluded, orders for Roman salt and grain were placed, with an advance in silver placed on the table. The Romans were delighted.

Leaving the Athenians and the Romans to work out the remaining details, Sherzada bid farewell to his colleagues. Most of the delegation would sail for home the following morning, except for Antonius who would remain behind to study the Athenian constitution, and Lucius Cincinnatus. A crew would soon arrive to take the warship he had just purchased back to Rome. Cincinnatus would be the first captain of a Roman naval ship, but he confided to Sherzada that sea-faring made him queasy. *A strange confession,* Sherzada thought, *coming from one of Rome's toughest military officers.* Like the Spartans, the Romans were expected to be fearless.

Sherzada was soon on his way with Aristeides. This time they walked north-eastwards up towards the hills above Athens, away from the sea. It was then he noticed the true scale of the destruction. And yet, this was a city rapidly returning to its past glory. Athens was busy resurrecting itself.

They continued to walk for a long while up a steep winding path, until they reached the top of a ridge called Immitus, where a magnificent villa stood.

Noticing Sherzada's expression, Aristeides whispered. 'Of course, the houses of the rich are repaired at a faster rate than those of the not so rich.'

They were ushered into the house by well-dressed slaves, and escorted through a marbled hall of a huge lobby to an expansive terrace that overlooked the sea. Sherzada could see the islet of Salamis at a distance, the place where the Greeks had won the greatest naval battle in history. And as he gazed north, he saw the beach of Marathon, where Datis' gamble failed and his father lost his life.

Just at that moment, someone joined them. A tall, attractive woman, about the same age as Gorgo, whose long reddish-blonde hair matched the colour of the shawl stylishly draped around her shoulders. The amber of her eyes was matched by that of her elegant *chiton* dress made out of fine silk, imported from the East, no doubt. Revealing parts of her body, her dress would not have raised many eyebrows in Sparta, but here in Athens, it was the type of thing that attracted gossip, if not scandal.

Yet she was very familiar. And then Sherzada recalled that earlier in the day, he had seen a new statue of the goddess Athena, the patron of Athens, being finished in the city centre. The statue may have been Athena's but the poise, the body and indeed the face was of this young beauty standing in front of him.

Aristeides bowed slightly to the young woman and turned to Sherzada. 'May I present the Lady Elpinice, daughter of Miltiades, victor of Marathon. She is Cimon's half-sister as well as the wife of Callias, our richest citizen,' he said.

Sherzada gazed at her in admiration. He had heard of Callias' famed ugliness. *How could he have so attractive a wife,* he thought to himself, wondering at the irony of the word *Callias* – 'beautiful' – fitting her so perfectly.

Aristeides announced, 'I need to attend to some personal matters. You must excuse me.' Then he winked at Sherzada and whispered in his ear, 'If you wish to save Pausanias, here is your chance.'

As Aristeides walked away, Sherzada turned to look back at Elpinice and noticed that she was not smiling.

'So, you are Sherzada,' she said in a sharp tone, staring into his eyes, 'the Saka warrior who fought for the Persians; the man who destroyed the Temple of Athena the Protectress, that had once stood upon our sacred Acropolis.'

Chapter 33

The Wisdom Of Athena

Villa of Callias, Mt. Immitus
Athens
The following day

Sherzada did not quite know how to respond. He hesitated, feeling a little embarrassed. Though he tried to say something, all that came out was mumbled sound.

Yet this was enough to make Miltiades' daughter burst into laughter. 'I just wanted to see your expression. As far as I am concerned, you did the city of Athens a great favour by destroying that eyesore – that sorry excuse for a building should never have been built in the first place. Now, you have given us an opportunity to construct something more appropriate in its place – something more beautiful – something that truly reflects the aspirations of the Athenians that will remain forever the symbol of our City.'

Elpinice went and sat down on a couch on the spacious balcony and invited Sherzada to sit beside her, which he did.

'I cannot blame you for burning down the buildings on the Acropolis,' she continued. 'Throwing your father's body into the sea was unforgivable. Actually, they tried to do the same to my father while he was still alive, even after he all he had done for Athens; even after he had saved her at Marathon. This Democracy of ours has a fickle and ugly face. The very same people of Athens who had once adored my father, wanted to punish him at the urging of that monster, Xanthippus. They would have certainly thrown my father off the Acropolis too, had he not agreed to pay fifty talents as indemnity. Fifty talents is more than annual income of a small city-state. My father did not have that sort of money. As it happened, a leg wound he had suffered during a campaign turned gangrenous and he died shortly afterwards with his debt unpaid.

'My half-brother Cimon was asked to pay his debt. When he said he could not, he was thrown into prison, leaving me alone to find a way to raise that money. It was then that Callias, the owner of many of the silver mines at Laurium, approached me with his offer – or rather, his proposal. He would pay the entire indemnity if I agreed to marry him. I did so, in part to preserve my family's honour, and in part also to preserve my own.'

'Your own?' Sherzada asked.

Elpinice smiled. 'My Lord, Cimon's mother was a Thracian princess. Mine was a daughter of a Dardanian chief. As a child, I was raised by my mother, but when she died in an epidemic, my father had me brought to Athens. But since my step-mother refused to take me in, my father arranged for my education elsewhere in the city.

'When my father died, and my step-mother returned to Thrace, Cimon asked me to come and live in his house. But it was not long before I understood his true intentions. My brother … my half-brother … has many great qualities. But he is also a complete degenerate. He did not invite me into his home to give me, his sister, shelter; he wanted to keep me as his lover. I have no taste for incest. So, when Callias made his proposal to marry me, it was not just my father's debt I was thinking of. I told Cimon to accept this arrangement too, if he did not want to spend the rest of his life languishing in prison.

'My Lord,' said Elpinice with a sigh, 'I love Athens, but I do not care much for its Democracy. It has no place for a woman – and certainly none for someone like me. Did you know that the democratic Assembly passed a law which decreed that women found walking out and about in public should be considered as prostitutes? The hypocrisy of the men in Athens is that they worship Athena – the goddess of wisdom and strategy, and yet they keep their own women locked up in their homes.'

She got up and walked across the balcony to look out to sea. Her hair blew in the breeze as she continued to speak. 'Because I am a woman who dabbles in politics, I am labelled a whore. But my interests are those of Athens, tempered, of course, with protecting the financial interests of my husband and promoting the political aspirations of my brother. It is I who caused the recent downfall of my enemy, Xanthippus … And then there was poor Themistocles. I was genuinely fond of him, but he too had to be sacrificed on the altar of expediency. Even in this Democracy of men, I can still manipulate things and there are times I am able to cast the deciding vote.

'Now tell me, my Lord, what brings you to Athens? I am sure it is something a little more interesting than negotiating a trade agreement.'

'Pausanias,' he said. 'Why are you after him?'

'He is a Spartan, after all,' she scoffed. 'Is that not reason enough? As if the Persians weren't enough; now we have to deal with a different type of Barbarian. Among the Greeks, only the Spartans are uncivilized. What do they know of philosophy? Do they go to the theatre? Do they have any opinion on architecture? Yes, they do make an effort at poetry, but does that really make them civilized? Civilization comes from sophistication of culture, from the refining of language, the development of literature, from the way you dress, the way you live, and the way you behave in society. The Spartans are a drab lot. All their men know about is the life of the barracks, and all their women know is how to produce sturdy babies. Their only strong point is dancing, my Lord. Civilizations, however, are rarely built around choreography.'

Elpinice continued to speak as she paced about the balcony, looking almost as beautiful to Sherzada as Gorgo had done the first day she had visited him in his prison. 'They do have a good army; I shall give them that. And Thermopylae was certainly impressive, if somewhat pointless. But our army is no less formidable. After all, we beat the Persians at Marathon, without any help from the Spartans. Had it not been for the Athenians, there would have been no Greek victory either at Salamis or Plataea, or even Mycale. How can the Spartans say that they are Greece's pre-eminent military power when none of these victories could have been possible without us? So why should we humble ourselves before them? Why should we entrust our security in their hands rather than our own? What do we owe these Spartans? Greece is secure only as long as Athens remains strong.

'Athens' strength lies not in the vineyards and olive groves of Attica, nor in the grand buildings of this City, nor in its great democratic Assembly or its eloquent orators, but on the waves of the Aegean. The sea is our life blood. It brings us trade and it brings us food. And when it does not we have a problem, as we do now with Pausanias.'

Sherzada nodded and thought for a moment. Then he said, 'My Lady, what if there is a way out? What if I can convince Pausanias to leave Byzantium peacefully?'

'Good luck to you, my Lord. A man as stubborn as young Pausanias will only leave that city in a coffin.'

'My Lady,' Sherzada entreated her, 'at least let me try. If you destroy Pausanias, you may further aggravate the relations between Athens and Sparta.'

'Spartans will shed no tears if he drops dead. Sparta is no longer concerned about her prodigal son.'

'You have just now told me, and eloquently so, why Athens should be free from Spartan influence,' he replied. 'By the same token, there are Spartans who are suspicious of Athens and her designs. Both your states stood against Persia together and won. Now every incident brings your two cities a step closer to confrontation. I have been told that Themistocles is in the Peloponnesus, visiting the enemies of the Spartans. Is he no different, in their eyes, than Pausanias is in yours? Are these two men just a couple of mavericks spinning out of control, or do they represent the growing fears and suspicions that Athenians and Spartans now have towards each other? Do you really think that a Sparta strong on land and an Athens strong at sea will keep out of each other's way? Sparta's army is always poised to invade your backyard in Attica and your fleet will soon have the capability to threaten Spartan soil. Where will this end?

'You are embarking on a dangerous path that can only lead to war, and a mutually destructive one at that. Neither of your cities will recover from such a conflict.'

'Indeed,' Elpinice nodded, 'it was the alliance of Athens and Sparta that saved Greece. Our patron goddess, Athena, is known for her wisdom. Its source is skilful intelligence – *Metis.* And it is Gorgo, I admit a little grudgingly, who has this. Ironic, isn't it, that Athena would grant her wisdom to a Spartan woman rather than an Athenian? She alone held Greece together at a time when it could have easily fallen apart. It is Queen Gorgo who won the war for us. But, alas, the Persian invasion is over now; so is Gorgo's day. It is time for us lesser mortals to shine in the sun. Gorgo grows weaker and the conspiracy against her advances by the day. Perhaps she is more in need of help than Pausanias.'

Elpinice stared again at the sea in a north-easterly direction, as if towards Byzantium, and said, 'The question is how to save Pausanias from himself. Seek out a traitor, my Lord, and that individual might help you find the answer.'

Chapter 34

The Prisoner Of Aphision

The Dungeon of Aphision
Outside Sparta
That evening

'He is a Royal Prince and a General of Sparta. Release him!' cried Gorgo.

The dungeon of Aphision was a dark and dingy place where recalcitrant Helots were kept and tortured before their inevitable execution. It was rare for a Spartan, much less a royal prince, to be incarcerated here. But to Euro's tormentors, nothing would have been more appropriate than this. 'My cousin has broken no law,' she insisted as she knelt on the ground to clean the wound on Euro's face.

Archidamus shook his head. 'Not from what I have heard. He armed Helots during the campaign in Thessaly against my grandfather's specific orders. He violated military conduct. He must be tried.'

'If Prince Euryanax is to be tried, then by his peers … his fellow generals in the War Council,' said Gorgo. 'But that does not warrant his torture. This is a clear violation of our laws.'

'He was not tortured,' said Pericleidas, smiling. 'He tried to escape by breaking these bars with his head, but as you can see, it did not work.' He pointed to the blood-stained bars of the dungeon.

'Prince Euryanax's disobedience of the King's instructions requires him to be tried in the Gerousia,' said Archidamus.

' … From which I am barred,' Gorgo cut him off, 'thanks to your grandfather!'

The ban was the price Gorgo had had to pay a year earlier to ensure Pausanias' acquittal when he was brought to trial for his activities in Byzantium.

But now Leotychidas himself was in trouble. He had been caught red-handed by his own commanders with Persian gold, reportedly stuck up his sleeves. He was immediately arrested, but on the eve of his trial had escaped to Tegea and sought refuge in a temple there. Given Sparta's alliance with Tegea, the Gerousia did not press them to hand him over.

'Still, it is not a crime,' Gorgo continued, 'to disobey a king who has been caught accepting bribes from the very enemies my cousin was fighting. It could be argued that Leotychidas' instructions were precisely to ensure a Spartan defeat in Thessaly, and because of Prince Euryanax's 'disobedience' our force returned undefeated.'

'You can argue whatever you wish, Majesty,' said Archidamus, 'but the decision will be that of the Gerousia.' He ordered Magnas to unlock Euro's chains. 'I will release him to the custody of the Ephors who will hold him until his trial tomorrow morning. You are free, Majesty, to spend some time with the prisoner before the guards transfer him to his new holding.'

Archidamus bowed to Gorgo, and as he was about to leave, turned and said, 'Since my grandfather has been stripped of his crown, the Ephors have upheld my right to succeed him as the Eurypontid King of Sparta. I hope you will come to my coronation.'

'Congratulations, Your Majesty,' she said. 'Sparta expects great things from you.'

Giving her a nod and a confused smile, Archidamus walked off with his companions.

Gorgo hurried to Euro's side and pulled him into an embrace. Quickly, Euro told her how he had been ordered by King Leotychidas to lead an overland column across Greece to support his maritime operations against the pro-Persian rulers of Thessaly. 'What I did not know at the time was that Leotychidas was secretly making deals with Aleuas, the ruler of Thessaly.

Aleuas had bribed him with Persian gold to leave Thessaly and ensure that Spartans never return. To do that, a plan was prepared under which Leotychidas would withdraw his naval force from Thessaly on some pretext or other, which would free up the Thessalians to destroy my column. The point being that if a Spartan army was destroyed in the north, it would deter us from sending more expeditions against the supporters of Persia in Greece.'

'Which is what would have happened …' Gorgo added.

'Precisely … had not I armed the Helot servants, we would not have been able to turn the tables on the enemy.'

'I do not have to be in the Gerousia to ensure your acquittal,' said Gorgo soothingly. 'I still have influence there as well as in the War Council.'

Euro shook his head. 'Eurybiadas is dead. Evaeneutus is still loyal but his loyalty is a divided one; Archidamus is his kinsman, after all. The loyalties of many of the generals are in doubt. And as for the Gerousia, they are easily swayed.'

Eurybiadas had died under mysterious circumstances, Gorgo recalled. But though it was hard to argue with Euro, Gorgo still knew that Evaeneutus was an honest man and would not fail to point out that there was no case against Euro.

But Euro did not see it that way. 'It's no use, Gorgo. They want my head and they will not stop short of anything before they have it. But I am only a means to an end; we all know who their real targets are.'

'*Strategos*,' called one of the guards, coming to lead an unchained Euro away into the night.

Chapter 35

Aria

Outside Chalcedon – Asiatic side of the Sea of Marmarra
Three days later

Sherzada stood on a hill, gazing at the scenery in front of him. Here, there was land behind water and water behind land, as the waterway of the Bosphorus straits snaked up to the Euxine Sea, dividing two continents in the process. And right there in front him across the water on the European side, stood Byzantium, Cleonice's city. He remembered the pretty Byzantine girl with the violet-blue eyes and wondered what her fate had been. Was she the woman Aristeides had spoken about?

Byzantium was lighting up as the sun began to set behind it. The city had been his destination and although right in front of him, he could go no further. As he sat gazing across the straits, one of his guards signalled that it was time to return to the Persian camp.

This camp had not been on his itinerary, but fate had brought him here a week earlier. His ship had been bound for Byzantium in these very waters, when a violent storm blew it off course. It would have surely sunk had not the crew made a heroic effort to get the vessel into port. This port was Persian-controlled Chalcedon, right across the water from Byzantium.

There, Persian soldiers had swarmed the ship and detained the passengers and crew. Such was the price any Greek ship unlucky enough to be blown off course had to pay. The ship and those found on board would normally be released after the payment of a fine and answering some questions for the benefit of Persian intelligence.

But Sherzada's case was different. Since somebody on the ship had identified him as some kind of ambassador, the soldiers had taken an unusual interest in him. The Persians were always suspicious of foreign diplomats travelling through their lands – and not without reason. There was a thin line between diplomacy and espionage.

The soldiers asked Sherzada to ride out with them. All foreign ambassadors had to be presented before the Governor, they told him. They rode half an hour out of town to arrive at a large military encampment, with grand tents set out on a large scale. A neat row of a dozen large tents indicated the presence of a high dignitary – presumably Persia's governor in the West.

It was one of these tents that Sherzada was taken to. Inside, there was no shortage of luxurious furnishings. Sherzada had forgotten how seriously the Persians took their hospitality. He had not even lay down to rest on a couch, when a long train of slaves came in with all sorts of fine foods. The other thing he had forgotten was how seriously the Persians took their food. It was delicious.

While he ate, Sherzada had begun to assess his situation. Were the Persians to discover his true identity, he would be a most unwelcome guest. He had enough respect for Persian intelligence to know that they would have been keeping track of him – to some extent. They would certainly be suspicious that Spartans would have released him unharmed. They would be curious, in the least, about his sudden presence on their territory in the guise of ambassador. The richness of the food made him so drowsy that he dozed off while still considering his predicament.

When he opened his eyes, the first thing that hit his senses was an alluring perfume. Delighting in its smells, he opened his eyes. Sitting beside him was an attractive woman in her thirties. She wore an elegant Persian dress and seemed to be drowning in jewellery.

'I am sorry to have startled you, my Lord. My name is Aria. My master sent me to see that you were being well taken care of.' Though she spoke flawless Persian, there was something clearly

European about her.

'I thank you, my Lady,' Sherzada said, 'for this most gracious hospitality. But you see, I am an ambassador from Rome and I urgently need to ...'

She interrupted him, in Latin. 'Rome? I spent some time there when I was younger. What a delightful place! So, what business does a representative of the Senate and People of Rome have all the way over here in Persia's backyard?'

Taken aback, Sherzada tried to think of something to say, but he fumbled.

Aria smiled and continued in Persian, 'Highness, I know perfectly well who you are. They say the Spartans freed you after you worked your magic on their young Queen. They say you have an eye for beautiful women.' She had spoken the last sentence in Attic Greek, with just a hint of a Dorian accent. *There was something very familiar about this woman*, Sherzada thought.

Moving even closer, she continued, 'Indeed, there are many rumours concerning you. They say at Plataea you conspired to deprive Lord Farandatiya of one of his choicest concubines.'

Sherzada realized that he must have a ridiculous expression on his face, for it caused Aria to burst out laughing. Seeing that she was making him uncomfortable, she gently moved away a little – though he almost wished she hadn't. 'Had it been a different time and place, I would have enjoyed knowing you, my Lord. But now I have someone I love just as your wife loved you. I remember her. She was truly the rarest of beauties. I am so sorry she passed away far too young. I met her once, a long time ago.'

Sherzada recalled Rán had once told him that she had been visited by a mysterious young woman who seemed to know everything about him. It was only much later that he had learned her true identity. 'You are Ariadne of Taras?'

'At your service,' Ariadne said with a smile. 'And it is indeed a pleasure to finally meet you, my Lord.'

'You were Datis' best spy,' said Sherzada. She was the only one of his operatives Datis ever spoke about. She had worked undercover in Athens, among other places, obtaining the most sensitive information from Greek leaders and secretly transmitting it to the Persians.

'Coming from you, my Lord, that is high praise indeed. Datis saved me from a life of destitution and slavery and persuaded me use my various skills to promote Persia's interests.'

'Datis once told me you conquered more Greek potentates by your charm than all of the Great King's generals combined.'

Aria blushed.

Sherzada continued, 'I have always wanted to ask you this. How did a Greek woman, and that too of Spartan blood, become Persia's best spy?'

Aria thought for a moment. 'I had my reasons, but let us say the Persians have treated me far better than the Greeks. Though the Greeks call them Barbarians, the Persians, I am convinced, are more cultured and civilized. I have no regrets for what I have done. But tell me, what are you *really* doing here?'

Sherzada decided to tell her the truth.

'So you want to see Pausanias, the man who spared your life at Plataea?' She switched to her native Doric Greek. 'Pity, you just missed him. He was here with us until last night.'

'What was he doing here?' Sherzada responded in the same dialect.

'That, I cannot tell you,' she replied.

'Then, at least, can you tell me how long I am to be kept here?'

'That is for my lord and master to decide.' Aria got up and headed for the entrance of the tent. 'But I ought to tell you, my Highness, you are under investigation for treason. He is unlikely to let you go until this matter is cleared up.'

As Ariadne turned to go, Sherzada asked her of whom she was speaking.

'Artabaz,' she said softly as she left his tent.

Chapter 36

Confessions Of A Genius

The Persian Military Camp
Outside Chalcedon
Two days later

Although Sherzada was a prisoner, he was free to move around – albeit under the watchful eyes of half a dozen heavily-armed guards – even outside the camp. He was required to return to his tent at dusk. And there he would invariably be welcomed by a sumptuous feast.

That evening as a spread of fine dishes was laid out before him in his tent, Sherzada pondered his predicament. Artabaz was away and nothing was likely to change until he returned. Though agitated and impatient, Sherzada fought to convince himself that there was nothing he could do except to wait. So he decided to have his dinner quickly before retiring to his unusually soft bed. But as he sat down at the table, he heard loud voices from outside the tent. A man could be heard shouting at the top of his voice, in very bad Persian, demanding to come inside.

Sherzada rose and politely asked the guards to let the visitor in. And in walked a short, heavy-set man of around fifty, with a bull-neck, unkempt ginger-blond hair and a scruffy greying beard. The man's dress indicated he was Greek and the flask in his hand suggested he had been drinking.

'Is this Gorgo's famous lover?' he quipped, in Attic Greek.

'I am Queen Gorgo's friend,' Sherzada replied in the same dialect, 'sadly not her lover.'

The man came and sat at the laden dinner table. 'Lucky man,' he whispered as took another swig from his flask.

'Whom do I have the privilege of addressing?'

'Themistocles, the son of Neocles, a humble citizen of Athens,' was the reply.

Sherzada's eyes widened. 'The victor of Salamis?'

A slight smile appeared on Themistocles' scowling face. He belched and responded, 'The very same.'

'What are you doing here, in the camp of the Persians?'

'I was about to ask the very same question.'

'I am not exactly here by choice,' Sherzada replied.

Themistocles chuckled. 'A clever excuse. Well, I hope you don't mind if I join you,' he said, helping himself to the venison and lamb kebabs laid out on the table. 'No need to stand on ceremony. Make yourself at home, my friend. What was your name again? Of course, "Scirzadatitus",' he said, massacring Sherzada's name. 'Aristeides told me about you. Any friend of Aristeides is a friend of mine, even if you are a Spartan-lover.'

'I am not a Spartan-lover, and you are not exactly Aristeides' friend.'

'I am drunk; you are wrong; and I am in no state to split hairs with you right now,' said Themistocles, between another hiccup and tucking into more food.

'If you don't mind my asking, what is Greece's greatest admiral doing in the camp of its hated enemy?'

'At least,' Themistocles responded, 'you have the decency to recognize me as Greece's greatest admiral. Many of my own countrymen have forgotten about all that.'

Sherzada pointed out that his very presence in the Persian camp would attract a death sentence in Athens. Themistocles calmly admitted he had been dealing with the Persians for a long time; he had pleased them and deceived them in equal measure and had got away with it too. 'As for my opponents back home, they will have to do better than that if they want my head.'

Sherzada pointed out that being in Artabaz's court was not the most patriotic act for an Athenian, especially for a person of Themistocles' stature, especially when Athenian troops were battling the Persians at Eion not very far away.

'Let Cimon just try to pull this one off,' he scoffed. 'That lecherous pup dares take my place in the hearts of the Athenian people.

'And still, Cimon was born with everything,' he continued with a sigh. 'His father was a hero; mine, a nobody. Both our mothers were Thracian; but his was a princess, mine a mere slave-girl. Had it not been for our Democracy, I would have still been an insignificant halfling. And had it not been for the sea, I would have never led Athens to greatness.'

Themistocles explained that he had been the first advocate of a strong navy. But the upper classes, fixated on the land from which they derived their wealth, opposed him. Why should they shift resources to building ships which would be oared by the poor? But all of that changed when a windfall of silver at the mines of Laurium was discovered. Then Athens no longer had an excuse not to build a navy. Still the landed gentry and the aristocracy put up a stiff resistance against his proposals to build two hundred warships. Leading the charge on behalf of the aristocrats was none other than Aristeides. The two of them, who had fought side by side at Marathon, fought an almighty political battle against each other. In the end, the numbers told. The poor, who outnumbered the rich, voted to support Themistocles' project – a fleet manned by the poor citizens of Athens that would rule the waves.

And just for good measures, Themistocles also secured Aristeides' ostracism. 'Pity,' said Themistocles. 'To this day Aristeides believes that it was the one vote he helped an illiterate man cast against him that sent him to exile. Little does he know the lengths I went to in order to get rid of him on that particular occasion. Of course, once he was out of the way, the aristocratic opposition crumbled and I went ahead with building my navy.

'Those very ships eventually saved Greece. The Oracle of Delphi said Athens would be saved by these "wooden walls". Who do you think bribed the Oracle to predict that? They say the

Spartans have a direct line to Delphi, as perhaps do the Persians. But we Athenians had been bribing the Oracle long before either of them figured out how. '

Themistocles took a large swig from his flask. 'It was I who lured the Persians into the trap at Salamis. And it was I who defeated the Persians at Salamis. So it is I, and not that upstart pipsqueak Pausanias, who has the right to claim to be the saviour of Greece. That immature little rascal spent most of the time at Plataea either prevaricating or arguing with his own commanders. Had it not been for the wise counsel of Aristeides, he would have brought disaster to Greece. It was thus us Athenians who won both Salamis and Plataea …'

But Sherzada interrupted, reminding him that the Athenians could not have the led the Greeks to victory at Salamis without Spartan support and the strategic vision of one person in particular.

'Your Queen Gorgo was indeed responsible for all of that … I stand … or rather, I sit … corrected!' he said, with a hiccup.

His eyes became misty. 'You know, Gorgo invited me to Sparta and when I came, she showered honours upon on me. I was crowned like a champion there; feted like a god. Gorgo honoured me more than the Athenians ever did. Though in doing so, she undermined the very basis of my political campaign in back in Athens. But yes, you are right my dear Sherazidius … it was she, not I, who won the war.'

'But then, my Lord,' Sherzada asked, 'why do you hate the Spartans so much?'

'I don't really hate them. I merely despise them for their arrogance. The Persians may be our enemies now, but they will not be our enemies forever. As Persian influence recedes in Greece and the Aegean, the void has to be filled by someone. It has to be the Athenians, not the Spartans. This Persian war is just a cover for Athens' naval hegemony of the Aegean. My idea, of course. I have been playing such games all my life. No point stopping now, my friend.'

With something of a struggle, Themistocles got up. 'It has been a real pleasure talking to you, Prince Sherodotus. I bid you good night.' With these words, he started to leave … And as he did so, he tripped, went down face first on the soft cushions and fell fast asleep.

Sherzada called the guards who brought in a litter to take him back to his tent. He could not help wondering at the irony as Persian soldiers carried away on their shoulders, almost like a hero, their once greatest enemy.

Chapter 37

Artabaz's Revenge

Persian Military Headquarters
Four days later

As he saw the sun set behind Byzantium across the narrow straits, Sherzada clenched his teeth in frustration. He was so close to his destination and yet reaching it seemed impossible. The Persians had been holding him in gilded captivity for more than a week. Of course, the thought of trying to swim across the straits to Byzantium often crossed his mind. But then again, he had a healthy respect for Persian archery.

His thoughts were interrupted by a familiar voice. 'There you are,' said the man, in Spartan dialect. 'I've been looking everywhere for you.'

It was Demaratus. Though still as fit as ever, he too seemed to have aged in the last couple of years. His hair had considerably greyed, and soft wrinkles had appeared on his handsome face. 'It is good to see you again. We have not seen each other since Xerxes' departure from Greece.'

When Sherzada asked how he located him, he replied, 'Artabaz is careful in that he rarely allows his guests to meet each other, but his wife, Ariadne, told me where to find you. She seems to be keeping an eye on you.'

'Have you seen Artabaz?' asked Sherzada. 'And do you have any idea why he's keeping me here?'

'His return is expected tonight,' said Demaratus. 'And your present situation, I believe, has something to do with Plataea. He believes you conspired with Alexander of Macedon to have the retreating Persian force massacred at the Strymon Crossing.'

'Had I done that,' said Sherzada, 'I would not have stayed behind and fought until I was captured ...'

'...Only to be released unharmed by my former countrymen, the Spartans, sometime later,' interrupted Demaratus. 'It looks all too suspicious, my friend.'

Demaratus continued, 'Initially, the blame was directed at Prince Burbaraz. Even the Great King was convinced that Prince Burbaraz was in league with his Macedonian brother-in-law and had conspired with him to destroy the Persian army. The fact that the Lady Gygaea had gone missing around that time added to these suspicions. So upon his return, Prince Burbaraz was put in chains and thrown into a dungeon. But he continued to plead his innocence. Burbaraz insisted he had no contact with Alexander; he did not know where his wife was; and the only one who had warned him about the Strymon crossing was yourself.

'Xerxes wanted to execute him, but Burbaraz was one of Queen Atossa's favourite nephews. So she interceded with her son, the Great King, to spare his life. Soon Lady Gygaea also returned, apparently from Illyria where she had been with relatives. She also vouched for her husband's loyalty. In an emotional speech before the Queen-mother and the Great King, she denounced her brother and insisted that neither she nor her husband had anything to do with the Strymon massacre. Persian intelligence could also find no evidence against Burbaraz. So he was freed, reinstated as governor, and united with his wife and children.

'In fact, everyone has forgotten the whole affair, except for Artabaz. The truth, my friend, is that Artabaz is still obsessed with Plataea – and Mardonius. You know better than I how Mardonius tried to humiliate Artabaz publicly, accusing him of cowardice. The greatest insult you could give a man like him. Then, to add near death to insult, Artabaz would have died at the Strymon had he not got the warning from Prince Burbaraz. So you can imagine his anger.

'Artabaz has always blamed Mardonius not just for the defeat at Plataea but for the entire botched Persian invasion – a view we all share. And now Artabaz has to deal with the aftermath of the Persian disaster in Greece. He resents cleaning up Mardonius' mess.'

They soon arrived at the Persian camp. 'Ironic, is it not,' asked Sherzada, 'that I who fought for them stand accused of treason, while you, who betrayed them, walk around freely?'

Demaratus laughed. 'Water under the bridge. Things have changed now. Whatever people like me might or might not have done in the past has been forgotten; except for Artabaz's obsession with Mardonius.'

And amid the marching of Artabaz's crack troops and the shouting of officers, Demaratus continued. 'In fact, Xerxes has been very kind to me. He has given me a kingdom to rule freely as long as I give him the required annual tribute. And now my kingdom is threatened by Athens and its allies. I am not the only Greek ruler who fears Athenian expansion. Even some of the Ionian cities who recently won their freedom by revolting against the Persians are wary of the Athenians.

'And then there is that other Athenian fixation – Democracy,' he said. 'They are trying to replace the rulers of the cities they 'liberate' with democracies. The Athenians claim that only democracies can support the interests of Greece, whereas oligarchies and monarchies will serve the interests of Persia. While I used to have some sympathy with that argument, I do not believe this argument any longer – nor do I trust the Athenians. They are becoming quite skilful at manipulating democracies for their own interests. Democracy or not, eventually each of these states will become subservient to the Athenian Assembly – a prospect as, or perhaps more, terrifying as being under Persian rule. So I have come to reassure Artabaz that my loyalties remain with Persia.'

'Ah, but will he believe you?'

'He has no choice. Artabaz now commands all the Persian forces in Ionia and neighbouring regions. But these are not sufficient to defend the whole of the Western Asiatic sea-board from the Hellespont to Caria against the Athenians and their allies. So he has to rely on the allies he can get along the coast. He needs people like me to create further obstacles for the Athenians.'

'And what of Pausanias? Does Artabaz need him also?'

'Pausanias is a different story,' said Demaratus. 'Artabaz is willing to give Pausanias a great deal if Pausanias would offer earth and water to Xerxes. But Pausanias refuses. As a result, all he has got from Artabaz is some funds to repair his tiny fleet and hire some mercenaries for Byzantium's defence. Artabaz has told Pausanias that more generous funds will be on hand if he formally "defects" to the Persians. Pausanias continues to resist.

'You see,' Demaratus continued, 'I gave up being a Spartan a long time ago, but Pausanias is still very much a Spartan. His dealings with the Persians are merely a marriage of convenience.'

Sherzada told Demaratus about his mission and how he ended up being detained on the wrong side of the Straits.

'Happy for me that you did,' said Demaratus, 'but do you think you can convince a young man as stubborn as Pausanias to do the very thing he would rather die than do?'

'I can at least try,' Sherzada responded, 'but only if Artabaz releases me from this wretched imprisonment.'

As they neared Sherzada's tent, Demaratus excused himself. So, alone, Sherzada had an early, though as ever delicious, dinner, with fowl and meat cooked with exotic vegetables, fragrant rice, and several varieties of bread. Sherzada finished his meal and went to sleep. When he awoke, over him stood a familiar figure. It was Artabaz. 'So good to see you again, old friend,' he said to Sherzada.

Artabaz sat down on Sherzada's bed next to him, as the latter uncomfortably pulled himself up to a sitting position. He came straight to the point. 'Ariadne tells me that you are keen on catching up with your friend Pausanias. But as you might have guessed, there is a little matter of the Strymon ambush that we need to resolve.'

Sherzada tried to plead his innocence by reminding Artabaz that the last time the two of them had seen each other was he was defending the ford at Plataea against a Spartan onslaught, but Artabaz merely smiled.

'Rumours are that you escaped from Sparta by seducing King Leonidas' widow,' he said. 'If I put that together with another rumour that you had killed Leonidas in battle earlier on, this was such an audacious act that very few people other than yourself could have pulled it off. Such is your reputation.

'But there is still a detail that does not fit,' said Artabaz. Sherzada quietly reached for the dagger he had been keeping under the sheets next to him by his pillow.

'Reliable eyewitnesses report,' continued Artabaz, 'that on the night before battle, you were visited in your tent by a Macedonian officer.'

'That was not a Macedonian officer, my Lord.'

Artabaz's angry stare told Sherzada that he did not believe him.

'It was a woman, my Lord,' Sherzada responded. 'To get into my tent unnoticed she wore a Greek helmet that masked her face and wore a long cloak that covered her body. She told my officers that she was a Macedonian cavalry officer with an important message to gain access to my tent.'

Artabaz's left eyebrow went up, he was silent for a long while ... and then he laughed. 'I would not have believed you were it not for your reputation. Women seem to seek you out, it seems. Be careful, my friend, they might get you killed, one day.'

After a deep sigh, Artabaz said, 'Excepting that one detail which you have now explained to me, I do not have any proof against you. In fact, on the contrary, I have evidence that supports your innocence.'

Sherzada's hand moved away from his dagger. 'What evidence, my Lord?'

'The word of Alexander of Macedon, no less.'

'Surely you would not believe one so treacherous as the Macedonian King?'

'I would not have,' said Artabaz. 'But Alexander and I have lately reconciled. Even as we speak, his forces are once again massing on the Strymon border, this time to attack the Athenians.'

Sherzada could not hide his astonishment, and so Artabaz went on. 'Let me tell you what I have to deal with. I have less than forty thousand troops and I have to defend Phrygia, Aeolia, Ionia, Caria, and Bythinia, not to mention Rhodes and the other Aegean islands still in our possession against the relentless attacks of the Athenians and their allies. I have asked King Xerxes for reinforcements but none are available; and moreover the treasury is nearly empty. We have money to bribe some of our foes, but not enough to raise and maintain armies. The fleet I have asked for will not be ready for another ten years. I simply don't have enough forces to repel the Athenians. I need to find creative means to defend Persian territories. And that is where Ariadne comes in. She is trying to create a spy network similar to Datis' for me.

'However, my problem is Thrace. The Athenians are there in strength. Cimon, the son of Miltiades, is also the nephew of the King of Thrace. So he is using his blood ties with Thrace's king to build up local support as well. Another Athenian fleet has been sighted near here, apparently closing in on Byzantium. But I can do nothing to stop it.

'Pausanias, unfortunately, will not be able to keep the Athenians at bay much longer. Once the Athenians take both Byzantium and Eion, Thrace will be theirs. And then they will try to force their way on to the Asiatic side – in fact, the very spot you and I are standing on right now. If they succeed, Persia will lose this entire sea-board.

'And that is where Alexander of Macedon comes in. Alexander

has long claimed Thracian soil as part of his kingdom. Now that Persia has all but evacuated Thrace and the Athenians are stepping in to fill the vacuum, Alexander has become alarmed. He sees his former allies – in fact, his favourite former allies – the Athenians, as a threat to his domain. So he has decided to attack them to take back what he thinks is his. He is here right now, asking for more money and weapons, which I shall give him, even if it causes me to empty my war chest. He has already cut off the Athenian land supplies along the Strymon border. His troops are getting into position as we speak, to attack them across the river. While I don't expect Alexander to take all of Thrace, I do expect him to stop the Athenians. Which is why I am helping him.

'When I asked Alexander about your alleged role in his earlier Strymon attack against us, he was very surprised that you knew about it at all. As far as he was concerned, it was a secret he had not shared with anyone beyond his inner circle in Macedon. And you have just clarified the story about the "Macedonian officer" in your tent. So, my friend, I owe you an apology.'

Finally, he would be free to leave.

'One last thing,' said Artabaz. 'The recent defeat that we suffered would not have happened were it not for Mardonius. We would not have invaded Greece in the first place and suffered the humiliation that we did.

'But this past week, Themistocles, Pausanias, and Alexander have all been at my court asking for my help. These are the best of the Greeks – their heroes. Yet each one of them bowed low to me. Each one of them promised to fight their former allies on my behalf. Though Leotychidas, the victor of Mycale, is not here, he has been my best agent and has taken the lion's share of my bribes. The greatest of the Greeks are doing my bidding and are helping to sow chaos in Greece. I have thus avenged Persia for its defeats at Salamis, Plataea, Mycale and the Strymon. Pity the nation that has such heroes; and pity the heroes that have such a nation.' Artabaz smiled a broad satisfied smile as he turned and walked out of the tent.

Sherzada could now finish his journey. His only hope was to reach Pausanias in time.

Chapter 38

The Ghost Of Cleonice

Byzantium
Summer, 477 BC
The following day

The ships docked north of Byzantium at first light. Demaratus had insisted on taking Sherzada with his small naval squadron, carefully avoiding the path of the much larger Athenian fleet to the south. Sherzada could not help reflecting on Elpinice's parting words that he must find a traitor to save Pausanias. Was his meeting Demaratus a sign or a simple coincidence?

They had to go a little further up along the Bosphorus Straits to secure safe landing. From there, Sherzada and Demaratus rode on horseback to the gates of Byzantium.

They would not have been allowed to enter the city, had an old Spartan soldier on guard duty not recognized Demaratus and let them in. As they entered the town, they saw feverish activity all around. Soldiers, mercenaries and militiamen were rushing to the battlements. Demaratus and Sherzada were taken to a tower above the southern walls. As they climbed, the reason for the tumult became clear – hundreds of Athenians were landing on the coast below. At the top of the tower, Sherzada found Pausanias looking down from the ramparts. He was wearing his long crimson Spartan cloak, but underneath he wore baggy trousers and a loose long-sleeved shirt of the Persian type. And Sherzada was still in his Roman toga.

Pausanias' handsome face reflected a gloomy weariness. He bowed slightly to Demaratus and welcomed Sherzada with a warm embrace. 'Two years ago, you and I met at Plataea. The man who brought you to me leads these Athenians against me today,' he said, pointing down to the Athenian marines as they jumped off their ships. 'I would not have won Plataea without Aristeides' support. You and I who were enemies then are here together as friends,' he said, 'and the one who was my friend is now my enemy.

'Now, please excuse me,' he said. 'I must see to our defences. You are of course welcome to stay but I suggest you leave soon. No point dying needlessly here. This is not your fight.'

Later that evening, against Pausanias' advice, the two guests dined with Pausanias and his officers. The food was as distinctly Persian as Pausanias' dress. Pausanias was in a better mood then. He described the Persians' dress as more practical than the Greek, and their food, delicious. There was no harm in adopting the more attractive aspects of a culture. Sherzada could not have agreed more. But soon the conversation between Pausanias and his men turned to military matters. Sherzada and Demaratus listened silently as they tried to assess the balance of forces. Apparently, Pausanias had only a few dozen Spartans who had volunteered to serve under him after he resigned his regency, a hundred or so Bosporan mercenaries – paid for with Persian gold – and a town militia a few hundred strong; in all, six hundred men. *Not enough to hold off Aristeides' three thousand Athenians,* Sherzada thought. As they ate, they learned a force of two thousand Thracian warriors was also on its way to support the Athenians. Cimon's maternal links were at work. The odds were stacking up against Pausanias. But he remained calm.

After dinner, Demaratus excused himself. War did not excite him the way it used to. He was, after all, a Spartan no longer. He was also a man who knew only too well the meaning of misfortune. Sherzada saw him off and then walked on to the palace terrace above Byzantium's fortifications, and gazed at the Athenian campfires below the city walls.

Pausianus appeared and sat down beside Sherzada, saying, 'I have often tried to make sense of all of this, but I cannot. Regrets, I certainly have, but I cannot blame myself for everything. If only the Athenians had left me alone.'

Sherzada reminded him that it was he who had cut off the Athenians' grain supplies.

'A trifle compared to what they did to me!' he said, a little hysterically. 'You must have heard the stories. I was arrogant. I mistreated people. I alienated our allies. I took a woman against her will and then killed her. I conspired with the Persians to fight against the Greeks. Athenian propaganda, all of it. They made me into nothing less than a monster.'

'Tell me the truth,' Sherzada suggested as gently as possible, watching the water below and realizing how little time they had. 'Tell me the whole story.'

Pausanias sighed. 'When we arrived here, the Persians were withdrawing from the European side. Except for Eion and Doriscus, they had abandoned all of Thrace; Byzantium, too. The war shifted to the Aegean Sea. The Athenians began to focus on liberating only those Aegean islands and Ionian cities that tended to favour their interests. Even then, I helped the Athenians as far as I could, but soon I began to see where this war was headed. With the Persians not going on the offensive and the Athenians bent on building an empire of their own in the Aegean under the guise of liberation and democracy, it was not a war of independence anymore.

'And ever since Plataea I had been smitten by Cleonice. I longed to see her again. Leading the Greek forces in the Aegean gave me that opportunity. While the Athenians were busy island-hopping, I brought a force here and seized Byzantium. Once in control of the city, I went straight to the house of Cleonice's parents with my soldiers. I demanded she come with me immediately. She refused. When I insisted, she picked up a dagger and pointed it at her own chest, saying that she had hated being a concubine of a Persian general and would not want to repeat the same experience with a Greek one. She ordered me to leave her house or she would plunge the dagger in her heart. I did as she said.

'But several weeks later she came to me and told me that she would agree to live with me but only as my wife, not as my slave-girl or my concubine. So I married her. We were very happy together. She gave me two sons – twins. The elder I named Pleistonax, for no other reason than taking the first part of Pleistarchus' name and combining with the last part of Euro's. Then I named the younger Cleomenes after Gorgo's father, my favourite uncle.

'When I took control of Byzantium, this town attracted many Greek soldiers, sailors and traders from Athens and other cities allied to us. But these people treated the locals very badly; cheating them, exploiting them, physically abusing and humiliating them and sometimes even killing them. Any Byzantine who dared to complain was dealt with harshly by these Greeks, many of them Athenians. I could stand this no longer. So I started putting on trial those who mistreated the local population and punished all those who were found guilty. Some were fined, some were imprisoned, others banished, and a few were even executed, but in each case the punishment matched the crime. People from our allied states started complaining about the way I was treating their citizens in Byzantium, forgetting that these very citizens had behaved wrongfully towards the Byzantines. But the Athenians, under Themistocles' influence, turned the whole episode on its head, accusing me of mistreating people.

'In any case, after the rumours against me reached Sparta, the Gerousia recalled me to answer charges that I was in league with the Persians and that I had abused Greek citizens. In spite of the best efforts of Leotychidas and his lackeys, they could not find an iota of evidence against me. They would have still gone ahead with prosecuting me, had Gorgo not drilled some sense into the Gerousia. I resigned my regency and left Sparta, returned here mainly because of Cleonice. I couldn't bear to live without her.

'When I returned, the Athenians were being led by Cimon and

he wanted to control Byzantium. So he sent assassins against me. One day, I got credible information that an assassin was in town. That night, I doubled my guards around my bedchamber. Cleonice was spending a few days with her parents and I did not expect her to return that night. But she decided to come back that very night, telling her parents that she was missing me. The guards let her through, and when she entered the bedchamber she accidentally overturned a lantern causing a small fire. She tried to wake me to warn me about the fire. But when I awoke, I saw the room on fire and a dark figure leaning over me. Expecting the worst, I reached for my sword and stabbed the figure. As she fell on me, I realized it was Cleonice. I had killed the woman I loved.'

Sherzada felt a stab of pain, remembering the girl who had pleaded with Pausanias to save his life.

It was some time before Pausanias could go on. *It was hard to believe his companion was a man still in his twenties,* thought Sherzada. He remembered his promise to Gorgo, and wondered how he would be able to save them both.

'It was after that I blocked off the Hellespont,' Pausanias continued. 'I refused to let through any ship carrying grain to Athens. I had to teach them a lesson. I wanted them to pay for what they made me do.

'But even here the Athenian lies haven't stopped. They say that the ghost of Cleonice is haunting me, driving me mad. I suppose the guilt of what I did to her is, but Byzantium represents everything Cleonice loved, and I will defend it with my life. These Athenians will pay dearly for their crimes.'

* * *

The next morning, Sherzada went up the tower again and saw Demaratus was already there, studying the Athenians. The city below was in a state of fear. Civilians were cowering in their homes and the defending troops were nervously hanging on to their weapons, waiting for the enemy to make his first move. But he didn't.

'Strange,' said Demaratus. 'Aristeides doesn't seem in a hurry to attack us. He hasn't brought out his siege engines or deployed his battlelines. I wonder what he is up to?'

'If Aristeides really wanted to attack us he would have done so by now,' mused Sherzada.

As they came down the tower, they found Pausanias on the ramparts encouraging his men. 'By Apollo,' he fumed, 'if Aristeides does not launch an assault by dusk, I will attack him where he stands and drive him and his Athenians into the sea.'

'Remember,' said Sherzada carefully, as he walked up to him. 'Aristeides is not like the other Athenians. He still considers you his friend.'

'If the man is my friend, he should take himself, his army and his ships out of here. Otherwise, let him attack me, and I will show him the folly of crossing a Spartan prince. I would rather burn this city down than hand it to Aristeides.'

Sherzada grabbed Pausanias by his collar. 'This is no heroic last stand! This is no Thermopylae. Is this not the city Cleonice loved? Do you want her parents to perish here; your sons too? I too have fought against adverse odds, but only when I had good troops behind me. How many Spartans do you have? Sixty? And your Bosporan mercenaries are good fighters, but they are more interested in Artabaz's gold than in defending Byzantium. And as for your citizens' militia, they are no match for the Athenians. So if it comes to a fight, Pausanias, you can rely only on your sixty Spartans. Against these you face three thousand battle-hardened Athenians and two thousand blood-thirsty Thracians.'

Pausanias gave an ugly laugh. 'Don't tell me you are in the pay of Aristeides? Returning a favour for saving your life at Plataea?'

Sherzada turned away in anger. Only Gorgo's mesmerizing

face before him gave him the patience to try again. 'Have you forgotten Gorgo? Have you forgotten Sparta? The Athenians are going to take this city one way or the other. If Cleonice means so much to you, and if you have the slightest regard for the affection Gorgo holds you in, you will take this opportunity Aristeides is giving you … and escape from here, return to Sparta, and regain your position as Regent.'

'I have no future there,' said Pausanias. 'Archidamus and his cronies have made sure of that.'

'Gorgo needs you. Don't tell me you have turned your back on Sparta and on her.'

'I shall gladly give up my life for Sparta. But it is Sparta that has forsaken me. Gorgo is under pressure and now Euryanax is a marked man.'

'Euryanax? What do you mean?' asked Sherzada.

Pausanias looked at Demaratus, and Demaratus explained how Euryanax had disobeyed Leotychidas' order not to arm the Helots while fighting in Thessaly, and how Leotychidas' arrest for accepting bribes from Aleuas of Thessaly had not prevented Euryanax's incarceration as soon as he returned to Sparta.

'Euryanax also escaped just before his trial,' said Demaratus. 'I have heard the Crypteia is sent to assassinate him. Gorgo is suspected of abetting his escape, though there is no proof that she did. Rumours abound about Archidamus' conspiracies against Gorgo and Pleistarchus.'

'This is the Sparta you wish me to return to?' asked Pausanias. 'Where one of my cousins is being hunted by the very men he and I led at Plataea; the other is slowly being stripped of her power and dignity; and my nephew, the King, is under threat from his own colleague. This is not the Sparta I once knew.'

Pausanias moved away from them, turning again to the defences of the city. But from his vantage point Sherzada had already seen the dejected looks on the faces of the city militiamen. From the windows and doors he could see people huddled together, terror plain in their eyes. Sherzada knew that Pausanias had seen this, too.

Pausanias stopped and without turning his back asked, 'If I were to leave here, where would I go? There is no place, other than the Persian court, which is out of the question. I have nowhere to go, except perhaps to Hades? As you can see, death is a very attractive option for me.'

Demaratus finally spoke. 'There is a Greek city in Ionia, a city called Colophon that has just liberated itself without any Athenian help. Its citizens hate the Persians, but they don't trust the Athenians either. They say that they don't want to replace Persian masters with Athenian ones. Moreover, they are well disposed to Sparta and Spartans. They will happily welcome you.'

Sherzada saw confusion in Pausanias' handsome face as he weighed his options. Going down fighting would certainly be heroic if completely pointless and Sherzada saw Pausanias was beginning to realize it too.

'Cleonice once told me about a dream she had about Byzantium becoming a great city and remaining so for centuries. It is certainly beautiful, just as she was.' Pausanias once again looked to all those below – anxious soldiers and frightened civilians – and then turned to Sherzada. 'Highness, Lord of the Sakas, *Legatus* of the Senate and People of Rome, and Guest-friend of the Royal Spartan House of the Agiadae, I beseech you to convey to Aristeides, *Strategos* of the armies of the Athenian People, on my behalf the following terms for the surrender of Byzantium ...'

Chapter 39

The 'Puppy's' Son

Royal Compound of the Eurypontidae
Limnae District
Sparta
The same night

Gorgo could not help wondering that this young woman in front of her had once been a spoilt girl with a short temper and a hard fist. She had become famous in all of Sparta for her pugilistic skills; in brawling she had broken many a nose – both male and female.

But on this night, she looked different. Gone was the long hair she used to tie up in a tight knot above her head. She had cut her hair very short in the wake of her nuptials.

Gorgo had trouble thinking of this young girl as a queen. In her late teens, she was a little younger than her husband Archidamus, and his half-aunt by blood. Lampito was the daughter of Leotychidas by his second wife. Leotychidas had ordained that the two should wed and they had done so dutifully.

Lampito went to fetch her husband and soon, Archidamus came out of his apartment, with his usual contrived smile. Gorgo could not help but notice how much of a weakling he looked in comparison to this tall brawny wife. His long hair was dishevelled as if he had lately risen from bed. Still, he chose to be maliciously cheerful. 'What a pleasant surprise! To what do I this nocturnal visit? Have you come to confess your involvement in cousin Euryanax's escape?'

'Not before you admit you played a part in your grandfather's treasonous activities.'

Archidamus' composure melted as he began to protest.

Gorgo calmed him down. 'I am here to talk to you about the murders of our senior generals, Eurybiadas and Evaeneutus included, as well as Theras, commander of the Knights. And his deputy has seemed to have lost his head, literally.'

Archidamus scoffed. 'Eurybiadas was knocked off his horse by a low-lying branch and fell headfirst into a ditch full of hard rocks. He should have known better than to ride a horse at his age, with his bad leg. Evaeneutus, my kinsman, died of drinking spoilt wine and he too ought to have known better. And for Theras, an unfortunate accident. And I am not really sure what happened to Iason. All these incidents are as untimely as they are unfortunate; that is all. '

As calmly as she could manage, Gorgo explained that Eurybiadas' body bore distinct signs of a struggle and it was not a question of his head being smashed on a rock, but of someone smashing his head in with a rock. Theras' death was also a cover up. Everyone knew that he was the best horseman in all of Sparta. And as for Evaeneutus, she asked Archidamus if he had ever seen him drinking alcohol, let alone being drunk. She knew he would not have touched any wine, bad or otherwise. She went on to mention two other cases of generals who had died under similarly suspicious circumstances; apparently from poison.

'Unfortunate coincidences, all,' insisted Archidamus.

'What about Taenarus?' she asked.

Archidamus professed ignorance.

How could he not know? she asked herself. Of the Messenian Helots who had served at Plataea, a hundred had been rounded up and marched off to the Temple of Poseidon at Taenarus in Messene with the false promise of being granted their freedom for their services to Sparta. Instead, they were massacred within the precincts of the Temple.

'Your friend Magnas was allegedly among the executioners. Surely he must have told you all about it,' she said.

'As far as I can recall, killing Helots is not a crime in Sparta.'

'But killing anyone in a temple is both a crime and a sin in Sparta. Your Majesty, do you know anything about your parents?'

The question seemed to have taken him aback. He frowned, but she continued anyway.

'You are the son of Zeuxidamus the son of Leotychidas, better known by his nickname *Kyniskus* – 'Puppy'. Your father was called Kyniskus because he was so gentle and loyal. Our Upbringing takes tender children and turns them into brutes. But that had no effect on your father. He remained always a gentle and kind soul. Though brave in battle, there was not a kinder and more wise man in Sparta. When he died, all of Sparta wept. And the Helots wept, for they loved him too.

'You were a baby in our care on the day your father died and your mother, my father's cousin, had left you in our house while she tended her sick husband. She died a few years later and on the day she died, I wept like I have not wept for anyone before, because like your father she too was loved by us and by all of Sparta.

'Your parents were decent and wise beyond their tender years. That is why Sparta expects much from you.

'There is something not quite right in this our kingdom of Sparta and you, the only adult king, have a responsibility to set things right. I have come to appeal to you, as your kinswoman and your subject, not as your adversary.'

But Archidamus shook his head. 'You Agiads and your silver tongues! You reduced my grandfather to the status of a puppet. Queen Gorgo, you have told me what you expect from me, now let me tell you what I would like to have from you. Hiero, the Prince of Syracuse, is on his way here to claim you as his bride. His is the most powerful of Greek states outside our mainland. I expect you to accept his offer and accompany him to Syracuse.'

'Why should I do that?' she asked, her voice sharp with indignation.

'A woman who has made a career out of manipulation and deception; and is not above using any means to achieve her ends, seems an ideal match for our ruthless and ambitious Syracusan prince, don't you think?

'I am jesting, of course,' he laughed, noticing her anger. 'After all, they say you have always placed Sparta's interests before your own. With your presence as the consort of the future ruler of Syracuse, Sparta will not only gain an important ally, we will extend our influence into Sicily and Italy.'

'And what will happen to my son when I am gone?'

'I shall protect him, of course.'

'As you have protected your late generals? Our senior-most bodyguards have been killed. Four of your Generals have been murdered. You have chased away a fifth, my cousin Euryanax. We are losing allies everywhere. Argos is becoming stronger while we are become increasingly friendless. Sparta is losing the goodwill of Tegea and every day we move closer to war with Athens. Do you really want to go down in history as the Spartan king who presided over our downfall? And what of the Helots? You appear to ignore that there is even a problem while your cronies go around massacring them. And you insist on this pointless feud with me and my family. Perhaps you would rather the world remember you as the grandson of a traitor than as the son of the most loved man in Sparta?'

Archidamus remained silent for a moment, perhaps contemplating the fate of his people, and himself. At least, that was what Gorgo dared to hope. As for the other – the suggestion she should be sold off for marriage – she would deal with that later. The fate of her people was hanging in the balance.

'Are you through, Queen Gorgo?' he said, finally. 'It's late and my wife is waiting for me. We have nothing left to discuss.'

For the first time, Gorgo found herself truly helpless.

Chapter 40

The World Turned Upside Down

Athenian military headquarters outside Byzantium
The following morning

A large circular shield of bronze hung inside the tent, bearing the black emblem of the Owl and the Olive, the symbols of his city. On the table lay his magnificent helmet painted gold and black, with a long horse-hair crest dyed in alternate gold and black stripes. And that was matched by his dress – golden breastplate, over a half-sleeved black tunic. He sat motionless on a chair as he attentively listened to Pausanias' terms for the surrender of Byzantium.

When Sherzada finished reading out the terms, Aristeides breathed a sigh of relief. 'You need not worry about my men harming any civilians. I am not fond of sacking and pillaging. And I will accept all of Pausanias' terms. As for Cleonice's parents, I shall personally pay my respects to them and reassure them of their safety and that of all of the citizens of Byzantium.' He paused, then asked, 'Is there anything else?'

Sherzada hesitated. 'Pausanias wants the Athenians to stop their propaganda against him.'

'And deprive the Athenian public of their most favourite pastime?' Aristeides chuckled. 'I'll do what can be done. However, one of the flaws of democracy is that you cannot keep people's mouths shut. So bad is Pausanias' reputation in Athens that it will be a long time before they stop saying unkind things about him.'

Aristeides rose and patted Sherzada on the back. 'You have saved Athenian lives, today, my friend … and those of others as well.'

'You also did well to stay your hand.'

'Well, I had three friends inside Byzantium,' Aristeides replied.

* * *

Sherzada rode back to Byzantium, where he once more found Pausanias. 'My Prince,' he said to Sherzada, 'there is one more favour I must ask of you.

'I am taking my infant sons, Pleistonax and Cleomenes, to Colophon for a little while. Their nurses, who are Helots trusted by my family, will accompany us. Once you are back in the Peloponnesus, I shall send the boys with them to you. You must take them and hand them to the care of my brother Nicomedes in Sparta, who is now Regent in my place. Tell Nicomedes that he must raise his nephews as his wards. When my sons are seven they will enter the *Agoge* – the Upbringing. They will grow up as Spartan warriors. Nicomedes must ensure this happens.

'My brother,' Pausanias continued, 'is very loyal and I know he will do this for me, provided you vouch for my sons' identity ... because no one else in Sparta knows of their existence.'

Promising to honour his request, Sherzada added, 'You must consider returning to Sparta, Pausanias. Gorgo needs you, even if you don't think you need her anymore. The two of you together can still out-manoeuvre Archidamus.'

'Not without Euryanax we can't. He was our real pillar of strength. He has always kept me on the right path. If you can somehow bring Euryanax back into the picture, and I have no idea how you will do that, I will consider returning to Sparta. But for all we know, he may already be dead. The Crypteia rarely misses its target ...'

Demaratus cut him off, saying, 'but then again, Euryanax was the Upbringing's best graduate. If anyone can outwit the Crypteia, it is he.'

Pausanias nodded and said to Sherzada, 'Return to Sparta, my

Prince. Help Euryanax get back to Sparta to support Gorgo. If you can do that, I too shall return. If you can't, do whatever is in your power to save her and her son. You are her last hope.'

That night, Pausanias' entourage left Byzantium by boat. Meanwhile, the Bosporan mercenaries, paid off with Persian gold, hurried towards their ships and sailed off in search of fresh employers and more gold; or simply, more gold. To cover their departure, the town militia dressed in helmets with long flowing crests and reddish cloaks. The appearance of a Spartan presence had to be maintained until the very end. Pausanias did not want to take any chances. After all, he was up against the Fox.

Still, for Sherzada, the Fox was 'Aristeides the Just,' and he knew the Athenian would keep his word.

In the morning, Sherzada rose at dawn and went down to receive the Athenians. As he watched the sun emerge from the waters of the Bosphorus, he caught sight of Aristeides approaching with his bodyguards. Sherzada escorted him to the house of Cleonice's parents, where Aristeides spoke kindly to them. His friendly words reassured them that neither they nor their city nor anyone in it was going to be harmed. This same message he delivered to a gathering of Byzantium's leading citizens whom he met with immediately afterwards. To make good his pledge, he kept most of his force outside the city, deploying only a tiny garrison inside the citadel, for it had been Pausanias' stronghold.

Once Aristeides had finished organizing his peaceful takeover of the city, Sherzada came to him to say goodbye. He found him poring over some documents. Sherzada told him that he needed to go, but Aristeides was preoccupied with other thoughts.

After a long while, Aristeides raised his head and told Sherzada the news. The Persian stronghold of Eion had also fallen a few days before, but only after overcoming incredible resistance. The Persian soldiers had fought to the last, inflicting heavy casualties on the Athenians. Hundreds of Cimon's men had perished taking its walls. And inside the citadel, no Persian – man, woman or child – was found alive. Once the walls were breached, all of the civilians had committed suicide, preferring to die than to become the slaves of the Greeks. Eion itself was left a smouldering shell. Burning the city to ground had been the last act of its Persian governor, Bogesh, before he too fell on his sword.

And now another war was flaring up in Thrace. Alexander's Macedonians, who only two years ago massacred the Persian stragglers from Plataea, were now attacking the Athenians at that very same crossing. Eion, which could have been a useful stronghold for the Athenians to protect the crossing, was but a charred ruin. Moreover, Alexander was using Persian gold to sow disaffection among the Thracian tribes, undermining Cimon's influence over them. The Macedonian King had also unleashed his soldiers against the Athenians all over Thrace, in a bid to weaken their foothold there and deny them the Thracian timber and silver they so badly wanted.

Aristeides shook his head. 'All of us were on the same side not so long ago. Did we fight for freedom only to go at each other's throats?'

Later, when Sherzada was ready to leave, Aristeides accompanied him to the port. They walked a while in silence, and then Aristeides spoke in a grave voice. 'I received a message from Elpinice. According to her source in Sparta, it appears this Helot business is becoming serious. And Euryanax's disappearance is being linked with increased restlessness among the Helots of Messene. I am sure this is adding to Gorgo's woes, if they weren't enough.'

Aristeides told Sherzada that Prince Hiero of Syracuse was coming to ask for Gorgo's hand. Sherzada knew about Hiero from his time in Italy; he was an unscrupulous, power-hungry man.

'I suspect Gorgo will not be pleased with this arrangement,'

Aristeides replied. 'Pleistarchus is still a boy and his Regent, Nicomedes, is not well-equipped to counter Archidamus' machinations.'

With a wrench, Sherzada changed the subject; thanking Aristeides for solving their 'Pausanias problem' in a happy way.

'I would love to claim credit for all of this. But it is Gorgo, not I, you should thank for orchestrating this,' said Aristeides.

'Gorgo?'

'After asking you to return to Greece from Italy,' Aristeides explained, 'Gorgo met with Elpinice in Megara. Elpinice agreed to convince Cimon to call off his assassins against Pausanias, and allow me to lead Athenian forces against Byzantium. She knew that of all Athenians, only I was sympathetic to Pausanias and would help him find a way out. And Demaratus' presence here was no coincidence, either. His task was to find a place Demaratus could escape to. However, Gorgo realized how difficult it would be to get Pausanias out of Byzantium alive. She said only you could convince him to leave Byzantium safely … you were the only one who could save his life.'

Looking back at the high walls of Byzantium, Aristeides said, 'Well, my friend, at least we did not make a mess of it like Cimon did at Eion. Eion is now useless to defend against Alexander's attacks. Byzantium is still intact. And that is all that matters to me.'

The two men finally reached Byzantium's usually busy port. Activity was beginning to pick up as merchant vessels and fishing boats were again being allowed in by the Athenian navy. Sherzada caught sight of the passenger vessel which was to take him away, docking close by.

'What will you do now?' Sherzada asked.

'I am tired of all of this. I shall await my replacement and then go into retirement; living off whatever crumbs my friends can throw at me.'

'That will not be necessary,' Sherzada responded. He still had an interest in the amber trade controlled by Scythian merchants at port of Olbia across the Euxine Sea. He reached into his bag and pulled out a parchment. 'Give this to the amber merchants in Olbia. It is a letter of credit. They will honour it and provide you with a generous sum of talents.'

At first the proud Aristeides refused to accept the parchment, but at Sherzada's insistence, he reluctantly agreed. He shook his friend's hand warmly. 'Thank you. And you … where will you go now?' he asked.

'I need to find Euryanax,' Sherzada admitted. 'I need both he and Pausanias back in Sparta if we are to help Gorgo fight Archidamus and his cronies.'

'Be careful, my friend. There is a vicious streak running through Sparta now. They are becoming more intolerant towards the Helots, and more suspicious of all foreign influence. King Archidamus believes that the only way he can lead Sparta is to remove the only obstacle on his way to greatness: Gorgo!'

Chapter 41

The Last Of The Messenians

The road to Mt. Ithome
Messene – South-western Peloponnesus
Late summer, 477 BC

The sun was shining in all its glory over Messene. It was a beautiful day. But Sherzada's mind was elsewhere. He was travelling in disguise so as not to arouse Spartan suspicions; pretending to be a merchant from Italy who had managed to get himself lost.

And as it turned out, the Spartans seemed to have no interest in foreigners who were careless enough to lose their way. Instead, all the soldiers he met seemed to be focusing on the Helots. Security was being tightened everywhere. Something was indeed afoot. Rumours were circulating that the Spartans had sent out not one but several Crypteia squads against the Helots, backed up, as Sherzada was witnessing, by their regular army. The large number of Spartan military patrols Sherzada came across were ample evidence of this. One story suggested that one of the Crypteia squads may even have killed its prey. But no one could confirm this report. The result was fear on the face of every Helot he came across. Fear that it might be their turn next.

But communicating with the Helots proved more difficult. While he had thought through how to evade Spartan suspicions, Sherzada had not really worked out how he would convince the Helots to lead him to Euryanax. Before leaving Italy for Athens, Sherzada had received a letter from Euro. This letter had no mention of Sparta, or Greek politics, or even Gorgo. It only mentioned one woman – a Helot woman – he had fallen in love with in the region of Mount Ithome in Messene. A woman whose beauty was reminiscent of that of Helen of Troy. Her name was Melissa.

If anyone knew where Euryanax could be, it was Melissa. But he had no idea where to start. He did not even know what she looked like, except that she was beautiful. Worse, the prevailing atmosphere of panic meant the Helots were too scared to talk to him. The moment he mentioned Melissa's name, they made polite excuses and hurried away. But the fact that nearly every Helot avoided answering his questions about Melissa only convinced Sherzada that he was on the right track.

As the sun set, he could see the town of Ithome above him, located on the top of a plateau-like mountain; bearing all the hallmarks of a natural fortress. Sherzada thought he would climb up in the morning and try his luck there. So that night he made himself a modest meal of dried meat and fruits and lay in the open beneath the stars to sleep, covered by his cloak.

When he woke, Sherzada could not see anything. He was blindfolded. His hands were tied behind his back. As he struggled to break loose, he felt two pairs of hands forcibly raise him up until he sat uncomfortably on his knees. He could hear men walking around him. They were speaking the rough dialect of the Helots. These were not the meek ones that he had become used to meeting in Sparta. These were the defiant, belligerent kind, at least from their talk. More alarming for him, they were discussing not whether they should kill him; but how. Each of his captors, in turn, came up with a more creative way of transporting him to his Maker. And each time a suggestion was made, there was laughter.

Then a loud female voice ordered them to be quiet. 'Do you want the entire Spartan army to descend on this cave, fools?'

There was silence.

The woman told the men to uncover Sherzada's blindfold. The light from the mouth of the cave blinded him for a moment. But soon his eyes became used to the environment. Though its mouth was very narrow, the cave itself was quite spacious. There were two separate passages extending inside the cave, through one of which the woman seemed to have appeared. All he could make out was her silhouette. Sherzada counted seven men in the cave, all armed. The two nearest were pointing their weapons at him.

'My name is Melissa of the clan Aristomenidae,' the woman said. 'I hear you have been asking about me.'

As she came closer, Sherzada could make out her features, her long flowing brown hair. Melissa reminded him of Gorgo, though she was taller, stronger in build, and sterner of tongue. She indeed had the beauty of Helen of Troy, just as Euro had described her. And after all, Helen was a Spartan of Achaean blood, not Dorian.

Melissa spoke Greek as someone who had received good education, unlike most of Helots who spoke a more vulgar vernacular.

As Sherzada's eyes became more attuned to the light in the cave, he found it more habitable than it had first appeared. There was even a table with some stools in the corner. Melissa pulled one over and sat down on it. 'Tell me, why have you been looking for me?'

'I am looking for Euryanax,' he said. 'I am here to help him.'

'Why should he need your help? How do I know you have not been sent here to kill him?'

When Sherzada told her that he was his friend, she simply responded. 'What greater treachery can there be than having a man die at the hands of a man he considers his friend?'

'Perhaps he does not need my help,' said Sherzada, 'or perhaps he does. I just need to understand what is going on. I am a foreigner who befriended him and his family. I helped to save Pausanias, as you might be aware, and I will gladly do the same for Euryanax.'

'He is one of us now. We are his family.

'My Lord, you have not been a Helot. You have no idea of the conditions we live under every day. At times, death is far more merciful than living the life of a Helot. And as you well know, any Spartan can legally kill a Helot with impunity. To add insult to injury, the Ephors also issue a directive to us to observe the law – Spartan Law; which basically means that we are supposed to behave ourselves even as our throats are being slit.

'Many of us are regularly beaten, and our women often raped, for no reason other than the Spartans reminding us that they are our masters. And they send the Crypteia to silence the few who dare to speak out or just to kill a random Helot only to remind us that they can.

'We are called 'Helots' because we are *Haliskomenoi* – 'captured people'. Our ancestors, once citizens of proud Greek kingdoms, were captured and enslaved by these Dorian Barbarians who now call themselves Spartans. Their ancestors invaded our lands some three hundred years ago. First they seized the Laconian kingdom and its capital, Sparta. They arrogated to themselves the names of those who once dwelt in the city of Helen and Menelaus, enslaving the original Spartans – who became the first Helots. Greedy and still hungry for more land, these self-proclaimed Spartans invaded this land, Messene, and after a bitter struggle brought it under their control.

'I am of royal blood. My mother's family claim descent from Helen and Menelaus, but on my father's side I am the direct descendant of Aristomenes, the last great King of Messene, who lived a hundred and fifty years ago. He led the last "Great Uprising" of the Messenians, and came very near to threatening Sparta itself. But eventually, the Spartans put down the "Uprising" and re-established the Helot system with a vengeance. Measures like the Crypteia were introduced to ensure we never rose up again. And the Spartans became even more brutal than before.

'My Lord,' she continued, 'I am the last of Aristomenes' line. My father was killed by the Crypteia last year, in spite of

Euryanax's best efforts to protect him. I had a younger brother whom I loved dearly. He died at Thermopylae along with other Helots, fighting proudly for the defence of Greece. Euryanax told me that you too fought at that battle. You must have witnessed the courage of the Messenians?'

'The Messenians fought with exceptional valour and they died with honour as warriors; our equals,' Sherzada said, and Melissa's face swelled with the same pride as he had seen in Gorgo's when he told her about Spartan courage at Thermopylae.

'My Lord, had the Messenians been free I would have been their queen. Had the Spartans not reduced us to slavery, Euryanax would have been king in Sparta. Imagine, a united kingdom of Sparta and Messene with free citizens and abundant resources. The Spartans would not have had to rule by terror at home and by bullying other nations abroad. But these Spartans do not see it that way. The time has come to take our future, our destiny, into our own hands. We have to take back our freedom. Nobody is going to give it us, certainly not these Spartans.'

'Why not try something different?' he asked. 'Why not seek the help of those in Sparta who sympathize with you?'

Melissa laughed. 'Who is mad enough to sympathize with the Helots in Sparta? The one Spartan king who did so, King Cleomenes, was declared insane and then murdered.

'The only Queen who dared to support us is his daughter Gorgo. And now she is under attack just because she dared to try to ban the wholesale slaughter of Helots. The Spartans are reverting to their old mindset. They are punishing even those Helots who fought for Sparta, massacring a hundred Helot veterans of Plataea at the Temple of Poseidon at Taenarus. What power and influence Gorgo had is all but lost, in large part due to her sympathies for us.

'If any Spartan could have made a difference for us Helots, it is Euryanax, but he too is hounded. No man has been more loyal to Sparta than him. This was the man who led Spartan armies to glory, and now the same Spartans are after his blood. Is this the Sparta you want us to make our peace with?'

'All I am saying is that leading this rag-tag group of young men against the Spartans would be suicide. Even if all the Helots of Laconia and Messene rise up – though I doubt all of them will – they will be torn apart by the Spartan army, the best in Greece.'

Melissa smiled. 'You think I don't know that, my Lord? I am very much aware of what we are up against. We have to take our time to plan, to train our young men, and then wait. Even if it takes a few more years, we shall wait for the perfect opportunity. And we shall rise up and bring down our oppressors. The Spartans have ruled over us for at least two hundred years, we can wait a few more before we make our bid for freedom.'

'Are you so sure that you can bring the greatest military power in Greece to its knees?' asked Sherzada. 'Are you certain that you can count on the support of every Helot in Messene or Laconia? I am sorry, but I don't think so. Not even with time.'

'So, my Lord, what would you have us do? Call the Spartans over and ask them to slaughter every single Helot man, woman and child? Because, I am sure, this would be a far better alternative than being in Spartan servitude forever. No, my Lord, there is no language which the Spartans understand other than force, and it is only through violence that we can free ourselves.'

Just then a familiar voice rang out from inside the cave. 'We will have to bide our time and find the right moment to strike.'

Though the figure that approached him was Euro, Sherzada could not have recognized him. His once long flowing hair was no more, his once magnificent beard had been replaced by a short stubble. He was dressed in the humble skins of a Helot – though the club in his hand gave an impression of a veritable Heracles.

Euro smiled as he came closer. 'I think my disguise is working. This afternoon you passed right in front of me.'

'Careful, my friend. Tempting fate is one thing I have learnt to avoid.'

'And how do you explain your present predicament?' he laughed, pointing at the rope that tied Sherzada's hands.

'Bad planning,' Sherzada admitted, with an embarrassed grimace.

Euro saw to Sherzada's binding, allowing him to stretch and move in comfort. Then his voice became grave. 'My friend, I once fought for freedom and I am going to fight for it again. But not as a Spartan. My fate is now bound with that of Melissa and her people. I will use all my knowledge and skill to prepare these lads, and many, many more like them in Messene, as well as Laconia, for our ultimate conflict with Sparta. I have been a general of Sparta and I know better than anyone how the Spartans fight.

'Forget about me,' he added. 'Go to Gorgo. She needs you now more than ever.'

Sherzada wanted to know more, but Euro hushed him.

He heard Melissa whisper into her husband's ear, 'We simply cannot allow our guest to walk out of this cave. He might alert the Spartans, even unintentionally, about our hiding place …'

'… Don't worry, Melissa,' said Euro. 'I know what to do with our friend.'

The last thing Sherzada saw was Euro's club coming down on him and then everything went dark.

Chapter 42

The Measure Of A Man

Outside Sparta
Late summer, 477 BC

Sherzada's head was still hurting a week later. He was getting tired of his Greek friends hitting him over the head as a means of getting him out of trouble. He was sure there were other ways.

He had woken a day and half later – perhaps he had been drugged as well – in a boat bound for the northern Peloponnesian city-state of Hermione. Everybody in the boat thought he had been drunk. This was Euro's way of getting him out of Messene undetected.

Once in Hermione, sure enough Pausanias' faithful Helots were waiting for him. They had come from Colophon, bringing Pleistonax and Cleomenes. As Sherzada had promised, he would take the infants to their relatives in Sparta.

When he met Cincinnatus, he was wearing only a tunic, but Sherzada recognized him from his shaved head and his perfect physique. Cincinnatus told him the Athenians had sold one of their triremes – their warships – to Rome and he had been asked to take the new ship home. When Sherzada asked him how his ship was getting on, given that neither he nor his crew had any prior maritime experience, he shrugged and replied, 'It hasn't sunk yet.'

Cincinnatus still doubted whether there was an enthusiasm back home for a navy. Romans tended to be land-lubbers, he said. But he thought it was a novel idea worth trying out. If he did not become the commander of a nascent Roman navy, Cincinnatus could always go back and work on his farm. Either was infinitely more exciting than spending long hours listening to boring speeches in the Senate, which he was now required to do as a newly enrolled Senator.

Cincinnatus told Sherzada that he was using the voyage home to train the crew. And they needed plenty of it. So he was taking his time, deliberating slowing his progress so that the men could become proficient as sailors and marines.

When Sherzada explained he was going to Sparta to help Queen Gorgo, Cincinnatus reminded him that he still held the privileges of a Roman ambassador, one of which was that Roman forces were obliged to come to his assistance should he need it. Since the next stop on their itinerary would be the Spartan coast, Cincinnatus said he was heading for a small island near Cythera where he could continue to train his men. He would remain there for a while should the need arise.

Before he left, Sherzada asked him the one question that had always bothered him about Lucius Quinctius Cincinnatus. 'Why do they call you *Cincinnatus* – 'curly'?' he asked. 'I have never seen your head unshaven. Is your hair really curly?'

Cincinnatus laughed. 'No my friend, it is in fact straight. The name was given to one of my ancestors for whatever reason and it stuck. Now every generation of his male descendants is condemned to carry it. In all likelihood it was a nickname – probably an ironic one. Do you remember old Caius Julius back in Rome? His family's nickname is Caesar – 'the hairy one' – and he is bald.'

They both laughed.

Later, Sherzada bought horses for himself and a cart with an overhead covering to protect the infants from the hot sun and carry their male Helot escort and the two nurses. But just as the group approached Sparta, the Helots insisted on completing the journey by foot. They feared Spartan retribution for Helots daring to ride on carts, no matter how humble, while ordinary Spartans travelled on foot.

So on the northern outskirts of Sparta, Sherzada disposed of the cart and they continued their journey on foot, while the infants cooperated by falling asleep. Sherzada took turns with the nurses carrying the infants. They headed straight for the Royal Compound of the Agiadae just inside the northern city limits.

Entering the compound, he saw a large gathering in its beautiful garden. Most of the men were, however, not dressed in the Spartan manner. Their cloaks were much shorter, and brighter, and their armour very ornate. However, it was their elaborately plumed helmets that made Sherzada smirk. He had not seen more theatrical military outfits.

In the centre stood a scrawny little man wearing a bronze breastplate that seemed a size too large for him. Though the woman he was addressing had her back to Sherzada, he knew it was Gorgo.

Gorgo was wearing a worn-out chiton dress of coarse material with a dark shawl. Her hair was un-brushed, somehow giving the impression that she had just got out of bed. Sherzada contrasted this with the last time he had seen her – the day he had left Sparta – when she had looked radiant in bright colours and expensive jewellery. He felt this had something to do with her guest.

The scrawny man was talking on and on, '… You Spartans are proud of your military prowess, but we Syracusans are second to none. I have led our armies to victory against powerful foes. I defeated an army of 300,000 Carthaginians at Himera. I crushed hordes of those treacherous Sikels at the base of Mount Etna. I destroyed the combined navies of Croton, Lucania and the Bruttium, and …'

Stifling a huge yawn, Gorgo cut him off. 'Forgive me, Prince Hiero, but from what I have heard, there were less than even 30,000 Carthaginians at the battle of Himera and you had at least twice that number of troops on your side. And the hordes of Sikels you crushed were only a few hundred hapless peasants who were inexperienced in combat. And as for destroying the combined fleets of Croton, Lucania and Bruttium, I have it on good authority that their total number did not exceed twenty warships compared to your two hundred. Impressive victories indeed, my Lord!'

Hiero turned red. 'Lady Gorgo, think carefully before mocking me. My brother Gelon is childless and on his death-bed. It is not long before I will become master of the most populous of all Greek states. My Lady, you are still young and beautiful, but that will not last forever. I offer unparalleled wealth and power. After all, you will be marrying the most powerful of Greek leaders and also the bravest. A real man! You would be a fool, madam, not to accept my proposal.'

'My Lord,' she said, 'I have tasted power and found it bitter. I have had wealth but it could not bring me happiness. And as for what makes a man, it is not power; it is not wealth; it is not destroying armies or sinking fleets; it is not even that thing between your legs. Do you know, my Lord, what is the true measure of a man?'

She walked a few steps forward, her head still lost in thought, waiting for his reply. When he did not speak, she suddenly turned and asked, 'Tell me, Highness, have you drunk the waters of the mighty Indus? Have you walked along the banks of the tempestuous Tiber? Have you gazed across the wondrous Nile? Were you at Thermopylae, my Prince, fighting among the heroes? Were you at Plataea deciding the fate of Greece? Were you at Fidenae with the Romans overcoming an adversary three times their size? Are you a leader who values wisdom over power? Are you a warrior who prefers peace to war? Are you a man of passion, my Lord? Are you a man obsessed? Do you have that hunger for adventure? Do you have that thirst for knowledge? Have you travelled to distant lands seeking nothing but the Truth? Tell me, Prince Hiero, have you ever thought of others more than for yourself? Do you know what it is like to love without condition? If not, then by what other measure can you truly call yourself a man?'

Hiero of Syracuse turned around, red-faced, and walked

away without a word, taking his flamboyantly dressed soldiers with him.

As Gorgo gossiped with her ladies-in-waiting, baby Cleomenes chose that very moment to wake. The howling cries of the infant betrayed Sherzada's hiding place at the edge of the garden.

She came round to investigate and seeing Sherzada with a babe in his arms, her eyes burned with rage.

'Whose baby is that?' demanded Gorgo of the little bundle he held in his arms.

'It's not what you think,' he smiled as he stepped forward, soothing Cleomenes.

Pleistonax began to howl equally loudly.

'That's what they all say,' she responded, clearly bemused. 'There are two of them?'

'Queen Gorgo,' said Sherzada, 'meet Prince Cleomenes, son of Pausanias and the Lady Cleonice, and this is his older brother Pleistonax.'

'Cleomenes!' Gorgo gasped, taking the infant into her arms, and bending to kiss the wailing Pleistonax. 'Pleistonax ... almost like Pleistarchus ... Pleistarchus will be thrilled to see his little cousins. We must go to him now. He has been ill.'

Sherzada followed Gorgo as she walked holding baby Cleomenes tightly and smiling at him, while he cradled Pleistonax, the Helots in tow.

As they approached Gorgo's apartment, Sherzada saw Pleistarchus come out. He had changed much in the last two years, older and taller than the little boy he had last seen. But he was looking very pale and weak. Still, Pleistarchus welcomed Sherzada with a broad smile. His face lit up as he saw the infants.

Gorgo turned to give the infants to their nurses so they could take them to the home of Pausanias' younger brother, Nicomedes, who would be their guardian from thenceforth. As she did so, her son collapsed on the ground.

Gorgo cried out. Sherzada picked up the lad and took him back to their apartment. As Sherzada was gently lowering him on to his bed, he smelled Pleistarchus' breath.

Gorgo managed to smile at last. 'I am so glad you came. I have a feeling this will get better now …' As she looked at the worried expression on Sherzada's face, her smile disappeared. '…What's wrong?'

'Pleistarchus has been poisoned.'

Chapter 43

To Kill A King

Sparta

Sherzada's words hit Gorgo like a bolt of lightning. 'This smell,' he said, 'this almondy smell. I have smelt it before on poison victims after they died. I am only surprised that he is not dead already.'

Gorgo gently touched her son's face as he lay on his bed. 'That is probably because I have been giving Pleistarchus potions to build his body's resistance against poisons,' she replied.

'You knew he was being poisoned?'

'I knew he was in danger of it,' said Gorgo, sitting down beside Pleistarchus. 'Father started using these when he sensed he might be assassinated. The potions I have come from a healer in Arcadia, but his knowledge and skills are limited.'

As Sherzada continued to examine Pleistarchus, he said, 'You did well, but there are many different types of poisons. They may have used more than one type. What you did may have slowed down the poison's effect, but he is still dying. We need to find a cure, and fast.'

Gorgo called to the servants to bring strips of wet cloth. And then she asked Sherzada what he could do to help.

'I know of one antidote,' he replied, 'which might neutralize the poison. But even that may only keep him alive a little longer. We still have to take him to a healer with greater skills than you or I.'

'Where will we find such a person? The skills of Spartan physicians are limited to combat injuries and I do not know of any healer who can treat poisons.'

He had an answer. 'Rán's injuries were treated by a number of expert physicians. One among them is an expert on poisons. He teaches at a school for physicians on the island of Cos. We must take Pleistarchus to him.'

'Then this is what we shall do.'

When Agathe and the other servant girls arrived with the wet strips to cool Pleistarchus' fever, Sherzada asked them to fetch the ingredients for his potion. While Gorgo tried to keep down the young King's fever with wet strips of cloth, Sherzada went with them to prepare the antidote. A little later, Sherzada returned with a jug full of the potion. Gorgo helped Pleistarchus sit up as he drank it. In a few hours, Pleistarchus gained some consciousness. He vomited a lot but Sherzada told her that it was some of the poison coming out. Soon afterwards, the heat in his body started to cool off and then he went back to sleep, breathing normally. Sherzada was confident that he would be much better by morning and would be fit to travel then. As her son's health improved, so did Gorgo's spirits.

Sherzada, meanwhile, thought he saw something outside. He lifted the blinds to get a better look but could not see anything in the darkness. He went to another window to check if Gorgo's guards were outside her apartment. They were. Perhaps Pleistarchus' predicament was making him imagine things that were simply not there.

As Sherzada sat down on the floor outside Pleistarchus' bedroom, Gorgo came and joined him. Sitting down beside him, she reminded him of the encounter at dawn when they had met five men outside the Temple of Athena taking down the bodies of the executed traitors. 'Those men,' she said, 'and those behind them are gaining power. They even have Archidamus under their influence and his jealousy against the Agiadae plays directly into their hands.

'These people, these reactionaries, want to take Sparta back to the past. A Sparta uncontaminated with dangerous new ideas. They say I have gone soft on the Helots.

'I found what you had written about the struggle between the

Patricians and the Plebs in your letters from Rome very interesting. If Sparta is to become truly great, we have to find a political compromise like the Romans are trying to. Just imagine! If we can get more Helots and the Perioiki to join our forces in return for concessions, we will not have to rely on our small army. It makes perfect military sense. But not just military. We shall have all those living within Spartan domains having a stake in the strength and welfare of Sparta. It makes political sense; and human sense.'

She got up, and let out a deep sigh. 'To do this I need my cousins beside me.' She turned to Sherzada. 'Thanks to you, Pausanias is safe, at least for now. But I am not sure … whether Euro is alive or dead?'

Sherzada smiled, but Gorgo hushed him by bending over and putting her index finger on his lips. 'That is all I need to know,' she whispered.

Sherzada whispered back, 'How did your father die?'

In hushed tones, Gorgo began to explain, starting with the last days of King Cleomenes' controversial life.

* * *

I remember Menander bringing my father the news. Father said that he could use the cover of patriotism to escape the charges with regard to the Sepeia massacre or the killing of the Persians but not that of bribing the Oracle of Delphi. His enemies had ensured that case against him was air-tight. He also knew what would follow. The trial would be used to impeach and dethrone him. He told me all of this before suddenly riding away in a hurry.

Soon, news arrived that Father was in Messene, raising an army of Helots to march on Sparta. For the Spartans it was unthinkable; not only because a Spartan king was marching on his own capital, but he was doing so at the head of an army of

Helots. As soon as he reached Arcadia, the Gerousia immediately dropped all charges against the King and invited him back.

Many began to fear Father and what he might do next. Some were convinced he was bent upon emancipating the Helots and ending the supremacy of Spartans within their own domains. Soon rumours started circulating that he was going mad. It was not long after that that he was declared insane and incarcerated. A day later, he was found dead. A Helot was swiftly executed for allegedly giving him the knife with which my father supposedly killed himself.

I did not believe the story. I had visited him only a couple of days before his death and had never seen him saner. Someone had ordered my father's murder. Only sixteen and newly wed to Cleomenes' half-brother Leonidas, I had no choice but turn to my husband. Leonidas promised he would look into the matter, but soon he, and all of Sparta, got embroiled in the Carneia incident around the time of Marathon.

And anyway, like most Spartans, Leonidas had seen only the madness, and never the method, in Father's policies. He did not understand any of it until we received Demaratus' message about the Persian invasion. It was only then Leonidas realized, almost a decade too late, what my father had been trying to do all along.

One night Leonidas came to me drunk and weeping bitterly, the first and last time I saw him in that state. He begged my forgiveness, saying he not only knew that my father would be killed, he was also a part of the conspiracy that had led to his death. When I refused him forgiveness, he left. Before he went, I told him that I had no intention of sharing his bed anymore.

Much later, after Thermopylae and just a few weeks before he himself took his own life, Cleombrotus, Pausanias' father, told me the whole story. Apparently, the two brothers saw Father as a dangerous man who wanted to ruin Spartan society and their laws. Their views were shared by the Ephors and a conspiracy was hatched to get rid of Father. Cleombrotus said in the beginning both he and Leonidas were reluctant to go along with the plan, but they finally agreed. Leotychidas was not involved in the plot because Leonidas neither liked him nor trusted him. So the Ephors went ahead and declared Father insane and later the murder was arranged in a way that would make it appear a suicide.

Around the time Leonidas first confessed his involvement in the death of my father, the Persian threat had begun to loom. Even though I hated Leonidas at the time, as a Spartan queen I continued to support him publicly. It was I who suggested to him the need to create a formal Greek alliance – the Hellenic League – which my father had always dreamed of. Leonidas took my advice and consolidated our alliance with Athens which Father had negotiated before his death, and brought others too within the fold. Those were heady days; exciting days. For once, the Greeks were acting the way my father had wanted them to.

After our abortive attempt to block the Persian advance at Tempe, Leonidas allowed me to work with the generals to find other ways to resist the Persians. My father had told me that it might be better to sacrifice a smaller part of an army in order to preserve the greater part of it, to buy time, to build up the defences and to wear the enemy down before a decisive confrontation. I had a plan, and I needed it to work.

Two things helped me. The first was the Carneia, which came soon after the Persian army entered Greece. I went to the Gerousia to remind the Spartans, in person, of the sacred duty to keep our army inactive for this period. The second was the one thing, other than the army, that my father had advised me to use sparingly and with great care.

I made a secret journey to Delphi on the beautiful slopes of Mount Parnassus, where I met with Gorgus, my father's friend. My father had told me that he was one of the few men in Greece whom I could trust. His strength was his discretion. Gorgus described himself as a broker in the business of influence and nothing was more influential in Greek politics than the Oracle of Apollo at Delphi. During that meeting, I gave him instructions along with a generous portion of my father's inheritance. He noted down word for word what I expected to hear from the Oracle.

Less than a week later, the Pythioi, our ambassadors to the Delphic Oracle, brought back a chilling message from the god Apollo as conveyed through his priestess in Delphi. And it was clear – either a Spartan king must die or Sparta would be destroyed. I watched Leonidas as the 'prophecy' was read aloud. I could see from his face that its significance had not been missed. As a religious man he realized the time for reckoning was at hand. He would have to die for Sparta to survive. His guilt would not have allowed him to reach any other conclusion.

And so Leonidas began to prepare for war. He had taken to heart everything I had told him about preserving the army, and decided to take a relatively small force to block the Persian advance. Our Greek allies were also asked to send troops. He justified the sending of this small force on the grounds that though the Carneia forbade general military activity, this prohibition would not apply to a tiny Spartan contingent already committed to its own destruction. Those who were already doomed could not invite a greater wrath from the gods, or so he rationalized. I could not help thinking at the time of the irony that Leonidas' suicide had been so meticulously planned, just like my father's.

Leonidas dismissed his bodyguard the *Hippeis* – three hundred of our best young warriors – and, instead, chose a force of three hundred veterans, all of whom had one thing in common. Each had a son who was about to complete the Upbringing. If the fathers perished, the sons could replace them in a matter of weeks. The army would be preserved and in principle the prohibition of the Carneia would not be violated.

When I saw the energy Leonidas was putting into the effort of training his small force, the way he was approaching his own death with so much courage and enthusiasm, as a Spartan wife I could not have been more proud of my husband. It was then I allowed him to share my bed once again. That was the closest I ever came to truly loving him. A part of me wanted to tell him all and save him, but somehow another part of me wanted my plan to work; to save Sparta and also to have my revenge. Perhaps too there was a feeling that Leonidas wanted to atone for his crime, and was looking forward to his death.

There arrived the day Leonidas came to say goodbye to Pleistarchus and me. Normally, custom dictated a mother or a wife would give the Spartan warrior his shield and tell him to *come back either with it or on it.* I wanted to say that to him as I gave him his shield. But what came out was something very different and very selfish. 'What am I expected to do if you don't come back?' I asked.

He smiled and said: 'Marry a good man who will treat you well, bear him strong children, and live a good life.' And he then went off to Thermopylae to die.

* * *

Gorgo looked at Sherzada and said, 'I do not know if your one God can forgive me, for I am not sure I can forgive myself.'

Just then the door slammed open. Gorgo got up with a start. Sherzada reached for his sword only to realise he had left it inside Pleistarchus' room. A Helot came crashing through the door. He stumbled and fell into the hearth room, as if he had been hurled inside. He was small and thin; his nose seemed to be broken, bleeding profusely.

Behind him came a tall hooded figure, carrying a short sword.

Chapter 44

The Children Of Chilon

Sparta

'Lampito?'

The tall Eurypontid Queen took off her hood to reveal her young, determined, face. 'This man came here to do you harm,' she said.

Lampito opened the door wide and showed Gorgo the two bodyguards posted outside her apartment lying on the ground. 'Poisoned, just like your son. And this man is one of those responsible.'

Gorgo still eyed Lampito with suspicion and continued to stare warily at the sword she was wielding. In her head, she was trying to comprehend why the consort of her opponent, Archidamus, would try to protect her.

Lampito went over the fallen man, who had only just begun to recover his senses, and prodded him with the sharp point of her sword.

The man stared at her, and then at Gorgo and Sherzada, with a terrified look. He was wearing something around his neck. He grabbed it and bit into it.

Sherzada tried to open his mouth to expel what he was trying to ingest. But it was too late. His body went into spasms and soon his mouth began to froth amid a strong almondy smell. The man was dead within moments.

Lampito sheathed her sword and sat down beside Gorgo and Sherzada and told them what had transpired. She began:

'I was out on my usual run at sunset. Now that I am a queen, I do not think it dignified to charge around when most people are up and about. Instead of running through town I take a route which takes me from the Limnae district across the bridge over to Aphision and then I run a circuit around the forest before joining the north road that heads back to Sparta.

It was not yet completely dark and I noticed a Helot running ahead – the same man who lies here before you. There was something suspicious about the way he was behaving. His gait was that of a spy, certainly not a Helot. And why he was hurrying into a forest which most Helots believed to be cursed by the ghosts of those of their kind executed at Aphision was beyond me. I was curious.

I quietly followed him deep into the heart of the forest. At a clearing, he was joined by several men. It was getting dark and all I could make out was that one of them was dressed like a Spartan warrior, complete with a long cloak and a helmet covering his face. The rest were hooded men who wore leather armour over their dark tunics. As soon as this fake Helot joined them, the Spartan took him to task.

'The boy King and his mother are not dead. Is that true?' he asked.

The 'Helot' explained that he had mixed poison into the breakfast milk of both the mother and son. But Queen Gorgo became distracted when she learnt that she was to be visited by the prince of Syracuse. She left her breakfast untouched saying that she had lost all her appetite. The young King, however, took a sip of the milk, but did not take any more, mistaking its slightly pungent taste for the milk going sour.

The Spartan became angry and said that even a modest amount of it could kill a grown man. But the 'Helot' reported that the dark Barbarian prince had returned and had helped prepare an antidote to save the young King.

The Spartan lost his temper and hit the man so hard that he fell to ground and then he kicked him several times. But once his temper cooled he asked of the latest status of the King, his mother and the Barbarian. The response was that all three were in the royal apartments, where the King was slowly recovering.

The Spartan said that they would have to strike tonight to finish them off. When one of the hooded men asked him what if their victims fled, he replied that they would track them down no matter where they went. 'By dawn, I shall have their heads. I swear it by the twelve gods of Olympus!'

Then the Spartan turned to the 'Helot' and said that he should go back and prepare the ground for their assault. His task was but to clear the way; the other assassins would finish the job.

But then he warned the 'Helot' not to get caught, for if he did a fate worse than death awaited him either at the hand of Queen Gorgo or his own. 'So if you find you have no way out, I expect you to choose the least worst of all the options.'

As the Spartan conspirator dispersed the men, I ran back to Archidamus. I found him with his usually coterie of courtiers and hangers on, and managed with some difficulty to drag him away into the garden where we could talk alone. I noticed that one of his friends, Pericleidas, was watching me closely. I took my husband to a secluded spot. And there I told him all that I had heard and seen.

My husband may have been blinded by his jealousy for you Agiads, but that night you came to tell him about all the suspicious goings on in Sparta had disturbed him, and myself as well. Now I had my own proof about the conspiracies afoot.

I told Archidamus to put aside his hatred for your House. I told him if these men could get rid of one queen and king, they could certainly do the same to the other pair, especially as we too share many of Queen Gorgo's sentiments. And then I said, 'And if Gorgo and Pleistarchus are killed ...'

'... the finger of blame will point at me.' Archidamus added that the successes of Cleomenes, Leonidas and Gorgo had cast a shadow over the Eurypontids and all he wanted was to reverse that by giving the Eurypontids their opportunity to shine. 'Like Gorgo, we are also the descendants of Chilon who taught us to use our heads rather than blindly follow the antiquated code of

Lycurgus. He wanted us to find solutions that were best suited for our times. But now I see I have devoted all my energies thus far in pursuing the wrong objectives.'

When I told him we could still make things right and stop this conspiracy, he shook his head. He said that reactionary feelings were running deep. His first instinct was to mobilize the Company of Knights, but ever since the deaths of Theras and Iason, he was certain that the reactionaries might even have infiltrated that most elite of Spartan military units. Instead of stopping the assassins, the conspirators within might abet them.

When I asked him what he could do to stop the conspirators, he bent his head and held it with both his hands and began to weep. He looked up to me with misty eyes and said,

'Ironic is it not that my name means "leader of the people," and here am I now leading no one. I am but a mere tool. And within the clique that is now trying to govern Sparta are extremists who will stop at nothing to get their way.'

Since he could not risk coming here without arousing suspicion of reactionaries amongst his entourage, he sent me alone to warn you.

I slipped through the guards and approached your apartment. But then I saw this man approach two of the guards and offer them some spiced wine, which the guards gladly took, only to fall dead in moments. It was then I attacked him and hurled him in here.'

* * *

'Queen Gorgo,' said Lampito. 'We were all blind. I realize now you have been right all along. But it is too late now. Your Majesty, you must flee at once.'

At that very moment, someone knocked hard on the door.

'Assassins don't knock.' Sherzada got up, walked over the door, and opened it.

It was Agathe, with a horrified expression on her face. Menander stood beside her, taut with anxiety. They had seen the bodies outside.

Sherzada signalled Menander to follow him into Pleistarchus' room. He said to Gorgo, 'We will get Pleistarchus; you and Agathe must fetch the horses.'

'Where are we going?'

'I have an idea. But first we must get out of Sparta,' he said.

Menander stepped forward. 'If it pleases you, Highness, I would like to come with you. I know the countryside well and will guide you to wherever you wish to go.'

Sherzada and Menander carried the still-weak Pleistarchus towards the stables nearby. Agathe, Lampito and Gorgo had come out with three horses. Sherzada noticed that Gorgo was carrying her father's shield and sword.

Pleistarchus was helped up to one of the horses and Menander mounted behind his King to give him support.

Sherzada mounted a second horse and turned to Lampito. 'My Queen, you must go over to the Regent Nicomedes and warn him about this.'

Gorgo nodded. 'Agathe, go along too, and make sure all others are out of harm's way, especially Pausanias' children and your own people.'

As Lampito was about to turn, Gorgo embraced her warmly. 'Thank you, for all you have done.'

Gorgo released her and mounted her horse, whereupon Lampito bowed and said, 'I would have done more for you, had it been in my power. Keep safe, *Megistu-Anassa*.'

Chapter 45

'Me Kheiron Beltiston'

Outside Sparta
That night

Sherzada led the party on the north-west road for several miles and then he circled westward towards the Taygetus range. With Menander's help, they followed a path along the foot of the range south. They circled the outskirts until they were on a path diametrically opposite to the road upon which they had left Sparta. Sherzada was taking his companions to the south-eastern corner of the Peloponnesus.

They rode hard until they reached the Laconian Forest near the coastline. Pleistarchus had started gaining consciousness but he was still tired. Sherzada suggested they take a break.

As Gorgo gave her son some water she asked Sherzada where they were going.

'To the beach at Boeae, opposite Cythera,' he said. 'There is a Roman warship anchored nearby. As soon as we get there, we will signal them and they will take us to Cos.'

'And after that?'

'I don't think it wise to return to Sparta any time soon. You may have to stay away for a while. You need to find a temporary home. What about Athens? I am sure Aristeides will give you protection; Elpinice, too.'

Gorgo shook her head. 'While I adore Aristeides and have become fond of Elpinice, I do not think I can trust the Athenians anymore. They are expanding their influence right across the Aegean. The island of Scyros and the city-state of Carystus have recently fallen to Athenian spears. This is only the beginning. It is as if an Athenian empire is replacing a Persian one in the Aegean.

'Just as you said the Persians fought for the Truth, the

Athenians are now doing the same in the name of Democracy. How can you impose Democracy at the point of spears? How can Athenians say they are fighting for freedom when they trample the rights of others? Forcing Aegean states to bow to them and become their vassals. People are being enslaved in the name of freedom, and I thought we Spartans were the only hypocrites in Greece.'

'Athens can afford to be hypocritical,' quipped Sherzada. 'The caches of silver, the proceeds of the slave trade, access to timber and iron makes Athens pre-eminent in the Aegean. It is the only power there. Weaker states have no choice but to submit. Athens can get away with this; Sparta cannot.

'Sparta is like a strong but brittle piece of metal,' he continued, as he helped Pleistarchus, looking a little better, back on to his horse. 'Difficult to break, but once broken, completely useless. To survive, Sparta has to be flexible, but I do not see that happening.'

Menander mounted up behind Pleistarchus, giving his young King support. After having helped Gorgo on to her horse, Sherzada got up on his and rode behind her.

He continued, 'The irony is that Persians, whom you have defeated, are never going to go away. Their symbol is a mythical bird called the *Huma*. Every time the Huma is seen to be destroyed, it reappears, often like the phoenix rising from the ashes. This is very much the nature of Persia. They are a proud and sophisticated people and as a civilization they know what it takes to survive. It is always a mistake to ignore the Persians, though at times it is unwise to take them too seriously. We who have lived next to them for centuries know a little about how to deal with them. Call them Persians, or Medes, or Parthians, or Iranians. Persia will rise again, and again, from the ashes. Even two or three thousand years from now, there will be a Persia in some shape or form. My question is: will there also be then a kingdom, a country, a land called Sparta?'

After almost two hours of riding, they finally reached the beach. There, Gorgo dismounted and spread a crimson cloak on the ground for Pleistarchus to lie on. Then Sherzada and Menander began collecting enough wood for three large fires.

'Hopefully, they can see these in Cythera,' said Sherzada, while Gorgo sat by her resting son.

Leaving Menander to look after the three bonfires, Sherzada walked to the top of a mound to get a better vantage point. The fires lit up the area, and so he reached into his satchel and took out a pen and parchment. He unrolled the parchment and started to write on it.

Once Pleistarchus had fallen asleep again, Gorgo climbed up the mound and sat next to Sherzada. 'What's that you are writing?' she asked.

'Oh, this is the book about the events I have witnessed here in Greece.'

Gorgo took the parchment from his hand and started to read it. After a while, she remarked, 'Just as I thought. Your account seems a little one-sided, don't you think?'

'Whatever do you mean?'

'It gives only your perspective.'

'You mean it needs a Greek perspective as well?'

'Or a woman's … you need to balance it somehow,' Gorgo replied.

Sherzada sighed and put away his writing material. 'Have you decided where you want to go?' he asked her.

'Frankly, I'd rather face death in Sparta than suffer the ignominy of being a Spartan exile in any other part of Greece. It just does not feel right.'

'But you also have to think of your son,' he said. 'Do you really want to return to Sparta to let the assassins have another go at him … and you as well?'

'So what should I do? Concede victory to my foes?'

'Sparta is about to embark on a disastrous path,' said

Sherzada. 'There is nothing you can do to stop it. All you will succeed in doing is putting your life at needless risk.'

Gorgo gave him a bitter look but one which also told him that he was right.

'You have done your best, Gorgo,' he continued. 'You have preserved the freedom of Sparta. You have saved Greece. But you cannot save Sparta from itself. There is nothing more you can do here.'

'Then where am I supposed to go?' she asked. 'With your Roman friends to this rather exotic Republic of theirs?'

Sherzada thought for a moment, and said, 'They would certainly treat you well. Even though they will never admit it, the Romans deeply admire both Athenians and Spartans. And no longer having a monarchy of their own, they are always fascinated by monarchs of other lands. But the problem is that Rome is surrounded by enemies and in a constant state of warfare. This is true all across Italy. It is worse even than Greece.'

'So, my Prince,' she asked. 'Where else can I go?'

'There is one more option,' he said with a half-smile. 'Once Pleistarchus has recovered, I shall leave for home. I plan to take a ship to the far side of the Euxine Sea – the land of the Western Scyths. From there, I shall make my way overland to my homeland in the Indus Valley, skirting around Persian lands. I would like you and Pleistarchus to accompany me back to my homeland.'

'Spartans are famous for carrying off women they intend to marry to their homes. I did not know that the Scythians had the same custom.' Gorgo's lips curled. 'Is this a marriage proposal, by any chance, my Prince?'

Sherzada shrugged his shoulders and mumbled something. Gorgo thought she had heard him say, '*Me kheiron beltiston!* – the least worst of all the options.'

'For it is the strangest marriage proposal I have ever heard!' she added.

Sherzada looked abashed. 'I have heard that you have not been very keen on accepting proposals lately …'

Suddenly, Menander cried out, 'Look: a ship is heading for us! It's a trireme.'

Sherzada quickly packed up his parchment and writing material into his satchel and got up to try to determine whether the vessel belonged to friend or foe. The ship lowered a boat with armed men who began to row towards them.

Hearing movement behind them, Sherzada turned and saw a dozen men wearing black leather jerkins over dark tunics. Many were masked and those who weren't did not look very friendly. They were rapidly moving towards him, and all were armed. These men were not Spartans. But behind them strode a Spartan warrior, his face covered by his helmet.

'Magnas,' Gorgo gasped. 'What do you want from us?'

'Your deaths, of course.'

Chapter 46

Farewell

Boeae Beach
South-eastern Laconia – Spartan territory
That night

'You are a coward and a traitor,' said Gorgo.

Magnas slowly took off his helmet and said, 'You are the traitor, Queen Gorgo, turning your back on what we Spartans hold dear and embracing any foreign idea and foreigner you happen to like.'

So incensed was she at his words, Gorgo picked up a heavy rock and hurled it at Magnas. He did not move away, probably thinking that the rock would fall short. It did not. It hit him squarely on the head, and he fell backwards with a yelp of pain.

His companions ran forwards towards Sherzada and Gorgo. Taking her by the hand, Sherzada brought her down from the mound towards Menander and the fires. The commotion had woken Pleistarchus. Weak though he appeared, he quickly rose and picked up Cleomenes' shield. Gorgo herself seized her father's sword, which she had left near where Pleistarchus had been laying. She came and stood beside her son.

Sherzada went forward to block the assailants. Swinging his long-sword over his head, he hit the nearest attacker with such force that the sword cut through his neck down to his chest. The man was dead before he fell to the ground. Experience had taught Sherzada that fighting assassins was easier than fighting trained warriors. Assassins thrived on the element of surprise. They liked to strike when their targets least expected it. But it was a completely different thing if their target was ready and able to strike back. And Sherzada was doing that ferociously; within moments, his sword claimed two more assailants.

Menander had also joined the fray and incapacitated one of the assassins. Pleistarchus smashed his shield into the head of another who lunged at him, stunning him. Gorgo took advantage of that moment to drive her sword into his groin. But the attackers kept on coming. Magnas, meanwhile, was sitting unhappily on the beach nursing his bleeding head.

The pressure of their numbers forced Sherzada and his companions to move back down the beach towards the waves. Gorgo realized that three of the assassins had circled around their rear. While two of them threw their javelins at her and Pleistarchus, the third rushed them. Pleistarchus skilfully deflected the first javelin with his shield and Gorgo, as she had been trained long ago, side-stepped away from the second javelin's trajectory barely a moment before it struck the space she had occupied and then with astounding agility swung around behind her son and forcefully drove her father's *xiphos* sword deep into the chest of third assassin, who was about to strike at Pleistarchus.

The two assassins threw another pair of javelins at Gorgo and her son. While Pleistarchus, protecting his mother with his own body, caught one of the javelins on the shield, she realized he could not turn in time to save himself from the second javelin and, having blocked Gorgo's path, she could do nothing to save him either.

At that moment, Menander threw himself in front of Pleistarchus, stopping the javelin with his body. He tried to take out the missile out of his chest, but it broke in his hand. With the shaft still protruding, he charged the two javelin throwers and killed them. However, before dying, one of the assassins slit his throat with his dagger. Menander fell lifeless on to the watery beach as Gorgo screamed his name.

Meanwhile, busy fighting off the other attackers, Sherzada was pulling back to where Gorgo and Pleistarchus stood. The waves were beginning to wash their ankles. Sherzada felt his feet sink into the wet sand as he made his stand beside the Queen and her son. The assassins too regrouped, preparing for another assault.

Just then, Sherzada saw another man emerge from the shadows behind Magnas. He was also a Spartan, wearing the long crimson cloak, carrying a spear in his hand. He was also wearing a face-covering helmet. The man slowly walked to where Magnas was sitting and then stopped.

'Damon,' said Magnas as he stood up, 'Where have you been? You should have been here earlier.'

'That is not Damon,' Gorgo whispered to Sherzada.

'Damon has been delayed; he sent me in his place.' The man took off his helmet.

'Pericleidas?' said Magnas, surprised. 'I was not expecting you here. But now that you are, you can help me finish this.'

Gorgo gasped. 'Surely not you? You were the youngest and best of our sea captains. You served with distinction at Salamis and Mycale. You are not like this man next to you, who refused to go on a single campaign so that he could chase the wives and daughters of those warriors risking life and limb for Sparta. You are a Spartan hero. Do not aid this coward in his act of treason.'

Magnas, still holding a piece of cloth over his head to stop the bleeding, said with a smile, 'How sad, my Queen. Even the best of Spartans have turned against you.

'Pericleidas,' Magnas continued, 'kindly do the honours.'

'With pleasure,' he responded. He slowly put on his helmet and grabbed his spear and moved forward. Then he turned around and thrust the spear into Magnas' chest so forcefully that it pierced his armour and his body. As the latter cried out and fell once more to the ground, Pericleidas took out his sword and thrust it into Magnas' throat.

The boat with the armed men was now close to shore. Sherzada heard one them shout, '*Ferratus*?'

He shouted, 'Is that you, Cincinnatus?'

'Aye,' responded a man in full armour with shaven head, as he jumped off the boat. The Romans were here.

Seeing that the tables had been turned, the assassins started to flee. However, Pericleidas caught one of them in the back with a powerful spear throw, and Sherzada dispatched another after chasing him down.

Daylight was breaking, as Cincinnatus and his men pulled the boat near.

Pericleidas came to Gorgo where she stood with Pleistarchus, and knelt down on one knee. 'Your Majesties,' he said, 'I beg your forgiveness. I had no choice but to pretend I was close to Magnas. I had suspected him of treasonous dealings for quite some time, including the deaths of our senior generals. But the only way I could uncover his activities was by being seen to be his accomplice. Still, Magnas only trusted Damon. He did not always include the rest of us in his plans.

'I knew something was afoot when I saw the alarmed look on Queen Lampito's face as I saw her talk to King Archidamus last night. I knew Magnas was up to something. I went over to Sthenelaidas and Cleandridas and forced them to surrender themselves to King Archidamus and tell him everything they knew, including the Argive connection. Magnas and Damon were in the pay of our old enemies. Even though Cleandridas is a hypocrite and Sthenelaidas an idiot, in their heart of hearts they did not share the hatred Damon and Magnas had for you.'

'Where is Damon?' asked Gorgo.

'He was coming to join Magnas. I made him tell me everything, and then I killed him.

'My loyalty is still with my Kings, Archidamus and Pleistarchus. Tonight, we have quashed just one conspiracy. But there is credible information about other plots against you. You and the King are not safe in Sparta, Majesty.'

Lifting her gown up to her ankles to avoid the waves, Gorgo walked toward the boat as the Romans helped Sherzada gently lay Pleistarchus in it. Pericleidas followed them as the waves began to flow at his legs.

'And what will you tell Archidamus?' Gorgo asked Pericleidas.

'Majesty, I shall tell him that Queen Gorgo has taken her ailing son to the Shrine of Asclepius the Healer in Epidaurus. No one pries around there, because it is also a leper colony. So as far as Sparta is concerned, King Pleistarchus is convalescing there. After a few years, if circumstances improve, you can return safely. If they do not, better you stay away. Sparta is not safe for you now.'

As Sherzada helped Gorgo to the boat, she turned to Pericleidas and said, 'Not long ago, I would have preferred to have died here. But this is no longer the Sparta for which Leonidas and his Three Hundred laid down their lives; nor the Sparta that won for Greece the most spectacular of its victories. Today, those same Greeks who stood by us at Thermopylae, Salamis and Plataea are turning against us,' and then she reached out to Menander's lifeless body, saying 'and still we continue to oppress and slaughter those who are most loyal to us. I, who fought so hard to protect Greece from the Persians, can do nothing to save it from itself. While I was fortunate enough to witness the zenith of Sparta's glory, I do not wish to see my son preside over the beginnings of its downfall. That is a burden your King Archidamus will now have to bear alone.'

Pericleidas bowed low, as the little boat took Gorgo, Sherzada and Pleistarchus to the Roman warship just as the sun was rising on the horizon. Once on board, the Romans made room for Pleistarchus to lie in the stern of their ship, and fixed a tarpaulin cover for shade, almost like a small tent. For now, he was safe.

Gorgo turned and saw Sherzada sitting nearby on the deck writing on his parchment. She walked over to him and sat down. Edging closer to him, she said, 'I have been thinking about your ultimatum.'

'You mean, my offer. And …?' he asked, with an expectant smile.

'My Prince, you ought to know me well enough by now to know I am partial neither to offers of marriage nor ultimatums of any kind.

'However,' she continued, 'I do have an ultimatum for you.'

'Oh! What is it?'

'If you want me to be a part of your life, if you want me to be your wife, you will have to share everything with me. Otherwise, you can drop Pleistarchus and me at Cos and continue home alone.'

'Of course I will share everything with you,' he said, with a slightly confused expression.

'In that case,' she said, 'I am delighted that you accept my ultimatum, my Prince.' Taking the pen from and parchment from his hand, she added, 'now, let me begin by adding a little woman's touch to this rather masculine story of yours.'

Postscript

Athens
Spring, 457 BC

To Queen Gorgo, from Elpinice,
Love, Honour and Greetings.
I am writing this letter twenty years after your 'disappearance'. It has taken me this long to trace your whereabouts at the other end of the Earth.

However, the news I have is not good.

The very year you left us, our dear friend Aristeides passed away. He had just returned from his stay at the Scythian port of Olbia. Thanks to Sherzada's help, he had made much fortune there, but it was barely enough to pay off his considerable debts. Though he died a poor man, his funeral, paid for from public coffers, rivalled that of kings.

Themistocles was finally forced into exile by his enemies at home. He eventually found his way to Asia, where the Persians made him King of Magnesia. The Persians, in the end, were more forgiving to him than the Athenians. Our great hero and democrat spent the rest of his years a despot, and a puppet of the Persians. Your cousin Pausanias, however, was not so lucky. Being repeatedly accused of conspiring with the Persians, he returned to Sparta once more to clear his name. However, facing an unfair trial and expecting no justice from the authorities, Pausanias fled to a Temple of Athena of the Brazen House for refuge. Archidamus tried to intervene to save him but was prevented from doing so by the reactionaries. They starved him to death. Now his young son Pleistonax reigns as Sparta's Agiad King.

After a bloody and inconclusive war with Macedon my brother made peace with King Alexander and focused his attention on the Persians. Luckily, court intrigues in Persepolis caused Artabazus to be temporarily removed and replaced by an incompetent governor. And in his absence, Cimon defeated the Persians at the Battle of Eurymedon. But soon after that, Artabazus was restored to his post and nullified our advances.

Some seven years ago, a terrible earthquake hit Sparta. The Spartans, so dismissive of architectural expertise, paid a terrible price for not reinforcing their dwellings. Seizing this opportunity, the Helots rose up in revolt. Some of them came very close to seizing Sparta itself had not Archidamus risen to the occasion. He finally asserted his authority, proving himself true to his name, and successfully led Sparta out of a dangerous situation. In a rousing his speech he recalled your memory, calling you Megisto-Anassa – 'Greatest of Queens' – and repeated your words about Sparta's warriors being her walls and their spear-points defining her frontiers. He was one of the young men whom you had seen off that night years before on the eve of Plataea. Archidamus then moved quickly to crush the Helot revolt, isolating their resistance to Mt. Ithome.

But Sparta had itself become isolated in the Peloponnese, all because of the influence of the reactionaries. Their insensitivity drove Tegea and other Arcadian cities into the arms of Argos, and they all joined forces, taking advantage of the Helot revolt to attack Sparta. Archidamus met them at the field of Dipeia, where he scored a decisive victory. Of the Peloponnesians, only the Mantineans fought on the side of the Spartans – and they did so with uncommon courage. They said it was their way of expiating the curse of cowardice placed on them at Gortys by your late husband, Leonidas. Almost the entire Mantinean force died fighting bravely at Dipeia, protecting the Spartan left flank. It is said that in their dying breaths they exhorted Leonidas to save them a place at his table; they said they were finally coming to dine among the heroes in Hades.

Archidamus followed this victory by sending Pericleidas to Athens to seek our support. Cimon, citing past Spartan services to Athens, prevailed upon our Democratic Assembly to let him lead an Athenian force, four thousand strong, along with siege equipment – which the Spartans lacked – against the rebel Helots besieged at Mt. Ithome.

Our intervention gave the Spartans the upper hand. At that point, the leader of the Helot rebels approached our soldiers and told them that the Helots were Greeks too. How could Athens support Eleutheria for Greece when it was helping Spartans to enslave and oppress fellow Greeks? Without doubt the leader of the revolt was none other than your cousin Euryanax. His words struck a chord with the Athenian soldiery, who threatened mutiny, much to the embarrassment of my brother. The Spartans, fearing that Athenians might support the Helots instead, asked Cimon and his troops to leave. This was effectively the end of the alliance between Athens and Sparta.

On his return to Athens, my brother was made a scapegoat for the whole affair and sent into exile. There have been calls for me to be exiled as well along with Cimon, because of my well-known sympathies for Sparta. Athens has now allied with Argos instead. I have no choice but to follow the prevailing political mood. So, on my suggestion, my husband Callias has travelled to Persia to negotiate a formal end to all hostilities between Athens and Persia. A peace will be concluded very soon, leaving us free to deal with Sparta. I hope you forgive me for doing this. I had no choice; I am an Athenian before I am a Greek.

And now as I write this letter, I am receiving reports of a serious confrontation developing between the armies of Athens and Sparta near a town called Tanagra on the Asopus River not far from Plataea. The Argives have sent an army to support our troops against yours. The forces on our side are led by Myronides, who had served under Aristeides at the battle of Plataea. Nicomedes, the Regent of Sparta, leads your army. The war Sherzada warned of is upon us.

I wish you and King Sherzada well on the other side of the world. I hope you are free from all this politics and bloodshed; though I very much doubt it. Some ten years ago, I have heard, King Xerxes was assassinated as a result of a court intrigue. His murder was linked to a scandal involving a beautiful young princess. I have recently learnt that very same princess now lives in King Sherzada's harem. I am dying to know the details. However, I must not be so insensitive. No doubt this situation causes you unease – But you must admit that we could not have lived in more momentous times.

Epilogue: The Legacy

Taxila
Lands of the Indus
Winter, 327 BC

A cold howling wind blew outside. Lying on a couch next to the fireplace, Alexander put down the manuscript that Kautilya had given him. The Macedonian King had been wintering in Taxila, as a guest of King Ambhi, training his men, and waiting for reinforcements from Macedon and Persia. Once they had arrived, weather permitting, he would march south to face Porus who was massing a huge army across the Hydapses – or the Jhelum as the locals called it. The great Macedonian conqueror picked his lyre and started to strum it.

As he played on the chords, he reflected on what he had just finished reading.

The letter from Elpinice matched what Alexander already knew about the origins of the series of conflicts – known as the Peloponnesian Wars – that would ultimately break the might of both Sparta and Athens, leaving the field free for Macedon to claim the spoils.

The manuscript also left other resonances, deeper than he had expected. Of course, his ancestor, Alexander son of Amyntas, had been something of a controversial figure, his nefarious dealings a well-kept family secret. And yet, had it not been for that Alexander's machinations, Macedon would never have become a truly independent kingdom. *The ends, as always, justified the means*, he thought.

Did Alexander not justify his war of conquest against Persia by saying that he was avenging Xerxes' invasion of Greece? This had made him, a Macedonian, a hero among Greeks.

After decades of internal dissensions, intrigue, and civil war, the Persian Empire had been weakened to the point of collapse.

The unfathomable riches of the still-great Empire were there for whoever could seize them. And that was the real reason behind Alexander's invasion of Asia – which began some eleven years before he reached the lands of the Indus.

Overthrowing the Persian Empire had not been enough. Alexander's lust for conquest and glory drove him ever eastwards. But here, on the other end of the world, he once again encountered troublesome people speaking Greek. And it was also in this cursed land that Alexander came close to knowing the true meaning of defeat.

As the sun came out and the wind eased, Alexander grabbed the manuscript and walked out in the courtyard. He mounted his horse and rode off into town, accompanied by his bodyguards – the Companions.

They asked him where he was going. He said simply, 'The university.'

The road led to a rather expansive campus set against the backdrop of pleasant hills. The buildings were small and not at all grand. Well-lit and airy, constructed with sun-baked bricks, they gave the impression that a lot of thought had gone into their construction.

Alexander was taken by one of the attendants to a long building and as he entered what appeared to be a large hall, he heard someone greet him in impeccable Greek.

'*Alexandros Megas*, welcome,' said a boy as he prostrated himself before the Macedonian King.

Alexandros Megas – 'Alexander the Great'. It was the first time anybody had called him that. The Macedonian King smiled at the boy, who was around fourteen. He stood over a pile of scrolls he had been evidently studying. On closer inspection, Alexander noticed that the boy was reading excerpts from Aristotle's *Politics*. He could not help smiling. Alexander could still remember the author, his former tutor, teaching him from this very book.

Just then, Kautilya emerged from the adjoining room. 'Majesty.' He smiled his usual broad smile and then bowed very low. 'What a great pleasure. You honour me by your presence here at my humble library,' he exclaimed excitedly. 'I am sorry, I did not know you were coming. Otherwise, I would have prepared a warm welcome for you.'

Alexander waved away his concern. 'I have just come to return your book. I shall be riding against Porus very soon.'

Kautilya gestured at the boy. 'Majesty, allow me to introduce to you my brightest pupil, Chandragupta Maurya. He is very fond of Greek treatises on politics.'

'He speaks excellent Greek.'

Kautilya asked Chandragupta to excuse them and the boy bowed obediently and left.

Alexander's eyes followed the boy through the window walking eagerly towards a woman – a very attractive woman in her thirties. But she was not Indian.

'Who is that?' he asked.

Kautilya looked outside and said, 'That, Majesty, is the boy's mother, Maura. Chandragupta was born out of wedlock, so he has given himself the surname Maurya after his mother. She is a former slave girl. People say she is a *Yavana* – a Greek.'

But to Alexander's experienced eyes, the woman was not Greek. She was clearly a native of the Balkans kingdoms to the north of Greece. Could she be an Illyrian? A Dardanian perhaps? Or even an Epirote ... just like Alexander's own mother?

Kautilya continued, saying, 'Chandragupta's mother is very ambitious for her son. She believes he has an appointment with destiny. She wants to prepare him for a promising future.'

'She reminds me so much of mine,' said Alexander, smiling as he watched Chandragupta walk into the tender embrace of his mother.

'The boy certainly has shown talent and potential from an early age. He knows much about politics and statecraft for one so young. That is why I have taken him under my wing. I want to teach him all I know.'

'And what of the boy's father?'

'Remember Aornos, Your Majesty? The fortress that would not fall,' said Kautilya.

'How can I forget,' Alexander muttered to himself.

'The Indian mercenary who betrayed Aornos to you. He is the boy's father. But Chandragupta's father refused to acknowledge him as his legal offspring, not because he was born out of wedlock but because he is not of pure Indian blood. The boy is part *Mleccha* and hence considered impure. At least, this is what his father and most Indians believe. As for me, I am not that narrow-minded. I believe new blood can inspire creativity.'

'And why did you and the boy's father help me? What is your interest in my success?' asked Alexander.

'Both of us are from the Kingdom of Magadh in the east. At different times, both of us have tried to overthrow the Nanda kings who rule there. My deformities are a result of the cruel torture I suffered at their hands. The boy's father is a claimant to the throne. He is the last survivor of the royal house of Magadh that was massacred by the Nandas when they seized power. Now we are both in exile, and like me he too is thirsting for revenge against the Nandas.'

Alexander was not amused. 'But you said that all I had to do was to defeat Porus and then India would fall at my feet. You never mentioned the Nandas before.'

'Majesty,' said Kautilya, nervously. 'Porus is the most successful military commander in India. If you beat him, the defeat of the Nandas will only be a matter of time and course. They will give in as soon as you march against them.'

Alexander was unmoved.

'What is the size of the Nanda army?' he asked.

Kautilya looked away. 'A hundred thousand men, twenty thousand chariots, and only a few hundred elephants; nothing that Alexander the Great cannot deal with.'

Alexander flew into a rage. 'What do you mean, nothing that Alexander the Great cannot deal with? I have just survived near defeat at the hands of those execrable Sakas, and there were not even that many of them. All I need is just one more "victory" like this one ... and then I am undone. Even if Porus puts up half as much resistance as these Sakas did, my army will simply refuse to move any further. There is already enough grumbling in the ranks. If I tell them that after Porus they have to meet an even larger army, they will simply abandon me and go home.'

Then Alexander thought a little and asked, 'Are you sure that there is no other kingdom in India besides that of Porus and the Nandas?'

Kautilya scratched his bald head and said, 'Actually, Your Majesty, I am not sure how many kingdoms there are in all of India. But once you have trounced Porus and overthrown the Nandas, no one would dare resist you.'

'I am not so sure about that,' said Alexander. 'My men are still wincing from the bloody nose the Sakas gave them. For the first time since I have led these men across Asia, I see signs of mutiny. For the first time, I have seen panic in their eyes. For the first time, I am afraid that I am beginning to fail them as a leader.'

'Let us defeat Porus, first,' said Kautilya, soothingly. 'But, Majesty, if I am not mistaken, you said you had come to return my book? How did you like it?'

'Very interesting,' Alexander replied. 'There is much in this book that I can relate to, but perhaps that is why it makes me uncomfortable. At least now I have answers to some of my questions, though not quite all.'

'I am pleased,' Kautilya said, 'that Your Majesty enjoyed this book.'

'While I enjoyed reading it, I did not like it. You were right; it is dangerous,' responded the Macedonian. 'I want this book, and all copies of it, destroyed.'

'Why, Majesty? If I may be bold to ask?' Kautilya enquired.

'Well, for a start it does not show my ancestor and namesake Alexander of Macedon in a favourable light. He is shown as a treacherous double-dealer. The book also raises the thorny question of whether we Macedonians are really Greek or not. Of course, we are not really … completely … Greek, but the myth of being Greek is important for me to maintain my empire. The book promotes the emancipation of slaves, which is very subversive. Then I also find his tendency to give political credit to women a little misguided. Even though my mother, Olympias, has had a disproportional influence over myself and my career, I don't think it is politically wise to advertise such details. Finally, all this talk about the one God. It will not go down well with my subjects, many of whom have already hailed me as a son of one god or another. This book has the potential of undoing everything I have worked for.'

Kautilya thought for a minute and then smiled. 'Your wish is my command, Majesty. I will see to it that all the copies are destroyed.' He took the manuscript from Alexander's hand and threw it into the fire in a nearby hearth.

'You are right that the emancipation of slaves is not a good idea. In India we have slaves and we also have castes. Everybody needs to know their place in society, especially those at the bottom. I also agree that the idea of one God is subversive. But then again, religion can always be exploited. I have been using my influence with the followers of a new cult called Buddhism to undermine the power of the Nandas. And yes, about women, I always say that their only role is to please and serve men. Giving them a role greater than that serves no one's interest.'

Alexander nodded in approval, and Kautilya bowed and excused himself. 'Let me bring the other copies of this manuscript so that we can burn them together.' He disappeared inside and brought another half a dozen copies. The two men then threw them into the fire.

As Alexander committed the last manuscript to the blaze, he asked Kautilya, 'How true do you think this story was? I mean, did this man really exist? What do you know about the real Sherzada? What happened to him?'

Kautilya smiled. 'Majesty, let us stretch our legs – it has become quite pleasant – and I shall tell you all I know.' He hobbled outside into the lush green countryside, followed by the Macedonian King.

As they left the university and walked through the cornfields towards the hills in the distance, Kautilya began, 'The story of Sherzada is shrouded in mystery. Had it not been for this book, none would have believed that he even existed. Now that the book is destroyed, I am sure he will be relegated to a category of legend, or even forgotten altogether.'

As they walked, Kautilya continued, 'His entire life is a subject of much debate. However, the accepted view is that he returned from the West accompanied by a foreign woman and her son. There is even one story of a possible second, younger wife that came along later. Then, there are different versions of what happened after he returned home. Again, the majority view seems to be that he united a divided kingdom. He became the King of the Sakas.

'As King, Sherzada extended the territory of his kingdom in every direction, more through negotiations than through war. The River Indus is locally called the Sindh after Sherzada's tribe, the Sindhic Sakas. In the end, even some of the former eastern territories of the Persian Empire like Gandhara, Arachosia and Gedrsosia recognized him as their overlord rather than the Persian King.

'Legends suggest,' Kautilya continued, 'that though he ruled wisely, some of his reforms did not go down too well with his people. His attempts to reform the caste system were not too popular, because the Sakas did not want their society destabilized by Sherzada's revolutionary ideas. His compassion towards the slaves and lower castes was seen as a sign of weakness. Finally, his worship of the one God alienated the priestly classes of the Sakas as well as of the local communities whom he brought into this confederal empire of his. They say he was killed in a conspiracy. But as I said, these are only some of the versions of the many legends about this man.'

'But ...' Alexander interrupted, 'do you actually think he convinced Queen Gorgo to come here with him all the way from Sparta? I find that hard to believe.'

'As do I,' responded Kautilya. 'Were it not for this.'

He led Alexander to a cypress grove. Beneath the tallest tree was a grave, simply marked in Greek: *PLEISTARCHOS BASILIEU SPARTIATIKON KAI GANDARION* – 'Pleistarchus, King of the Spartans and the Gandharans'.

As Alexander looked at the grave in astonishment, Kautilya pointed to the limestone hills on the horizon in front of them. 'Somewhere at the base of those hills is another grave with a headstone with a strange inscription, part Greek, part Scythian. The writing has almost faded now, but people believe that the translation of the original inscription on the headstone began: *Here lies Gorgo, Queen of the Sakas and the Spartans. Daughter of a King, Wife of Kings, Mother of Kings ...*'

And then Kautilya gazed at the hills above and said, '... and it was on top of those very hills that Sherzada finished writing his book ...'

Characters

Aeschylus, Athenian playwright
Agathe, Helot chambermaid of Gorgo
Alexander I, son of Amyntas – King of Macedon; ancestor of Alexander the Great
Alexander III 'the Great' – King of Macedon, conqueror of the Persian Empire in the 4th Century BC
Aranth Telumnas, Etruscan ruler of Veii
Ariadne of Taras, wife of Artabaz, former Greek spy
Arimnestus, Spartan general
Aristeides 'the Just', Athenian general and politician
Aristodemus, Spartan warrior, survivor of the battle of Thermopylae
Artabaz (also **Artabazus**), Persian general
Asopodorus, Theban cavalry commander
Aulus Antonious, Roman military officer
Burbaraz (also **Bubares**), Persian Prince and general; cousin of King Xerxes
Callias, wealthy Athenian businessman and politician; husband of Elpinice
Cato, Marcus Porcius, Roman senator
Chandragupta Maurya, pupil of Kautilya, future founder of the Mauryan Empire in India
Cimon, son of Miltiades, Athenian general and politician
Cincinnatus, Lucius Quinctius, Roman military officer
Cleandridas, Spartan conspirator
Cleomenes, Agiad King of Sparta, father of Gorgo
Cleonice, a young Byzantine woman captured by the Persians
Cleophis, Saka Queen of the Swat Valley
Damon, Spartan conspirator
Decius Mus ('the Mouse') **Publius**, Roman centurion
Demaratus, former Eurypontid King of Sparta, and advisor to King Xerxes of Persia

Elpinice, daughter of Miltiades and half-sister of Cimon
Euryanax or **Euro**, Spartan Prince, cousin of Gorgo
Eurybiadas, Spartan Admiral and confidant of Gorgo
Evaeneutus, Spartan general and relative of King Leotychidas
Gorgo, Queen of Sparta, daughter of King Cleomenes, widow of King Leonidas and mother of the child-King Pleistarchus
Gunnarr, Scandian warrior, father of Rán
Gygaea, Princess of Macedon, sister of Alexander I and wife of Prince Burbaraz
Hild, Scanian-scythian *Valkyrie* squadron commander
Iason, deputy commander of the Company of Knights
Ione, daughter of Aristodemus
Kautilya, ('the Crafty One') also known as **Vishnugupta Chanakiya**, Indian philosopher and politician
Khorrem, son of Mashista and nephew of Xerxes, a commander of the *Anusiya* – the 'Immortals'
Lampito, Eurypontid princess, daughter of King Leotychidas
Leonidas, Agiad King of Sparta, husband of Gorgo
Leotychidas, Eurypontid King of Sparta
Magnas, Spartan reactionary
Marcus Fabius Vibulanus, Roman Consul
Mardonius, son of Gobryas, Persian viceroy in Greece and cousin and brother-in-law of Xerxes
Mashista or **Masistes**, Persian Prince, brother of Xerxes
Mashistiyun or **Masistius**, Persian cavalry commander at Plataea
Melissa of the Aristomenidae, wife of Euryanax
Menander, Helot servant of Gorgo, father of Agathe
Nicomedes, brother of Pausanias
Pausanias, Regent for Pleistarchus, cousin of Gorgo
Pericleidas, Spartan naval officer
Phaenippus, Athenian Ambassador, and former Head of State of Athens
Pheidippides, Athenian envoy and Olympic champion

Pleistarchus, Agiad King of Sparta, son of Gorgo and Leonidas
Rán, Scandian-Scythian *Valkyrie*, Sherzada's first love
Sherzada, Crown-Prince of the Sakas of the Indus Valley
Sthenelaidas, Spartan reactionary
Themistocles, Athenian statesman and general, credited as the genius behind the Greek victory at the Battle of Salamis
Theras, Commander of the Company of the Knights
Velia Vellai, Etruscan ruler of Velathri
Xanthippus, Athenian politician and admiral
Xerxes or **Khashayarshah**, Persian King of Kings, son of Darius

Glossary

Agiadae – one of the two royal houses of Sparta

Agoge (Greek) 'upbringing' – Spartan military education and training system

Agora (Greek) – marketplace

Ahura-Mazda (Persian) – Supreme Zoroastrian Deity

Alae (Latin) – 'wing' – military unit of between 3,000 to 5,000 men

Alpha (Greek) – first letter of the Greek alphabet

Alopex (Greek) – 'fox'

Amarygian (or *Haumavarga*) Sakas – Asiatic Scythian tribe whose home base was north of the Oxus River in Central Asia

Amylcae – one of the five villages or districts of Sparta

Andreia (Greek) – 'bravery' or 'courage'

Androphogoi (Greek) – 'Man-Eaters' – a tribe existing on the north-western edges of the Scythian domains

Anusiya (Persian) – 'The Companions' – elite bodyguard of the Great King of Persia, formed entirely from the ranks of the nobility. The Greeks called them the 'Immortals'

Arachosia – ancient land straddling the mountainous area between what is now Pakistan and Afghanistan

Arta (Persian) – 'truth' or 'righteousness'

Ashkayavana (Sanskrit) – 'Horse Greeks' (a tribe of the northern Indus Valley)

Assur – land of Assyria

Assyrians – ancient kingdom that ruled much of the Near East before the rise of the Persians

Bastarnae – Germanic tribe, located in the 5th Century BC on the western Baltic coast

Black Cloaks – mysterious tribe existing to the west of the Scythian domains; possible ancestors of the Alans who later invaded the Roman Empire

Caelian – one of the Seven Hills of Rome

Carneia (Greek) – Spartan / Greek religious festival

Cissians – Persian-speaking inhabitants of Elam [see: *Elam*]

Cushites – an African people originally living on the upper Nile valley who had been driven westward by ancient Egyptian invasions into what is now Ethiopia and Somalia

Crypteia (Greek) – Spartan secret assassination squad comprising new military graduates

Dadicans – tribe living in what is now north-western Pakistan

Dahae – Asiatic Scythian tribe which spoke a dialect similar to Persian

Dardania – a Balkan region straddling modern Eastern Serbia, Kosovo and western Macedonia

Deimos (Greek) – 'terror'

Elam – southern region of ancient Iran (straddling the modern regions of south-eastern Iraq and south-western Iran)

Eleutheria (Greek) – 'freedom'

Ephor (Greek) – [*Literally*: Overseer]; one of five elected senior magistrates of Sparta

Epirote – a person from Epirus, an ancient Balkan kingdom controlling a region shared today between north-western Greece and southern Albania

Epynomous Archon – in Athens, the title of the senior *Archon* (Ruler) who was elected for a one term as Head of State

Eurypontidae – one of the two royal houses of Sparta

Gandhara – ancient kingdom spanning the Kabul and Swat River valleys (in South Asia)

Gedrsosia – ancient kingdom corresponding to the Baluchistan regions of Iran and Pakistan

Gerousia (Greek) – [*Literally*: The Council of Elders]; the highest law-making body in Sparta comprising of legislators who were over the age of 60

Haliskomenoi (Greek) – captive or conquered people

Hegemon (Greek) – 'leader'

Helots (Greek) – collective slaves of the Spartan state

Himation (Greek) – shawl or outer covering draped over a dress

Hippeis (Greek) – [*Literally*: horsemen]; 'The Knights' – Sparta's elite cavalry unit which also served as the Kings' bodyguards

Homioi (Greek) – 'similar ones' or 'those who are alike'. Also interpreted as 'peers.' This was another word to describe the *Spartiates*, the full citizens of Sparta

Hubris (Greek) – 'extreme pride' or 'arrogance'

Hyacinthia (Greek) – Spartan religious festival

Hypomeiones (Greeks) – [*Literally*: the inferiors]; Spartans who had lost their civic rights

Illyrians – a people inhabiting what is now the south-western Balkans including parts of Albania, Serbia, Montenegro and southern Croatia

'*Invincibles*' (*Shikast Napazir* in Persian) – Persian military unit comprising victorious veterans

Ismenian Band – Theban military unit named after the sacred spring of Ismene near Thebes

Khopesh (Ancient Egyptian) – sickle-sword originating in Egypt and North Africa

Kyniskus (Greek) – 'Puppy'; nickname of Archidamus' father

Kynosoura – one of the five villages or districts of Sparta

Lacedaemon – official name of the Spartan domains

Laconia – eastern province of Sparta, where the city itself was located

Lambda (Greek) – Greek alphabet, equivalent of the letter 'L'

Laukhme mi (Etruscan) – my King

Legatus (Latin) – 'ambassador'

Libertas (Latin) – 'liberty'

Libyans – ancient name for all Berber-speaking peoples

Limnae – one of the five villages or districts of Sparta

Lion Guard – elite military unit that protected the Lion Gate – the main entrance to the citadel of Mycenae

Lycurgan Code – legal code enacted by Lycurgus (who lived between 820 and 730 BC), the law-giver of Sparta

Lydia – a powerful ancient kingdom in what is now western

Turkey

Mahasigareis (Iranic dialect) – double-handed battle-axe

Mard-Khwaar (Iranic dialect) – 'Man-Eaters' [see: *Androphogoi*]

Megas (Greek) – 'the Great'

Medes – people from Media, a former kingdom once located in what is now north-western Iran and northern Iraq

Mesoa – one of the five villages or districts of Sparta

Messene – western province of Sparta, a formed kingdom seized by the Spartans around the 9th Century BC and, subsequently, a scene of frequent Helot uprisings

Metis (Greek) – 'cleverness' or 'cunning'

Mleccha (Vedic Sanskrit) – 'Barbarian' or 'foreigner'

Molon Labe (Greek) – 'come and take (them)'

Monophthalmus (Greek) – 'one-eyed'

Mothax [Plural: *Mothoi*] (Doric Greek) – 'bastard', son of a Spartan father and a helot mother

Navarch (Greek) – 'commander of the ships', admiral

Neuri – tribe living in the forests of Carpathia – one of many associated with the origins of the werewolf legend

Pactyans – a people living along what is now the borders of Afghanistan and Pakistan – possibly the ancestors of the Pashtuns

Paean (Greek) – song of praise or triumph; also a battle-cry

Parthia – a region in north-eastern Iran

Patria (Latin) – 'country'

Patrician (Latin) – 'person of high birth' or 'nobleman'

Peplos (Greek) – body-length women's dress in Ancient Greece made of long tubular cloth; popular in Sparta

Perioiki (Greek) – Outlanders; people living on the edges. The Perioiki dwelled on the edges of Spartan territories. They were free people, but without political rights. They were engaged in trade, handicrafts, and agriculture. They were also required to provide troops for Sparta in time of war or crisis

Phobos (Greek) – 'fear'

Peltasts (Greek) – Greek infantry that served as light infantry

Pitana – one of the five villages or districts of Sparta

Plebeians [From: *Plebes*] (Latin) – the common people of Ancient Rome

Puraparaseanna (Ancient Persian) – 'land beyond the mountains'; what is now northern Pakistan

Pythioi (Greek) – the two Spartan special ambassadors (one chosen by each king) to the Oracle of Apollo at Delphi

Ra'senna – name by which the Etruscans referred to themselves

Sakas (or: *Sacae*) – Eastern or Asiatic Scythians who spoke an Iranic dialect related to ancient Persian and Sanskrit

Sarmatian – European Scythian tribe, famed for their armoured horsemen

Scandians – Germanic tribe settled in what is now Denmark and southern Sweden

Scytale (Greek) – [*literally*: baton]; in Spartan military cryptography this was a tool used to perform a transposition cipher, consisting of a cylinder with a strip of parchment wound around it on which the secret message was written

Scyths or *Scythians* – nomadic Indo-European peoples of Iranic origin who roamed the great Eurasian plains

Skiritae (Greek) – inhabitants of the northern borders of Spartan territory; served as border rangers in the Spartan military structure

Spartiates (Greek) – Spartan citizens with full rights and obligations. Another word to describe the *Homioi*

Strategos (Greek) – 'general'

Sublician – bridge in Rome where the legendary Roman officer Horatius held off an attack by the forces of the Etruscan warlord Laris Pu-ra'senna (Lars Porsenna)

Suraseni – a people populating parts of Punjab, in what is now Pakistan and India

Symposion (Greek) – [*Literally*: drinking party]; a party where men could pursue intellectual discussion and other pleasures

Syssitionoi (Greek) – [Singular: *syssitia*]; Dining halls where Spartan men, presumably from the same military unit, dined together – a precursor to future military messes

Tigrakhaudas – tribe of European Scythians famous for their pointed hats

Trierarch (Greek) [*Literally*: commander of a *trireme* warship] – the equivalent of a naval captain

Xenia (Greek) – Code of guest-friendship (See *Xenos*)

Xenos (Greek) – [*Literally,* stranger]; 'guest-friend', a stranger who was hosted by a Greek and treated as a member of the family

Xiphos (Greek) [Plural: *Xiphé*] – double-edged short sword, preferred by the Spartans

Yavanas (Sanskrit / Indic dialects) – 'Greeks'

Zilath (Etruscan) – 'Ruler'

Acknowledgements

This is a story of a remarkable young queen that I found hidden in between the lines of Herodotus – the one variously known as the Father of History and the Father of Lies. It is to him I owe my greatest debt for this work. Other ancients to whom I am indebted include Livy, Plutarch, and Thucydides.

As I am to the ancient, I too am immensely indebted to our modern giants of Antiquity, namely my former teacher, Professor Barry Strauss of Cornell and, my friend, Professor Paul Cartledge of Cambridge. I would especially like to acknowledge the influence of Tom Holland, whose *Persian Fire* was one of the main inspirations of this novel, to whom I am personally grateful for being so open with me.

I am also indebted to Peter Green; the two Robins – Waterfield and Lane Fox; – and especially to Victor Davis Hanson, whose brilliant scholarship I have admired far more than his politics, and yet both have been equally critical influences in motivating me to write this novel.

I would also like to acknowledge here the influence of several modern authors who have written about Sparta, including John Carr, W.G. Forrest, Nigel M. Kennell, J.F. Lazenby and Scott M. Rusch, as well as John. R. Hale's impressive work on Athens. I also wish to acknowledge the works of John Keegan and Richard Holmes and their keen insights on the nature of combat and warfare.

Among the novelists to whom I owe the greatest debt is Steven Pressfield, the influence of whose great novels, *Gates of Fire* and *Last of the Amazons* can clearly be seen in this story. If imitation is the best form of flattery, this can be seen in the colour of Cleonice's eyes, in a quip about the Argives by Cleomenes, and in the reference the alluring presence of Amazons along the northern edges of the Greek world; the credit for all of these is Mr Pressfield's.

Though my story takes a very different tack than the Leonidas trilogy of Helena P. Schafer, and deliberately so, I would like to acknowledge my debt to her scholarship and writing.

I wish to warmly thank Sam Barone, whose generous encouragement I have greatly appreciated. I also acknowledge the influence of both Valerio Massimo Manfredi and Bernard Cornwell in writing this novel.

In this list, I should also mention the movie *300* (Zack Snyder, directing) as well as its sequel, *300: Rise of an Empire* (Noam Murro, directing), in spite of my reservations about their portrayals of events and personalities. I also want to acknowledge the influence of Travis Tritt's lyrics from his song 'The day the sun stood still' (from the musical, *The Civil War* – lyrics by Jack Murphy) in Prince Khorrem's poem on Thermopylae.

Above all, I have nothing but gratitude to those whose support has been the bedrock of this project. In this regard, I want to thank Hannah Vaughan Lee who painstakingly went through repeated iterations of this novel and carefully guided me along the way and my editor, Claire Wingfield, whose professional support and encouragement saw this project through to its successful conclusion. I also wish to mention the support of Charlie Wilson, Natalie Braine, Terry Edge, and Gillian Stern, all of whom helped to shape this book.

Among others, I wish to acknowledge the encouragement and contribution of Lucy Chester, Peter Wright, Suzy Price, Andrea Volfova, Marlene Nilsson, Marco Kalbusch, Ingrid Koeck and Imran Ahmed Siddiqui, whose individual and collective advice helped shape the story into the one it eventually became.

Above all, I would like to thank my family for their unwavering support.

Author's Note

'In war,' wrote the playwright Aeschylus, 'truth is the first casualty.' And indeed, history is often written by the victors. In writing this book, I have tried to address two issues. One is to try to present a more balanced picture of events, and that role is primarily given to Sherzada who acts as Gorgo's foil and sees things from a different point of view. The second is to present an alternative explanation of a well-known story. The Greeks could not have defeated the Persians without a central figure organizing their resistance. And Gorgo, in my view, fits this role perfectly. That she did this by following her father's apparently mad policies was too compelling a story for me to resist telling. Rather than seeing him as a mad king, I see him as a visionary and a great practitioner of *realpolitik*, something very few Greeks of that era understood. King Cleomenes has been the great unsung hero of ancient Sparta. The story of Gorgo cannot be divorced from that of her father.

Gorgo and her son mysteriously disappear from history not very long after the defeat of the Persians. In this novel, I have tried to offer one explanation of what might have happened to them, as well as the origins of how Sparta and Athens begin to descend down a path which leads them to disastrous conflict that will ultimately sap Sparta's power and end its predominance in Greece.

While the vast majority of the characters are based on actual historical figures, a very small minority are fictional – among them, Sherzada. He might appear as an historical anomaly, but not an entirely implausible one. Such a person could well have existed. In a world when time and again, the notion of a clash of civilizations has almost become a foregone conclusion, this novel tries to challenge many notions that continue to dog our political thinking.

Like Gorgo, Sherzada too represents an alternative reading of history. It is well-established that the Sakas established themselves in the Indus Valley in the first century AD. However, some ancient texts date their presence in the Northern part of the sub-continent even earlier. The ruins of a city called Sakala near modern Sialkot in Pakistan tantalizingly points in that direction. I have also challenged the widely held view that the Persian conquered what are now the Punjab and the Khyber Pakhtunkhwa provinces of Pakistan during the reign of King Darius. Instead, I suggest that while the Sakas of the Indus accepted the Persians as their overlords, they did not accept Persian occupation.

The fact that Greek influences reached the Indus Valley before Alexander the Great can be discerned from a variety of sources which indicate far more inter-cultural interactions across a wider area of the globe than is generally accepted.

As to the names and places, where possible I have – with some exceptions – used the Latinized as opposed to the Grecianised spelling. Thus Cleonike is Cleonice, Thraiki is Thrace, Kleomenes is Cleomenes, and Pleistarkhos is Pleistarchus, to give just a few examples. I have also tried, where possible, to 'Persianize' the names of the Persian characters rather than use the Grecianised versions that have come down to us in History. So Mardonius is Mardauniya, Artabazus is Artabaz and Bubares is Burbaraz, etc. In some cases, my 'Persianized' names are only an approximation of what they must have been in reality.

As for military formations, I have tried to describe them in modern terms only for the sake of simplicity. Deliberately avoiding the rich and often inconclusive academic debate about the size and composition of Spartan military units like *Lochoi* and *Morae*, I have assumed that a *Lochos* is the smaller military unit comprising around 300 troops – roughly the size of a modern army company – and the *Mora* around 600–800 men, roughly equal to a modern battalion. Since each of the urban districts of Sparta were expected to provide troops, I named each multibattalion regiment after its home district – hence the mention of the Kynosoura Regiment. All of this is to provide a modern reference to help those who are interested in understanding how the Spartan army would have been organized at that particular time.

I have used a similar method to describe other military units. A typical Greek battalion, I have assumed, would be roughly the same as a Spartan one, between 600 and 800 men. A Persian battalion, however, would notionally be 1,000 strong. The ancient cavalry equivalent of an infantry battalion would be a regiment, though it might contain far fewer men. It is not clear whether the Greeks had brigade-sized units, though some evidence suggests that they did. A brigade equivalent in all Greek armies would be a composed of several *Morae* or similar battalion-sized units, totalling between 3,000 and 5,000 men. Often, this was the size of a typical Spartan force on campaign. The Latin infantry *Alla* or a Roman Legion of the time would also be the same strength as a brigade and have been described as such in this novel.

On the subject of Roman history, I have deviated from the widely accepted Varronian Chronology (presented by Marcus Terrentius Varro) by three years, having the consulship of Marcus Fabius Vibullanus and Gnaeus Manlius in 477 BC instead of 480 BC. This is more in line with the dates presented by Livy. Whilst a decisive battle between the Romans and the Etruscans is mentioned by Livy, it is not given a name. I have called it the Battle of the Fields of Fidenae.

As for the other major battles, most, like Thermopylae and Plataea, did indeed take place. However, Gortys is fictional but would not have been out of place in the Peloponnesus of that era where Spartans sought to reassert their dominance time and again.

Some of the apparently stranger roles in this novel are also based on historic precedents. It is conceivable, for example, for a famous playwright like Aeschylus to serve as an inexperienced naval captain, just as a generation later the popular playwright Sophocles – without any significant military experience – was elected as a general to serve alongside the brilliant Athenian statesman, Pericles, son of Xanthippus. As in the case of Aeschylus in this novel, Sophocles' duties were largely confined to diplomacy.

I have also put into Gorgo's mouth some quotes, particularly the 'If!' remark in the first chapter, which were attributed to later Spartans. However, there is no reason to assume that Gorgo did not make similar statements.

Finally, some characters have a minor role in this one, but are linked to future novels in which they will play a far more prominent role. A prequel is in the works.

TOP HAT
BOOKS

Historical fiction that lives.

We publish fiction that captures the contrasts, the achievements, the optimism and the radicalism of ordinary and extraordinary times across the world.

We're open to all time periods and we strive to go beyond the narrow, foggy slums of Victorian London. Where are the tales of the people of fifteenth century Australasia? The stories of eighth century India? The voices from Africa, Arabia, cities and forests, deserts and towns? Our books thrill, excite, delight and inspire.

The genres will be broad but clear. Whether we're publishing romance, thrillers, crime, or something else entirely, the unifying themes are timescale and enthusiasm. These books will be a celebration of the chaotic power of the human spirit in difficult times. The reader, when they finish, will snap the book closed with a satisfied smile.